BOMBAY GARDENS

by
Jameela Siddiqi

Rubu,

with love Jameela
(Asma to
you)

26 . 8 . 06

Published in collaboration with Lulu.com
Copyright ©Jameela Siddiqi, 2006

ISBN 1-4116-9890-1

Text and Headings in Times New Roman 12 and 16 pt

Cover design by Lulu Gallery
Photograph Asia Maghouze

for
Peter Nazareth

Characters
INDIA – the 16th Century Fairy Tale:

Princess Jagwati – an insomniac Princess
Rangeelay Khan – a mysterious musician who puts her to sleep

UGANDA – 1955 - 1972
At Naran Villa
Naranbhai – small-time businessman and ambitious landlord
Sushilaben – his first wife, still in residence
"Mad Girl" Kirti – his daughter by his first wife
Nalini – his widowed older sister
Mohini and Sohini – twin-sisters, his nieces and daughters of Nalini
Bharat The Useless Nephew – son of Nalini
Geeta (Mrs) Naranbhai – his second wife
Doctor, Dentist & Lawyer – his three young sons by his second wife
Kamini Masi – former film star, spinster aunt of the second wife
Jannasani – the African houseboy
Juma – the junior houseboy

The tenants at Bombay Gardens
Pandit Suddenly – Naranbhai's best friend
Satish the Bachelor – refuses to marry unless "Dream Girl" presents herself
Shahbanu Hussein – the new tenant who causes male pulses to race faster
Saira – Shahbanu's beautiful daughter
Virjibhai the Compounder – a widower who is universally liked
Bimla – Virjibhai's older daughter turned housekeeper
Kamla—Virjibhai's younger daughter, dreaming of being a doctor
Tony D'Sa – the drunk, disgraced and fired from work
Mrs D'Sa – his wife, main breadwinner, piano teacher and cake maker
D'Sa Numbers 1 to 11 – the D'Sa children, known only by numbers

Others
Hazari Baba [of Amroha] – Saver of Souls, Mender of Hearts
Raushan – Naranbhai's chief enemy, married to an African politician
Sam – Raushan's husband
Dr Dawawallah – kindly Parsee doctor, employer of Virjibhai
The Dictator – former soldier who stages a military coup
Mama Safia – Qur'an teacher

LONDON, UK   2000
Camilla – expelled Ugandan-Asian woman, aspiring to be a writer
Grumpy Old Man – Camilla's grumpy brother-in-law
Much Younger Wife – Camilla's older sister and wife of the Grump
Baby – an Indian woman with an African accent

PROLOGUE

PRINCESS WAKEFUL - a true story from India, circa. 1563

"Once upon a time there was a Princess. (Why can't I start with those words? All my childhood stories always began like that.)"

Why is she talking to herself in the middle of a story she has submitted for a competition? Is she crazy?

"She was the only child of a much-loved and benevolent King. Everybody bowed and scraped to the King but the King bowed only before his daughter -- Rajkumari Jagwati -- the apple of his eye and the sole legacy of his favourite wife, the dead Queen.

Princess Jagwati's every whim was his command. She could twist him around her little finger if she so wished but, most unusually for princesses, Rajkumari Jagwati was a very reasonable and sweet-natured sort of young lady who seldom took advantage of her powerful position. And, the King loved her all the more for this. We all know that when princesses get their own way, something dreadful always happens.

The King was loved by his subjects and, while other neighbouring kingdoms were constantly fending off rebellions, the King of Kanchanpur continued to be enormously popular and secure in his Kingdom. It was one of the happiest kingdoms in all of Indian history until the unexpected happened.

No, it didn't happen as a result of political insurgency, or foreign invasion, or famine, or flood or some other natural disaster. It happened because Rajkumari

Jagwati forgot that natural knack of how to fall asleep.

At first, it was seen as a one-off. She had spent the night tossing and turning, unable to sleep a wink. On the following night, one of her senior attendants made her drink a special hot milk concoction of herbs and nuts -- said to soothe the nerves and induce sleep. But she spent a second night wide-awake and then, another, and another...

Healers and quacks of all kinds had appeared and prescribed the most outrageous concoctions for putting the Princess to sleep and, many of these, she'd had to actually swallow. Animal blood, urine, horse-hair, the placenta of a first-time mother who had to have been the first-born of her parents, dog-vomit... *(too many to mention without the author feeling sick -- reader/editor, please make up some more!)* "

I'm sure she meant to take that out -- how did it get left in the final version? What sort of serious wannabe writer issues direct orders to her readers and editors?

"When ten months had passed and the Princess hadn't slept a wink, the King grew very concerned about his only daughter's declining health. She was still only seventeen, but she had dark circles under her eyes and her irritability for lack of sleep had grown so severe that one by one most of her attendants had deserted their duties and disappeared. They could no longer work for a young woman who threw sharp objects at them.

The King was very sad. His beautiful, sweet-tempered daughter had turned into a hollow-faced, trembling, stammering, stuttering witch with not a sweet word for anyone.

(That's what lack of sleep can do to a human being - prince or pauper. Sleep is a great equaliser. The ability to sleep has been granted in equal measure to all human beings and, ironically, more often than not it is the rich who complain of insomnia whilst the poor are only too happy to rest their tired bones after a hard day's work.)

More notes to herself in parenthesis? I'm sure this is not the final version! Perhaps she sent in the wrong draft by mistake?

It was when the King had given up all hope of his daughter ever being able to sleep again that one of his advisors suggested a radical method they hadn't yet been tried. Traditional medicine-men, quacks, magicians, exorcists, and other such dubious characters he advised, should now be banned from the palace. Instead, he advised, the King should look to the oldest and best medicine to calm and soothe a sick body and help return it to its natural rhythm: Music. He suggested that the King should hold a musical contest. Musicians from all over the Kingdom, and beyond, should be invited to sing or play for the Princess. A podium, surrounded by a diaphanous curtain, should be erected in her bedchamber, some distance from the foot of her bed, so that while she lay down, a musician would sit behind that curtain and sing, or play. Whomsoever managed to put the Princess to sleep should be given her hand in marriage, along with half the Kingdom of Kanchanpur.

The musical contest was announced and they came in hundreds, nay thousands, from all over the Kingdom, and beyond. One by one, they played, they sang. All the songs were lullabies but while all over the palace the King, his courtiers and the many servants dozed -- and some even started snoring -- the Princess grew more and more wakeful. Some of the music was so bad that it made her scream and shout and throw various objects at the musicians. No, it wasn't working.

Finally, the King decided to leave things to fate and declared the musical contest closed because it had made the Princess even more sick. No more musicians please! The King would just have to get used to a daughter who was thin, shrivelled, bad tempered and wide-awake at all times. He could only hope and pray that death would come and soon end her suffering.

It was after the King became thus resigned to fate that a completely unknown musician presented himself at court. The King's attendants asked him to leave: "Please, go. If the King sets eyes on another musician, he's likely to order your execution -- that is, if the Princess herself doesn't kill you first…pleaseleave. The contest is closed. Music didn't work!"

"*My* music will work," said the mysterious, unknown musician.

"Big-headed fellow!" laughed the courtiers. "What makes you think your music will work? The greatest musicians of this Kingdom and beyond have failed. What's so special about you?"

"Nothing special. The rest of them sing for kings and princesses. I sing only for God. When God is thus invoked, human beings are bound to find rest -- and peace," answered the long bearded though young musician.

The courtiers were intrigued by the remark but they couldn't risk annoying the King by letting him into the Princess's bedchamber against orders, so they asked him to leave.

The handsome young musician, Rangeelay Khan, followed orders. He left the palace, but did not leave the palace grounds. He made his way into that part of the garden that lay directly below the Princess's quarters. He sat under a tree close to a fragrant flowering shrub known as "Raat ki Rani" (Queen of the Night) and began singing.

Some minutes later, on hearing his distant strains, the Princess began to get drowsy in her room. Her few remaining attendants noted this with joy and immediately set out to find the magic voice. They led him to the Princess's bedchamber where he was placed on the podium and concealed by the diaphanous curtain just as all the other musicians had been. From here, he continued to sing.
That night, the Princess slept for the first time in over a year."

Hey! This story is beginning to ring a bell -- no, it's more than a bell: it's a deafening roar, like thunder!

"So, the mysterious young musician had succeeded where thousands had failed. But does he get to marry the princess? No, he ends up being sentenced to death. Why? How?
Call me if you want to know the rest of the story!"

What? Is she mad? And all this time I've had to live with the guilt of sabotaging her manuscript when she has hijacked *my* story -- a story that wasn't even all there!

What amazes me is that she tells the story up to the same point that I know it. How does she know this story? And why is she withholding the end? Surely, she sent it in an incomplete version by mistake..?

DOUBLE TROUBLE (1955)

"Lean more towards each other...smile more...no that's too much...smile less. Don't look at the camera. Look to the right - no, no, to the left! Left, no, no, right! I mean my right - no, *your* right!"

Mohini and Sohini were draped in heavy silk saris as they stood in front of a crudely painted backdrop depicting a garden, framed by velvet-effect drapes in maroon tied on either side with large yellow bows. Neat rows of flower pots ascended along either side of the stone steps, getting smaller and smaller, seeming to lead to infinity.

Patel the photographer kept disappearing under a black cloth emerging from time to time to issue more instructions. Looking at him, one got the impression that he had spent most of his life thus, enveloped by a black cloth and peeping out from it only when some urgent directorial order was required.

"No, too much to the right! More left.... forget it. That makes you both cross-eyed! "

It went on like that for a good few minutes.

Naranbhai wriggled uneasily in the rickety wooden folding chair positioned behind the camera:

"What's all this left-right-left-right? Is this an army parade or what? Just make sure their eyes look big-big and their faces look fair-fair. That is all I want."

"I know, I know," said Patel the photographer, miffed that someone was trying to teach him his job. "I've done many of these you know? It is more usual to do them one at a time. Close-up only. Eye-drops. I use eye-drops to dilate the pupils. Eyes look bigger, more beautiful. You know, photo is first and last chance to see...."

"Just do what you're being paid to do and get on with it..." Naranbhai retorted impatiently and then, becoming suddenly aware of his favourite deities, the terrible-twin lords Rahu and Ketu, nestling reassuringly in his sweaty palm he calmed down, somewhat. These tiny, bulbous figurines of Rahu and Ketu, always had this effect on him. Naranbhai would often joke: "I have all the gods, right here, in my hand."

What harm could possibly come to a man who always had God with him? Remembering this all-important truth, Naranbhai even managed to smile a bit. No doubt the photographer was stupid in the extreme and determined to make a square meal out of a straightforward shoot. And all the while the girls' noses were getting shinier and shinier. There was nothing for it, but to sit and wait and be patient. He was glad he'd brought his Rahu and Ketu with him. But then he always took them everywhere. He'd had them since the age of ten and they had accompanied him on every important mission. Most people considered the twin-gods to be demonic. But Naranbhai had inherited the bulbous little statuettes from his long-dead mother who had told him that the two figurines, carried together, always ensured one of a healthy, balanced life. The balance was wrought by their two distinct characters -- Rahu was the lord of joy and bounty, Ketu, the naughtier one, was the lord of reversals in fortunes. Everything in life was about duality and it was best to carry both together so that each would counter-balance and moderate the impact of the other. Everybody knows too much joy, or wealth, is bad for you. Where Rahu brings expansion, Ketu causes contraction, and together they ensure that man does not get too happy or too full of himself. Highs and lows are avoided and the middle-state - called "contentment" - is successfully achieved. Contentment: that for which man has striven since Day One.

The minutes ticked away in Patel's cramped photo studio. The airless heat and blinding light in the poky little place at the back of the photographic shop was really beginning to get to Naranbhai. He began to regret the whole project. And yet, only two days ago, he had thought he had come up with the most brilliant idea of all time. Why get the doe-eyed girls photographed individually for prospective bridegrooms? Why not send a joint photo and see which - if any - gets picked? Presented with not just one, but *two* beauties within the same photo, a boy's parents were sure to feel obliged to pick at least one. Choice. As in business, consumers were duped more easily if there was a choice. If they had picked one brand of washing powder out of a possible thirty-seven, then they felt they had exercised some sort of power and it made them happier about the purchase. And marriage, after all, was a serious transaction. Naranbhai had been very pleased with himself for applying his business acumen to the ins and outs of the risky marriage business. Even so, on hearing about his idea, his second wife had, as usual, tried to pour cold water over the scheme. He told her that submitting a single shot of just one girl certainly meant a clear Yes, or a definite No, whereas his *unique* idea of a double-shot was sure to yield fruit. Even so, the second Mrs Naranbhai had her doubts: "When you do things double-double like that, then trouble also comes double-double!"

BUY ONE, GET ONE FREE

"You won't get a better offer than this. Two for the price of one," said the toothless old woman. She specialised in fixing up marriages.

"Yes...yes...but I want to know more about the family," protested Naranbhai lamely, not so much because he was against the match, but because it had all seemed so quick and easy, he felt he ought to raise some imaginary objection.

The miraculous arrangement was a direct result of his double-photo brainwave and concerned his twin nieces Mohini and Sohini, aged sixteen. They were the daughters of his widowed sister Nalini, who along with her three children, had been returned by her in-laws to live with him since they had no more use for her after the death of her husband some years earlier.

"So, you say these two brothers have agreed to marry the sisters? At the same ceremony? Double-wedding? All in one day? And only one dowry divided into two because they are going to be living in the same house? Sounds too good! Too good to be true."

"I tell you, it's never going to happen again. These sort of offers don't come everyday," the toothless old hag was determined to push the deal to a conclusion and collect her double commission from both parties without delay.

"What are you waiting for, hain?" she asked Naranbhai again.

The matchmaker had carried a recent photograph of the twins, posing in front of a painted garden, their arms inter-linked and their heads tilted towards each other. One girl was staring into the space on the left while the other looked blankly to her right. This enigmatic, pensive pose had been presented to a distinguished family of merchants in another town. The boy in question had had some difficulty making up his mind between the two girls - not least because they looked almost identical. Fearing that his hesitation might result in a rejection of both, the toothless old hag had persuaded the boy's parents to take both the girls for two of their sons. For this ingenious brainwave she clearly expected an additional bonus and commission from Naranbhai.

"What could be better, I ask you? Both girls will live in the same house and be a support for each other in times of trouble..."

"Trouble? You mean there is likely to be trouble?" Naranbhai decided to latch on to the word frequently used by his second wife, hoping to unearth some potential trouble-causing factor that might result in a reduced commission for the toothless match-making wonder.

But the woman was not to be trifled with. Matchmaking was the only profession she had known and it was one she executed with near-perfection in this East African country where Indian communities were scattered far and wide over many towns and inaccessible villages. Parents had very precise, clearly defined requirements for their children's prospective marriage partners. These requirements defined exact tribe, race, religion, caste, age, height, weight, hair, teeth and last, but by no means least, a fair skin. For the girls, that is. A man could be dark, but girls had to be fair unless they were planning to spend the rest of their lives on the proverbial shelf. Locating all these highly desirable qualities in a potential marriage partner was no mean feat. And not everyone could afford a passage to India where prospective marriage partners were supposed to be two a penny owing to extreme poverty. That is why professional matchmakers were so important. Over the years, the old woman affectionately known as 'Laggan-Masi' when things went right and 'old toothless hag-witch-churayl' when things went wrong, had made it her business to keep herself well informed on as many households as possible. This information was limited to the economic and social standing of various families and the numbers of marriageable boys and girls within each household. And it was an ever-changing databank of facts and figures. Baby girls born today, would be menstruating in a little over a decade and baby boys would be earning good wages in two decades -- or would've taken over their fathers' businesses. The gathering and updating of such information required a sharp brain, perfect memory recall for names and numbers and an extensive network of contacts. But this was by no means a daunting a task for the old hag given that her chief pastime was the collection and dissemination of gossip.

Information on girls was easy. She only needed to know their ages - of which she would sometimes take the liberty of knocking off two or three years - and a recent photograph as proof of big-big eyes and a white-white skin. And virginity? That was no problem at all. The old hag claimed to be able to tell by the way they walked whether or not they were soiled in that vital department.

When she saw Naranbhai furiously gripping at the statuettes of the twin-gods in his palm, the old hag regretted having brought up the word 'Trouble.'

"Anyway, why are you dwelling on all this trouble-trouble nonsense? Trust in God - er gods - and in me. A pair of brothers wishing to marry a pair sisters - what could be more natural?" she coaxed, ever mindful of her fee, and now beginning to get just a bit irritated with Naranbhai's over-cautious attitude. So she put the case more forecefully:

"Just think of the savings! Just one set of invitation cards. Only one wedding meal. One set of pandits. The house to be decorated just once. All over in one go. How many parents or uncles dare even dream of such convenience?"

Only Mrs Naranbhai, Naranbhai's second wife, shelling peas on the large swing in the middle of the verandah, remained unimpressed: "Double-double means trouble also double-double."

Her sister-in-law, the widow Nalini, hovering close by said to no one in particular:

"Jealous. She just doesn't want any happiness for me, or my daughters. Plain jealous, nothing else!"

AN EASY WAY OUT

In many parts of India, marriage custom dictates a compulsory ritual visit by the new bride to her old parental home a month or so after the wedding. Indians settlers in East Africa observed such customs with great relish, determined to remain connected to their cultural past. Although couched as a compassionate act and justified in terms of the girl's inevitable homesickness and the need to be with her own people, it is in fact a cleverly construed ceremony designed to enact an easy annulment of the marriage if the bride has in any way proved unsatisfactory. The main requirement of this first visit back to the parental home is that the bride may not return to her in-laws' home of her own accord or accompanied by anyone other than her husband. This all-important rule was designed to give newly married men an honourable OUT. Traditional societies with no legislation for divorce always devised other quaint little customs for giving a man an honourable exit route. All the man would have to do is to simply not show up to escort the wife back home. In such an eventuality, tradition defined by dignity dictates no questions be asked, and no recriminations made. The boys and their families are, quite literally, "off the hook," while the newly married girl's life is now well and truly tantamount to a fate worse than death. Far worse than being a widow and considerably worse than never having married at all. Now she is soiled, "spoiled" - touched and tainted by the caresses of a man who no longer wants her. Worse still, and having tasted the forbidden fruit and therefore assumed to have developed a voracious appetite for it, she is viewed as fair game by other men, while for other respectable women she is shamelessness personified -- given her alleged readiness for sexual activity.

Mohini and Sohini returned for their ritual first visit to the Naranbhai household with great pomp and ceremony. There was feasting and dancing. Their mother, Nalini the widow and, both their aunts - the two wives of Naranbhai - awaited their arrival at the front door with a thali bearing various auspicious spices and substances. The girls arrived, looking a shade heavier, with a kind of radiant glow about them - the kind attributed to the legitimate loss of virginity; a look that was met with much approval and meaningful head-nodding by the older women.

"Don't they look happy?" the aunts remarked.

Their widow mother wiped away a tear and waving her arms around both their heads, cracked her knuckles over her temples in an effort to ward off evil.

Neighbourhood women who had gathered for this home-coming looked on with envy as the two girls, both a shade fatter and overdressed to kill, entered their old house for what was thought to be a brief, seven-day reunion with their family. This kind of enforced separation from a new husband was said to increase the ardour. Absence makes the heart…

But, six months later, their husbands still hadn't shown up to escort them back home.

At first their mother, and Naranbhai himself, lied about it shamelessly.

"Next week, next week," they had said for the first few weeks. Then the story changed:

"We've told them to wait a bit. We can't bear to be parted from the girls just yet. After all, they have to live there for the rest of their lives so why deprive us of them so early?"

In time, neighbours and friends decided it was more tactful to not bring up the question, and when a few more months had gone by, it was clear the young husbands had no use for their new wives and were most certainly not coming back for them.

The Naranbhai household then changed its tune and a new version of events was broadcast for the benefit of the curious and nosy.

"Boys, these days! Can't recognise a real jewel when they see one! We don't want our girls to go back to such a household where they are treated worse than servants. Their husbands wanted to come and get them, we said NO. We need time to think it over."

But behind closed doors it was a very different story. Day after day, night after night, Mohini and Sohini were badgered with a barrage of questioning:

"What? What is wrong? What happened? Can't you two even make a simple thing like a marriage in a well-to-do family of shopkeepers work? What did you do? What did you say? Have you been answering back? Were you disobedient? Did you sleep too much? Did your tongues wag needlessly? What? What?"

It went on like that with every single adult member of the household challenging the girls at every step, and the second Mrs Naranbhai never ceasing to remind her husband that trouble had, indeed, come double-double.

Mohini and Sohini were silent. They just stood together, or sat together, their heads lowered with shame. One stared at a fixed spot to the right, while the other stared left - gazing into space and saying nothing - silent as that fateful double photograph.

Month after month, the girls remained silent. All efforts at getting to the bottom of their mysterious, short-lived, double-marriage break up remained in vain.

One morning, the African houseboy Jannasani found the two girls at the far end of the backyard. Their bodies stone cold, their hands covered in blood, a sharp razor soaked in congealed blood that had mingled together from both corpses.

"Perhaps it is for the best."

Afterwards, nobody could remember who had said it first.

At the joint funeral ceremony of his nieces, Mrs Naranbhai quite needlessly whispered to her husband:"I told you, if you do things double-double, trouble also comes double-double."

The double-suicide was not at first seen as a tragedy. Within the Naranbhai household its shame factor was more potent than any considerations of loss of life. And, further afield, the event was remembered far less as a sad waste of young lives and more for its essential moral message: even two fair-skinned, doe-eyed girls from a respectable household can fail to charm their husbands. In time, the story acquired a shorthand of its own: wayward young girls appearing in any way daring with regard to marriage and children were often warned:"Remember Mohini-Sohini?" Girls who refused to do their share of the housework were reprimanded:"Mohini-Sohini, don't forget!" Girls who preferred to skive off to the cinema instead of helping their mothers and aunts with younger children were cautioned: "Mohini-Sohini!"

Even so, that fateful double-shot of the doe-eyed twins, blown up poster-sized and framed, now occupied a prominent place in Naran Villa. Their mother, the widow Nalini, dutifully garlanded the picture with fresh flowers, every single day.

A VERY SPECIAL RELATIONSHIP

There ought to be a special word to describe the relationship between people who have never met but have occupied the same living space at different times. I know there is no such word in English, or in any of the African languages I know. There may well be one in the hundreds of Indian languages that my Indian (and Pakistani) friends in London keep telling me about. I have heard Indian languages are immensely rich in describing every single ambivalent state known to man. Perhaps that is why Indians are so complicated? And perhaps that is also why wherever they live on this planet, they retain a unique identity and a herding instinct unknown to other races. But hey, what would I know about Indians? I am only Indian by race. I was raised as an African girl, in a small village in East Africa. And, in my country in East Africa, being Indian had, at one time, been the biggest crime one could commit.

Then again, what is "Indian"? I remember reading somewhere that 'Indian' has become the *one* modern word that cannot be used without further clarification: Indian? What kind of Indian? West Indian? Red Indian? Brown-Indian, Muslim-Indian? Indian-Indian? Goan-Indian? Christian-Indian? East African Indian? British Indian? Indian by virtue of having a brown skin although monolingual in English only? What kind of English? English with an Indian accent, or East London accent - or then again a Lancashire, Yorkshire or Scottish accent? In Britain, these sort of Indians were affectionately known as 'coconuts' - Brown on the outside, White inside. But, in my country, whether Brown or White, inside or outside, Indians were considered criminals -- just for being Indian! But why didn't anybody notice that I, too, was Indian?

I know I'm not quite normal. In fact, I'm almost completely screwed up. I don't know about other people's childhoods but mine consisted, largely, of perpetual boredom. School hours were erratic -- sometimes there was no school. All the Indian teachers had left and there weren't enough African teachers to take over. I was at home quite a lot but my mother would not allow me to do any housework or soil my hands. She had all her sons -- my older

17

African brothers -- waiting on me, hand and foot, day and night. It was in those long hours of doing nothing that I first became aware of these unknown songs, persistently playing in my head. Gradually, the songs provided the perfect soundtrack for my hours and hours of gazing at photographs of perfect strangers. These were pictures left behind by the Indian people who lived in this house until 1972. For lack of anything better to do, I started a scrapbook and, as and when I found a picture, I would stick it into my book and try to give each picture a story. I tried to assemble it like a sequence of events but, not knowing the full facts, it didn't quite work.

There was one photograph in particular that intrigued me. Of course, it didn't fit my scrapbook because it was blown up poster-size, and framed. Two Indian girls - they could be identical twins - wearing their best saris and posing in front of a crudely painted studio back drop. I've never seen anyone look quite so enigmatic. One stared blankly to the left of camera, the other to the right. There were no other big group photos. How strange to have had only this one enlarged. I know Indians always lived in large families, particularly if they had large houses, such as the one we moved into when I was six. I still have some of those photographs. The scrapbook has long since ended up tattered, but I carried a few of those strange photos with me, all the way to London. But not that one I just mentioned -- of the two identical girls -- because that was huge. Mama Safia had it removed from the wall the moment we moved into the house. Human images were forbidden in Islam, she said. It was too big for me to take and hide so it knocked around our backyard for a bit. And then, one day, it disappeared. The next time I saw it, it was hanging on the wall of the small house of the Quran school caretaker. He had one of those houses arranged barrack-fashion, not far from our big house. He was a tall, thin, wiry man who hardly ever spoke and exuded an air of mystery. Of the smaller pictures which I hid in case Mama Safia made me throw them away, there was one of a tree and also a picture of that big swinging hammock on the verandah. But the seat is empty, although the swing appears to be in motion. That swing was still there when we came to the house and it was my favourite place for day-dreaming.

It was while puzzling over these photos in my childhood that I first became aware of the songs in my head. I then realised they had always been there. A melodious female voice in what I think is an Indian language. Why do I have Indians songs running through my head?

As I said, what would I know about Indians - or "the Wahindi" as they were known - in that part of East Africa? All I knew was that they'd all been booted out of the country by a courageous Dictator -- also known as our Champion Liberator and Enemy Number One of the British Empire. (In later years he was known only as *our* country's Enemy Number One!) I was about five or six years old at the time and much too young to read newspapers. The Wahindi had all got out within two months under a sentence of death, leaving behind their grand hill-top mansions, their social clubs, their shops and businesses, their places of worship and all their smart, airy, town houses with those spacious backyards and gardens. And, I suppose, a few photographs got left behind in the rush to get out. But if all the Wahindi got kicked out, why did I get left behind?

When I was growing up, I remember the elders saying that now that all the Wahindi had gone and the most malignant cancer disabling our country had been rooted out, our country was going to be a sort of paradise on earth. It was already "The Pearl of Africa"; now it was also going to be "The Garden of Eden." Sure enough, at least from my childish point of view, things were definitely improving. For a start, we moved out of our village and came to the bright city lights. We were given this large, pink-and-green, double-storey house in the capital city -- a city named after an animal, and built on seven hills, just like Rome. Our Dictator had just received a massive helping hand from some Arab government or the other, to set up Qur'an schools -- or madrassas -- all over the country. Children were to be trained to fight Imperialism in all its guises. And, under the new arrangement, my mother became one of his star Qur'an teachers.

I say "mother" but she is not my real mother. . My life is a series of "yes-buts". I know, but I don't know. I am, but I am not. She was a black African, and I was a Muhindi. That much I've always known. She more or less said it once. When her other children - all older and all boys - were being punished for some naughtiness for which we had all been equally guilty, she excluded me from the disciplinary procedure. She always treated me with respect and deference. Is it my imagination, or is she a little scared of me? Once, when I really pushed her to explain, she said: "You are a gift from Allah! You didn't come from my womb, you came from Him! You are in my very special care. If I say a harsh word to you, I'm answerable to Allah."

"But don't all children come from Allah?" I asked her. She silenced me with a slight gesture of her hand, and went back to reading her Qur'an. And, once again, I'm left wondering. Wondering, as to how did I, an Indian-Muhindi girl, come to be in the care of an African woman? And why did she treat me like a princess? And how can I ever forget the way she sprang into action over that other matter - the only other highlight of my childhood? I must tell you about the mysterious man with a long beard and wearing clean white robes who would appear in our backyard, now and then, and tell me the same story over and over again. He always began at the beginning and ended at the same point. It was the story of an Indian princess who had forgotten how to sleep. And her father had arranged a musical contest so that whichever musician succeeded in putting her to sleep would have her hand in marriage. And, finally, one musician succeeded…

And then I don't know what happened. He never told the story beyond that point because he stopped coming to our backyard. It was after my mother had read some special Quranic verses and blown her breath over me in the hope that I would stop talking to myself.

I told her I wasn't talking to myself. I told her about the man, but she refused to believe me.

REVENGE IS SWEET

Talking of princesses, I have a confession. We've all dreamed of that moment when our most despised enemy is at our mercy. There can't be a more empowering feeling in the world. I guess our leader, the military dictator, must have also felt that sweetness when he had the Wahindi writhing – their money, big cars and flashy houses unable to comfort them. I've always wanted to savour that feeling against some hated enemy. And, my chance finally came. No, not in childhood -- I didn't have any enemies then -- but years later, in London.

I had, very unwisely, entered into an affair with a married man. When Simon first ended our affair and decided to start afresh with his wife, I sustained myself on numerous fantasies as to how I would settle the score with the woman who had triumphed over me and blown my world to pieces. And then, some years later, when I thought my bitterness had abated, there she was, by a neat twist of fate.

I guess I've always felt powerless. A wannabe writer who finished up as a PA in a short-story magazine office. I have always wanted to write, but I never manage to get started. Every time I finish reading a good book, I immediately sit down and start writing something of my own. But it's not easy. Once, I even managed to write one whole paragraph of a novel, beginning with the words: "Last night I dreamed I went to Bombay Gardens again..." Yuck!

How do other people do it? How do they sustain that self-confidence that somebody's going to want to read their outpourings? Confidence unfailingly deserts me, again and again, and I go back to my mundane life, feeling sure that someday I will sit down and write that book. In the meantime, I drudge along in a glorified secretarial role as Personal Assistant to the editor of a short story magazine. We have an annual prize for new, unpublished writers. They submit short stories of less than five thousand words and, if they win, the story gets published in our magazine. There's only a small cash prize, but it is a prestigious award in that publishers then look at the new writer with much interest. Our prize, provided by a reputable Trust, has resulted in

21

many unknown, previously unpublished authors finding the spotlight turned onto them.

How could I have thought that by taking such a job I would eventually wind up as a writer? As an employee, I'm not even allowed to enter these competitions. My job is to open the mail, look over the entries, register them, check for all enclosures and then put everything in a file for my boss to farm out to professional readers. We had had over three hundred entries. Of these, fifty were to be short-listed and sent out to big-time celebrity authors and critics for a final evaluation. Those that didn't make it to the short-list were re-checked by a panel of preliminary readers and editors. And, it was my job to ensure that their manuscripts reached the right people.

When I saw the application form and manuscript from a Camilla Perkins, the name immediately drove me into a fury. But, here, at last, was a chance to stand in her way. I had reason to believe she was the same Camilla -- Simon's wife -- *the* Camilla who had become the chief obstacle in the path of true love, or at least what I had thought was the path to the love of my life. In those days I used to think that of these treacherous, twisting, turning lanes at least *one* will lead straight to Simon's heart. But no, apparently not while Camilla was still in this world. After all, she had stood in my way for a good five years and, eventually, she had won. Her husband had gone back to her, leaving me high and dry. Now I was going to get even. Having dealt my fragile ego every kind of blow, she was now muscling into my territory: I could not stand by and watch her become a writer. She had already won the man. Why should she also win the prize?

As I wrote that standard letter of rejection to Camilla Perkins, I felt completely vindicated. Fate was giving me a chance to stand in her way, and I had to grab that opportunity. But, how I wish I had at least read her story before smuggling it out of that pile of entries for the short story prize. I was so frightened of leaving it lying around the office -- in case one of the other PAs saw it and decided to put in the "To Read" pile -- that I actually smuggled it into my brief case and took it home. I hid it in my closet, in case there was ever a fuss and somebody came to search my house. I was getting paranoid. But then, as I've already told you, I'm not completely sane.

I hid the manuscript and, in a few days, I forgot all about the incident. But I did feel a strange kind of peace in thwarting one of Camilla's ambitions after she had so ruthlessly destroyed everything I had lived and hoped for. Yeah, I've always been a bit sick, but my mind was finally at rest. Perhaps here, at last, was a cure for my sickness?

And then, fate played a very cruel trick. I chanced upon Camilla's manuscript package while clearing out my closet for a friend's Church jumble sale and, as the papers fell out of the manila folder, the title of her story caught my eye. Six months ago, I was so enraged at seeing her name that I didn't even bother to check the story she had submitted. And, today, the title stirred something in me: "Wakeful Princess". And, sitting right there on the floor in front of my closet, I started to read it...

How did she know this story? It's not a well-known story and I've never found it in any of the Indian sources I've checked. I asked various Indian scholars in London if they knew the legend of the Princess Jagwati and the mysterious musician Rangeelay Khan but I drew a blank. I knew the story, but only up to a point. And nobody had been able tell me what happened beyond that point. Camilla's manuscript told the story in great detail, but again, it was only up to that point. And, she had the cheek to finish her story with the words: "If you want to know the rest, call me!" She had stopped at that same point as the mysterious bearded man who used to come and tell it to me in the backyard before my mother ended his visits with the power of her Qur'anic verses.

Her entry would never have made it to the short-list because no publisher likes to be bullied by an author. It's tantamount to saying to the publisher: "If you agree to publish it, I'll give you the ending; otherwise, why should I? If you don't want to publish it, why the hell should you want to know how it ends?"

But, never mind her Bolshi attitude and all that, I wanted to know how and where she had encountered the story. How could an Englishwoman have heard of an old Indian legend that I only encountered when a mysterious, long-bearded man in snow-white visited me on those hot, sultry afternoons when I had nothing else to do? I decided to call her...

What was I to say if and when I called her? I spent a few days chewing it over and then, one day, I finally plucked up the courage. I just had to know -- one way or the other:

"Hello? Is that Camilla Perkins?"

"Yes, speaking," she said.

"I'm sorry to call you like this, but it's about your short story --- the prize --- the one you entered for some months ago...about a wakeful princess? Sorry, I know, you didn't win, but I was one of the readers...yes on the panel of judges...yes, yes... The reason I'm calling is I was intrigued by your story...it's just that I think I know that story...or at least I know part of it. Is it a true story? Did you read it somewhere...or was it told to you? Sorry I don't mean you've plagiarised...of course you wrote it...I just wondered...Can we meet? I need to talk to you."

I haven't done too well. I sound too incoherent, somewhat flustered...will she know I'm guilty?

There's an uneasy silence at the other end. Some people have this way of enforcing a pause so that you feel pressurised to speak. So, I have to say more:

"Look, I know this is really irregular, you see I've come across that story...no, no, not in a book...what? A film? You're saying there was a film about it? Sorry, I've never seen an Indian film in my life...no, I was told that story as a child, but I was never told the ending... err...no, not in India, somewhere in East Africa. No, I can't really tell you who told me the story...it's kind of weird..."

Suddenly, her tone changes completely. From a stony indifference, she turns positively warm.

"Sure, let's meet! What did you say your name was, again?" she asks.

I hadn't given her a name. The only name I could come up with was a rather ridiculous one but it was something my African mother had always called me: "Baby. I'm called Baby," I said. How could I give her my real name? Simon might have mentioned it in one of their many quarrels over me. Or, at least I hope they quarrelled over me. The "other" woman longs for some kind of acknowledgement, however negative the context.

"Baby? Oh, that's nice! Unusual! Very original! When and where do you want to meet?" she asks. I'm dumbfounded. I hadn't expected it to be so easy. So she answers her own question:

"I suggest we meet at...on..."

MOON SONG

A month had passed since the double funeral of Mohini and Sohini, and it was full moon again. Here, in equatorial East Africa, the moon could look very big on certain nights, almost as though it were a circular hot air balloon, hovering, just before its descent to the ground. And, in the silvery night, Naranbhai's daughter by his first marriage, only ever known as "Mad Girl," had, as usual, broken free of all those who tried to restrain her. She had managed to reach the rooftop terrace of Naran Villa from where she sang her special moon songs, as she was inclined to, every full moon. She chided her imagined Beloved for being no more than a reflection of the Full Moon in the water-pot of her heart. He, whom she thought resided in her heart, had turned out to be only as unreachable as the Full Moon. This sad fact set the scene for some poignant poetic verse on the nature of deception and illusion.

It was believed the moon got larger when she sang, a rumour that caused a Dictator of later years to demand her arrest and detention because being able to control the size of the moon was a skill he very much coveted.

Whenever she sang, it was as though someone had poured liquid gold over the silvery moonlight. A strange hush would descend on the tropical grasslands and all creatures, great and small, would fall silent at the magic of her voice. But, while the universe itself stood still, the entire household at Naran Villa would be galvanised into its emergency routine. Every household member abandoned whatever else they were doing and began to close doors and windows to prevent curious onlookers from gathering outside the house. The Naranbhais' African houseboy, Jannasani, was sent racing up the stairs to the terrace from where he had to drag the girl and bring her back into the house. This, he usually accomplished, but not without a prolonged struggle from the Mad Girl.

Nobody knew where the Mad Girl's songs came from. They certainly weren't from amongst the hundreds of Indian film songs that were popular at that time, but how could she have made them up? For instance, there was that intriguing one she sang about having flown to earth -- on bent and battered wings -- but her feet, to this day, not having touched this earth. Another verse in that song spoke of sleep, and how she had "stolen" somebody's sleep, but the punishment for her theft had been to lie awake -- night after night.

It was the same routine every Full Moon. The Mad Girl would sing, and she would eventually be subdued and brought under control. Then she would sit on her bed, rocking her curled up body back and forth, and humming quietly -- all night -- for she never slept -- presumably a punishment for having stolen somebody's sleep.

It was hard to know whether the songs were about her, or about somebody else.

She sang the same song for a few moons and then changed to another song.

Today, she sang a new one. It was a song about how her song was so fragile that it was only meant to reside in her listeners' hearts:

"Don't hold it in your hand -- it might fall, and shatter beyond all repair -- that's how fragile my song is. It can live in your heart, or then, it can be touched by your lips…but don't ever try to hold it in your hands…"

The songs seemed to touch everybody in varying degrees except her father, Naranbhai. He was convinced that her caterwauling amounted to nothing more, and nothing less, than drawing attention to his misfortune at having fathered a mad daughter. He would hang his head with shame, and dread the next gathering of his cronies on the verandah of the family home, Naran Villa. His friends, such as they were, would gather at teatime to discuss important matters. Amongst the regulars were Dhanjibhai the grocer, Butt, a Muslim-Punjabi garage owner and Naranbhai's own tenant and friend, the part-time pandit Dixit, usually only known as "Pandit Suddenly." Of all the men, Naranbhai felt most intimidated by Pandit Suddenly who had actually read a few fat books in English, making it difficult for Naranbhai to establish his hegemony during these discussions.

27

What was it with the daughters of his household? The misdoings of a daughter always prevent a father from holding his head up high. The nieces, Mohini and Sohini had done nothing except bring shame on the family and his own daughter, a wild, uncouth, cross-eyed creature had done little else except cause him immense discomfort every single month, with her caterwauling. It was as though every single girl who ever lived under his roof had been cursed. Whenever he thought this, he would tighten his grip on the mini-statuettes of his twin-gods Rahu and Ketu with renewed determination, as though imploring the gods to turn the tables on his fate as a shamed father. And, uncannily enough, whenever he tightened his grasp on Rahu-Ketu the Mad Girl would sing a verse that ended with the words:

"Is God only your God? Is He not also *my* God?"

THEY'RE PLAYING OUR SONG!

Our efforts at unravelling our own stories can end up with those stories being woven into other people's lives. Or, what we've always thought of as *our* song, can also be somebody else's song!

I was early for my meeting with Camilla Perkins. I stood outside the tube station in the Asian ghetto area in north-west London as she'd asked. I had a good twenty minutes to kill. At first I paid no attention to the song becoming louder and clearer in my head. I've had this particular song running in my head for as long as I can remember. It took some time before I realised it wasn't in my head but that it was coming from the direction of an Indian record shop, across the road. Without thinking, I crossed the road and entered the shop. Sure enough, that was the source of the music.

This was the very first time I had heard that song - in that same voice - outside my head. The excitement was too much to bear. So it did exist! I hadn't just been imagining it all these years.

I walked up to the shop-owner and said: "Can you tell me more about that song? I'd like to buy that disc, but I also want to know the history of that song...."

He stared at me blankly.

"What?" he said. "You don't know this song? It's one of the most famous film songs of the early seventies! What's it with you Anglicised Indians? Always pretending ignorance about your own culture. Shame, shame."

I was very taken aback. A complete stranger, having a dig at me about my ignorance of Indian culture. I felt like telling him to mind his own business, but then I decided to eat humble pie and let him educate me.

"Honestly, I'm not pretending," I said as calmly as possible. "I have heard that song in my head, day and night and now..."

"Of course you have!" he interrupted. "I just told you it's a famous film song..."

"No, you don't understand. I haven't heard it anywhere for real. I've only been haunted by it. Day and night. There were no Indian songs or films where I was growing up. In fact, by the time

29

I was six or so, all the Asians had been thrown out of my country. I know I look Indian, but I was raised as an African..." I stopped suddenly. Why am I relating my life story to a complete stranger in a record shop?

I looked at my watch and realised Camilla would be arriving any minute. I hastily paid for the CD which featured "my song" and darted across the road again.

I was suddenly accosted by an Indian woman in well-cut trousers and a long black cardigan. A large red dot was stuck to the middle of her forehead:

"Hello, I'm Camilla", she said extending her hand at the same time. How the hell did she recognise me? OK, so I'd said I'd be in a beige raincoat, but there were at least another two dozen passers by in the same M&S raincoat. But that question was completely eclipsed by my shock and surprise at Camilla being Indian. I didn't even bother to hide the fact: what was an obviously Indian-Hindu doing with an English name? I was stupid enough to ask her that rather impertinent question.

"Oh," she replied, in a casual tone, "in this country, nobody can pronounce my real name. Anyway, my surname is Perkins. Married an Englishman, you know? So I thought 'Camilla Perkins' has a rather nice ring to it, don't you think?" And, before I can ask another question, she gets all chatty again.

"Have you been record shopping?" she asks with an easy familiarity as though we were old, old friends. I'm still shocked and speechless at finding an Indian woman instead of an English one. I numbly take out the CD from my bag and show it to her, while mechanically saying: "I don't know about the rest. I just bought it for Track 9...."

"Oh that! Of course! How amazing you like this song! It has a very special meaning for me. You know, it saved my life, quite literally...come, let's find somewhere for coffee...err, have you had lunch yet?"

She led me into one of those Bhajjia Houses on Ealing Road, Wembley.

No sooner had we sat down than she immediately launched into a wildly chequered account of what appeared to be her life history, interspersed with details of her current activities in London. She had secured some funding from an arts organisation and was looking for Ugandan Asians to tell their stories for a project called "Voices of Expulsion."

I'm furious! She's probably doing this to get free material for a book. 'Ugandan Asians', indeed! What's even remotely Ugandan about them? They're all the rage now. Yes, yes, those that we called "Economy-Milking Wahindi", are called "Hardworking Ugandan Asians" in Britain and are involved in all sorts of business and artistic activities. I guess Uganda's loss is Britain's gain.

So, not having made it as a writer she's dabbling in various other projects hoping to do something that could eventually be turned into a book. I can smell a frustrated writer a mile off. It takes one to know one. I suspect that like me, Camilla is also in some kind of rut. I can't help thinking that, like me, she too dreams of some vastly creative career, but has ended up a frustrated housewife...

When she had finished babbling about her current project, she asked: "And you? Where are you from? India or Pakistan?"

I told her, almost apologetically, that I was from East Africa. I felt she wanted to be the only one "from" there. The rest of us had to be from somewhere else. But, unless I'm imagining it, she's delighted.

"Wow! What a co-incidence!" she says, chummily.

I really hadn't expected to find so much in common with Camilla. I thought we only had Simon in common. But no, not only is she Indian like me, but we were both born, and brought up in the same country in what used to be British East Africa.

That Simon bastard must've had a thing about displaced Indian woman. I've always wanted to know more about these people who were originally from my country. I was from among them, but I wasn't one of them. It had never bothered me before now, but ever since the death of my African mother, I had become obsessed with finding out about my real family - my real mother. Why did she give me away? What was her story? I had no leads.

"So, you were you in the Expulsion, I take it?" she asks, bossily.

"No. I was a child of six when the Expulsion happened and I lived with an African family. I was the daughter of "Mama Safia", one of the country's top Qur'an teachers. "

"No wonder! You feel guilty about not being expelled, right?" she sounds relieved, and continues with some relish: "You feel left out of all the drama, yes? Ugandan Asians who were students in England or India in 1972 are even more cut up than the expelled ones. Would you like something with your coffee?

The coffee arrived and she prattled on:

"I know, you must feel terrible, and very guilty at not being expelled. You must feel like you've betrayed the whole race by being exempted...how can you live with that?"

Bloody presumptious woman! I stay calm and reply in flat, even tones:

"No, not at all. How could I have been expelled? I had an African mother and five African brothers. Why should I feel guilty? Nobody questioned my citizenship status or ordered me to leave. Neither did anyone comment on my being Indian after all the Indians had got out. I came to Britain in 1984 -- nearly sixteen years ago -- to go to University. And then I settled here. She - Mama Safia - insisted I study abroad and then try to get a work permit and stay on because, at that time, my country was going to the dogs."

"So! African mother, eh? That means you're of mixed race -- we call them "Chautharas." I must admit, you don't look very Chauthara-- you're fairer than me...and very straight hair, just like a real Indian....still, being Chauthara is very hard, it's even worse than....."

"I'm NOT of mixed race. I am an Indian....."

"Oh come on! You have to face it! Your Indian father probably had his fun with your African mother and then abandoned her! Bastards all these Indian men. I'd rather be a lesbian than marry an Indian. That's why I married an English...."

"No, no, it wasn't like that at all. Both my parents were Indian, but I somehow ended up being raised by a very nice African woman....you know...I just told you, about Mama Safia. She taught Muslim children to read the Qur'an...."

"Oh, you're just in the great African River!" Camilla's voice had a teasing undertone. I didn't like this kind of familiarity on such a short acquaintance.

"I....I don't know what you mean," I said coldly.

"Great African river. The Nile. De Nile. Denial. Ha-ha-ha, don't you geddit?"

Camilla thinks it's very funny to mock the African accent. And it's a direct taunt at my Ugandan-English accent. Why is that funny for her? It's no more and no less funny than her sing-song Indian English accent. God! She's even more irritating than Simon had led me to believe.

"Now, tell me, what's your *real* name? How can anyone be called 'Baby'? You must have a real name."

"That is my real name," I replied trying to stay as calm as possible. "Mama Safia only ever called me Baby."

"But what does it say on your birth certificate?" she asked as though she were a senior immigration officer at Heathrow's Arrival point.

"Don't know! I've never seen my birth certificate. Don't think I ever had one..."

"That more or less proves you're a Chauthara. Anyway...er...listen to me, er...Baby," she squirms at having to use my name. "You have to accept facts. That sort of thing went on all the time. Indian men considered it their birthright to have sex with African women. And the result was babies like you. Unless you accept that, how can you even begin to start tracing your Indian father?"

"I have no interest in tracing anyone! I'm telling you, my mother and my father were Indian. I was just given to Mama Safia. I don't know why or how or by whom. I don't even know if they gave me away or...."

"Why are you so sure you're all-Indian? OK, I admit, you have a very fair skin....in fact, now I think about it, you look almost exactly like that Bollywood actress --- Kitty Complex --

no, no I'm not kidding. That's her name!" she starts giggling. It's obviously very amusing for her that someone with my East African accent could resemble a big Bombay star. No doubt, Muhindis think it's a great honour to look like one of their Bombay Bimbo screen goddesses.

"I'm sorry I don't know much about Indian films or film stars. I don't speak any Indian language...."

"So how come you like that Indian song?" she asked patronisingly.

"I've heard it in my head -- day and night -- for as long as I can remember," I reply, quite truthfully. She giggles.

"But you speak English just like an African..." she says accusingly, as though it were a crime to do so. Bloody woman! This is the same woman whose existence made my life a living hell! She's even more infuriating than Simon had painted her. He had only ever referred to her as "Camilla". The crafty bugger had never told me that she was Indian, or that she was from somewhere in East Africa. Obviously, he didn't want me to see his "pattern."

"Of course I speak like an African. How else would I speak? I speak English and Swahili. My mother spoke beautiful Swahili. I can understand Luganda. I don't know any Indian languages. I was raised in an African village and I had no contact with Indians. It was only after the Indians were expelled we moved to a very big house in the capital city," I said, feeling my patience running out. This isn't going at all as I planned. I was supposed to be asking the questions. She has put me on the defensive.

At the mention of "house" I see she is genuinely curious: She asks: "Where was the house? Which area of the city?"

"The area had been renamed -- long name -- it was supposed to cobble together the name of our Dictator and Liberator and that of one of his chief benefactors -- some rich Arab guy. In the old days -- or at least that's what the elders said -- the entire area was known by some other name and the large house that we eventually moved to, was set some distance away from a few smaller houses that were all joined up together, and......"

I stopped suddenly. I thought I saw more than a flicker of recognition on her face. Yes, those words had certainly made an impact.

Suddenly, I've got her. I have this feeling I know something that she wants to know -- even more badly than I want the rest of the princess story. So, I change the subject and come back to the original reason for our meeting:

"Now, that story you wrote about the sleepless Princess. Tell me, did you just make that up or...?"

"Tell me more about that house first. Can you remember what the area was called in the old days?"

I decided to ignore the question.

KILL THIS MUSIC!

Of course I remember the old Indian name of that area where we came to live in 1973. But I don't feel like telling her. I'm still annoyed that she implied I was the illegitimate child of an Afro-Asian coupling. How *dare* she?

Apart from my physical appearance, I had almost conclusive proof that I was pure Indian. See this thing I wear around my neck? This is not African. It's Indian! And, Mama Safia says it's been with me since I was a baby. She says it was clenched in my fist when I first arrived and, to save it from getting lost, she threaded it onto a chain and put it round my neck. And that's where it has remained. In the past, I'd never worried too much about my Indian parents. I was far more concerned about these songs in my head. On getting to London, the songs had started to get louder and louder and I had tried various things to get to the bottom of the mystery. The GP sent me to the local hospital for a consultation and the hospital psychiatrist recommended I see a "Culture-Specific Therapist". Culture specific? Specific to *which* culture?

"I want the songs to stop," I had said to the Indian-lady shrink in one of London's Asian-dominated areas for treating freaks, flunkies and junkies. Once I'd said it out aloud, I realised how ridiculous it sounded. Does she think I'm completely loopy and cuckoo? She is silent. I must make my point more forcefully:

"I have this singing racing through my head, day and night -- the same song, again and again, and it's driving me round the bend. And sometimes I catch myself singing along. It's completely stupid! It's a language I don't even understand! I want to know how the songs got there."

"What sort of singing?" she asks finally. I think she's trying very hard not to laugh.

I told her the songs were all in a woman's voice. A very sweet voice, but hey, who wants to hear this din day and night? Nothing is clear-cut in my life. Other people are one thing or another. They are this, or that. But I'm always "this-but." Yes, but not

36

quite. I am Indian by race, but I speak no Indian languages. So what the fuck are these Indian songs doing in my head?

The songs go on and on. Sometimes they put me to sleep - at completely the wrong time of day, and sometimes they make me wide awake, even in the dead of night.

"How long has this been going on?" the shrink asks, stifling what I'm sure is a giggle.

I tell her that I'm certain I've heard them while I was in somebody's womb, waiting for death. And it came. One day, I, the foetus, started to die. But when I reached the other side of the claustrophobic birth canal, I found death was called "Life". What I had imagined was called dying, was actually known on earth as "being born." Earthlings know absolutely nothing, yet they think they know it all. Here, rebirth is called "death"!

"Hmm..." is all she can say, in that annoying, professional non-committal way. I can tell by the look on her face that she thinks I'm completely mad.

"What about your childhood? Tell me more about that..."

What am I to tell her? Apart from being bored most of the time, all I remember is that lovely man in white robes, his eyes twinkling as he arrived in our backyard, from time to time. He would tell me a story. The same story, over and over again. But, he never finished the story.

Other than that, my childhood fantasy world was dominated by two things: the strains of hundreds of tuneful though meaningless songs continuously churning in my head, and some photographs -- of unknown people, fossilised by time and shrouded in mystery. These Indians obviously had a need to record every single mundane and momentous event for posterity. But why was I so drawn to these photographs of strangers? Perhaps because my own family - or at least the one in which I grew up - did not have a single picture of any of us. My mother, a strict Muslim, said images of humans were forbidden in Islam. Image-worship was "haram." Only Allah was worthy of worship and adulation. So, once I had found these mysterious photographs, I kept them hidden. After all these years, I still had some of those photographs. I carried them all the way to England. Why?

Perhaps it was because I had spent such a large part of my childhood gazing at them and trying to reconstruct the past. Somebody else's past had merged into my present...

HUMILIATING DEFEAT

According to Naranbhai, a young woman could circumnavigate the globe, swim all the oceans single-handed, write three bestsellers in a row -- or, even develop a foolproof cure for cancer. But until and unless she was safely married off, she was a complete failure and a source of never-ending shame for her parents and elders. While the Mohini-Sohini business had done nothing to alter Naranbhai's personal philosophy of immobilising wayward young women by the shackles of marriage, it had had far reaching consequences for Naranbhai's political aspirations. The double-suicide of his nieces had happened just four weeks before the Town Council elections. Had the elections been just two weeks away, then there's a good chance that Naranbhai would have done well out of the sympathy vote. But four weeks is a long time in local politics. It's a whole extra fortnight of speculation during which blame can be apportioned, with or without full knowledge of the facts. Basically, the people of his own community, as well as those outside, had concluded that Naranbhai had embarked on an extremely ill-researched double-marriage for his nieces just to economise on costs.

Until the tragic suicides had interrupted his normal daily routine, Naranbhai's whole life had become one of trying to get the one and only seat reserved for an Asian candidate on the town's all-important body, the Town Council. In a radical departure from the usual committees of Whites and their appointed stooges telling everybody else what to do, the White colonial government had embarked on a tokenistic gesture to admit *one* Asian member to the Council. It was a pretty humdrum sort of post, carrying no salary and no real power. Its main function was to put forward the Asian-business-community point of view in all vital matters such as the putting up of shop signs in different languages and the regular collection of rubbish. But Naranbhai had treated the proposed post as no less important than that of the President of the USA. Whoever was to win this new, powerful office was going to be no less than a god - or goddess - for Naranbhai's chief opponent was a formidable Indian lady of equally formidable proportions known as Raushan. She was married to a much younger man who never spoke in his wife's presence and who seemed to live in perpetual fear of his older, much smarter, wife. This fact alone had caused Naranbhai and his supporters to conclude that nobody in their right minds could vote for such a pants-clad man-eater. But, far worse than being older and taller than her husband, she had married an educated *Black* man in grand style and had never ceased to remind every Asian she met that she had done this to set a good example of racial integration. She had even implied that by doing so, she had performed a supreme sacrifice on behalf of the entire Asian community, and that all Asians would somehow benefit by her alliance with a bright, young, upcoming teacher-aspiring-to-politician. By a curious process known only to the many contradictory forces of colonialism, for an Asian woman to marry an educated, 'upper class' Black, suddenly catapulted the couple to an unofficial "European" status. They lived in a nice house in the European residential area (provided by the Government, of course) and in seven years of marriage, had produced three beautiful, clever children. Raushan's mother was known to dote on her grandchildren and to boast to all and sundry: "Children come out so beautiful when the races are mixed. And so clever! So, so clever!"

Raushan's Town Council campaign had been fought along the lines that only *she* could truly represent the Asian population and look after its best interests for the future. The 20th century was more than half way through but "these Indians" still behaved as though they were in some 19th century village in India. She had all but declared the rest of the Indians (and Pakistanis) much too backward in their thinking and inclined to get girls married off at a young age instead of educating them to stand on their own two feet. Raushan had taken full advantage of the Mohini-Sohini incident by making her meek, mouse like husband drive his Bottle Green VW Beetle up and down the town's Main Street with a crackling loud-speaker bellowing out her distorted, but powerful tones:

"Now, you have all seen his ideas. See what would happen if he was in charge? If HE had his way, every single girl in this town would be married off to the first unsuitable man who was available and then, in her own shame, kill herself. This is the 20th century! Which century are these people living in? Education, education, education! That's what our girls need. Vote for me, and I assure you..."

Raushan's strutting about and lecturing all and sundry on the principles of inter-racial marriages being the only way to a safer world, had caused Naranbhai to comment to his own inner circle of cronies:

"You don't have to marry into a different race to get on with them. If everybody starts marrying someone of a different colour, then what will become of the world?"

By "world", Naranbhai of course, always meant his own little world and how that appeared to be constantly crumbling in the face of mindless atrocities like education for girls, which invariably resulted in spinsterhood. And now, to make matters worse, a woman was to sit on the prestigious Town Council. That fact alone, in his view, proved that the world had turned topy-turvy -- or to put it in his own language, it was a clear case of "Ulti-Ganga" (the Ganges had started flowing backwards.)

The pedantic Pandit Suddenly never missed an opportunity to pontificate: "But this is *Africa*, Naranbhai! If you must cite a great river, it should be The Nile, not the Ganges!"

Naranbhai shot him a cold look: "Just because we live in Africa doesn't mean we forget the holy rivers of India. If you were a proper Pandit instead of a part-time one, you would understand. When women are put in charge of things, it is the beginning of the end. Women function best with the restraining influence of a husband. Only, in this case the husband is an upstart schoolteacher who behaves like he is a future Prime Minister. And, just because he's black, he acts like her slave. Nothing like an obedient husband in tow to make her feel even more powerful!"

And, with that, he tightened his grasp on his twin-gods, Rahu-Ketu, constantly being rolled in the sweaty palm of his right hand.

In the days to come, and with the world about to end, he would need his gods all the more.

PRINCESS ELIZABETH

The formidable Raushan and the ambitious Mr Naranbhai had been long-standing enemies. Naranbhai had despised her from the moment he first laid eyes on her. At that time, she was newly married to the good-looking, much younger black African chap called Sam. The couple's car had broken down in one of the side streets leading off Main Road, and instead of letting her *man* sort it out, Raushan had begun kicking the car at various strategic spots with her high-heeled sandals, resulting in the car immediately starting up again. As she was doing this, Sam stood around helplessly sucking on an ice-lolly. Naranbhai took an instant dislike to the woman soon to be intensified when she was hand picked to play a pivotal role in an upcoming Royal visit.

Three years earlier, (before the Mohini-Sohini debacle and, Naranbhai's resulting election defeat) it was announced that the British Princess Elizabeth was soon to visit the small town on her latest Commonwealth tour. Naranbhai's joy knew no bounds as he imagined that his then brand new tour company would pick up some prestigious exposure by overseeing the tour details for the Princess who was sure to be taken to the country's biggest Game Park. The Bus Company consisted of no more than one clapped out bus, and a rather sullen African bus driver who was inclined to often not show up on duty. Even so, the so-called Bus Company had managed to safely take, and return, a few parties of tourists to the country's many scenic spots and national parks. Now and then, small groups of people would be taken to the spectacular Falls, and other areas of interest, but it wasn't yet a thriving business. But now, with a Royal Visit coming up, Naranbhai was convinced that new business from this visit would catapult his khattara bus to name and fame by virtue of one of the seats having been occupied by a Royal behind.

But the dreaded Raushan, in her role as social secretary and self-appointed co-ordinator-yes-woman to the many White officials who were in charge of the visit, decided to keep Naranbhai and his khattara bus a million miles from getting anywhere near the Royal party. Naranbhai was convinced that Raushan had only secured this important organisational role because long before she had bullied the gullible Sam into marrying her, she had been the lover of a number of White-skinned officials. All of Raushan's life was immorality personified as far as Naranbhai was concerned. Even so, he had written to her putting his battered bus at her disposal to take the royal party to the biggest national Game Park. When four weeks had passed, and there was still no reply, he decided to eat humble pie and approach the formidable Raushan directly with his offer. He ran into her at the town's only bank and came straight to the point:

"Princess Elizabeth - will she be visiting Murchison Falls? How is she getting there? My bus you know - we have done tours for over a year now. I can cancel all bookings and make bus available....absolutely free.....all I need is for my company to be mentioned....."

"Sorry, all arrangements are already in place," Raushan had said smugly.

"So, how is she getting there?" he had asked sheepishly.

"Top secret!" she had said smugly. "The Princess, what she will do, where she will go - is not to be disclosed to just any aandu-paandu who comes nosing around. Everything is in hand. All arrangements are progressing smoothly. Actual details - top secret!"

Later that day, in trying to impress his second wife that he knew something about the Princess's detailed schedule, he repeated Raushan's words: "Secret you know - top secret!"

"Yes, yes," said the unimpressed Mrs Naranbhai impatiently. "So secret, that probably even Raushan knows nothing about it. But likes to wind you up - and you just fall for it. You like to think of yourself as smart-smart, clever-clever, but you are taken in so easily! A child could fool you, a mere child...never mind a woman who has eaten her way through several grown men....."

A few weeks later it emerged that there was to be a special dinner hosted by the Town Council in honour of the Princess and attendance was by invitation only. Naranbhai had not received an invitation. As the day of the visit drew closer, the town was being furiously cleaned up. Pavements were hosed with high-speed jets of water and buildings were being re-painted. Red White and Blue

44

bunting was being hung to run from lamppost to lamppost, and across every shop doorway. Raushan personally went to each and every Indian shop and house and virtually ordered them to show some patriotism. The husband Sam had to drive her around in a car full of union jacks and bunting tied up in bundles which she would thrust at the shopkeepers and bark: "Here, get this hung up - now - this minute! Show some patriotism for our great, kind, civilised, rulers! God Save the King and err…also the Princess!"

In time, it was learnt that in the forty-eight or so hours of her visit to this country, Princess Elizabeth would open a new maternity clinic and lay the foundation stone for a new kindergarten school. She would also visit a botanical garden just outside the capital, and then attend a display of tribal dancing. After that she was to visit the country's largest Game Park. A banquet at the Town Hall was to be the finale of this flying visit. Naranbhai felt the blood pounding at his temples every time he imagined Raushan, no doubt in full African regalia, sitting next to the Princess at the banquet. And, he felt sure, Raushan was sure to tag along on the Game Park visit and pretend to know everything about every animal, appointing herself the official guide for the tour, when *his* Bus Company had done so much to promote and popularise these venues for visitors from abroad.

But then fate waved its magic wand. The Princess's visit was cancelled. While she was still in the neighbouring country on the first leg of her tour of East Africa, her father, the King of England, had died and she was to return to Britain immediately and take over her duties as Queen.

Naranbhai's joy knew no bounds. Never mind the King's death, at least Raushan would stop strutting about like a peacock and declaring herself the Princess's new best friend.

The next time he saw Raushan, he couldn't stop himself from asking: "So, are you going to the Coronation in London? No? Why not? Didn't the Princess send you a *personal* invitation?"

While the flags and bunting were hastily being pulled down so the African country could go into mourning for the death of a British monarch, Naranbhai never lost an opportunity to say: "See? When the right people are not involved in something, it can never happen. It's God's will!" And Naranbhai would grasp, with renewed faith, at his twin-gods, as ever cupped in the palm of his right hand.

Having secured such a delicious victory by the direct intervention of the heavens, Naranbhai felt he had overcome Raushan for good and, when some years later, the Town Council seat came up, he felt sure God would be on his side again. But the Mohini-Sohini disaster had cost him dearly and had allowed Raushan to steal a march on him, all over again.

REGATHERING THE TROOPS

Having fully vented his disappointment at the election result but refusing to be beaten down, Naranbhai soon started to make other plans. He liked to think of himself as a big-time business tycoon, but actually, most of this business ideas, (and businesses) had crashed as monumental fiascos. Being a poor relation of an extremely wealthy family, Naranbhai was resistant to the idea of working for a salary. To be a wage slave would be an unbearable come down. However ill-fated his business schemes, "businessman" seemed a far more befitting label. He deluded himself as having many fingers in many pies, but at the present moment in time, all he owned was a small set of ramshackle houses, arranged barrack-fashion and rather grandly called "Bombay Gardens." But, apart from elephant grass growing wild and unruly, there was nothing in the immediate vicinity to even vaguely suggest a garden. A crudely painted sign identified the premises as *"BOMBAY GARDENS - residences for decent peoples only - Rats not allowed"*

Now rented out to poorer Indian families, the houses had originally served as staff quarters for the many servants and attendants who had been attached to Naranbhai's ancestral home, Naran Villa, which stood a short walk away from Bombay Gardens. A narrow mud-track that ran parallel to an open gutter linked the two. The Indian servants, who had originally inhabited Bombay Gardens, had been brought over from India, in the good old days when Naran Villa had served as his grandfather's "town house" and when immigration was unrestricted. Naranbhai often observed, with a great deal of bitterness, how the descendants of some of those original servants were now far richer than himself. Unlike most other Indian settler-industrialist families, who had usually prospered with the passage of time, the Naranbhais had gradually seen a downturn in their fortunes. The reason? Lack of family unity. Although considered vastly wealthy compared to his poorer, Bombay Gardens tenants, Naranbhai was, nevertheless, one of many poor relations of a once distinguished industrialist family. The usual family squabbles in the previous generation had left him with only a small share of the original booty. His share had included the pink-and-green Naran Villa, a double-storey house with a curved front, its walls painted pink with dark green window frames. In its heyday it had been a sort of feudal manor. Now, through Naranbhai's unfailing efforts although Naran Villa was once again very much a centre of community activity and the headquarters of important decisions, it was one of his most cherished dreams to resurrect the glory and grandeur of the old days. The old days were actually not that old. Naranbhai's grandfather had come to East Africa as a middle-aged man. It had been a short-term strategy, and the family myth still prevailed. They were here to make money, gather up the gains and go back to India to live like kings. Naranbhai had been brought up to think of East Africa as a foreign land, where he was supposed to make his fortune and quit. And, two generations on, Naranbhai still bought into the myth of someday returning home. But he wasn't sure what he would be returning to. This East African country was scheduled for Independence. Plans were already underway. In Naranbhai's mind, that momentous event was to have been the watershed for the end of his African adventure. Until that happened, he needed to make as much money as he could because, after Independence, when power was handed over to the Blacks, they were sure to obstruct Indian enterprise and ambition. He had to make his fortune fast, but how? All his business schemes had failed, the latest being a cinema, "Naran Talkies" which had been forced to shut down on grounds of loose ceiling plaster which frequently landed on the heads of cinema goers when they were least expecting it. Soon, the ceiling was letting in sizeable quantities of water. During the showing of a classic 1940s Indian film, "Barsaat" ("Rain"), patrons were awe-struck at having rain fall on their heads while a monsoon shower poured in the film. A few days after that incident, the British colonial government forced the closure of the cinema owing to public safety concerns.

Although comfortably well off, Naranbhai was still largely dependent on his Bombay Gardens' tenants paying the rent on time. And, being poorer Indians, they frequently had all the normal excuses. Virjibhai the Compounder's pay was late. Satish the Bachelor – with all his talk of finding "Dream Girl" -- had spent his entire salary on gramophone records that month. Mr D'Sa had drunk all his wife's hard-earned money while her back had been turned decorating a cake. And then there was his best-friend and tenant, the part-time Pandit Suddenly, pleading poverty on ground of being a holy man. More and more these days, Pandit Suddenly had taken to pulling rank over Naranbhai on grounds of having read more English books. Even so, his Hindi and Gujarati speech was peppered with only one English word: *suddenly*. Hence his nickname.

Virjibhai the Compounder had taken out a huge vima - life insurance policy - so that his two daughters would be well provided for in the event of his death. Whilst appreciating Virjibhai's far-sightedness, Naranbhai was perturbed about this. It wouldn't be right for unmarried young women to come into so much money. He should urge Virjibhai to put *him* in charge of their funds if, God forbid, anything tragic were to happen. Girls who barely knew how to tie a sari round their waists should not be made economically independent. And then, that drunk D'Sa's weekly drama of beating his wife black and blue was just not on! It might set a very bad example for impressionable young women who might well go off the idea of marriage. Where would society be without marriage?

No, recently there had been too many irregularities at Bombay Gardens and Naranbhai meant to crack the whip and, once more, bring things under control.And, that house number 9 which still stood vacant would have to be rented out soon.

It was money down the drain to have a property sitting empty. He would have to get someone very decent and morally upright to live there. And this time, with this new tenant, he would call the shots from the start. It was hard to bring them to heel once they'd lived there too long. The next person who came to see him about the vacant house would be subjected to the full works. And with a renewed determination he smiled at the little figurines of Rahu and Ketu, the twin-gods who ensured man of a balanced life whenever he was caught between opposing forces.

BOMBAY GARDENS

While Camilla gazed at me, expectantly, I pretended not to be able to remember the old Indian name of the area we had moved to in 1973. How could I forget such a simple name? I decided to dramatise my efforts at remembering the name. I placed both my hands over my temples and suddenly said: "...something Gardens! That's what it used to be called. And the big house near it had another name, but the letters had fallen off the front gate by the time we came..."

Camilla is visibly perturbed. I ignore her expression, and continue:

"We lived in the big pink-and-green house with a big, semi-circular verandah on the front and the smaller houses nearby -- a sort of compound, almost like a barracks. It had become a Muslim school. My mother was a sort of headmistress of the school...

"Do you really not remember the old name of those smaller houses? It wasn't *Bombay* Gardens, was it?" she asks, her voice quivering slightly.

"Er...maybe....Bombay....it could have been the name of some other Indian city. Maybe it was Bombay Gardens... why? Did you know Bombay Gardens? Or anybody who lived there?" I asked Camilla, knowing that she is infuriated at my pretence.

"No, no, of course not, not at all. I was just struck by the name..."

She's lying! I know she's lying. There's nothing to be struck about. In the old days, various residential areas in our towns were named after Indian cities. Mama Safia once told me that the Asians had completely Indianised our cities - or at least those parts of it that hadn't been Europeanised. And the richer Indians were always falling over one another to move out of the Indian areas and into European ones. Apparently, in those days, Sunday evenings on the High Street made the place look like it was somewhere in India. Mama Safia said the Indians wore their finest clothes and paraded up and down the High Street to show them to other Indians.

"So, how did you come to live there -- er---Bombay Gardens, did you say?" she asked finally, trying to sound casual but her hands were trembling as she took a long sip from her glass of Evian water which she had ordered straight after the coffee and cake.

"I just told you. Some Islamic Foundation from Kuwait or Saudi Arabia or somewhere like that, poured money into the country and this whole residential area was bought up by them. Our Dictator wanted us to be seen as an Islamic country, although the majority of people were Christian. Anyway, various Saudi-trained mullahs started to arrive. It was around that time Mama Safia was invited to leave the village and move into this big house. The Qur'an school was just a short walk from there. Our house was huge...the largest house I've ever lived in. There were seven large bedrooms...."

"Was it furnished?" asked Camilla. I can sense she wants more information on the house and this is just an opener. I'm going to reveal a little, but not all. At that point I decided to tell her about the photographs, the photographs that had haunted my childhood. But I wanted to lead up to it slowly. She's all ears now, and I can take my time:

"Well, there were a few things lying around the house. The Indians had not been allowed to take all their belongings. And there was a death sentence for those who tried to wilfully destroy their things. But, before they left, some of them were able to sell many household items, I believe. I remember Mama Safia grumbling that they hadn't left a single light bulb in place! There was some very basic stuff like a dining table and some old beds and mattresses, but it was all quite dilapidated when we arrived. There was overgrown grass and the garden was a complete mess. The house had clearly seen better days. As a child, I was always bored because Mama Safia never allowed me to do any housework. Her sons did everything. She said she didn't want me soiling my hands. I was cut out for something different. The boys waited on me, hand and foot, and got an immediate rollicking if my washing wasn't done or my smart cotton frocks not pressed. And then, when I said, I'd like to sit in on her Qur'an teaching, she refused. She told me, quite explicitly, that that was not for me. She said I was a different religion and that I would learn about that later, when I was grown up. She had no wish to make me lose the religion of my ancestors. I was Hindu, she would say, pointing to the chain I wore around my neck. So, not having anything to do, I used to nose around the house in the afternoons. I only went to school some mornings and then too, more often than not, I would return home if the teachers hadn't turned up. And, one very hot and sultry afternoon, when I was trying to open an extra window which was high up, I climbed up on a table. As I did so, I noticed a tattered old photo album on top of the old-fashioned wardrobe. They obviously hadn't sold this mahogany cupboard, or it was too heavy for anyone to carry..."

"Album? With photos?" she's all excited again.

"Most of them had been removed. But they'd missed three..." I said casually.

"Real photos? What did they show?" Camilla is making a very poor job of containing her excitement. Yes, it has worked. She's hooked now.

"Did I *look* at them? You're kidding, surely! My whole childhood was spent obsessed by these photographs of strangers...complete strangers....people who had lived in this house, and then been booted out of the country."

I'm determined to spin it out. I go off on a favourite philosophical tangent of my own:

"There ought to be a special word describing the relationship between strangers who have occupied the same house at different times. You know, they have eaten, cooked, slept, fucked and shat in the same spaces, watched by the same walls. There should be some word describing this kind of intimacy...for instance..."

It's working. Camilla has another bottle of water and not only that, she has now also produced a packet of cigarettes from her handbag, although the small Indian Café is clearly marked 'No Smoking.' She points it towards me.

"No, thank you," I said. "I don't smoke, and I'd rather you didn't because there are no windows here...please...if you don't mind."

She frowns and puts away the cigarettes. She'll do anything I ask, because I know things that she wants to know. And that's without even the slightest inkling that I was the woman who carried on with her husband for a full five years!

"So," I resumed, matter-of-factly. "Forget Bombay Gardens or whatever it was called in the old days. What I sometimes wonder is how I came to be raised by an African woman. Why was I given to Mama Safia? Don't get me wrong, I loved her very much...."

"Err...yes...err...what?" Camilla was miles away. Suddenly, coming to, she asked:

"Why didn't you ask this...err...this Mama Safia?"

"She's dead now. Losing a mother can open up all sorts of wounds one hadn't previously noticed. When Mama Safia died, a whole part of me died with her. And I began wondering about the part that was left behind. Who was I? What was this body? In whose womb did it take root? Who pushed me out into this world? And, having done that, why did she have to give me away? It's a huge question, if you think about it. Mothers carry you inside their body, for a full nine months and feed you their own blood. Fathers contribute a drop of semen to the process. Previously, I hadn't fully realised the oddity of being an Indian in an African family. These things only surface when one is nearing thirty. Ask any shrink -- most weirdos, flunkies and junkies end up with a shrink only *after* their 30th birthday."

Camilla is thoughtful. Finally she says: "Oh, I don't know, I was very close to my father. He was both, mother and father to me. I can honestly say I never missed my mother -- but then I had an older sister. What about the rest of your family? You said you had lots of African brothers. Didn't any of them know how you came to join their family?"

"No, not really. I didn't talk much to my brothers. They were all much older and always busy. I was really only close to one brother -- the youngest. He was the one who joined the army. He died. Well, he was killed -- for failing to carry out orders. Anyway, by the time I realised that my situation had been an odd one, Mama Safia was dying of cancer. One of her sons brought her to London for treatment, and although I sat by her bedside, day and night, there was no way I could have raised anything like this. And now she's gone. The one woman who knew all the answers has gone."

MAMA SAFIA

Mama Safia was a beautiful woman -- in every sense of the word. But she was beautiful at the wrong time, and in the wrong place. A mysterious tribe directly descended from the Persians was said to live in seclusion somewhere on the island of Zanzibar. The people of this tribe were taller and lighter skinned than most of the population along the East African coast. Inter-marriages with other tribes were rare, but girls being girls, anything is possible. Mama Safia was most definitely partly of this mysterious tribal extraction. And that part of her which was not from the Persian originated tribe, was most probably Arabian or possibly even Portuguese, or perhaps a mixture of all of those. She was lighter-skinned than most Indians, but was still classified "Black African." She had made the irreversible error of coming into this world fifty years too early. Had she been a young woman in the Europe of the early 1980s or 90s, she would most certainly have been a regular fixture on the catwalks of Milan and Paris or, at the very least, a frequent, emaciated apparition on the cover of Vogue. She was very tall -- for a woman -- with long limbs, elongated torso and a shiny brown-black-ebony complexion. A well-placed, clearly visible black beauty spot on the right of her chin, just below the lips. Gigantic brown eyes, naturally up-curling eyelashes, and a prominent forehead which would have been covered with dark curls in cloud-formations had it not been for the restraining influence of her headscarf. In the privacy of her own house, when the scarf would sometimes be removed in female company, the clouds of hair would accentuate her high cheek-bones in a way that poets could only dream of and artists could only ever produce from their imagination

Mama Safia - whose name meant "Mother of Safia" was known as such because of her oldest daughter, Safia. Although she was, indisputably, the Mother of Safia she was, nevertheless, a victim of her unacknowledged beauty which had become a major obstacle to her finding domestic employment when she fell on hard times. No Indian woman was so stupid as to employ a beautiful African female servant!

After her husband died, Mama Safia had had no option but to try and earn a living. But, door upon door was slammed on seeing her beautiful face. Finally, she started to make a few shillings by teaching Indian Muslim children to read the Qur'an. For this, she travelled twice a week by bus -- all the way to the capital where the children of Indian Muslims were taught to recite the Holy book parrot fashion. The job brought in just enough money to feed and send her five sons -- the bane of her existence -- to reasonably well-equipped schools.

Years ago, long before she married, a mysterious sage in her island homeland of Zanzibar had told her that she would have enormous good fortune but only if she became the mother of at least *one* baby girl. He was a strange, elusive creature and nobody really knew whether he was real or not. Some said he was a homeless storyteller. Yet others maintained he was a restless Indian spirit of hundreds of years ago, who had met a violent and totally unjustified death. But then, the Island was full of such beings: here one moment, gone the next. A heady scent would announce their arrival and a mere rustle of fabric would denote their departure. Such things were part and parcel of life. It was said that these spirits had feet pointing backwards, but since nobody had succeeded in ever seeing his feet -- owing to his long white robes -- nobody could be too sure.

Years later, when Mama Safia married and moved into the interior of East Africa, her first child was a girl. Sure enough, her fortune soared. A few hours after she'd given birth to Safia, her husband was promoted from school gardener to Chief Caretaker of the entire premises of a private nursery, primary and secondary grammar school complex. And, in a radical departure from the norm, they were given a cosy little house in the school compound since her husband's duties required him to be on the premises 24 hours a day. Normally, at this point in time there were strict rules about live-in female dependants -- wives or otherwise. But the school authorities had decided that Imrozi could bring his wife and baby to live with him. Mama Safia was convinced this was the good-luck magic of the baby-girl playing out, exactly as predicted by that old sage in Zanzibar. Soon after Safia started walking, Mama Safia went on to have five boys in quick succession. The boys were all named after the days of the week and, by lucky chance, had all been born - in the correct order - on different weekdays.

The lucky mascot-daughter, Safia, died -- most tragically, in 1961, aged just 14. Unable to bear the grief of the death of his only daughter, her father died during her funeral. Dazed and numbed with grief, Mama Safia did not fail to register that her good luck had gone with the departing daughter. She took her five sons and went to Imrozi's village some miles away. Imrozi's elderly uncle accommodated her. She promised him it would be a temporary arrangement -- only until such time as she had saved enough money to take her children and go back to Zanzibar. The uncle was in no hurry to push her out: she was beautiful and her five sons were quite the perfect unpaid taskforce. She gave in to his sexual demands and, eventually, even started praying she would conceive another daughter so her fortunes could be reversed again. As time went on, and Zanzibar was plunged into a political crisis, she felt less and less inclined to return. Soon, what had begun as rape - the lustful conquest of the powerless - had turned into an unofficial marriage -- of sorts....

When Imorzi's old uncle died, there were no other claimants so Mama Safia just remained in his house. They had sufficient garden produce for food and a little bit extra to sell by the roadside, but there was no money for the boys to go to school. That's when she had started teaching the Qur'an, first to African Muslim children in nearby villages and then, her fame gradually spread to the larger cities from where Indian Muslims started sending a car for her.

Some of the villagers were convinced that the limousines carried Mama Safia to altogether different kinds of duties that had to be performed for Indian men. Little could anyone have guessed that her knowledge of the Qur'an -- and her ability to impart this knowledge -- was to secure for her a most comfortable and lucrative future once the country came under the rule of a Muslim dictator who decided to kick the Indians out.

SAVED BY A SONG

"Actually I'm really glad I've met you," I said this with renewed warmth to Camilla. I had started feeling somewhat sorry for her -- not because of what I had done to her, but because her Expulsion from the country of her birth suddenly dawned on me. Up until now, "Expulsion" had just been a catchword in my mind. It was something someone did to somebody else. It was a historical event. And it had had severe consequences for my country. I had never, ever reckoned with the individual personal trauma it might have caused those who were being expelled. I didn't even think of them as individuals; I thought of them as a group, a racial group....

I had come a long way from my initial reason for the meeting with Camilla. This was the wife of my ex-lover, and this was the woman whose short story manuscript I had smuggled out of the pile of entries from the "To Read" file. Suddenly, it looked like she might have the missing pieces of the puzzle of my life. I should show more sympathy and try to extract more information about the old days:

"I'm so sorry you were expelled from the country of your birth. You must have been quite young. Tell me, what was it like?"

"A nightmare! A complete and utter bloody nightmare! How strange you say you have songs in your head bothering you all day. Strangely enough, if it hadn't been for the songs of a strange man, I might never have come out alive."

"What man? What was his name? An Indian?"

"I guess so -- it's all gone a bit hazy. But he used to tell this story -- that was the story I eventually wrote for the competition. Funny thing is, I can't remember the ending. Perhaps I was never told the ending? Now, you might well ask how a mediaeval Indian story figures in 20th century colonial Africa, but I'm telling you..."

"If he told you the story, how come he never told you the ending?" I ask.

"I'm sure he did -- he must have -- he promised. It's possible he told it, after I'd left the area. You see, for a while, I had to live somewhere else. It's a very long story...*story*! Everything's a bloody story in my life!"

"But that's really good for a writer, isn't it? Now, why did you decide to submit that story without an ending? To the magazine, I mean..."

"I know I shouldn't have sent it in without an ending, but.... I don't know. Anyway, some years after the Expulsion, there was this big film -- from Bollywood -- featuring the same story - the story of the Princess who had lost the knack of being able to sleep....it's a real story - an old Indian one -- but films never get these things right. They always change historical facts because they have financiers to please -- happy ever after, and all that." She falls silent.

"So, what happens in the film?" I ask.

"You'll have to come to my house and see the video someday - err..no, you cant. I haven't got it. I lent it to my brother-in-law and he watches it ten times a day! Never gave it back!" she grumbles.

"What about the rest your family? Where are they?" I ask.

"No family. My parents died while I was still young. I only have one sister - married, to a much, much older man. About thirty-five years older. A complete and utter nightmare! Makes her life a complete misery. I keep telling her to leave him, but she can't - you know, Indian women. Apparently, during the Expulsion he did her some huge favour and now she's stuck with him. She feels bad about leaving him. Like I was saved by that song, she was saved by marrying the Grumpy Old Man."

"Arranged marriage?" I asked, thinking it was a fairly logical question.

"Why do you people think Indians only have arranged marriages?" she screams.

I note the reference to "you people". She has now promoted me from black to honorary white. And, I am neither. She can see I am the same colour as her

I change the subject: "Does your sister live in London?"

"Yes, she lives with her Grumpy Old Man. And "Grumpy" is the under-statement of the year!"

A PARCEL

(a suburb of north London, 2000)

"But what can it be?" the Grumpy Old Man was predictably agitated.

Something unusual had happened. The postman had apparently brought a parcel. But the old man had been in the bathroom and his wife had been wrapped up in the deafening grind of the washing machine. The postman had left a card saying there was a parcel to sign for, and collect, from the main North London sorting office, some ten minutes' walk away.

"For me? But how can it be for me? Who would send me a parcel?" he grumbled.

"Who is it? What is it?" his wife emerged from the small laundry area behind the kitchen, a heap of socks in one hand. She always got their socks mixed up. He wore black socks all day and, so did she. Their feet were roughly the same size. Socks and a bulky cardigan that belted at the waist were the only two concessions she made to the British weather. Otherwise her attire remained unchanged, as it had been all her adult life -- a sari: Polyester for home and silk for going out. There was a time when she would have worn a crisp cotton sari at home. But in Britain, such traditional luxuries as pure cotton were impractical. Washing, ironing, starching. Polyester could just be thrown into the washing machine with everything else, and since she spent the best part of her day hovering somewhere near that machine, it seemed like no extra burden to have to wash four or five saris every week. It was her favourite chore because, quite apart from anything else, the sight of her bra hooks tangled into the elastic of his underpants, was the only thing vaguely reminiscent of what had once been a lukewarm erotic bond between them.

All in all, she had adjusted very well to living in London, unlike those other East African Asian women who had become used to spacious houses and half a dozen servants and for whom, drudging away in closed-doors Britain was like a life-sentence. But for the likes of her, it was a definite improvement, not least because of the convenience of household gadgets - vacuum

60

cleaners, washing machines, microwaves, to say nothing of pre-packaged foods and ready crushed garlic and ginger. But her husband had got grumpier and grumpier during their twenty-eight years in Britain. He still entertained notions of some day returning to East Africa.

"To do what, exactly?" his wife would ask, trying not to sound too sarcastic and always remembering to add: "When you were there you used to fantasise about returning to India. Now we are here, you want to go back to Africa. What for? Who is waiting there for you?"

"The life.That's real life.You call this life?" he would grumble.

"Life is what you make of it. If you do useful things, life feels worth living. All you do is sit around all day and watch TV and video and then blame life for not being interesting enough," she would retort, noting with a sense of despair that when life did offer up something unusual or interesting - like a surprise parcel from an unknown source - he chose to view it as a sinister twist threatening to undermine his safe, cosy, daily routine. While she mused over his grumpiness, for the millionth time during their married life of twenty-eight years, he thought with some bitterness and resentment: "Now the ant has learnt to fly. She used to be meek as a mouse - and look at her now. This living in England business has really made her too big for her boots - and socks!"

Still grumbling, the old man held the official white postcard close to his eyes:

"It's a parcel, and it says it's for me," the old man said to his wife.

"So, what's the problem?" she asked impatiently.

"Yes, yes, but who would want to send..."

"Just go and sign for it and get it and then you might just find out who sent it," his wife said impatiently.

But the old man was still shaking his head.

"I don't know - this has never happened before. How do I know if it's safe to open? It might be a bomb."

"Don't be ridiculous," his wife scolded him and dumping the dozens of pairs of socks in his arms moved forward to take a look at the card herself.

"That's right - it's got your name and it definitely says 'parcel.'

So now she pretends to know how to read English, thought the old man.

He stood staring at the card that his much-younger wife had now put down on the hall table.

"Come on, get your shoes on! Aren't you going to go and get it? I'm dying to know what it is and who sent it!"

Typical woman, he thought! Always excited by surprises and parcels and presents. How can the same God who made Man also have made Woman?

"It can't be right. I'm not expecting anyone to send anything. Such things are dangerous. It might be something for which someone wants money. It's better not to collect. In this country they just send things and it says Free-No Obligation. You put it to one side and forget all about it. A month later they send a bill. Two months later they send threatening letters. Six months later they send the bailiffs. Anyway, if it was legal, whoever it's from, would've phoned to say they are sending something."

"Not necessarily. It might be a surprise present. Why don't you just go and collect it? It will make a good outing for you."

She relished any opportunity, however brief, to get him out from under her feet.

But he was still hovering uncertainly while at the same time studying the card with a concentrated frown as though staring at it extra hard would bring some illumination as to the identity of the sender of the parcel.

"It says here they will keep at it at the sorting office for two weeks from now," he said suspiciously.

"So? You can go and get it today, can't you? Or even tomorrow. But go today - go now in fact. I want to know what it is."

"Why do women always get so excited with parcels and presents?" he said with some irritation. "I'm thinking of all the safety factors, and all you care about is to know what it is! Women are so greedy and short-sighted!"

"Look, it's not even for me - it's for you! What is it to me? I just thought it might be nice if you go and get it. Take a nice walk. Might cheer you up a bit."

"I don't need cheering up. I'm fine as I am. I wish this hadn't happened. It makes me worried, and disturbs my whole routine!"

"What routine? TV, TV, TV, food, TV, TV, toilet, TV, TV food, TV, bed. That routine?"

He left the hall sulkily and went back to his armchair in front of the TV. She entered the living room:

"Look, would you like me to go and get it? I could do some shopping on the way."

"Oh no! Not more shopping. You went only yesterday. What are we going to do with all these things?"

"What do you mean 'what are we going to do'? What do you think I do with all the stuff? It's to make *your* life more comfortable. Have you ever wondered why your towels are never torn and there's always tea and coffee and biscuits in the kitchen? Do you think it just falls out from the ceiling? And the vegetables I cook? Do you think I pick them in the garden, if that small backyard can be called a garden? I have to go out and get these things for us to eat. It's bad enough you never come with me, or even offer to carry the load back home. And then you go on like I'm doing all this for me. Taunting me all day."

"OK, foodstuffs and all that, I know, I know, but where's the need to have twelve different tea-pots when you never use them? And that flower vase you came home with the other day? What about that?"

"It's for flowers."

"That's what I mean. You're the kind who would buy dog-food just because it's on Special Offer - whether we have a dog or not! You've bought a vase, so now you'll go out and buy flowers. And they'll die in a week, and then you'll buy some more. What a waste of money! "

"They won't die in a week. I've seen some really nice silk and plastic ones. They'll last longer than you!"

63

And with that bitterly accurate statement, she left him in front of his TV ads and went back to the kitchen. She had already resolved to pick up that postcard herself and walk to the sorting office later on that afternoon when her chores were done.

In the afternoon, she put on a clean pair of black socks and threw a thicker white cardigan over her sari. Rearing to go complete with plastic shopping basket in hand, she stopped at the small hall table to pick up the post office postcard.

It had disappeared.

THE PLOT THICKENS

"Where's that postcard about the parcel?" the young wife asked her grumpy old husband. The early afternoon, in typical British fashion, was turning grey and threatening to produce a drizzle - just as she thought she might set out shopping and then on to the post office.

"What card?" the grumpy old man asked evasively.

"Oh come on, that one, you know? Where is it?"

"I threw it out," he said, without looking at her.

"Why? Are you mad?"

"Those sort of things mean trouble. I don't want any trouble. I want life to be just the same," he answered.

She was exasperated: "Oh how could you do that? Come on, where is it? I will go and collect it."

"There is no need. I don't want it. It's addressed to me, it's nothing to do with you."

She decided to leave him sulking. He clearly wanted to be persuaded and coaxed into getting it. She decided not to play the game. He had obviously hidden the card in some safe place. She didn't believe for a moment that he could have thrown it out. She knew her husband quite well. He might pretend to be intolerant or ill-tempered, but he was actually a very soft-hearted person and gullible in the extreme. In his youth and even well into middle age, he had fallen for every kind of sob story and had always stood by those he felt had been unjustly treated. His protective instincts towards beautiful young women had sometimes bordered on the ridiculous. Isn't that how she had managed to wheedle her way into his heart?

No, no, it wasn't like that at all. She had never loved him - never even thought about him in that way. He was only a sort of exit-visa when political troubles came and she needed to get out of East Africa -- fast. And now, years after the crisis had passed and she was safe, she still stuck by him -- through some inexplicable sense of guilt.

When the two-week deadline in which to collect the parcel was nearly up, she decided to ask him about it just one more time:

"Where is that card from the postman? Do you want me to get the parcel for you?"

"No, I told you I've thrown it out. I want nothing more to do with mystery parcels. It might be a bomb, or it might be drugs. I don't want any trouble."

"Don't be so dramatic. It might be something from India," she said.

"I don't know anyone in India," he replied morosely.

"OK, someone else then. Someone from here."

"They would have phoned."

"They might have wanted to surprise you."

"I'm too old for surprises."

JASMINE & ROSES

(1955)

Still smarting over the Mohini-Sohini fiasco and his resulting election defeat, landlord Naranbhai scrutinised the woman who stood before him on the front verandah of Naran Villa. She was slim, of medium height, clad in a shocking-pink nylon sari with a tight, skin-fitting blouse that showed just a bit too much of the midriff. Her hair was coiled up high above her head, but a few strands had, one suspected very deliberately, been left to hang loose down either side of her face. There was a single pink rose tucked into the figure-of-eight style coil, arranged high above her neck. Pink crystal earrings, glittering like jewels in the morning sun and almost brushing over her shoulders, dangled languidly from her ears. Her wrists were littered with dozens of pink glass bangles interspersed with a few gold ones. At the very end of one wrist, a loose fitting gold bracelet arched down on the back of her lily-white hand. The bracelet was constructed round a single solid chain of gold from which hung various miniatures of well-known monuments fashioned in solid gold: Big Ben, the Eiffel Tower, the Taj Mahal and the Leaning Tower of Pisa. He noticed her palms were stained with fading henna and her long, pointed fingernails painted shocking pink.

Naranbhai sized her up quickly: fashionable, modern, and possibly quite well off. Probably in her early thirties, but trying to look twenty-two. Too much make-up, but underneath it all she was something of a natural beauty. Good bone structure with high cheekbones. A bit too bold perhaps. After all, she had come here all by herself. Otherwise she looked like a fairly respectable woman, despite the fact that she made direct eye contact when talking to him when the correct form would have been to lower her eyes out of respect and modesty. In any case, she was very fair-skinned - almost white in fact - so she must be a decent sort. That was the Naranbhai way of assessing a person's character.

Naranbhai knew she had come about the house. A three-roomed house was at present vacant in his exclusive and much sought-after complex of small houses rather ambitiously named Bombay Gardens. The absence of anything even vaguely amounting to a garden had not prevented Naranbhai from calling his ramshackle property by that rather evocative name. Only in small town land-locked East Africa could a barrack-like rectangular arrangement of small houses all of which opened their backdoors onto a shared, unpaved backyard, so mercilessly come to be associated with a name that conjured up images of a dirty, dusty and overcrowded Indian port city. Hence the addition of the luscious word 'Gardens', but apart from the odd potted plant wilting with thirst in the blazing afternoon sunshine, there was nothing to suggest a garden in the usual sense of the word. Emboldened by Naranbhai's imaginative and defiant description of his property, various other richer Indian settlers went on to construct small colonies of houses for poorer Indians. The tenants of these houses were usually people with low-paid jobs, or poorer relations who were on monthly allowances from richer ones. Such settlements, where doll-sized houses were available at an affordable rent,were usually called Delhi Gardens,Poona Gardens, Bangalore Gardens, Mysore Gardens, Madras Gardens, Benares Gardens, Calcutta Gardens. A particularly squalid one in the hottest, most arid part of the country was rather ridiculously called Simla Gardens.

Naranbhai and the other landlords were of the view that Indians on lower incomes should live in places named after exotic-sounding Indian cities. And well-to-do property-owning ones like themselves, should live in large, rambling multi- storey houses they called "Villas." The word 'villa' was either preceded by their own name, or that of one of their distinguished ancestors. The Indian intelligentsia, usually dismissed by the Naranbhai classes as being too shameless and westernised, mostly resided in rent-free government or private corporate housing, situated on leafy avenues named after British statesmen. In later years, when British rule came to an end, the same roads were re-named after newly appointed Black politicians, For Naranbhai, that was the ultimate come down in life. Once you had lived on a road named after someone with a white skin, however shameless the White race, how could you then live on a road named after a depraved and highly sexed Black native called something like "sammy-jomwaga-wanga" without a complete and irreversible loss of dignity and status?

Naranbhai and his extended family consisted chiefly of a first wife who had borne him a mad daughter and a second wife who had presented him with three healthy sons. Apart from the two wives, there were various female dependents on all sides of the family, all under the same roof in the huge Naran Villa, a pink double-storey building with green doors and window frames. From a distance the house gave the impression of a gaudy pink-and-green iced cake. And it seemed when the icing was being prepared, little bottles of food colouring had somehow accidentally spilled into the mixture, making the pink just a bit too pink and making the green positively jungle-like. The house had a semi-circular front resulting in a curved front verandah where Naranbhai was mostly to be found either rocking gently on a big swing or stretched out in a green-and-white striped deck chair with a copy of the 'Argus' over his head, dreaming up his latest business venture.

But now, as the fashionable woman in the shocking pink sari stood facing him on the verandah, he sat up straight and motioned her to take a seat on the large swing. She declined and remained standing, looking him straight in the eye.

Naran Villa was a short walking distance from Bombay Gardens. It stood on a clearing with wild, elephant grass on all sides. A narrow dirt track that ran parallel to an open gutter down below was the best and quickest route between Naran Villa and Bombay Gardens, taking less than three minutes on foot. Naranbhai believed in living close to his tenants. That was the only way to keep an eye on them. A sign at the front of his rented houses declared that they were only meant for "decent peoples" and he made sure that decency was observed in every sense of the word. Unmarried women or those unfettered by a restraining male presence in the household were not welcome as tenants. Naranbhai believed that women had to be supervised by fathers or husbands -- or failing that, even other senior males. That was the only way for society to remain decent and untainted by the influences that had so corrupted the western world. Women had to be custodians of shame and men had to be their guardians to ensure that they executed this God-given duty without the slightest bit of shirking.

"So, what does your husband do?" he finally asked the woman, having looked her up and down, and just a bit annoyed with his eyes that kept wanting to rest on her hint of a cleavage, filtering through the glass-nylon. And, unable to stop himself, he suddenly sighed, with all the pathos of legendary lovers through the ages.

The woman looked at him with renewed interest. Naranbhai looked back at her, still awaiting an answer. But instead of answering the question, she said:

"When you sigh suddenly, for no reason at all, it means somebody, somewhere has suddenly felt a surge of pain.....they winced in that very moment when you..."

Naranbhai felt his heart racing. A beautiful woman, and a poetic one at that...

But he composed himself hurriedly and decided to press on with the business in hand. He reminded himself he was a tough cookie and poetry-shoetry could not budge him from his astute business sense. He grasped at his figurines of the twin gods Rahu and Ketu and spoke with renewed strength:

"Be that as it may, I asked you a question: what does your husband do?" he asked officiously.

"He is a salesman. He travels a lot. That is why I have to look after everything else," she explained in a voice that reminded him of warm honey swirling into and then slowly becoming undistinguishable from thick, yellowing cream. He tightened his fist over the twin-gods as though appealing to them for more strength.

"Yes, I see..." he said, clearing his throat and unsure how to proceed. Finally he said: "Normally I don't do this kind of business with women. I prefer to talk to the man of the house. Send him to see me."

"He will return very late at night and then he will be off on safari again. He has to go to all the villages. Stays away many nights. I need to move house on my own otherwise we will be homeless," she replied. More honey went into the thick cream.

"And your reason for leaving your present accommodation? Any references?" he demanded bureaucratically.

"It's not big enough. My daughter is growing up and needs her own room...... .to study," she added as an afterthought.

"I see. Very good, very good. Good studying is important. But not too much studying for girls, eh? Other children?"

"No others. Just one girl."

"So why do you need a three-roomed house?"

"A sitting room, our room and then a room for her," explained the woman.

"You know Bombay Gardens is for decent peoples only? I hope your daughter is well behaved. Under your control, yes?"

"Oh yes, of course. I'm very strict with her."

"And the neighbours won't like it if there are male visitors when your husband is not at home, you understand?" He had to keep raising objections although somewhere deep inside he had already capitulated to the honey and warm, thick cream.

"Yes, yes, of course. But my brothers will be coming sometimes..."

"Brothers?How many brothers?" demanded Naranbhai, already smelling a rat, and dismayed to note that the thought of any male, whether related to her not, was already having the unwelcome effect of making him feel extremely insecure.

"Three - no, four....sorry five, no, six brothers. And of course many, many cousins."

"All men?" he asked possessively.

"Yes, all men in my family. I was the only girl," she answered gently patting the sweat on her neck with the end of her transparent glass-nylon sari. Naranbhai watched the glistening drops disappear leaving a sort of translucent sheen on her milky white skin. The cream and honey feeling started to return, only this time it had found a way out of his heart and was shooting towards the loins. He fought back in the only way he knew, by being even more officious and bureaucratic.

"What caste?" he asked. "Bombay Gardens is for higher castes only."

"I am a Muslim bhai-jaan,"she said softly, even apologetically.

"Oh, I see, I see," Naranbhai buckled down quickly for fear of offending someone of another religion and then briskly added. "No harm in that. Many of my good friends are Muslim. Like Police Chief Inspector Amin...err..Ay-men. Very nice, very nice indeed." And then, as a sudden afterthought he asked: "I hope you will not be slaughtering any cows?"

"No, no, never bhai-jaan. You see, we hardly ever eat meat," she explained.

The panic on Naranbhai's face was difficult to conceal:

"You're not...not.. from a mixed religion marriage, are you?"

In Naranbhai's view such a marriage would make her morally suspect.

"No, not at all, tauba, tauba, God forbid! We are pure Muslim, *pure*," she said proudly.

"Very good, very good!" Naranbhai was clearly thrilled. It was too good to be true. A respectable Muslim couple with just one well behaved, studious, teenage daughter and all nearly vegetarian to boot! There had to be a catch.

"You have one month's advance rent?" he demanded feeling sure the woman would mumble some excuse about having to get it from somewhere, some other time. Instead she reached into her pink plastic handbag and produced five hundred and fifty shillings - a hundred and fifty more than she needed to.

"I hope I brought enough," she said breathlessly. "I wanted to be sure we get the house."

Naranbhai's eyes gleamed at the mint-condition notes. He grabbed them from her and quickly began inspecting them for irregularities.

When he was satisfied they were real, he said: "Yes, yes, all right. Seeing as you are a woman alone, and your husband far away travelling, it is my duty to help you. I always help all my tenants." And then emboldened by her having addressing him as "bhai-jaan" he added, "You may look upon me as your real brother. You may move in as soon as you like."

He greedily started counting the notes, while the woman, Shahbanu Hussein, looking clearly relieved and delighted, ran off to make arrangements for the move. But Naranbhai was dismayed to find that fingering the notes did not give him as much pleasure as was usually associated with this most pleasant of activities. Instead, he found to his annoyance, he was feeling strangely excited and mildly aroused for an altogether different reason. Maybe it was his partiality to cream and honey? Then again, perhaps it was her perfume lingering so alluringly somewhere between those crisp notes? The notes were all green, but already to his mind's eye, they appeared shocking pink. And they no longer seemed to be made of paper, but of glass-nylon.

He buried his nose into the notes while at the same time reaching for his twin-gods, Rahu and Ketu, and started silently praying to give him strength to meet the challenges that must now, surely, lie ahead.

NARAN VILLA

Balance of Power

Naranbhai sank back into his green and white stripy deck chair and decided that the faint smell of jasmine and roses left lingering behind by his new tenant was really quite agreeable. He fanned the notes and fluttered them holding them up to his face to intensify the perfume. The morning breeze was still fresh. The mid-morning heat had yet to descend, and the combination of a golden morning, money in hand, a taste of honey in the mouth and an intoxicating perfume left behind by the swishing of pink glass-nylon, made Naranbhai count his blessings. On the whole, life hadn't been too bad. The combined, complementary strengths of his twin-gods Rahu and Ketu had always served him well and kept things fairly balanced: Rahu's good luck and Ketu's mischievous reversals and their mutual neutralisation of one another's extreme impacts, had ensured that life was anything but dull. However severe a problem, it never lasted too long -- as long as both gods remained in one's possession.

Naranbhai thought of himself as magnanimous in the extreme and felt he made many allowances for his tenants. The younger Mrs Naranbhai, his second wife, often chided him: "Soon you will make us move out and live under a tree so your precious tenants can take over Naran Villa, rent-free!"

He loved it when she exaggerated his generosity. It made him feel big and reckless -- the last of the great spenders. In truth, Naranbhai was neither miserly, nor a big spender. All in all, he usually struck a perfect balance between the two extremes. Shahbanu's arrival and his incessant need to impress her now threatened to upset that balance. Yet, the rent from Bombay Gardens was his only income. Over the years, he had embarked, without much success, on various other money-making ventures. A bus company consisting of just one, semi-mobile bus had proved a major disaster. And a cinema for mainly showing Indian films had had to close down because of a leaking ceiling. The repairs were going to cost Naranbhai thousands of shillings he didn't have. That entire debacle had caused Naranbhai nothing but headaches. Even so, he was determined that his financial situation should improve, and that in the months to come, the cinema should re-open in one of the grandest openings ever seen this side of the equator. It was in connection with this dream that his latest business project had first begun to take shape. He had, gradually and very craftily, increased the rents bit by bit on Bombay Gardens and his financial situation had, somewhat improved over the years. But then the number of dependants at Naran Villa had also increased steadily.

Although Naranbhai was given to occasional morose feelings at the prospect of heading a household consisting largely of argumentative women, he still had a childlike quality in that the slightest diversion could make him look on the bright side. So, when an attractive, pleasant smelling woman in a perfectly co-ordinated sari and skin-tight choli topped with matching dangling earrings had entered his orbit carrying enough cash to pay an advance on rent, he decided life was, on the whole, quite good to him. Always delighted to accept a new subject with ready cash, he was wont to sit down and calculate the takings all over again, multiplying them by twelve and mentally adding the figure into his annual income. And then, when he was satisfied that he was making more than enough to feed and maintain his large household with its many squabbling females, he felt unusually charitable towards the sari-clad battle-axes who filled his house with endless tittering, chattering, squealing, wailing, sobbing and giggling.

But today he realised, with something of a pang, that he felt well disposed towards the entire world for some other, quite inexplicable reason. It wasn't just the money. It dawned on him, with some vague, bittersweet regret, that the rent amount multiplied by twelve and added to his annual income did not bring as much satisfaction as the faint smell of jasmine and roses that lingered on the notes. He brushed the notes across his face and let his nose sink into their evocative fragrance. He toyed with the idea of keeping the money separate from his other stash, of never spending it, then quickly checked himself for turning into something of an old fool.

He quickly brushed off any dreamy, impractical ideas induced by her fragrance and folded the notes ready for the iron safe that sat by his bedside. There were expenses to meet - argumentative mouths to feed. And then there was his original, highly innovative business idea - his latest - yet to be implemented. That would involve untold expense. It was something the like of which had never been witnessed - not only in the small town, but also on the whole of the African continent. And, to date, it was still a secret -- a secret he hugged close to his chest for fear of being overtaken by other richer, more influential people.

"Money isn't everything," he often congratulated himself for his new idea. "One needs vision. One must see big-big. And then have the courage to do big-big work. What I've thought of this time, is big, big, big!"

The second Mrs Naranbhai had got used to this kind of talk and in keeping with her wet-blanket, bubble-bursting reputation had said: "Big-big idea also means big-big trouble when it all goes wrong!"

"I would have been a great man if I had the right kind of wife," he would tease her.

"So? What's stopping you? You already have two. Why not bring one more to encourage you in big-big ideas?" she would say with mock bitterness.

"A man can move mountains if a woman believes in him," Naranbhai would sigh.

"And who says the mountains need moving?" she would retort. Although she was not educated in the normal sense of the word, there wasn't topic under the sun on which the second wife didn't always get the final word.

Naranbhai was unquestionably the supreme head of his household but it was a position that was not entirely without its drawbacks. His authority and rule generally worked better with his tenants than with the women of Naran Villa. Whenever the women quarrelled amongst themselves, Naranbhai could do little except stand aside and watch. But the smallest crisis in Bombay Gardens often called for his personal intervention and afforded him a clear opportunity to stage a staggering display of his qualities of statesmanship. Like when Virjibhai the Compounder suddenly lost his wife to a mysterious fever and Naranbhai was able to organise and officiate at the funeral. Or when Mr D'Sa the drunk went missing for five whole days and Naranbhai was able to enlist the help of his police contacts in tracking down the drunken wastrel. He hadn't forgotten how Mrs D'Sa had beamed with pleasure on seeing her useless husband return and their normal routine of her being beaten up by his leather-belt once or twice a week resumed to assure everyone that everything was quite normal again.

And then there was that time when Satish the Bachelor was in need of a Dream Girl to marry and Naranbhai was able to line-up the choicest specimens from his wide circle of friends and acquaintances. For each of these projects, Emperor Naranbhai was able to take on the role of project manager and, for this glory, he was eternally grateful to his tenants. His task was made easier by the fact that the multiple crises in Bombay Gardens seldom had any personal reference to him whilst the quarrels in his own house were very much a direct result of his two marriages.

The chief protagonists in the Naran Villa house-wars were the older Mrs Naranbhai - Naranbhai's first wife now known only as Sushilaben -the official "Mrs" pre-fix being used only for her opponent, the second Mrs Naranbhai. The second wife maintained she was entitled to the 'Mrs' part since the older wife was no longer active, either in household management or in the sexual sense of the word. The older wife had borne him a mad daughter and both mother and daughter were now utterly dependent on Naranbhai's goodwill and the pretended generosity of his bossy second wife. The second wife, (who always insisted on being addressed as *Mrs* Naranbhai,) and who had appeared on the scene seven years after the first one, had produced three healthy sons. Naranbhai was deeply indebted to her performance in this respect. He regarded three strong and healthy boys in quick succession, one after another, as no mean feat in a world where bossy wives were more and more inclined to present one with girl-children, along with all the headaches of expensive marriages. But Mrs Naranbhai had done him proud and presented him with not one, or two, but THREE male heirs - already earmarked for Doctor, Dentist and Lawyer.

"I don't have just one or two, but *three* tickets for entry to heaven," he would boast to his cronies, referring to the vital fact that his final funeral rites would be more than adequately performed by such a numerous and efficient contingent of male descendants.

The fertile, second Mrs Naranbhai had also brought with her, as part of her dowry, a spinster aunt from India, who had once been known as "Kamini Devi -Venus of the Silver Screen." Now shrivelled up and wrinkled with unhealthy curiosity of the kind that emanates from extreme nosiness, and bearing visible scars of disillusionment and bitterness, it was hard to imagine that she had, at one time, been a beautiful woman - a leading light of the silver screen in its silent days. But then the talkies came and her crow-like voice proved utterly unacceptable to critics and audiences alike. And although once dubbed "Venus", as soon as they'd heard her jarring tones, they decided she was extremely ugly as well. Her entire family had lived on her earnings during the silent era, but they had fallen on hard times once her film career came to a sudden halt. After a few short-lived, unsuccessful liaisons with lesser aristocrats, Kamini Devi, now known only as Kamini Masi, took to the northern Indian hills, donning a saffron sari and fingering her prayer beads in an effort to lead the life of a jogan (a female ascetic.) But when her niece, the future second Mrs Naranbhai, was to marry a rich man and move to Africa, Kamini Masi was coaxed out of her hermetic ashram to accompany the new bride to the Dark Continent and help her settle into her new home. The visit had been intended as a six-month trip, or until such time as the new bride had adjusted to her surroundings. That had been over ten years ago, but Kamini Masi, who had taken to East Africa like a Tilapia to the Nile did not, as yet, show any signs of leaving.

Naranbhai himself had welcomed the aunt Kamini's presence in his house, not least because, his first wife was still in residence at Naran Villa and thick as thieves with his widowed older sister Nalini. Nalini was the mother of the unfortunate twins Mohini

78

and Sohini. Naranbhai reasoned, quite astutely, that if his new wife also had a female relative of her own to use as emotional blotting paper, then it would keep a balance and ensure peace between the two wives. So it came about that each wife was secured with a female ally of her own. By and large this balance of power had worked quite well. The second Mrs Naranbhai, by having an aunt of her own on the premises, had not focussed her attentions unduly on the first wife, Sushilaben, who remained more or less confined to her rooms tending to her daughter, the Mad Girl. She had been named "Kirti" some days after her birth, but nobody ever referred to her as Kirti. In spite of having such a beautiful name, Kirti was only ever known as the Mad Girl.

Although a monumental tragedy and a source of never-ending shame and sense of inadequacy, in practical terms the Mad Girl was really no trouble and usually spent the day sitting on her bed with her head lowered and gently swaying from side to side singing softly to herself. But once a month when the moon was full, the Mad Girl went quite berserk and the entire household was galvanised into a well-rehearsed routine. Doors were locked, windows closed and curtains drawn as the Mad Girl tried to wrest free of those who attempted to restrain her. Unfailingly, and as though overcome by some powerful, invisible force, she would break free and head straight for the flat roof terrace at the top of the house. From there, she would gaze up at the moon and sing in a loud, melodious voice until Naranbhai, her mother Sushilaben and Jannasani the African houseboy, dragged her back to her room and locked her in. She would then remain there, softly whimpering and singing through the night.

As far as anybody could remember, the Mad Girl had never, ever slept. Occasionally, she would stop singing and hold an intriguing whispered dialogue with a being only she appeared to be able to see:

"Why didn't you come yesterday? Where were you?" she would whisper to the invisible one over and over again before breaking into song.

The river remains thirsty, a dark, deep secret,
Easily uttered, but never understood.

79

Naranbhai would hang his head with shame as his daughter's melodious voice reached him on the verandah below. Whenever his friends came to visit and the men sat on the verandah slurping their tea from saucers, discussing politics and business and philosophy, he would hope against hope that the Mad Girl would not choose to break into song. But she always seemed to make a point of singing in an even louder voice, and she always chose words that uncannily seemed to elucidate the topic under discussion. On these occasions she sang a great deal more expertly. Naranbhai's cronies enjoyed his discomfort in between slurping and burping on their tea. But they did have the good grace to pretend to not have heard the singing as they ruminated over the consequences for Indian businessmen once the British left and this land-locked African country was handed back to its people. Whenever the independence theme was under discussion, Mad Girl would sing of chains that bind the feet. And how those chains would someday turn to cotton wool and blow off, light and wispy, in the gentle early evening breeze.

CONSUMMATION

There were several theories about The Mad Girl, and how she came to be mad. But nobody really knew for sure. Bombay Gardens could only speculate, while only one, or perhaps two, people in Naran Villa probably knew the truth. There was a school of thought that maintained that Kirti the Mad Girl had been born perfectly normal and had only become mad after her father had so callously taken on a second wife. But, there was another, altogether more delicious (and favourite) theory. Apparently, when Naranbhai and the Mad Girl's mother Sushilaben first got married, (he had gone to India for this) an astrologer had cautioned Naranbhai's old grandmother that the new couple should be kept apart for a whole nine days (and nights) and prevented from indulging in conjugal bliss. Otherwise, the astrologer is supposed to have said, Naranbhai would be struck dead within the first six months of marriage.

The most sensible thing would, of course, have been to delay the actual wedding by nine days, but the logistics were horrendous. Scores of relatives had made complicated arrangements to attend the festivities. Naranbhai's grandmother also feared that requesting a delay would upset Sushila's parents, since the wedding had already been delayed twice - once when Naranbhai's uncle died and then again when heavy rains had made the roads quite impassable. It could not be delayed again. Furthermore, she had been advised that while she had to keep the couple apart somehow, for a whole nine days, she could not disclose the reason for this to anyone, least of all to the bride and groom.

So, it was alleged, that when a coy, young Sushilaben dressed in red and gold entered the bridal chamber and Naranbhai followed sheepishly a few minutes later, fast on his heels came his old grandmother. She had already had her bed put in the middle of their twin beds. She came in without a word, lay down on her bed, covered her head with a sheet and said: "Now, go to sleep children. You must both be very tired."

That first night, neither Naranbhai nor his bride Sushilaben dared to say anything. They barely looked at one another, and since they were both quite tired anyway after days of protracted wedding ceremonies, it seemed a sensible idea to just go to sleep. And, with Naranbhai's grandmother so firmly and determinedly lying between them, there was little else they could have done.

But when the same thing happened on the second night, the bride felt most definitely put out while Naranbhai himself was completely mystified by his grandmother's behaviour. She had taken care of him ever since his mother (her daughter,) had died. There had always been a good understanding between grandmother and grandson, so he completely failed to see why she was behaving in this unreasonable manner, especially when she herself had been so keen to get him married. She had been the one to choose the girl, out of several dozen girls. And she had chosen Sushila because when asked to sing for the traditional inspection ceremony, Sushila had, rather shyly, sung a bhajjan featuring the twin-gods Rahu and Ketu, the opposing forces in all of Creation. That had clinched it for the old grandmother. Rahu-Ketu were her grandson's favourite deities and this was a clear sign from those very gods.

Naranbhai finally plucked up courage to quiz his grandmother over her strange nocturnal behaviour. Why did she insist on sleeping in the middle of him and his bride? He asked to speak to her alone.

"Not now, not now, " his grandmother said casually. "It's late and I'm tired. Tomorrow, tomorrow," and she turned over and deliberately started snoring.

Naranbahi sat up on his bed and looking across the heap that was his grandmother's sleeping form, and gazed longingly towards his bride. She turned to face him and he gestured to her to step out onto the roof terrace, signalling that he would follow. She started to creep out slowly, bangles jangling, earrings tinkling, sari rustling, silver anklets chiming. But she got no further than the bedroom door, securely padlocked from the inside. She stood at the door, uncertain what to do. She turned around and gestured helplessly to Naranbhai. He merely put his hand to his forehead in a gesture of complete despair. Finally, the bride slowly shook her grandmother-in-law awake, pleading that she needed to go to the bathroom. The grandmother (although fully alert) woke up feigning sleepiness.

"What? Who? Oh, you. I said to you, beti, you must always go before we lock up for the night. Now you have to walk across the backyard - snakes and Bhagwan knows what else," she grumbled.

She insisted on standing guard outside the tin-shed while the new bride pretended to be using the lavatory at the far end of the backyard.

After a few minutes she spoke up: "Finished? Come on, hurry up, I'm cold!"

"Don't wait for me, Ma. I'll be OK. You go back," the girl said as softly as possible.

"No, I have to lock up, come on!"

"I'll lock up Ma, you go," she tried feebly again.

But the old woman wasn't budging. She took astrological advice very seriously. These unknown forces were not to be messed around with.

The two women returned to the bedroom and Naranbhai was still sitting on the bed, puzzling over an explanation for his grandmother's strange behaviour.

The following day he managed to slip his bride a note (hoping to God she knew how to read) asking her to say to his grandmother that she was feeling unwell and needed to be taken to a doctor.

At first, the grandmother was extremely suspicious. But then, not wanting to take any chances, she agreed to let Naranbhai take the girl to see a lady-doctor in the big town some twenty miles from their village. She waited with them at the bus stop, as a cautionary measure, reminding herself that in this day and age anything was possible given that the bus stop was fairly deserted. Once they had boarded the bus, she decided she could leave them alone. They were hardly likely to embark on conjugals in the middle of a crowded bus.

Sushila and Naranbhai sat in complete silence on the bus. When it stopped at the next village to pick up more passengers, they alighted, and without a word to one another walked straight towards the ruins of an old palace surrounded by tall grass. They remained here for about two hours, well hidden by the long stalks of grass. Later, they boarded the same bus, headed back home.

As soon as they entered the house, the grandmother accosted them.

"What, what, what? What did the lady doctor say?"

"Nothing serious," Naranbhai replied evasively. "Just weakness. She had an injection. We have to go again tomorrow for another injection."

"Again? Injection? Oh no! Must be serious. I'll come too."

"No need, Ma," he said hurriedly. "She needs a series of these injections to build up her strength, and then she'll be fine."

But his grandmother had already started to smell the proverbial rat, not helped by the fact that she spied a bit of grass sticking to young Suhsilaben's lavishly oiled and tightly plaited shiny hair. She confided her fears to the astrologer who simply said that if her suspicions were correct, then that would be that. In other words, the end was nigh!

Naranbhai and his bride Sushilaben continued to do the daily rounds of the ruins. On the tenth day after the wedding, Naranbhai's grandmother moved her bed out of their room. They were thrilled and mystified. Suddenly, it seemed they were free to do as they wished and nice though it seemed, they both had to admit it had been more exciting out in the open, stealthily buried in the grass behind the stone ruins. But soon after their consummation was official, it was time for Naranbhai to return to East Africa with his new bride. They departed on a steamer exactly thirty days after the wedding. Unknown to anyone Sushilaben was then, already, twenty-eight days' pregnant.

LOVE IN RUINS

1942

The young Naranbhai, understandably, had not really noticed
his surroundings whilst consummating his marriage to Sushila.
The place that had afforded shelter and a degree of privacy to the
young couple was the site of some old palace, now in ruins, with
bits of stone monuments, here and there, jutting out from the
overgrown grass. It was obviously not an important monument
otherwise it would have been sealed off as a national heritage site.
The exact place where he had lain with his bride was just below a
strange slab of a wall -- almost like a rectangular pillar. Standing
by itself, about 7 feet tall and three feet wide with a depth of two
or three feet. There was no inscription. Perhaps it was a pillar left
over from a series of pillars that held up some huge Darbar of a
former king? Did they have rectangular pillars in those days?

The rectangular pillar just stood there, eerie and silent, while
Naranbhai and his bride lay shielded by it, totally absorbed in one
another. Had Naranbhai, in the midst of his unbridled lust, looked
up for just a second, he might have been able to make out the
form a slender young woman. He would have seen that she was
barefoot, her clothes ragged and her hair matted with lice. She
was sitting at the base of the pillar, her head resting against its
cold stone, whispering a song. It was almost as though she was
singing it for someone who was buried, though still alive, within
that stone monument.

At one point, out of the corner of his eye, Naranbhai did think
he saw something move quickly, but he didn't really dwell on it.
He had his own imminent ecstasy - and an insatiable young bride
- to see to. And then, suddenly overcome by guilt that although he
was legally married to the woman, he had had to drag her away
into the wilderness as one would an illicit mistress, he began to
lose his vigour. The mind can be a man's worst enemy in
sustaining the strength and ardour that is vital to good loving. For
a moment it seemed he wouldn't be able to carry on. Sushila
gazed into his eyes, her face close to his. Something in her eyes
made him regain his strength. Or maybe it was a small voice,
perhaps in his mind, or perhaps from somewhere behind the

pillar, which seemed to be saying: "Go on, go on! You must, you must! You must finish what you are doing, otherwise how will I ever be born?"

But, of course, he had no recollection of anything so bizarre. Memory is a strange creature. It selects and edits only that which we are able to live with.

Yes, those had been eight very strange days indeed. Those hot midmornings in the wilderness, when Naranbhai and Sushila just couldn't get enough of each other. But now, he always resisted the temptation to think back to those days. He was not entirely comfortable with any erotic memory that confirmed his one-time physical desire for the same Sushila, now Sushila*ben*, mother of a mad daughter, living under his roof as a retired wife. He had long since married a second time, and often chided himself that his lustful thoughts - and of these there could be many, on average, three times a minute or so - should focus only on his current wife, the second Mrs Naranbhai, and nobody else. But, in another unexpected twist of fate, these days those carnal thoughts were being invaded by a barely discernible cleavage that lay beneath some shocking pink glass-nylon....

KNOW THINE ENEMY

From the very day Shahbanu moved into Bombay Gardens the entire area was completely transformed by the frequent presence of an unusually large number of impressive cars. Ford Prefect, Anglia and, on one or two occasions, even a sleek black Mercedes, with its steering wheel on the wrong side. Naranbhai was extremely gratified to see the results of taking in a classy tenant. He toyed with the idea of raising the rents for the houses. After all, where else could one get to live at such a low rent and have such nice big cars parked outside?

Mrs Naranbhai was curious about Shahbanu from the moment she noticed her husband gazing distractedly into space while stroking his face with the new bank notes. She had already decided on a strategy of not letting anyone get an inkling of her suspicions. But then, when she learnt that the new lady tenant was not only a fair-skinned vegetarian Muslim but that she also had an absent husband, Mrs Naranbhai could hold it in no longer.

"What kind of man leaves a fair-skinned wife to her own devices, eh?" she asked her ally and live-in aunt, the ex-film star Kamini, Venus of the Silent Era. It had been noted by many that Kamini was an incessant chatterbox, perhaps desperately trying to make up for all those years of forced silence on the silver screen.

"Something definitely going on there if you ask me, something very black in the daal," Kamini replied dramatically to her niece's question, wearing an over-acted expression dating from Indian cinema's silent era.

And that seemed to be the only encouragement Mrs Naranbhai needed. Ever a woman of action as opposed to speculation, she immediately went into fuss-mode and started muttering, "They've just moved in. Can't expect them to cook straightaway - only human decency...neighbourliness. So what if they are tenants? So what if she is a Muslim? Muslims are also human. Landlords must set good example..."

Muttering thus to herself, she proceeded to load a large metal thali with numerous little bowls bearing ample portions of the regular Naranbhai lunch. Dal, vegetable curries of three different kinds, rice, chapatties, chutneys, pickles, papards and throwing a large clean cloth over the tray made the long-suffering Jannasani carry it walking some distance behind her to nearby Bombay Gardens. Jannasani was the black house boy who had probably originally been christened "Johnson". Either that, or he had worked for a White master who had insisted he take his surname. Many servants with unpronounceable names were told that they'd have better job prospects by being called Tom, Dick or Harry. Jannasani, as was his wont, simply followed orders - or had developed that brilliant knack of conveying the impression that he *always* followed orders - even when he was doing something off his own bat.

The tray was received with surprise and delight at the other end, although a moment of awkwardness ensued while a distinguished looking gentleman caller stood aside uneasily while Mrs Naranbhai waited for an introduction. The food-bearing mercy mission - a hallmark of the Naranbhais - was designed for the sole purpose of serving as a preliminary investigation of new tenants.

"Your brother?" Mrs Naranbhai asked finally, unable to suppress her curiosity about the good-looking Asian gentleman, "Helping you to move in? How nice!"

"Er...yes, brother. Yes, helping.... My brother, yes..." Shahbanu agreed eagerly while the man gazed intently out of the small sitting room window, pretending to have found some object of extreme interest.

Mrs Naranbhai noted, with some dismay, that Shahbanu's distinctive voice which had registered as cream-and-honey with her husband, was actually a sort of "Welcome to my brothel" tone: hushed, breathless, enticing, conspiratorial.

"And your daughter? Will I get to meet her?" Mrs Naranbhai persisted.

"She's in the bathroom. Just getting ready...." Shahbanu began and then stopped abruptly as she caught the man looking at his watch. "Won't be long...." she added hastily to the man

"Oh, I see!" Mrs Naranbhai gleamed with pride and satisfaction at her own powers of deductive reasoning: "So! Uncle waiting to take niece for an outing, eh? Girls! I tell you. They take forever to get ready -- but how would I know? God only gave me boys. Three boys you know?" she informed Shahbanu proudly, adding: "One will be doctor, one dentist and one lawyer."

Shahbanu was impressed: "How old?" she asked.

"Nine, seven and five," Mrs Naranbhai replied.

Shahbanu could not hide her surprise that a man of Naranbhai's seniority should have children of such a young age. In time she was to learn from the Goan lady, Mrs D'Sa who lived next door, that the present Mrs Naranbhai had only been in residence for the last ten years or so. The previous Mrs Naranbhai, Sushilaben, had failed to produce a male heir and as such Naranbhai had exercised an ancient right to take on a new wife. The sullen Sushilaben had produced just one mentally retarded daughter, Kirti, known only as the "Mad Girl," and that mother and daughter were confined to an upper storey in Naran Villa. Naranbhai paid all their expenses but Sushilaben was under strict orders to refrain from exercising any kind of authority over the household. She had been ordered, explicitly, to show the utmost subservience in the presence of the current Mrs Naranbhai, who ruled the roost on grounds of having brought into the world not one or two, but *three* healthy boys for Mr Naranbhai.

"Hindus you know," Mrs D'Sa had offered by way of explanation. "They have to have boys otherwise they can't go to heaven."

On this point alone, the Roman Catholic Mrs D'Sa and the Muslim Shahbanu felt a bonding that is derived from a mutual sense of superiority. Thank God we are not Hindu. But then Mrs D'Sa went and spoilt it all by needlessly pointing out, "Baby-boy or no baby-boy, Muslim men can take four wives anyway. At least Hindus need a good reason," and then realising that her remark may have caused some offence she jokingly added: "Just imagine the other way round! I have enough trouble with one husband. Who wants four and all, hey?"

Mrs Naranbhai's tray of food was taken into Shahbanu's bare kitchen and Jannasani was ordered to get back to Naran Villa and go about his many duties.

"Lazy as hell he is," Mrs Naranbhai said jovially. "Difficult to get good servants these days. At least he is not a thief, and he doesn't smell too much. Only when he smokes those dreadful local cigarettes - "

But Shahbanu failed to respond to Mrs Naranbhai's comments on lazy black servants and their smoking habits. Mrs Naranbhai, having positioned herself on Shahbanu's brand new plastic-covered sofa in the hope of a long chat during which more information would be gleaned, asked various nosy questions but Shahbanu was being consistently monosyllabic in her replies. Frustrated by her lack of progress, Mrs Naranbhai stood up to go. She assumed the air of one who had just remembered some urgent and vital task:

"Can't just sit around here! So much to do! The entire household depends on me. If I'm not there, everything falls apart. Must go. Can't expect you to offer me tea or anything. You have, after all, just moved in. My mother would never even take a glass of water in a Muslim house, but we are different. As long as it's not meat or fish or other dead flesh, we eat anything, anywhere. Must leave you to enjoy your lunch. Please send the girl to the house if you need any more of anything, like pickles or...."

Shahbanu suddenly relaxed and the realisation that the tiresome Mrs Naranbhai was about to leave brought a spontaneous smile on her face. The sense of relief made her animated and for lack of anything better, she said: "Oh? Really? Thank you, thank you very much!"

Mrs Naranbhai was put out by the enthusiastic response. She had simply done the normal thing of inviting Shahbanu to send for second helpings of lunch in case the quantities she had brought were insufficient. It was customary to offer second helpings to guests, even if they weren't eating at your house. But no person of good breeding was expected to take up the offer and appear greedy for more. So Mrs Naranbhai was truly amazed that Shahbanu, on such a short acquaintance, could jump so eagerly at seconds. Bad form!

She hoped against hope that Shahbanu would not expect daily feeding in double-helpings, and would realise that this was a one-

90

off gesture reserved only for those who had newly moved in, or a generosity offered in the event of illness or death. It was customary for neighbours to send trays of food on such momentous occasions.

VIRTUE & BEAUTY

Naranbhai had always shown a definite weakness for women, a kind of gallantry in the old fashioned sense which made him grab their shopping bags, hold open doors, vacate seats and generally pander to their every whim. This gallantry was not generally extended to any of his wives, or his own mad daughter. It was strictly reserved for other people's wives and other people's daughters.

The very first evening after Shahbanu had moved into Bombay Gardens and drawn many gasps from all and sundry, Naranbhai already felt a degree of ownership towards the new woman tenant. When he came out onto the verandah of Naran Villa for the usual early evening chat with his cronies, they looked at him with renewed respect and envy.

"Naranbhai, how lucky for you to have such a fair and beautiful tenant," one of the men said wistfully.

Another added: "Just like a film star! Oh God, what wouldn't I give for..."

"Hey you!" reprimanded Naranbhai. "No bad-eyeing of my tenants. Her husband travels all the time and I consider myself in charge of her welfare in his absence. I will not tolerate any indecent thoughts about her. From today, she is like my - err...my sister. She calls me 'bhai-jaan' - brother, you know? Came to see me herself to fix up the rent and everything. Poor woman, husband travelling all the time and she having to do man's work. Tut-tut, what a world we live in!" he concluded with genuine compassion for the married-but-to-all-intents-and-purposes-single Shahbanu Hussein.

"Naranbhai, err...have you err...actually met her husband?" asked Pandit Suddenly.

"No, not yet. But soon, one day, I'm sure I will, I will..."

Even as he said it, he most sincerely wished that Shahbanu's husband, whoever and wherever he was, would just be struck by lightning, leaving the way clear for Naranbhai to comfort her in her bereavement.

Pandit Suddenly was determined to pursue his line of inquiry:

"Naranbhai, it's just that...when a woman suddenly says her husband is always suddenly travelling, we should be alert...you know what I mean?" he reduced the last few words to a whisper.

"No I don't know what you mean!" Naranbhai said coldly.

Although he didn't like the idea of Shahbanu having any kind of husband - present or absent - neither did he want to encourage the kind of talk that cast any doubt over her impeccable beauty because a woman without virtue, could never truly be considered beautiful.

After two weeks had lapsed and the Naranbhais' tray and its many small metal containers of different curries still hadn't been returned from Shahbanu's, Mrs Naranbhai concluded that the woman was extremely ill bred. She lost no time in pointing in this out to her newly smitten husband:

"These Muslims, you know? They love our food, but no manners! Trays and utensils from other people's houses should be returned promptly, and filled with other food on return. Those are the rules. Everybody knows that. Even when I send something to Mrs D'Sa - although they are of a different religion - she promptly returns all utensils with a few raisins if nothing else. They are so poor and yet..."

Naranbhai waved his arms impatiently. "What are you now on about woman? I'll buy you a new tray and some more bowls...."

"That's not the point!" she retorted. "When neighbours send food, it is only good manners to return their dishes promptly...."

"She's just moved in. Give her a chance," Naranbhai said, as ever defensive of his beautiful tenant and irritated in the extreme that his battle-axe of a second wife should draw attention to Shahbanu's lack of etiquette. That beautiful, elegant, fair lady was nothing short of an epitome of good manners and good breeding.

That same afternoon, a beautiful young woman of about fifteen or so, presented herself at Naran Villa bearing a tray covered in a hand-embroidered cloth. Mrs Naranbhai immediately recognised her own tray cover and gathered the girl must be Shahbanu's daughter Saira. She leapt forward to receive the offerings. Naranbhai looked at her triumphantly as though to say: "See? What did I tell you? Just give it time...."

Even as he thought this, he remained wonder-struck by Saira's youthful beauty, in every way a younger, firmer imitation of the delectable Shahbanu herself.

Mrs Naranbhai removed the cloth eagerly only to find various metal bowls and other containers, all empty, badly rinsed and untidily piled on the tray. Her dismay was clear. After Saira had left, she dug into her husband again.

"Can you believe it? She sends the bakulis back empty - completely empty - except for stale traces of food.....at least she could have scoured them...."

"What are you grumbling about now?" Naranbhai challenged. "Only this morning you were grieving the loss of your tray and your bowls. Now that they're back, you're still grumbling."

"Poor show, very poor show," muttered Mrs Naranbhai.

This was well before Naran Villa and Bombay Gardens had learnt that Shahbanu never ever produced any real food and both mother and daughter appeared to live on fruit juice, instant coffee and biscuits. It was a truth that caused Mrs Naranbhai even more consternation. How could a woman, who never produced delicious home-made edibles, ever be considered attractive by men? And yet Shahbanu, in just a little over two weeks, appeared to have every single specimen of the human male species dancing attendance on her. Bachelor Satish had put his khattara car at Shahbanu's disposal and was less and less willing to run Mrs Naranbhai into town. Pandit Suddenly had taken to changing into a clean dhoti every day. And even the drunken D'Sa would bow every time Shahbanu passed by him in the backyard to make her way to the bathrooms at the far end of the backyard. Men were, indeed, utterly gullible creatures, concluded Mrs Naranbhai in a conversation with her ex film star aunt.

The aunt Kamini, most tactlessly, responded: "Yes, my dear niece. You know all about that, don't you? How many women succeed in marrying an already married man, hain? Don't worry - - you're well ahead of the others!"

WHOSE BRIDE?

For Mrs Naranbhai, becoming the second wife of a man ten years older than herself, who still had his original wife in residence was, believe it or not, the best possible escape from a fate that otherwise didn't bear thinking about. How exactly this had come about, nobody was too sure. That was always the way in claustrophobic, small town communities. Assumptions were made, and conjectures arrived at with vast leaps in logic. The missing bits were filled in with whatever assumptions matched the moral and cultural prejudices of the speculators themselves. Cryptic remarks spanning over many years were pieced together and deductive reasoning was applied with meticulous attention to inconsistencies spotted in the official version, as offered by the protagonist of the scandal in question. The story carried from year to year, acquiring more colouring and texture and, as time went on, beliefs intensified -- and re-intensified. Sometimes these stories carried such legendary proportions that it was impossible to know whether it had actually happened, or whether it was the plot of some Indian film of the 1950s. Either life imitated art, or art itself was inspired by life. Often there was certainly no way of knowing which was which. And so it was with the question of how Mrs Naranbhai had come to become Naranbhai's second wife. A story had emerged over the eleven years or so that they had been together, and once the details were perfected and found to be satisfactory - as a story - it soon became the official version. That is the way it is with history. It all depends on who's telling the story and, to a larger extent, it depends on the recipients of that story.

It was said that when the second Mrs Naranbhai was still known only as Geeta, and had just turned 17 (sometime in the late 1940s,) a marriage had been arranged for her according to tradition. Of course she hadn't seen or met her husband-to-be. But some of his female relatives had checked her out, looking her up and down - pulling at her plait to ensure it was real, and had asked her to open her mouth so her teeth could be counted. They picked Geeta out of the dozen or so girls they'd personally inspected. All that the young Geeta knew about her husband was that he was not deaf, dumb, blind or lame, and that he was twenty years old. In those days girls had to consent to any marriage on the grounds that the 'boy' in question appeared to have no physical disability. His family lived in an Indian town several hundred miles from the village.The various wedding ceremonies - detailed and prolonged - had gone off without a hitch and as the bridal party departed on the final evening with the new bride in tow, she was even mildly excited at the prospect of impending sexual intimacy with a complete stranger.They still hadn't met or spoken. She hadn't dared to look up at him and he, even if he wanted to, could not have seen her owing to the full, heavy gold-embroidered gunghat (veil) over her face. The gunghat was held in place by thick garlands of flowers, and within the gunghat, her features further obscured by ornate jewellery - a teeka over her brow and a gigantic nose-ring almost covering the lower half of her face. They settled into the back seat of a heavily adorned car, driven by the groom's Uncle. A male cousin sat in the front, while various other relatives and wedding party guests were to return by train. The car sped along smoothly for a while,but, thirty minutes into the journey, there was a multiple car crash. Tragic though it may seem, the real tragedy was that the other two cars were also carrying bride-and-groom pairs in the back. All three brides were in red and gold, and all three were heavily gunghatted. One of the brides and one of the grooms died on the spot. The two pairs that survived, miraculously sustaining only minor injuries, were rushed to hospital.And then,due to some inexplicable bureaucratic error, enhanced by the fact that neither groom would have recognised his own bride - or vice versa - each bride wound up with the other's groom. And since the two families didn't really know each other, upon discharge from hospital, each pair departed to their separate destinations.

The future Mrs Naranbhai arrived at what she thought was her new home all weak and quite a bit shaken, one arm in a sling. Her new husband or the man she thought was her husband - was a pleasant, talkative young man who did not immediately throw himself at her. Quite apart from the fact that he was extremely talkative and loved the sound of his own voice, he still had a bandage on his head. He gathered she was still in shock, so he just concentrated on making friends and getting to know her. They talked all night. He told her he was going to start studying to become a lawyer. He bragged about how he could have become a professional cricket player if he'd wanted to. He spoke of aunts and uncles - brothers and sisters. He talked of his favourite food. She remained shy, but managed to ask intelligent questions about everything. She coaxed him to talk more and more. The young man was in heaven! He had found the perfect wife. A good listener was always good wife-material for an ambitious young man. But even the best listeners can sometimes doze off, and that is exactly what Geeta did, just before sunrise...

One of his aunts arrived the following morning. One look at the bride and she screamed and fainted. When they revived her with splashes of cold water and smelling salts, she exclaimed: "But who is *she*? This is not the one we went to see..."

Nobody took her seriously at first. But the aunt was insistent that this young girl was a complete stranger. "She's not the one with whom he took the sacred rounds of the fire. She's not the one with whom those mantras were read. Oh God! Who is she? And they spent the night together...Hey Ram! Ram, Ram!"

Once all the hysteria had died down, the budding young lawyer-hopeful assured everyone that he had only chatted to her and that no "harm" had been done. All that remained was to locate her real in-laws and deliver her to them as soon as possible.

It ought to have been the proverbial happy ending, but it was also an ending with a twist. While one surviving bride had had a happy reunion with her over-talkative, lawyer-to-be husband, the other surviving bride, Geeta, had been rejected by her husband - as well as his entire family - on grounds of having spent a whole night with a man who was not her husband.

"But we just talked. He didn't lay a finger on me," she protested.

It was not believed. How could a normal, healthy man just talk all night? And what on earth was there to talk about? He, aspiring to be a lawyer and she, barely primary school educated? No, she was soiled. Second-hand goods - a complete disgrace not only to her family, but the community at large. And, by the same token, a source of shame and disgrace for the entire province, the whole country and a blot on the good name of Indian womanhood.

It was the worst possible predicament for a young Indian girl. Married, but as good as widowed. Virgin, but tainted on account of having spent *one* night talking with a stranger. She was not allowed to take on the widow's garb.That would've been blasphemous since her husband was still alive. Remarriage - even if such a radical thing had been allowed - was completely out of the question because it was assumed she had lost her virginity to someone other than her husband - hussy! It really was a fate worse than death. And, the future Mrs Naranbhai, had chosen this fate rather than the death that Mohini and Sohini -- her future husband's twin nieces -- were to choose some years later, in 1955, in a not too dissimilar situation.

As identical twins, Mohini and Sohini had been married off to a pair of brothers.The brothers looked vastly different, so the girls were supposed to know which was which. But heavily veiled throughout the joint wedding ceremony, Mohini and Sohini had somehow ended up spending the night with one another's husbands. The husbands should have known better, but they pleaded that the girls looked exactly alike and it was a natural mistake.Even so, when the mistake was discovered, neither husband was prepared to have his original wife back. And nor could the twins stay on with the man that each thought was her respective husband because, the sacred words had been said with a different one.But, on that occasion, a long-established post-marital ritual, necessitating a compulsory visit by the bride to her parental home a month after the marriage, came to the rescue and the impasse was solved. After the first ritual bridal visit, both brothers decided not to bother to escort their wives back home, since both women were now tainted beyond repair.

Unlike Geeta - the future second Mrs Naranbhai - Mohini and Sohini had been intelligent enough to choose death over the fate that might have awaited them as married-but-single women.

A MEETING AT GOD'S HOUSE

The future second Mrs Naranbhai, however, was an altogether different kind of woman even by the standards of those days. She kept protesting her innocence in the belief that eventually, somebody would believe her. After the dreadful bridal mix-up was sorted out, she was returned to live with her parents. But they were equally disgusted with her for having spent a night with a complete stranger, yet so petulantly insistent on her virginity. There was only one thing for it. She decided to go to the hills and live like a jogan. Her maternal aunt Kamini had taken that path into the hills when her short-lived film career and all the peripheral romantic activities around that had failed. And it seemed to have worked for her. Or at least it had stopped the tongues wagging. Once a fallen woman was prepared to live out the rest of her years in seclusion and service to God, then all her imagined sins could be forgiven.

So, at the tender age of 17 and a bit, Geeta went to Haridwar to join Kamini Masi. Aunt and niece were at peace. Kamini Masi was completely supportive and understanding of her young niece's predicament -- the injustice of it all.

Just before her 18th birthday, and a day before she was to take the final vows to join an order of celibate jogans, a mysterious stranger arrived from Africa. In India, people belived the most ridiculous stories about Africa. The "Dark Continent" was said to be full of man-eating tribes who lived in jungles but the few, brave Indians who had gone there and tamed the wilderness, were said to be laden with gold from head to toe. "Their pots and pans are made of gold and diamonds can be picked up along the way, any time you go for a walk!" It was rumoured that the mysterious stranger was one of the richest Indians in Africa - descended from a distinguished family of industrialists -and had probably come on a special pilgrimage of thanksgiving because his many businesses in East Africa were making lots of money. Little could anyone have guessed that his pilgrimage was just the latest in a series of antidotes that had been prescribed in connection with the madness of his one and only daughter.

Geeta had been barely aware of the stranger's presence in the vicinity when their eyes met across a long, steep, flight of temple stairs. He was descending, having just offered his supplications and having made yet another plea for a son. His marriage had so far only resulted in one mad daughter. As he descended the treacherous stone-steps, she was ascending for her daily audience with a deity. This was her final day of internship. On the very next day, she was to take the vows that would render her a celibate and ascetic for life.

The bright sunshine outside the temple made the man from Africa slightly dizzy. He faltered on the uneven, support-less stairs, and would have fallen had it not been for a young jogan in a saffron sari quickly by his side, offering him the end of her sari to wipe off the sweat that had broken out on his brow.

Yes, fate had intervened. It was like Geeta was being given one last chance to rejoin the human race instead of condemning herself to the lonely life of a jogan. The man, for his part, was convinced that this young woman was the answer to all his prayers. She would give him a male heir. It was a sign from God. Just the fact that they had met in such a holy place, and that too at the threshold of the holiest of all temples, had convinced him that this was a match made in heaven.

But nobody really knew the full story of that first encounter between husband and second-wife-to-be. There were many versions of the truth. But this was the favourite version. Beyond that, it wasn't even clear if Naranbhai had actually married her at some stage, or had, somewhere along the line, just started referring to her as his "wife."

A SENSE OF ADVENTURE

The second Mrs Naranbhai and her aunt Kamini masi (ex film star of the silent era) both felt like pioneers conquering new territory when their ship touched the Eastern Coast of Africa. Modern day, jet-age travellers can never fully appreciate the mystery and sheer delight of the first sighting of a coastline from the sea. The dim, majestic outline of mountains, rising in the distance, and the gradual, very gradual, solidification of land, distinguishing itself from the sea. Approaching it thus, one feels like an interplanetary traveller approaching new worlds. Aunt and niece watched in awe as land came closer...and closer...

Once the ship had docked, they got off to take the train into the interior. Mrs Naranbhai's head was reeling with the sights and sounds. She had seen numerous white people in India, but she had never ever seen a black person for real. Naranbhai had already gone on ahead of them, to see to various formalities, and then send for the two women. Besides, he had to prepare his first wife, Sushilaben, for the shocking news that he had met and married another woman in India, because God had guided him to do so. To the local authorities he had been able to say that he had converted to a kind of Islam which allowed him to marry more than once by a fixed term contract for the specific purpose of acquiring a male heir. And, this East African country, although ruled by the British, was one where polygamy was already known and widely practised. It co-existed side-by-side with the teachings of the Christian missionaries, and, as such, the authorities were not totally averse to such a request. As long as Naranbhai was not involved in any nationalistic, trouble-making activity, they couldn't care less about the number of wives. A number of Indian men already had unofficial second wives - usually African - in the bush.

Having got off the ship and whizzing along towards the interior on a train, the clearest thing the junior Mrs Naranbhai remembered thinking at the time was that this was a beautiful country, but what a pity about the natives. Why did they have to be so dark? How could one know whether they were clean or not? With such dark skin how do you tell dirt apart from skin colour?

Did they wash? How did they know when all the dirt had washed off? Did the water turn black? So why were the rivers and lakes so clear and sparkly blue? Still trying to puzzle it out, she said to her aunt:

"So green, everywhere you look greenery and greenery. And red soil. Just look at it! I've never seen so many banana trees in my life. Such a nice place! Pity the natives can't be sent to live somewhere else. Do you think they'll bother us? Is it true they eat humans? I hope they don't come near us."

Aunt Kamini, never one to play down a situation but, wherever possible, to always dramatise it further and add as much mirch-masala as possible, lost no time in adding to her niece's fears:

"Don't worry, beloved niece. If any of them touches you, or if you happen to brush past one with a black skin, don't worry. Just wash your hands exactly sixty-seven times and you'll be purified again. That is what we used to do in India if we happened to touch an achhut (untouchable) by mistake. And if you're making pickles or anything like that, make sure there's no kaalias (blackies) in the vicinity. Even their shadow must not be allowed to fall where you are making achaar. I think Naranbhai said there's a black servant in the house. Be careful. Oh, and used sanitary towels... these must always be burnt. An enemy must never ever be allowed to possess a trace of your menstrual blood...."

How "Black" came to mean "enemy" was not explained.

Mrs Naranbhai wondered how she would cope with a black servant actually moving around and working in her new home. She had been told it was a very, very large house and other relatives also lived in. How she wished her new servant could be Indian. There was nothing quite so satisfying as having someone of your own race to boss around. But an Indian servant would have been out of the question. Those days had long gone. Indians no longer came to East Africa to work as domestic servants or labourers. They had now been promoted to the mercantile-middle-class, a class much needed by the British rulers. When you are a ruler, it is no fun to have peasants alone. A middle-class with all its normal middle-class greed and aspiration makes it easier to navigate affairs -- to administer, manipulate, divide and rule.

102

Sure, in the not-too-distant future a black middle-class would emerge but, for the time being, the Indians would have to do. Once they'd served their purpose, they could be dumped, or moved on to some other colonial holding, to play the same role all over again. Perhaps, some day, if all else failed, they could be invited to Mother Britain to drive the buses and set up corner shops that would remain open after hours. The white working classes were getting grumpy about working beyond six p.m. in the evening. Just an idea. It would probably never happen. These people with their saris and dhotis and chappals would never be able to live in temperate zones. When they'd served their function in the newer colonies of Africa, it was widely expected they would go back to India -- richer than they'd started out -- and pick up where they'd left off.

There were quite a lot of other Indians on the same train. Some had lived in East Africa for years and years and were simply returning after short holidays or wedding trips back to the homeland. One of these women, a great expert on East Africa, was able to enlighten Aunt Kamini and her niece with the indisputable authority of one who actually *knows*.

"There's a King, you know? A real black King!" said one of the women, quickly adding: "Listen, sister and daughter, whenever you go out, wrap your saris well over your chest and arms. These natives just snatch at gold chains and bracelets."

Mrs Naranbhai automatically reached for the end part of her sari and immediately wrapped it tightly around herself to cover up her newly acquired wedding jewellery and absently started wondering if she would ever get to see this native King.

"A black King? Can blacks become Kings?" the niece looked doubtful. And then remembering the Maharajas of her own land she asked. "What does this King wear, do you think?"

"Probably nothing. All these savages roam around naked you know? No shame!" Aunt Kamini answered.

"What's his name, this King?" she asked the other women passengers. They looked at one another and could not produce his name.

"No name," one said finally. "He's just known as King. His father and grandfathers were also known as KING. They are a fierce people. Their women are said to be very beautiful -- according to our men, but I don't see how that can be. How can black be beautiful? But men you know....blinded by lust, they don't care what they stick their thing into..."

Mrs Naranbhai winced at the prospect of her new husband sticking his "thing" into anything other than her. Her thoughts turned to the King again. She wanted to know more about him and the women were only too pleased to enlighten her:

"He's supposed to be very handsome and has many wives," and then lowering her voice to a conspiratorial whisper, she added: "One of his favourite mistresses is supposed to be an Indian. A Muslim lady. But then, these Muslim women never care about being one of many......"

The Aunt Kamini interrupted her, not wishing to discuss the sore subject of multiple wives, and asked:

"But the country is under British rule. So, is this king over, or under the British?"

Nobody knew for sure.

Mrs Naranbhai felt cheated. Naranbhai had told her they were going to live in a "British" country. A country where Whites were in charge and Indians, as long as they behaved themselves and kept out of national politics were free to make money. He hadn't really explained the position of the King. What if she were to suddenly run into him? Would she have to bow down or kneel? How could one do that for a black man? It was one thing to have agreed to live in the same house as a previous wife but to also have to live under the rulership of a black King? Suddenly, she wasn't sure she had made the right decision. She should have insisted that if Naranbhai wanted her for her womb - to produce a baby-boy - then she should have insisted on remaining in India, and insisted that he move to India. A country with black servants and a black King? How would one know which was which? Don't they all look alike?

But, in the next few weeks, Mrs Naranbhai was to learn, to her utmost relief, that life in British East Africa was not all about battling with the natives. In fact, one didn't even need to see them -- save as domestic servants or the odd vegetable vendor who came to the door. The rest of the time, she and her aunt Kamini quite forgot that they were not in India. In fact, East Africa was her making. A vastly improved lifestyle, married to one of the relatively richer men, and no shame to carry from that previous, scandalous episode of having spent an entire night with a stranger whom she had wrongly assumed was her husband.

SECOND WIFE SYNDROME

It was common knowledge that Sushilaben's initial reaction to her husband taking a second wife had been to swallow some rat poison. But the thought of what would become of the Mad Girl left at the mercy of a battle-axe stepmother had prevented her from taking such a drastic action. And then there had been the widow Nalini's intervention. Nalini, the slightly older sister of Naranbhai, and mother of the twins Mohini and Sohini, had, quite astutely, advised her best-friend-cum-sister-in-law that the wisest course of action was to stay put and make life as difficult as possible for the new wife. It was far better to remain on the premises and exercise an intangible control over things. It was also a wise course of action to remain as gracious, welcoming and soft-spoken as possible, so that Naranbhai would feel nagged and pressurised *only* by the new wife whereas the older one would appear charitable and reasonable in the extreme. It was sure to increase her chances of a reconciliation if she could be seen to be the more amenable, understanding one.

It was, indeed, excellent advice and Sushilaben had done well to take heed. But it wasn't always easy. By and large she managed to appear more reasonable than the second Mrs Naranbhai but, from time to time, things got so completely out of hand that both wives, supported by their respective female allies, came to blows - but only verbally. The situation was very well balanced by each wife having a female ally of her own. Sushilaben's ally and sister-in-law, mother of the doomed twins Mohini-Sohini was also mother to Bharat, more commonly known as Naranbhai's Useless Nephew.

In later years, the Useless Nephew was to prove quite useful, albeit momentarily.

The second Mrs Naranbhai, for her part, was no fool. Having been with Naranbhai for ten years, it had certainly not escaped her notice that since Shahbanu had moved into Bombay Gardens, her husband had started spending longer and longer in front of the mirror. Recently, he had also taken to using a blackening lotion on his slightly greying hair. It was foul smelling stuff that left greasy charcoal stains on pillow covers and towels, and indeed wherever Naranbhai happened to rest his head. Only yesterday, while playfully putting his head in her lap (as men tend to do when they are enamoured of someone else,) he had left a big, black blotch on her best sky-blue sari. In the past, she had teased him about his slightly greying hair and, being a fair bit younger, had urged him to start colouring it so that people would not laugh at her for being lumbered with an old man. She had even teasingly sung: "Main ka karoon Ram, muje buddha millgaya" (Help me God, I'm stuck with an old man.) But then he had scolded her for harbouring such superficial values and even held discourses on the virtues of learning to age gracefully. So all of a sudden, why the hell was he preening himself and pouting at the mirror and leaving messy, big black patches all over the place? For Mrs Naranbhai, it could only mean one thing: his heart had been set to do "dhak-dhak" by a younger, more beautiful woman.

Being his second wife, with the older first wife still in residence, Mrs Naranbhai suffered from the classic second-wife-insecurity syndrome. This was a double-edged fear. On the one hand, she lived in the constant dread that one day he would, somehow, fall in love with this first wife all over again. On the other, there was always the possibility that a man who could so readily bypass his first wife could surely do the same with the second one if another diversion presented itself. It was only *then* that a second wife realised that the imaginary threat of the first wife was far better than being confronted with the real challenge of an entirely new, much younger, much prettier woman. And, it was for this reason, that soon after the arrival of Shahbanu in Bombay Gardens, the younger Mrs Naranbhai sought to reopen a dialogue with Naranbhai's first wife, Sushilaben, mother of the Mad Girl. But if the second Mrs Naranbhai was nobody's fool, then Sushilaben, was certainly no mug and correctly guessed the reason for the younger wife's overtures. And, even if by some oversight she hadn't, then her chief ally and Naranbhai's widow-sister Nalini, would soon have put her right:

"See? She's running scared now!" Nalini would enlighten Sushilaben.

"Yes, she has every reason. Shahbanu is very pretty," Sushilaben would say, trying not to sound too pleased at this unexpected good fortune in the ongoing power battles of Naran Villa.

"Those who cause pain to others must some day expect to taste the same," Nalini would philosophise.

"Still, I hope the situation doesn't get out of control," Sushilaben would say in a conciliatory mood. At some level she liked things to be exactly as they were. The uneasy balance was somehow manageable without yet another party entering the fray.

Mrs Naranbhai lingered outside Sushilaben's bedroom door. Not being too used to being friendly, she merely simpered and smiled and ended up saying something banal like:

"Did you like today's lunch? Shall I have something special prepared for you for dinner? What would the Mad Girl like?"

But before Sushilaben could reply, Nalini had pounce on the second wife:

"Yes, yes, and add poison to it as well! Since when have you cared about what Sushilaben or Mad Girl like to eat, eh? Come on, we all know why you are stewing!"

Sushilaben would reprimand her sister-in-law and ally: "Please Naliniben, she is only trying to be friendly. We mustn't be so arrogant that we can't even appreciate a kind gesture." And turning to her rival she would say: "Thank you. Very nice lunch. Perhaps chapatties instead of puris this evening?"

"Hahahahaha" Nalini would laugh heartily. "She is as flattened as a chapatti herself. See, see… the puffiness of puris has all gone now" she would chortle, rather pleased with herself for equating complex emotional states to different kinds of home made breads.

At such times, Sushilaben despaired of her ally Nalini. Sure, Nalini had provided her with unending support and encouragement and had stood by her through thick and thin, but she was dismayed to see that even the tragic double-suicide of her twin daughters Mohini-Sohini had done nothing to blunt Nalini's razor-sharp tongue. As far as Sushilaben was concerned, her husband's second wife had, for whatever reason, extended a hand of friendship and it was her duty to at least try and be polite if not to reciprocate the gesture.

"Don't mind her, please. Come, come in and sit down," she said pleasantly.

As Mrs Naranbhai started to come in and sit on the bed with the first wife, the ally Nalini immediately made herself more comfortable expecting to be given some snippets of the younger wife's fears and concerns. At the same time, Mrs Naranbhai's own ally, the film-star aunt Kamini also appeared to see why all the women had gathered in the older wife's room. Soon, all four were sharing shredded supaari (arreca nut) and seated chatting and giggling like schoolgirls, a situation that would normally have caused panic of the first degree in Naranbhai. Nothing filled him with greater terror than that the women of his household should become chums. But, on this occasion he had other, more pleasant thoughts to occupy him as he painstakingly applied more blackening lotion to his hair, only vaguely aware of chattering, giggling females in some part of the big house. He dismissed it as mere background noise and proceeded to arrange his hair sideways in an attempt to cover up the balding patch that had started to form at the top of his head.

Meanwhile, in Sushilaben's room the high-spirited conversation was rather dangerously headed towards something like comparing notes:

"He's always playing with those fat little statuettes of Rahu and Ketu. I've told him a thousand times he should put them on a chain and wear them, but no. Always in his hands, always, always," giggled Mrs Naranbhai.

"Yes, he always twiddles with them when he is nervous, or excited about something," the older wife enlightened her with clear overtones of 'I've known him longer than you have.'

Nalini, of course, had to jump in and prove that she, being his older sister, had known him even longer than both the wives put together:

"Yes, once when he had nearly arrived at school for an exam, he came all the way back home just because he'd forgotten to take his gods with him. They belonged to our mother you know. It's the only thing he has of hers. She gave them to him when she was dying. Typhoid."

It was a well-known story, but Nalini had to repeat it to prove that she had known Naranbhai since childhood.

On her deathbed, Naranbhai's mother, aged only 34 or so, had reiterated her grandfather's advice: "Son, always aim to keep the forces balanced. There is good and there is evil. There is joy, and there is sorrow. One without the other makes no sense. Without sorrow, how would we recognise joy? And without joy, there really would be no point in continuing to live. So, a bit of each at all times, and never losing sight of the fact that there is no such thing as non-stop joy or non-stop sorrow. Each preceedes -- and succeeds -- the other. No one state lasts forever. It is never worth getting too worked up about either. Nothing stays the same and the man who recognises this ever-changing state of flux -- learns to stay on even keel and remain unmoved by the highs and lows of life. Carry these, always. They are not good luck charms. They are symbols of the gods of joy and sorrow, riches and poverty, bounty and famine, plenty and little. And they will serve to remind you that it is not worth getting puffed out with joy, nor beaten down by loss or sorrow."

That is how Naranbhai had always told the story of his mother's deathbed speech. But, it was generally thought by all and sundry, but particularly by the second Mrs Naranbhai, that the speech had been elaborately embroidered over the years.

Mrs Naranbhai hated her husband's habit of "fiddling" -- as she called it -- with the two bulbous little figures of the twin gods Rahu and Ketu. Measuring an inch each, they were fashioned out of real, solid gold and she was convinced they would end up being stolen. Although both deities had a little loop over their heads for threading through a chain, Naranbhai refused to wear them thus. He thought chains and other such items of jewellery would make him look effeminate. Instead, he clattered the figurines in the palms of his hands whenever he was worried, anxious or bored. Or, when he needed to remind himself that life was a curious mixture of gains and losses although, in recent years, he had had nothing but loss, loss and loss.

"He spent most of our wedding night under the bed searching for those little statues," Sushilaben suddenly revealed in

mischievous tones. "Nalini had told me about his obsession with
the little gods, so as soon as I got a chance, I hid them from him.
When he realised they were missing he was so upset, he
completely forgot he had just been married and there was a bride
waiting on his bed for him. He just searched high and low, barely
aware that I was even in the room."

"And then what happened?" Mrs Naranbhai asked nervously,
not too sure she wanted to know. Any mention of her husband and
his first wife on their wedding night, made her extremely
insecure.

"Oh, I finally took pity on him and said they were hidden
inside my blouse -- one in each breast -- and he proceeded to rip
open my...."

She stopped suddenly, pretending to blush at the memory,
while Nalini and Kamini giggled and tut-tutted at the impropriety
of it all. Only Mrs Naranbhai went completely quiet, wishing she
had never asked the question. There was only way to equalise the
score:

"On our wedding night he left his figurines on the dressing
table. For once, they weren't nestling in his hands. He realised it
was an important occasion and his hands would be needed for
other things."

She stopped to see if this juicy disclosure had had any impact
on the older wife. Sushilaben's expression remained unchanged,
but Nalini was suddenly back to her old belligerent self:

"Hey Ram! How can you sit here and talk about your wedding
night? Have you no shame?" she yelled at Mrs Naranbhai.

"Well, *she* did - you let *her* talk about her wedding night..."
Mrs Naranbhai protested feebly.

"That's completely different! She was -- *is* -- his FIRST wife!"
Nalini offered by way of twisted logic. The aunt Kamini decided
it was time for her to go in to bat in her official capacity as ally to
the second wife:

"*Why* is it different? You mean to tell me my niece's marriage
was not a real marriage? He married her, you know, right and
proper! Round the fire, with all the mantras. She's not his
mistress, you know? He didn't elope with her."

"So are you suggesting he eloped with Sushilaben?" Nalini barked back.

"She still wants him. Why else would she be telling stories about *their* wedding night?" Kamini challenged.

"Is she not even entitled to her memories? Your hussy of a niece comes and takes her husband from under her nose and she is not even entitled to remember the happy times she had with him?" Nalini's voice broke and she wiped away an imaginary tear with the end of her widow's white cotton sari.

"Get your facts right," barked Kamini. "He came after my niece. She didn't go begging to be made his wife. He came, looking for a young woman to give him sons. What's *your* best-friend given him except one mad daughter?"

As always, only the allies had done all the mud-slinging up until now, but as soon as the Mad Girl was mentioned, both the Naranbhai wives joined in and soon, all four women, two against two, were shouting at the top of their voices. The shouting came to an abrupt halt when the Mad Girl, whose name always came up in any row between the women, turned over in her bed, sat up, and began singing. She sang of how youth was just a fleeting moment, and life itself a few minutes. But the night was long, too long... This, she sang, was the basic mystery of life. So why not live and let live before death comes to claim its debt?

Elsewhere in the house, Naranbhai was admiring himself in front of the mirror for the hundredth time, when he became aware of raised voices and screaming, abruptly brought to an end by the Mad Girl's song. He smiled to himself. The women were at loggerheads again. Wonderful! Things were back to normal. In an ever-changing world it is always reassuring to find that some things always remain the same.

IN A STEW

(North London, 2000)

"Every aandu-paandu has now come to Britain and become a big man!" the Grumpy Old Man was on his usual favourite subject. Britain ought to be a haven for the truly sophisticated and wise - even the gentlemanly in the old-fashioned sense - but, instead, it had turned into a kind of rubbish tip for every hustler, every con man and everybody but everybody was trying to illegally enter the country. The Arabs were taking over the smarter parts and turning them into Beiruts and Kuwaits. The Caribbean Blacks were turning every street corner into a slum - and ganja stall. The Indians were unbearable with their slippery-glittery saris worn under scruffy duffle coats. The Chinese were selling half-baked medical knowledge and getting very rich in the process. The riches were so tempting that many Chinese had been prepared to travel in airless containers at the back of lorries, risking death by suffocation, just to get to Britain and make money. The Irani exiles from the former Shah's Iran were doing atrocious things to the English way of life: the men were selling gaudy carpets and the women were teaching females of all nationalities that the ideal of femininity was a hair-free body. Hair was only allowed on the head - and nowhere else. From everywhere else it was tugged and pulled in a manner that would make the most horrific torture-chamber ritual seem like a short and most pleasant holiday. The Grumpy Old Man knew these things because his wife's disgrace-of-a-sister, Camilla, was a regular frequenter of these Irani-owned beauty parlours. Here, she would pay good money to let somebody cover her entire body with burning hot wax, which, when cool and hard would be ripped off savagely, sticky-tape-fashion.

"It's true what our elders said," the old man had remarked on over-hearing Camilla give her sister a blow-by-blow account of her latest depilatory adventure.

The Grumpy Old Man said: "Money was supposed to be for making life more comfortable. But in the final days of the world, there would be a tendency for people to pay money for pain - for making life *less* comfortable." And that would launch him into how White men paid large sums of money to professional women to inflict pain on them. Since his "reading" consisted largely of tabloid rags, and his English was still very seriously limited, he mostly only read the headlines and looked (with pretended distaste) at the pictures of naked women. As a result, his English vocabulary was more fluent in the sensational. And he always had any number of outlandish examples to support his theories. But on the subject of foreigners in Britain, for the Grumpy Old Man, the Pakistanis were the worst of all, with their mullahs feeding dangerous ideas to impressionable young minds. Why did the richest and most nationalistic, patriotic Pakistanis always live in Hampstead, Knightsbridge, St John's Wood - in fact anywhere but Pakistan itself? And why was Britain so keen to appear 'humanitarian' to the Bosnians and Albanians and Kosovas who, according to the Grumpy Old Man, were no better than common thugs?

"Don't say that," pacified his young wife, as usual. "We too came here because we had no where else to go. And just because you didn't do as well as the others, that's no reason to pronounce them all criminals. Most of these people did good because they worked hard."

He felt she was, as ever, having a jibe at his sitting around doing nothing all day.

"My health, you know. My health just went down the drain with this climate."

"I like this cold climate. It gives me energy," his wife contradicted. "And I certainly don't miss the flies or cockroaches. I like doing my own housework. I'd always done housework anyway, but it's so much easier in this country, with all the facilities and the machines."

"Machines don't necessarily mean progress. What about the human spirit? That has been all but killed off by your mechanised existence. People don't know about courtesy anymore. Nobody has time. Nobody takes the trouble to look in on the sick. Even one's own children only visit at Bank Holidays or Christmas."

"But when they do visit, you grumble so much. No wonder they keep away."

"Why do you always twist everything around to make out like it's my fault? If it weren't for me, where would you be?" As soon as he'd said it, he regretted the taunting question. Sure enough, she replied, without a moment's hesitation:

"If it weren't for you, I might well have stood on my own two feet several years ago, and made something more of my life than just cooking and washing for you. If you had left us alone...."

"OK, OK, " he interrupted impatiently. "At least I was there in your final hour of need. What would YOU have done if I had not agreed to your plan?"

"There is nothing I could have done, but if you hadn't interfered in my life in the first place, I might not have been in that impossible situation," she said with undisguised bitterness.

"It amazes me how you've learnt to talk and answer back. You used to be completely quiet and well behaved. A perfect Indian woman! Look at you now! It's true what they say. Women cackle more and more as they get older. And when they learn to do it in more than one language - then that is truly the end, believe me!"

"I'm still 30 years younger than you. And it's true what they say about men as well - they grumble more and more as they get older."

They fell into an easy silence. That always happened to married couples. With practice, over the years, their many disagreements were not for resolving, but to serve as an essential means of communication. Often it was the only kind of communication left, with other areas of contact gradually withering away. Finally, she broke the silence in the only way she knew:

"What would you like for dinner? Should I just mix up all those vegetables again? We could have it as a mild stew - not good for you to have spicy curries all the time. Or would you prefer -?"

"Why must you always ask me about dinner just after I've had tea? You do it on purpose. You always ask about the next meal when you know I'm tanked up with the last one. That way, you hope, I won't request anything too difficult. Typical! What else do you have to do all day? Too much for you aren't I? Just one poor

115

old man - with a small appetite - needing regular feeding and you think it's a big burden. After everything I've done for you! Don't talk to me about dinner now. Ask me half an hour before dinner, when I'll be really hungry."

"And then you'll say I never have anything ready on time!" She turned on her heel and announced she was popping out for a cup of tea with the Muslim woman who lived next door. He didn't approve of his wife's friendship with their Muslim neighbour. Muslims were dangerous people. Every single Muslim household was likely to be a hotbed and training camp for suicide pilots. He would never, ever, trust Muslims again. The bloody woman next door had, at one time, owed him a lot of money. He loved to bring this up again and again.

"Oh, come on!" said his wife. "She *did* return it, in the end."

"Yes, in the end. Not even in the end, after the end. And she returned it at the current exchange rate. In the days I had given it to her it was worth more than five hundred pounds sterling. But she waited until the exchange rate was in her favour - and one British pound equalled thousands of East African shillings. Then she gives me a paltry fifty pounds, or some such thing. I will never forget it!"

His wife left the room. He began searching for the TV remote control

He sat staring at the TV screen. He reached for the remote control and started channel hopping again. Finally, he gave up and hit the video "play" button.

There she was - Kitty Complex - Kitty indeed! Mad as a Hatter, in the umpteenth showing of one of her most successful films of the early seventies. Now in her forties, she had also turned her hand to production, and every single one of her films began with an invocation to Rahu, the God of Bounty. The Grumpy Old Man considered it out and out blasphemy that anyone should use one of *his* favourite gods for such frivolous and irreverent purposes. And, once again, he felt an immense satisfaction at having something else to stew about.

DIVORCING IN STYLE

I had gone silent on Camilla when she urged me, once again, to tell her more about the photographs I found in that house. Camilla had just started telling me what an awful, unbearable grump her older sister had married while she, herself, had had the good sense to marry an Englishman.

I swallow hard, hoping she won't have noticed the lump in my throat, and for lack of anything better to say, I blurt out, "Good, good. I'm very happy for you...."

"We're divorced now. No, no, don't be sad for me. It was all very amicable. If I'd married an Indian it would never have been so civilised. Chauvinist bastards, all of them!"

Divorced? Did she say "divorced"? My mouth has gone dry and the room is spinning. Bastard indeed! He divorced her? And all that time he was trying to break it off with me he was doing this big guilt-trip number...had to go back to her....can't leave her.... God! What a slimy, lying, treacherous cad! Camilla is, thankfully, unaware of the storm raging in my heart...she continues:

"Even though he left me for another woman, I don't really mind," she says. "How can a man help falling in love? He fell in love with me, and then, some years later, he fell in love with someone else. But then Simon was always falling in love. At one time he had three of them on the go -- all at once -- and I used to have to help him to dodge the phone calls. We were a team -- husband-and-wife -- so how could I mind? And, he always kept me in the picture. He never lied..."

I feel sick. I was one of many? And she was privy to all his sexual dalliances? Sick woman! She's obviously making huge allowances because he was English. Yes, the colonial mentality rules! I suppose she still feels grateful that he married her in the first place. Yet Simon used to tell me that she threatened suicide every time he broached the subject of their failed marriage and proposed a "trial separation." And once, he had said, she even took an overdose of sleeping tablets. That was the time he and I were going away to Amsterdam -- he pretending to have some business. Apparently she took an overdose and he cancelled the trip. I had booked non-returnable cheap flights on *my* credit card.

"Yeah," continues Camilla. "He often double-booked the women and then turned to me with a little-boy-lost look to bail him out. There was that time when some chick got it into her head that he would do a whole Friday-to-Monday with her in Amsterdam. Imagine! Some stupid woman being so naïve as to think a married man could slip away for *four* whole days. On that occasion, I advised him to say that his wife had had a medical emergency -- overdose, not sure if deliberate -- just to make it more dramatic. That's how I got him out of that one."

I can feel my lunch returning upwards. So, Simon, aided by his wife, was lying to me all along. How could I have been so naïve as to think that a man who is prepared to cheat on his wife would not, also, cheat on his mistress? Wait! He wasn't even cheating on her! She was in on it. He was only cheating his other women while *she* watched the fun and became his spin-doctor. And to think I hated her so much when all the time it was Simon who was messing me around?

I suddenly feel very sorry for Camilla. What a sham of a marriage! No, no, I feel more sorry for myself. She appears to have emerged pretty unruffled out of all this. Seems she was a co-conspirator in most of his extra-marital affairs. Sick, sick, sick!

"But then," I try to say calmly, "if you got on so well, why did you have to get divorced?"

"Ah well, all good things must come to an end. He was in love with someone else and I had to let him go."

I'm gutted! Someone else! Not me, but someone *else*...

"So...so...you're divorced?" That's all I manage to say, and then, for lack of anything more intelligent, and to cover up the fact that I'm flustered by this revelation I add:

"Was your family very upset you got divorced?"

"You don't know my brother-in-law, the Grumpy Old Man," she says. "When I was single he used to grump and grump about how I was no better than a whore running loose -- just asking for trouble. Then, when I did get married, he grumped even more because I'd married someone of a different race and religion. The

Grumpy Old Man thinks marriage is about settling down. Yet, we know all sorts of people who have become nothing but unsettled by marriage. In his view, "settled" is the only state respectable women can be, and it usually involves being with a man. Even if it's completely the wrong man he must be of the right skin-colour and worship the same God! 'Single' is the dirtiest word in the Grumpy Old Man's dictionary. I could circumnavigate the globe. Swim all the oceans. Solve the Middle East problem single-handed. Discover a new planet. Even find a cure for cancer. But until such time as I married a person of the right age, race, height, religion and language, he had me classified as a randy woman of loose morals! When I had turned 22, he was already saying I was well past a medically safe age for bearing children. Thirty years ago, the same people said this to girls of fifteen - they were told if they left it, even for another month, then they would give birth to abnormal babies. Girls of eleven used to be married off to men of 65 in India, and it was all said to be in accordance with God's wishes. At 19 you were supposed to have the menopause - no, no, I exaggerate, what am I saying? There isn't even a word for 'menopause' in any Indian language - "

For the first time in our meeting, I realise she is much more than the frumpy housewife of my ex-lover.

"So, your brother-in-law should have been thrilled when you and your English husband -- (I pretend to not remember his name) -- got divorced?"

"No, he wasn't thrilled. Divorce is far worse! He didn't talk to me for six months after that. Yet, you don't know what kind of man he was in the old days....the things I could tell you about him....one rule for men, another for women...."

"So how did your sister end up married to him?" I ask.

"Oh, very long story! This bloody Expulsion again! I tell you, there are thousands and thousands of stories about this Expulsion, and behind each story there's another few thousand stories. And, you have no idea how much rubbish I've heard since I started actively meeting other Ugandan Asians. Half of them want to be victims. Others say the Expulsion was the best thing that could have happened to them. Then there are those who make up the most horrendous lies about their grand past. Some were no better than coolies, living in overcrowded slums alongside smelly gutters. But they hoodwink the Brits. into thinking that they all lived in grand houses and had one servant to polish the shoes and another to tie up their shoelaces. And I'm telling you, these Brits. know absolutely nothing about it. They screwed up everyone, and then sent their VSOs to screw everyone else who hadn't yet been screwed -- quite literally. But they knew nothing about what things were like on a day-to-day level. Even when it all came to such a bitter end for us, the only thing the Brits cared about was to dig up dirt on Idi Amin. The tabloids lapped it all up. Sometimes I think they must've paid him a handsome amount for agreeing to become their court jester. His outrageous, idiotic pronouncements on exploitation, colonialism, neo-colonialism, were a great diversion from what was really going on. But the newer generation doesn't even care about that anymore. And, as for you African-Africans, you haven't a clue!"

Suddenly I was a "You African" -- just because I don't speak any Indian language. She is a curious bag of contradictions: proud of her race, but determined to stand apart from it and appoint herself its most objective orator.

DAMSEL IN DISTRESS

In less than a week after Shahbanu moved in to Bombay Gardens, a sleepy Naran Villa had been awakened in the dead of night with Shahbanu's persistent rattling of its thick-chained gate.

"Is anyone there, please? Please open up! This is an emergency! Jannasani! Jannasani!"

Jannasani was renowned for sleeping through almost anything. Mrs Naranbhai was often heard to say he could sleep through earthquakes, floods and even the actual end of the world. But since none of these calamities had so far occurred in this part of the world, Mrs Naranbhai was probably speaking figuratively. Or at least that's what Shahbanu hoped, in this, her most desperate hour of need. And since Jannsani's little cupboard of a room was at the far end of the Naran Villa backyard and she was rattling at the front gate, there was a less than remote chance he would hear her. Mrs Naranbhai had risen first, but afraid of opening the door in case it was black savages on the rampage, she had woken up Naranbhai who, armed with a folded black umbrella had cautiously stepped into the room of his first wife, Sushilaben, which overlooked the front gate.

"Yes, who is it please?" he had asked in English, using a strong, clear voice, pretending he wasn't at all afraid of intruders in the middle of the night.

"It's me bhai-jaan," came Shahbanu's little-girl voice. When he finally opened the front door, and came out to unchain the gate, Mrs Naranbhai followed, fast on his heels, Shahbanu appeared in the cool dark night, tousled hair and minus make-up, elegant and lily-like in a white satin dressing gown. Mr Naranbhai felt decidedly scruffy and unpresentable in his dhoti and white vest, while Mrs Naranbhai made a private note with a great deal of venom that the Shahbanu woman managed to look quite delectable and alluring, even without the help of jewellery or make up.

"The lights - they've all gone. I'm so afraid of the dark, Bhaijaan. Can you help? I know nothing about electricity."

Before Naranbhai could play Knight in Shining Armour armed with fuses and pliers, Mrs Naranbhai, blood pressure rising, barked. "Lights have gone? All lights? Have you tried using the switch? What about bulb? Change the bulb!"

"I've never done that. I don't know how. Anyway, I don't have any light bulbs. We've only just moved in - half the things are still packed...." She would probably have gone on and on with the helpless female act if Naranbhai hadn't, at once, sprung into action.

"Nothing to fear! You just stay where you are. I'm coming over.....did you really walk all by yourself in this dark night? You shouldn't do that! You really should think about connecting a telephone. I'll look into it for you...." And chuntering thus, he disappeared into the house to get dressed. A few minutes later, armed with fuses, matches and an emergency kerosene lamp, he prepared to accompany Shahbanu on the short walk back to Bombay Gardens.

"You're never going there just because a bulb might have blown," Mrs Naranbhai said in disbelief, and then realising that that was exactly what he was planning to do, and even appeared to be looking forward to it, she immediately added, "Wait, I'm coming too..."

"What will you do there? What do you know about electricity? Anyway, it will take you too long to get dressed..."

Even as he said it he realised, with some dismay, that Mrs Naranbhai would not have to get dressed as she always slept fully dressed in her sari, tight choli (bodice), underskirt and all. So, he changed his tack:

"No, no! No need for you to tail along on this chilly night. I will go and help our tenant. It is my responsibility. I am, afer all, the landlord..." and he shot out before his second wife could raise any other objections.

LET THERE BE A LIGHT BULB

Naranbhai felt like the most blessed creature in the universe as he respectfully walked two steps behind the distressed Shahbanu along the narrow, snake-like mud-track that ran parallel to the open sewer which stank more than usual that night, but all Naranbhai could smell was jasmine and roses. As it was, the mud track was so narrow that two sets of feet could not walk alongside each other. When walking with Mrs Naranbhai, he always marched out ahead, but with Shahbanu, he remained respectfully, and protectively three steps behind. He tried to make conversation as they took the short walk from Naran Villa to Bombay Gardens to sort out her lights.

"Too much - too much for you to handle all by yourself. Your husband should really come home and take care of such things - " Naranbhai began.

"He can't. He's working. He comes home for such short periods anyway, I can't very well start giving him tasks as soon as he steps in, can I?" she pouted.

"You are a such a considerate person. A considerate wife is a very rare thing, believe me. He is a lucky man," Naranbhai pronounced wistfully, wishing more than ever that the absent husband would meet with a car crash when next headed homewards. Then he added, "You know, I think God made you and then threw away the mould. He made none other like you - " and then, clearly embarrassed at himself because he'd never paid such a direct compliment to anyone of either sex in his entire life, he fell silent for the rest of the short walk.

Shahbanu entered the darkened house first, and quickly lit a candle. As the flame rose and strengthened it threw a warming light on her face as she bent over the candle. Naranbhai drew a sharp breath at seeing her in candlelight for the very first time. He stood transfixed, until she thrust the candle at him, saying: "Here, this will help you see better. Not sure where you need to look first -- fuse-box? Where is it?"

"Err - yes - err - fuse box, very good idea," Naranbhai was still quite distracted at being alone with her by candlelight.

"Fuse-box!" he repeated, as though he'd just had a brilliant idea. He was here to act as trouble-shooter. This was his chance to show masculine efficiency and ingratiate himself. He rapidly set about performing various heroic tasks like finding the light switch and turning it on and off in rapid succession while at the same time pretending to listen out for something unusual. Then he went towards the kitchen where he inspected various things -- none of which had the remotest connection with electricity. He really wasn't at all sure what he was meant to be doing. Still, he felt obliged to appear as though he were carrying out some thorough investigative work, while Shahbanu followed him, candle in hand, expectantly waiting for him to make a pronouncement on the possible root of the trouble. Just then, a hint of a shadowy figure was seen outside the sitting room window and Naranbhai almost let out a scream. But before his vocal chords could do anything about it, Shahbanu had yelped like a frightened animal and proceeded to wrap herself, ivy-fashion, around his paunchy body.

In a few seconds, the tall wiry form of Jannasani stood in the warm, orange-yellow candle-glow in the small sitting room, staring at the embracing couple without emotion.

"What the hell are you doing here?" Naranbhai barked.

"Mama - (meaning Mrs Naranbhai, mistress of the household,) Mama said I should come and help you," he replied matter-of-factly, while at the same time rubbing his sleepy eyes.

While Naranbhai stood stupefied at how determined his wife must've been to actually succeed in waking up Jannasani at this ungodly hour, Shahbanu had, gently and most apologetically, disengaged herself from Naranbhai's body.

"Sorry, bhai-jaan, so-so sorry," she said in a much rehearsed, little-girl voice. "I became so afraid, I just didn't think -"

"It's all right, it's all right," he said, trying to sound as dispassionate as possible, as though beautiful young women clinging to him by candlelight in the dead of night were a fairly common and frequent occurrence in his life.

Jannasani produced a light bulb and Naranbhai snatched it from him. Looking around for something to stand on, he felt he could happily have strangled the house boy on the spot as

Jannasani said: "Let me do it, Bwana. I am much taller. I can reach without anything to stand on."

Naranbhai's humiliation was complete. Not only had the house boy appeared with a solution, but was now also going to execute it. The glorious moment of trouble-shooting heroism that Naranbhai has so desired for himself was going to be denied him, thanks to the interfering house boy. He handed him the bulb, a bitter expression on his face, and then pretended to supervise its correct insertion into the bulb holder:

"Careful, now. Make sure it doesn't break before you put it in. Take out the old bulb first - don't hold it too tight...!"

Shahbanu smiled quietly, and she was still smiling when, a few seconds later, Jannasani turned on the light switch and the small sitting room was suddenly, and almost blindingly, awash with a 100-watt light.

THE INQUISITION

On the short walk back to Bombay Gardens, Naranbhai was fretting and fuming over the best choice for Jannasani's punishment. But a little voice inside his head kept reminding him that Jannsani was, after all, only following Mrs Naranbhai's orders. If anyone was responsible for stealing his moment of glory then it was his battle-axe second wife, and not the house boy. Besides, Naranbhai also realised that it had been Jannasani's slow, silent, shadowy way of appearing in places that had sent Shahbanu flying straight into Naranbhai's arms. If Jannasani had walked upright, with loud footsteps clearly announcing his arrival, then Naranbhai might have never had the good fortune of enjoying her embrace -- however short-lived. No, it was Jannsani he had to thank for that impromptu bonus of a moment, and far from doling out any punishment, it was Jannasani he would have to bribe -- and sweeten -- so as to ensure that the all-too-brief intertwining with Shahbanu was not reported back to Mrs Naranbhai.

Predictably, Mrs Naranbhai was wide-awake when Naranbhai got back to Naran Villa. He made sure Jannasani went straight to his closet-sized room at the far end of the backyard and was given no opportunity to be subjected to an interrogation by the mistress of the house. As Naranbhai prepared for bed, his second wife asked:

"So what about before Jannsani turned up with the bulb I sent?" she asked, unashamedly nosy. "What happened?"

"Er - nothing, nothing happened. I was just trying to fix the light when - "

"What? In the dark? How could you see in the dark?"

"Well, not pitch-dark. Shahbanu had very kindly lit a candle. She is a most resourceful woman, you know? Very efficient!"

Mrs Naranbhai, though still youngish, but more than just a bit overweight, felt her blood pressure rising again.

"Candle, hain?"

"Yes, candle, what else?" Naranbhai replied, beginning to get just a little annoyed.

"You and her, all alone by candlelight, hain?"

126

"Not for long. You made sure of that, didn't you?" he said with undisguised bitterness.

She giggled girlishly, and made the all-too-familiar advance towards him. He recoiled sulking a bit and choosing to retire to his own room that night.

As he sat on his bed he mused that his second wife was a sort of consecrated obstacle; almost like a giant-sized paperweight that was put onto thousands of pieces of irregularly sized sheets of paper, keeping everything in its place. He knew that the raising of this paperweight would result in the most unruly disintegration of the forces that often held a man together. Although frustrated in the extreme, and his heart still definitely pulling towards Shahbanu's bewitching charms, he had to admit that it was Mrs Naranbhai who was, somehow, holding his world together.

Isn't that why men had invented marriage?

AN OASIS

After Shahbanu's arrival in Bombay Gardens, the first hint of 'garden' emerged amidst the small houses that joined up to form a rectangle with one side missing. Laid out barrack fashion, the fourth side of the rectangle was walled off with a wooden door providing a back entrance to the complex. The gate was left open during the day and locked at night, the residents taking it in turns to ensure that this was done by eleven o'clock each night. And, more often than not, it was Satish the Bachelor who ended up doing the final locking up each night, always being the last to get in, the many charms of the Black Cat club keeping him out late, night after night.

The street facing side of the rectangle contained the two largest houses - three bedrooms each. Shahbanu had one of these houses and a very large family of Indian shoe-repairers had the other. Both sides of the rectangle featured two identical smaller houses - one with one room and another with two rooms - with no windows except those overlooking onto the central backyard - a largish clearing of space onto which all the backdoors opened. Facing one another across the yard, the houses were mirror images of each other. The two roomed houses were occupied by the widower, Virjibhai the Compounder on one side, and the large D'Sa family on the other. The one room property was occupied by Satish the Bachelor on one side, and Pandit Suddenly on the other. Two bathrooms - one for men, one for women - and a row of three flushing lavatories were placed against the inside of the wall, separated by sheets of corrugated iron, which served as dividing wall, roof and door. The bathroom facilities, shared between seven households, were considered quite adequate by the standards of poorer Indians in those days. The back wall, made of concrete, had once been painted white, but the paint was now peeling, weathered with patches of yellow and rust. It was about six feet high and into its ledge large, jagged pieces of broken brown and green glass, once part of beer bottles, had been sunken, presumably while the cement was still wet, serving as a deterrent for potential after-hours intruders.

Into this yellowing bleakness came Shahbanu in shocking pink, with all her colourful flowering plants, and the previously bleak communal backyard was now ablaze with cheerful greenery and colourful fragrance. She had moved in with several dozen large clay pots bearing plants and flowers of every shade and scent. These, she had lined up all along her outer walls at the front of the house, facing the main road, as well as along the wall facing on the backyard. Cuttings were generously offered to neighbours, who being unused to such refinement, welcomed Shahbanu's guidance in potting, planting, and tending to the miniature versions of Shahbanu's bigger displays of greenery and blazing colours. It was a common sight in the mid-morning sunshine -- and in the fading early evening light -- to see Shahbanu watering and tidying not only her own plants but also all those occupying the backyard-sakati. She would break off dead leaves, crunching them into the palm of her hand. If there hadn't been much rain, she would spray each and every leaf using a kind of pump that others, less refined, would only have associated with DDT. She would pour ribbons of water out of a large kerosene tin with the water spluttering over the parched earth which in turn would give off a delicious aroma, grateful to have its thirst quenched. Most exciting of all, she had introduced an exotic shrub with small green and white flowers. The flowers only opened and gave off a seductive scent after sunset and, on being asked their name, Shahbanu had said: "Queen of the Night". They were usually worn as garlands around coiled hair, and were said to be an essential accessory in the art of seduction. Mrs Naranbhai had, quite predictably, commented that a Queen of the Night was bound to rely on the Queen of the Night.

In time, the whole barracks-style settlement acquired a new kind of manicured veneer, much to Naranbhai's delight. He was thrilled that his rented-out property was at last beginning to become true to its name. And, given the smart cars that her many male visitors arrived in, and with the area now turning as lush as the Hanging Gardens of Babylon, Naranbhai once again considered raising the rents. But he had lost a lot of his sharpness in money matters. Ever since Shahbanu's transformational arrival, he had other things to occupy his mind.

From time to time Naranbhai would appear in Bombay Gardens during the mid-morning to inspect the 'garden' and after commenting on each and every plant would accept a glass of home made juice from one of the neighbours. Bombay Gardens' residents were too poor to afford bottled or fizzy drinks. Instead, real fruit juice, laced with ice hastily begged from Naran Villa, was offered with profuse apologies.

"Never mind, never mind," Naranbhai would say and down the freshly squeezed orange, passion-fruit or mango juice with the heroic air of one who had just been offered some dubious tribal delicacy laced with animal excretions.

"Never mind, never mind. It is offered with love. That is what counts. I am a simple man," he would eulogise of his own courage. "I can fit in anywhere..."

Afterwards, the tenants would all agree amongst themselves that their landlord was, indeed, a man of the greatest simplicity and humility.

"Imagine! A rich man like him, accepting mere fruit juice in our poor houses. He is great indeed."

Yes, life had certainly looked up, not just for the neighbourhood, but also for Naranbhai, personally. But, if there was one thing that perturbed him it was this: more and more, these days, whenever he showed up at Bombay Gardens, his best-friend and tenant, the part-time Pandit, (usually known as Pandit Suddenly) was always hovering somewhere not too far from Shahbanu. One morning, Naranbhai saw them both seated on low stools in the sakati, with Shahbanu's hand in his. His face was bent intently over her palm like he was tracing the movements of some microscopic creature. Shahbanu sat smiling while her beautiful, lily-white hand, palm facing upwards, rested on the Pandit's left thigh. Naranbhai's felt a pounding in his temples as he quickly moved over to where the two were seated. Before he could say anything, Shahbanu informed him in her wonderstuck, slightly breathless, little-girl-caught-in-a-brothel voice:

"See, Pandit-ji is reading my palm! Isn't that nice of him? I've always wanted to have my palm read...he is so good. He has already told me so much that is absolutely true..."

Bloody typical, thought Naranbhai. All these sexually frustrated pandit-types usually profess knowledge of some or the other magical art just to be able to touch up a beautiful woman. He seethed inwardly, but decided to play it cool:

"So, what has he told you, our beloved Pandit here?" he asked, trying to sound as casual as possible. "Has he told you that you will meet a tall, dark, handsome stranger?" he asked sarcastically while at the same time pulling in his paunch and trying to stand very tall.

She ignored his mocking tone and carried on gazing at the Pandit's face while the latter's brow became knitted as though he had just spotted something exceptionally revealing and unusual. She waited on tenterhooks. The Pandit decided to spin out the tension:

"Most interesting, most interesting," he said finally, without bothering to elaborate on what was interesting. Shahbanu kept watching him, while Naranbhai asked in a mocking tone:

"So are you going to tell her what is interesting, or are you just going to go on talking to yourself, hain?"

"Very, very interesting. I've never seen a heart-line like this one. And, suddenly I wonder....ah! Here it is! How amazing!" The Pandit was determined to enjoy his big moment.

"What? What is interesting?" Naranbhai barked.

"Confidential! Palmist must keep client confidence. I will tell her in private, suddenly. Not with you here!" he replied.

Naranbhai felt the blood pounding against his temples again, and his mouth suddenly felt like a stretch of the Sahara Desert. And, to add insult to injury, Shahbanu said to Pandit Suddenly:

"Pandit-ji, come into my house. It's quite private there. You can tell me everything in there...would you like some fresh lime juice?"

Pandit Suddenly rose like a schoolboy who had just been summoned to scrub the back of his favourite female teacher in her bath, shooting Naranbhai an undisguised look of triumph. As he and Shahbanu disappeared into her house leaving Naranbhai in the sakati, the Pandit turned back once more and gave Naranbhai one more pitying look. A disgusted Naranbhai turned on his heels and started the short walk back to Naran Villa, the mid-morning sun now beating down with a force that matched his rising anger. He waved his black umbrella in a menacing way as he walked back, beating the space before him and imagining the Pandit's behind suspended somewhere on the spot where his umbrella was doing the merciless thrashing.

He arrived fuming and fretting on the verandah of Naran Villa. Mrs Naranbhai was swaying gently on the big swing, stringing some runner beans. On seeing him she said:

"What's the point of taking an umbrella with you and then not using it? It's to shield your khopri (balding head) from the sun, not for waving about in front of you like a sword..."

"If you had seen what I have just seen, you too would want to slash the bastard's head off...."

"Who are you talking about? Who has upset you now?"

"That bloody fake Pandit. That good-for-nothing pretender..."

"But he's your best-friend...?"

"Exactly! *My* best-friend! And do you know what I've just seen? He was holding Shahbanu's hand and then sweet-talked her into letting him into her house -- in front of me -- no shame -- right before my eyes! He disappeared with her into her house under the pretext of predicting her future. Such a crook! He should be locked up!"

Mrs Naranbhai smiled smugly: "So what it is it you? It's not like Shahbanu is an innocent virgin! She's a married woman. A married woman whose husband is nowhere to be seen. So what if she's entertaining the Pandit? Why is your bum burning?"

Mrs Naranbhai was thrilled that the Pandit, in his amorous ambitions, appeared to be making some headway with Shahbanu. It would show Naranbhai that Shahbanu was everybody's and anybody's. To push the point home, she added:

"Only the other day, she was getting into Satish's car on the pretext of a visit to the doctor. She sat in the front, and she was laughing and joking with him...."

She stopped, with some satisfaction, to observe Naranbhai's obvious discomfort.

"It's a neighbourly thing to do. And how could she have sat in the back? Didn't Satish remove that backseat to give our crook Pandit to use as a sofa? But, this Pandit, pretending he knows how to read palms, was squeezing her hand, I tell you squeezing it! Her soft, white, delicate hand in his ugly, hairy paw! I could have killed him!"

"But what's it to *you*?" Mrs Naranbhai asked jealously.

"She's my tenant. And her welfare is my concern. I don't want it getting about that the women of Bombay Gardens are being marauded by the wandering hands of our Pandit and others. Decency must be observed at all times. I think I'll have to have words with him..." he trailed off, still seething at the memory of the look the Pandit had given him just before disappearing into Shahbanu's house.

He raised his folded umbrella at the memory, and Mrs Naranbhai ducked.

DEMONS & SAINTS

Shahbanu brought much more than greenery and fragrant flowers to Bombay Gardens. Apart from triggering off the dormant hormones of the semi-potent, she also brought an ambience of holiness. She appeared to be a devout woman and an entirely new kind of dawn and dusk culture ensued. At dusk, as the flocks of birds flew towards the setting sun and street lamps were beginning to be lit, a mist of incense smoke mingled with the fragrance of flowers creating an awesome stillness which announced that prayer rituals were imminent. The evening scent of Shahbanu's Raat ki Rani flowers grew headier as the shadows gathered, and, led by Shahbanu, everyone prayed - separately. As soon as Shahbanu's white-chaddar clad form was seen in the window of the sitting room, others hastened towards their own houses to perform rituals of their own.

Shahbanu's fragile form clad in white and praying in the sitting room window which faced east, had became quite a common sight in Bombay Gardens. The Hindus looked on with respect and reverence and took an even bigger delight in performing their own prayer rituals at the same time. Nothing as catching as a general, widespread sense of holiness at dusk, and Shahbanu's lone form, seemingly lost in the meditation of God, reminded others that they had been remiss in not remembering God often enough.

Naranbhai beamed with pride.

"What a nice thing," he boasted to his friends. "Brings such a nice feeling to the place. When God is regularly remembered His blessings can only make everyone more prosperous," and he would clasp his twin-god statuettes, always cupped in the palm of his right hand, with renewed faith.

"Yes, but the cars start coming as soon as she finishes praying," objected Mrs Naranbhai, as usual averse to any idea that painted Shahbanu in a positive light.

"So? You want them to come during her prayers?" Naranbhai was sensitive in the extreme if any doubts were cast on Shahbanu's apparent holiness.

134

"It is only right that she should first remember God and *then* her people come to see her..." he would explain, in his capacity as self-appointed defence counsel.

"Yes, but how do we know they are really *her* people? There are never any women. Only men. And some of them look like Chautharas (mixed race, Afro-Asian.) They go in one by one and come out one by one," Mrs Naranbhai's ally, Kamini Masi, always sided with her niece. That, after all, was her chief function within the household.

"So what? You want them to come all at once? And of course they are all men. She was the only female in their family. She has told me so herself."

Naranbhai was keen to show that he and Shahbanu had discussed personal matters in great detail and that he was especially privileged to know her entire life's history. But in truth, he had only ever had that one proper audience with her, when she had come to see him about the house. The rest, he had invented gradually, over a period of time, giving Shahbanu a kind of re-constructed past that made her seem a few short steps away from a cross between Joan of Arc and the Indian saint-mystic-poetess Meera Bai.

Shahbanu's other neighbours were equally welcoming of her presence. She had style. She had class. Each and every neighbourhood woman tried to model herself on the mysterious, enigmatic Shahbanu. Soon, various heads emerged in a crude imitation of Shahbanu's distinctive coiled coiffure, sporting a figure-of-eight design with two loose strands falling down either side of her face. Their sari blouses gradually became shorter, hitched up to just under the bust-line. But where Shahbanu revealed a slim, shapely waist measuring some 23 inches, in Mrs Naranbhai's case two or three solid pads of creased flesh - a bit like a blown up insect body showing various segments, and not entirely unlike the Michelin tyre ad - were visible in all their undulating glory. Earrings became longer and dangled to brush against shoulders, and the traditional Indian gold studs were hastily put away in preference for plastic baubles of various shades and designs. In time, Bombay Gardens came to be known as a residential area for fashion-conscious women, all of whom took great pains to match their glass and plastic jewellery to the colours of their saris and other costumes.

These dressing up rituals reached their peak on Sundays when every female sported her best clothes with jewellery to match, for the traditional promenade up and down the town's main street. For the ignorant onlooker it might have seemed a pretty futile exercise, all dressed up and nowhere to go, save to walk up and down the main road. But for the townspeople these early Sunday evening jaunts became the highpoint of their weekly social calendar. Nothing much happened on these walks. You simply got dressed up and walked along with all the family and met other families doing the same. It was customary to stop, exchange greetings and gossip, admire mutual outfits and then carry on walking, foaming at the mouth if you happened to have spotted a rival in a superior ensemble.

Largely Indian crowds bobbing around in their best outfits had become such a fixture on Sunday evenings that a Dictator of later years was known to have remarked to one of his side-kick chamchas: "Tell me, where am I? Is this my capital city, or have I been transported by a magic carpet to Bombay? Thee-hee-hee-hee-hee...."

He may have laughed heartily at the time, but it was no laughing matter, as history was soon to show....

Only Shahbanu was conspicuously absent from these Sunday walks. Both Shahbanu and her daughter looked extremely elegant on Sundays when a larger than usual number of cars pulled up outside Bombay Gardens from about five onwards.

"They seem to get too many visitors," Mrs Naranbhai commented to Mrs D'Sa in a casual sort of way. She was clearly fishing in the hope that Mrs D'Sa, who had the house adjoining Shahbanu's, would be able to shed some light on the exact nature of these frequent visits by extremely distinguished looking men.

Mrs D'Sa, a Roman Catholic Goan, was the mother of eleven children and the long-suffering victim of an alcoholic husband. Once a week or so, usually on a Saturday, her drunken husband would beat her in the communal backyard, in front of the toilets, for all to see. After the beatings, she would whine and cry in pain while he stood some distance away muttering obscenities in their native tongue, Konkani, while Mrs D'Sa started to slowly and painfully make her way back into the house. Half an hour later she would emerge in the backyard again and summon him to dinner. He would follow her into the house, swearing and cursing. Then he would sit down to dinner after which his loud sobs - punctuated only by hiccuping, burping and singing - could be heard all over the courtyard. "Oh Danny Boy....." was the only song he ever sang. And, it was usually on the same night as the beatings that the D'Sas would have sex. The entire process was so noisy that Bombay Gardens' mothers would cover their children's ears with blankets. But within the house, the D'Sa children giggled under their blankets. Very often they would sit up in pure delight, hugging and congratulating one another if there was the slightest sound bearing testimony to the fact that their parents were getting on rather well.

The D'Sa Saturday ritual had become such a commonplace event that when one Saturday the beating didn't happen, various neighbours called in to see if Tony D'Sa was feeling all right. On that occasion they were informed by a tearful Mrs D'Sa that he was down with a bad bout of malaria. After a tense few days when the neighbours learnt that Mr D'Sa was up and about again, there was a general sense of relief for 'poor Mrs D'Sa' and the beatings resumed once again.

The D'Sas had, at one time, been very comfortably well off. They had lived in one of the smarter houses on the lower slopes of the European residential hills. The house came with Mr D'Sa's job -- Senior X-ray technician in the country's largest hospital. But he was fired after falsifying and mixing up the X-ray results in return for a bribe. Once caught and disgraced, the rest of the Goan community decided to steer clear of the D'Sas. Honesty - at least as an official policy - was a big one with this community. And although it was D'Sa who had done the dastardly deed, the community decided to ostracise poor Mrs D'Sa as well. Officially, the Roman Catholic Goans stood opposed to divorce, but they were extremely unforgiving towards a woman who happened to be married to "such a crook." A woman carried the sins of her man and was seen as equally - if not more - responsible for any financial hanky-panky. After he was fired from an extremely well paid job, Tony D'Sa sank into a deep depression and took to drink in a big way. While his drinking and gambling debts mounted, Mrs D'Sa had had to take charge as main breadwinner. A small, two-roomed house in Bombay Gardens was all she could afford and, Naranbhai, although at first reluctant to take pig-eating Christian tenants, had taken pity on her and her many children -- at that time only six of them -- and allowed her to move in.

"Children are from God after all, never mind which God," he had rationalised for the benefit of potential objectors. But there hadn't been too many objections. Christianity was, after all, the religion of White supremacy and its practitioners were considered superior for many reasons, not least their fluency in English. Their non-Christian Indian neighbours had welcomed the family with open arms whereas its own kith and kin had turned its back on the fallen-from-grace D'Sas.

The ragged D'Sa children, equally fluent in English and in the Gujarati they'd picked up from playing with other Indian children, made a perfect vision of the classic Dickensian urchin. The brood ranged in age from eighteen months to twelve years, but apart from the youngest and the oldest, it was difficult to tell the rest of them apart. The younger D'Sas were all clones of one another and even the fact of being male or female seemed to make no difference to their almost identical appearances. Mr and Mrs D'Sa only referred to the children by number: Number One, Number Two, Number Three.....

It was an ingenious invention to save remembering several different names of identical looking little people.

Mrs D'Sa supported the entire family out of the money she earned from giving piano lessons, mostly to European girls and those from middle-class Goan and Parsi families. She usually went to their grand houses for this task, but some pupils also came to her small house for lessons. Her piano filled most of the small D'Sa sitting room, which, afer dark, also doubled up as a bedroom for five of the eleven children. The other six slept scattered about between the parents' small bedroom and the small hallway leading to the back door. After about seven every evening, the D'Sa house had the look and feel of a mattress store crossed with a morgue.

Apart from the Baby Grand which dominated the sitting room, Mrs D'Sa's other cherished possession, purchased out of her piano-teaching money, was an electric Baby Belling oven, with her baking skills supplementing the piano income and making up the shortfall in the children's school fees. In spite of limited resources, the D'Sa children were enrolled in a special private school run by nuns, where Latin and French and RE were compulsory.

Very few homes had ovens at this time, which had led Mrs D'Sa to wisely invest in one. She baked cakes and other delicacies for the townspeople at the rate of a shilling an hour. Quite often people would mix their own cakes, turn the mixture into a tin, and then send it to be baked. But for birthdays and other big occasions, Mrs D'Sa undertook to prepare and deliver the completed item. On such occasions the piano would be closed and covered with a thick bed sheet over which Mrs D'Sa would place various preparations in readiness for decorating the cakes. No one had dared imagine the full implications of having various bowls of icing sugar and numerous other sugary delicacies in the midst of eleven children all of whom would hover at the covered piano with great expectations. Grubby fingers stealthily dug into bowls, and, according to Mrs Naranbhai, lice probably flew and fell from little scalps while Mrs D'Sa's back was turned. Despite these surreptitious mouthfuls, the children would, nevertheless, still stick around for the official privilege of being allowed to lick the bowls clean.

The Naranbhais were among her regular customers and Mrs D'Sa had turned out cakes in various shapes over the years for the Doctor, Lawyer and Dentist's birthdays. Even so, Mrs Naranbhai, the proud mother of the three boys, had always found it difficult to conduct a meaningful conversation with the Goan woman - 'meaningful' in Mrs Naranbhai's terms being a conversation that provided the maximum amount of contentious information about other people.

Mrs D'Sa, true to Goan custom, refused to speak Gujarati or any other Indian language, although if the truth be told, she probably understood every single word. Mrs Naranbhai's own English was hopelessly limited. The only common language between the two women was Swahili, and since Mrs Naranbhai had only ever spoken that language to her Black houseboys, her command of Swahili was more fluent in the imperative than in the business of digging up dirt on other Indians:

"Plenty visitors -- gaari mingi sana," Mrs Naranbahi would say in her kitchen Swahili, pointing her face in the direction of Shahbanu's house. Shahbanu was not only a source of gossip and never-ending mystery, but of late, on seeing her husband's immense interest in black dye for his greying hair, Mrs Naranbhai had made it a top priority to gather as much information as possible about this enigmatic woman.

"Yes lots of visitors. Very sociable lady, very popular," Mrs D'Sa would readily agree.

"Do what they?" Mrs Naranbhai would probe.

"Si-jui...don't know - not sure," Mrs D'Sa would reply.

Mrs Naranbhai decided this was a hopeless course of action and the best move would be to drop in on Shahbanu unexpectedly on the pretext of taking her some tasty dish while the male visitors were present.

Mrs Naranbhai proceeded to do so one Sunday, urging the rest of the family to go ahead with their usual Sunday promenade into town and promising to catch up with them later. She banged hard on Shahbanu's door but there was no reply although loud music could be heard from within. Mrs Naranbhai, as yet unaccustomed to the sound of Elvis Presley, just thought of the music as "English noise." She waited a while but the door remained closed. Shamelessly she hung around outside, pretending to admire some new potted plant. Eventually the door was opened and a most distinguished-looking African man, of medium height, emerged. He nodded quickly in acknowledgement of her greeting, got into his black Mercedes, and sped away.

The fact of the man being African gave Mrs Naranbhai all the ammunition she needed for the timebeing. She had often argued that even if they were indeed her brothers, then they were certainly very dutiful ones, to visit their sister, every Sunday, unaccompanied by wife or family. As every sister can testify, brothers, once married, are less and less inclined to visit sisters. But now, she confronted Naranbhai with her latest finding:

"So! Tell me! How is one of her brothers is black?"

"Some Indians are very dark," Naranbhai said without much conviction and secretly much perturbed by this new twist.

A SERIES OF EXPLOSIONS

"You have to be very careful whom you suddenly let into your life," Pandit Suddenly was cautioning the delectable Shahbanu. "Sometimes, too much beauty is a disadvantage. It attracts the wrong kind of man -- the kind of man who falls suddenly for beauty and nothing else. And then, just as suddenly, he grows tired: either someone more beautiful suddenly comes along, or your beauty suddenly fades in his eyes because he gets used to seeing so much of you...suddenly."

"That's all very interesting, Pandit-ji, but *suddenly*, why are telling me all this?" Shahbanu batted her eyelashes in an affected manner and proceeded to do what she did best: play dumb.

"I'm just telling -- I consider it my duty, as your neighbour and as a Pandit, man of God -- that you should suddenly be aware of the wicked ways of the world...."

"Thank you Pandit-ji, most kind of you. I will remain alert, as always. A woman all alone has to be....."

"That is exactly why I'm suddenly saying you should not remain all alone....you should have an understanding with someone who watches over you -- only as a brother, of course -- particularly since your esteemed husband is away so much......"

As he spoke, Pandit Suddenly realised that it wasn't so much that Shahbanu's alleged husband was always allegedly travelling - he was, in fact, completely absent. To date, nobody had ever set eyes upon him. And, Shahbanu's habit of giving, what the Pandit thought of as "inviting looks," to landlord Naranbhai, was causing Pandit Suddenly a great deal of consternation. Without naming names, he proceeded with the sermon:

"Now, certain men -- not a million miles from here. they will never give up what they already have just to make room for you. He will never leave his wife...er...wives...."

"Why should anyone leave their wife for me? Who is asking them to leave? I'm not that stupid! Who wants to be stuck with any man, day in day out? I would much rather they remain with the wife. For me, the best kind of husband is an absent husband. That way, it is much more romantic. Otherwise, the wife turns into a constant nag and the other woman remains an elusive, desirable mystery. My husband and I only have very brief meetings -- sometimes just once every three months....."

Pandit Suddenly's was trembling with awe -- partly because of her boast that absent husbands suited her fine but mostly because she sounded so blasé about keeping other people's husbands constantly on the go -- buzzing around her like flies.

"Yes, yes..." he said vaguely, without knowing what he was agreeing with. "Just a small caution. I thought I should point out a few things. Afterwards, if anything should happen, I would never be able to forgive myself. As a man of God, it is my duty to caution you about, about, er....you know, certain wives can become very, very jealous and there's no knowing what they might....."

"Pandit-ji, if you're a man of God, I too have my faith and Allah has always protected me. My intentions are good. If women get jealous of me -- without good reason -- then God knows what is in my heart, no matter what those women think..." Shahbanu was waxing lyrical.

"Yes, very good, very good!" chimed in Pandit Suddenly. "You remain true to your err...err...Allah, and don't pay any attention to all the gossip. A good woman like you can never come to any harm....particularly when you have friends like me, watching over you."

"Yes, Pandit-ji, indeed," Shahbanu pouted and produced an extra soft, creamy voice to maximise the impact. "I thank Allah everyday that I've got a neighbour like you. One both, spiritual and worldly, and one who cares about my welfare. I am blessed."

"And I am blessed too. I am the perfect er...friend...sorry, brother, for you. At least there is no jealous wife on the horizon -- let alone *two* wives! I never married..."

"Why, Pandit-ji, why? Pandits are allowed to marry, aren't they?" Shahbanu did her breathless-little-girl-caught-in-a-brothel-voice again.

"Of course they are! But for me, the right woman never came along. Many wrong women came. You know, nothing like power to turn women on -- greedy women who wanted to enjoy the perks of being a Pandit's wife....?"

Shahbanu restrained herself from asking 'What perks?' She was too polite to ask a direct question like that. Free incense sticks and a few free meals here and there did not qualify as 'perks' in Shahbanu's way of thinking.

"Yes, yes, Pandit-ji," she said instead. "Very bad idea to marry the wrong woman just for the sake of being married. A distinguished -- and educated -- man like you must have had thousands of women after him. Most noble of you to not be tempted! Anybody else would've fallen for it, if nothing, just to have a built-in housekeeper and cook by day, and then at night...err...night..."

"I'm perfectly capable of doing my own cooking!" Pandit Suddenly decided to use this as an opener to list his many qualifications. And, he grew so boastful about all the dishes he could prepare that, before he knew it, he had promised to let Shahbanu partake of his meals whenever he had no other plans. Shahbanu, who had never even successfully boiled an egg in her life, concluded she had done very well out of this little chat she'd had with the lovely Pandit-next-door and, in the days that followed, she was sent many plates of all kinds of edibles, lovingly prepared by the Pandit.

No sooner had Pandit Suddenly turned into Shahbanu's free food delivery service, than Satish the Bachelor offered to lend her some of his Indian film records. She feigned a polite interest but told Satish she preferred "English" music. Shahbanu's passion for "English" music was limited to the songs of Elvis Presley. When she had politely turned down his offer, Satish reiterated something he had told her from day one:

"My car is always at your disposal. OK, it doesn't always start and these days the passenger side door is jammed, but any time you want to go anywhere, I want you to promise me that you will call on my services. No need to arrange a taxi or to walk in this heat. Your beautiful face will turn blacker than Africans if you walk in the sun!"

"Shoooo sheeweet of you Satish-babu!" Shahbanu cooed. "Very kind, of course I'll let you know...by the way, are you free today after four? I need to go to the doctor...."

"Of course, of course!" piped up Satish, thrilled that his offer had been taken up so promptly. In his excitement, he quite forgot that he had promised to ferry Mrs Naranbhai to the tailor where she was to have an important fitting session for three brand new ensembles, being put together for her to wear at the various ceremonies for the wedding of Dhanjibhai the grocer's niece.

At five minutes to four that afternoon, Mrs Naranbhai was pacing up and down the Naran Villa verandah in readiness for Satish. Unable to contain the excitement mounting within her at the thought of the delicious fitting-session that awaited her at the tailors', she began walking along the mud-track that led to Bombay Gardens. It would save Satish the bother of having to drive around the long way to pick her up. She would present herself at his house and they could go from there.

She arrived at Bombay Gardens just in time to see Shahbanu gathering up her sari and climbing into the driving seat of Satish's khattara car, before sliding over to the passenger seat. Beads of sweat broke out on her forehead as she watched the scene. Satish suddenly spotted her but still didn't remember his promise to drive her to the tailor that early evening. Instead, he nodded a polite greeting and prepared to get into the car. Shahbanu turned and started rolling down the glass on the passenger window. It worked by turning the handle until the glass jammed and then turning it the other way until it loosened and gave. Nothing about Satish's car was straightforward, but it had the honour of being the only car in Bombay Gardens. Shahbanu called through the half-open window: "Hello Mrs Naranbhai? Going anywhere? Need a lift? Plenty of room in the back....but no seat you know......squeeze in with me, in the front?"

Mrs Naranbhai felt the sweat trickle down the back of her neck. So now bloody Shahbanu was treating it like it was *her* car! Satish jumped in and after a few explosions and jerks, the car moved off and sped away after a belch and a hiccup or two. Soon, they were gliding along -- give or take a few bangs --and Satish felt a great deal of satisfaction at having a beautiful woman sitting so close to him in the small Ford Prefect. He slowed down a bit so that as many people as possible would see this wonderful sight. At

145

the same time, he made a mental note to trade in the khattara and get himself a decent car at the first opportunity. How on earth could he hope to look the romantic, dashing hero that he was if he proceeded everywhere by a series of explosions?

Mrs Naranbhai stomped back to Naran Villa and dug straight into her husband:

"If only you would learn to drive -- or at least buy a car and engage a driver for me -- I wouldn't have gone through such humiliation. Brazenly, before my eyes, she gets into his car and goes off...offering me a lift like it was *her* car! How can you put me through this? Don't you see a woman of my standing needs her own transport...?"

Naranbhai never did manage to learn how to drive, and he was very nervous about driving in heavy traffic. In this part of the world, at this conjecture in history, "heavy traffic" meant that you weren't alone on the road. There was at least one other car, or lorry, within sight. Naranbhai had been extremely unlucky with cars, or indeed anything that moved on four wheels. His now defunct Bus Company bus had given him nothing but headaches. And, some years ago, when Naranbhai's cinema had been a thriving business, and he had purchased a second hand black Mercedes and engaged a driver to ferry him back and forth from the cinema, the driver had made off with the car. It was thought he must have gone to the Congo, sold the vehicle and retired on the proceeds.

Normally, Mrs Naranbhai's demands for a car would've raked up all this blood-boiling stuff from the past. But today, on hearing that Shahbanu had gone off in Satish's clapped out car had completely obliterated Naranbhai's past gripes with motorised transport. He had something much more urgent on his mind: the possibility of Shahbanu getting too close to Satish the Bachelor. So, instead of pacifying the second wife, yet again, over the car business, he said: "That Satish is getting too much! High time we found him a girl...."

"What girl? He only wants his "Dream Girl"!" Mrs Naranbhai barked. "Dream Girl" had become the catchphrase for Satish's notions of an ideal wife.

"Dream Girl or no Dream Girl, I'm going to have a very stern talk with him. I do not want any unmarried tenants -- men or women -- occupying my property! Such things breed immorality..."

"Then you'll have to ask the Pandit to get married as well..." taunted Mrs Naranbhai, fully aware of rubbing salt into his wounds. If Satish was running around burning petrol on ferrying Shahbanu all over town, then it was no secret that Pandit Suddenly was burning a great deal of cooking oil -- and KCC pure butter-ghee -- in producing numerous edibles for Shahbanu. As an afterthought she added, quite unkindly:

"And you? Look at you! Can't drive, can't cook! You don't stand a chance with her!"

And before he could reply, she had hollered for Jannasani to go and fetch her a taxi.

PANDIT SUDDENLY: SUN & MOON

Satish the Bachelor occupied one of one-room houses in Bombay Gardens and facing him directly across the backyard was the identical dwelling of Pandit Suddenly. His real name was Dixit and he had originally been a school master in a village in North India. He had come over to East Africa by sea, on a whim, without having secured a contract for a teaching job. The Brits, although pretty keen on teachers from North India, were nevertheless sticklers when it came to teaching qualifications. A mere degree in an appropriate subject was not sufficient. A documented teaching qualification, such as the B. Ed. Degree or, at least a certificate from a recognised Teachers' Training College, was a must. The Pandit hadn't known that. Back in India, his 'panditry' alone had been sufficient to wield the cane and terrorise ragged village children into memorising Wordsworth or Coleridge. On arrival in East Africa he found, to his dismay, that the schools were not exactly desperate for teachers and that there were already large numbers of Indian teachers in place -- with the right qualifications. His meagre savings were fast dwindling, and he would have starved had it not been for the fortunate discovery by someone that he was something of a pandit as well. Soon, people began consulting him on various family matters - an intervention here, a prayer there. And then they would make their offerings - oil, coconut, rice, sweets and fresh and dried fruit. And then, when the Pandit felt he was indispensable to the many rituals surrounding births, marriages and deaths, he grew a bit more ambitious. One day, he said to the faithful: "Don't bring me only rice and coconuts. I need clothes. The evenings are suddenly chilly. Bring me a shawl, suddenly, or a sweater. Suddenly, a bicycle would also help me to get around."

And, they did. Quite suddenly!

One day, a particularly distressed group of visitors had gone to him over the matter of their wayward teenage daughter who was determined to elope with her beloved who was of a different caste. On that occasion, the Pandit had cleverly managed to talk her out of it. When the family stood around offering profuse thanks, and at the same time wondering how to head back home, so late at night, from the Pandit's then abode -- on the outskirts of town -- he said to them:

"If you really want to thank me, then suddenly please help me to find somewhere inexpensive in town."

And, the family, who were acquainted with Naranbhai, persuaded that landord that the acquisition of such a wise person, albeit at a reduced rent, would be a boon for Bombay Gardens. And, as a pandit, his presence would ensure that the highest Indian moral standards would be upheld at all times. For a nominal rent, the Pandit moved into the one-room dwelling and despite being a lowly tenant, gradually became Naranbhai's best friend. Naranbhai was in awe of Pandit Suddenly, not least because the chap could read English. Among his few belongings - mostly religious paraphernalia and various pandit-style gizmos for performing religious rituals - there were a few impressive looking books in the English language that the Pandit had, no doubt, carried over from India. Naranbhai didn't know any of these books but assumed that anyone who had read such things must, indeed, be a very clever man. All the fat English books were in an extremely sorry state and none of the covers or titles had survived the ravages of time except for a play about Joan of Arc. Although the only English word to creep into the Pandit's Hindi or Gujarati in the interests of extra emphasis was the word "suddenly" - at both opportune and inoppurtune moments - the Pandit was, neverthless, considered something of an authority on the English language. Pandit Suddenly could oppose Naranbhai on vital matters and still get away with it. Such was the power of an English education! Whenever they had their semi-friendly spars on some trifling matter, Pandit Suddenly was quick to quote from Bernard Shaw or Yeats. And since no one in the immediate vicinity knew what he was talking about, the argument generally ended with a consensus that as a Hindu Pandit and a man who read fat books in English with small print, Pandit Suddenly must be right.

The Pandit had a daily early morning ritual of saluting the sun. At daybreak, he would stand in the communal backyard, hands enjoined, and mutter some magical words with eyes closed. Then he would hold up a container of water as though an offering to the

Sun and proceed to pour the water over his head. From here it would trickle down his face while he continued muttering the magical words.This kind of ritual might have been quite a sensible thing to perform at midday when cool water trickling down one's face would bring untold satisfaction against the midday sun. But to do it at the crack of dawn, when the air was still chilly, was, indeed, a sign of utter piety and devotion.

Early risers had learned not to interrupt the Pandit's rituals. On one or two occasions when one of the D'Sa children had unwittingly asked: "Pandit, what are your doing? Why are you doing that?"the Pandit had barked back:"Why are you interrupting me so suddenly? Suddenly why do I have to explain what I am doing? Is this a tamasha or a circus? Now, be off, suddenly, all of you!"

The words 'sun and moon' were sometimes also added to the pandit's nickname for both these heavenly bodies were of paramount importance in his day-to-day life. He had been known to say, on more than one occasion, that the moon was the most important thing in relation to human beings and their life and body cycles. The moon, he said, affected all bodies of water. Tidal waves, the feeding cycles of oysters and many other things. And since the human body was 85% water, how could it escape the impact of the moon? To bring the argument closer to home, he often cited the Mad Girl's extra-frenzied singing around the time of the full moon. This, he said, was surely related to her menstrual cycle. Naranbhai was quite sceptical of the Pandit's sweeping theories about heavenly bodies. He was convinced that his mad daughter sang for no purpose other than to embarrass her father and his family's good name. But he never dared to contradict the Pandit who was also something of an astrologer. On this, and certain classics of English Literature, nobody could argue with the Pandit.

The moon, the Pandit had said, was "suddenly" even more important than the sun, because it took the sun's light in a measured and considered way. It did this so that people could look at it directly, whereas looking the sun in the eye was quite out of the question. The moon was not interested in its own glory.

It existed for the express purpose of exalting the sun and basking in its reflected glory. This, he said was a Divine symbol and a clear hint from God as to how women should behave in their relationships with men. And, every so often, he would gather a group of women and girls and read to them from some obscure scriptures on the role of the Hindu wife:

"...a wife should always look upon him as her God, should lavish on him all her attention and care, paying no heed whatsoever to his character and giving him no cause whatsoever for displeasure..."

The Pandit observed a sort of lunar calendar. So, according to his calculations, it wasn't 1950-something, soon to be 1960, but more like the year 17736 or some such unfathomable number. Someone had once quizzed him on the exact calculation and he had retorted: "Suddenly why are you interested in all this, hain? Just to make fun of me? Be off with you, suddenly, time-waster!"

The Pandit's birthday was another oddity. It happened on a different day each year. On that day, he would let word slip - usually through one of the young D'Sas - that it was his special day. And devotees were expected to turn up with the usual offerings of fruit and flowers. And, on each such birthday, he would say that according to his own predictions, he would most certainly live to see his thousandth moon. The Pandit had told all and sundry that back in his village, in India, the only birthday that counted for a man was (suddenly) the birthday that marked his thousandth moon. This was a decent life expectancy. Any more than this, was sheer greed. It was a decent man indeed who lived to see his thousandth moon. Nobody knew the Pandit's exact age, but by all guesstimates his thousandth moon celebration was thought to be some fifteen years away. But nobody could have guessed that he would not live to celebrate his thousandth moon. And, with a sort of Divine poetic justice, his end, when it came in 1972, fell on the day of his 999th Moon!

DISGRACEFUL DAUGHTERS IN LAW

Life in late 1990s north London was far from ideal for the Grumpy Old Man. It had turned into nothing short of a tedious list of dos and don'ts. He couldn't eat this, or that. Basically, he couldn't eat any of his favourite foods, either on grounds of sugar content, or fat content, or both. He had been prescribed to take long walks. He hated walking. His one and only friend, an eldery man who was originally from Nairobi and whom he'd met at the local diabetic clinic, was dead. The man had been taking one of his prescribed diabetic walks when a van, turning a sharp corner had knocked him over and killed him. The incident had caused the Grumpy Old Man to stop going for walks.

He found it difficult to fill the day. He often wondered how he had passed the time in previous years. How could he once have thought that time just whizzed by too fast? How could he ever have said there weren't enough hours in the day or enough days in the week? Was that really the case? How could it be, when now, it was a major feat to get from 10 o'clock in the morning to lunchtime?

His thoughts kept turning to all those things she kept in neat rows of airtight tins - things that he was not allowed to eat.

"Why the hell do you get so much if I am not allowed to eat any of it?" he would ask resentfully, eyeing the sweetmeats, Bombay mixes, little fried puris and savouries of all kinds.

"Just in case - in case of guests," she would reply.

"But nobody ever visits us - even the children only come once in a blue moon," he would say dejectedly.

"That's what happens when children get married and have their own lives. It is only to be expected," she would say sensibly.

"Just because they are married shouldn't mean they forget their father. It all depends on who they marry," he would grumble:

His wife would try to change the topic as she sensed he was, once again, keen to find fault with his daughters-in-law, who in his eyes were mostly to blame for everything on grounds of being from different races and religions.

"If you don't marry your own kind, there is no hope for culture or tradition," he would say with finality.

"But what is 'own kind' these days? Am I your own kind?" It was a valid point, but not one that he ever wished to discuss at any length. She would elaborate:

"All the Asian children in this country now go to the same type of schools and speak the same kind of slang English. Just by choosing another *Asian* for a partner they feel they are being old-fashioned and traditional. Religion is not that important for them, so why make it an issue? As long as they marry good people, what does it matter?"

"It matters a lot!"he would retort."Just listen to you.Just because you been in the UK for a few years you think you are white."

Without a doubt, much of his bitterness came from not being occupied.His wife seemed to keep,somehow, constantly occupied. He envied her constant activity, although he was often at a loss to identify the end product of her seemingly never-ending labours. It seemed amazing to him that someone who had no young children to attend to, or a full time job or profession, or even a part-time one, could make herself so busy all day. She was always hovering somewhere between the kitchen and the small area at the back of the kitchen where a washing machine and dryer were in constant toil. How on earth could just two adults of generally clean habits produce so much dirty linen? Had they really got through all those towels? One long sari after another would go into the machine and, an hour later, emerge out of it again. How could she get through so many saris? They hardly ever went out. Not like the old days, in East Africa, when every weekend saw many birthdays, weddings, religious rituals.

If she wasn't doing mountains of laundry then she was out on the local high street. Shopping was one of her passions. She hunted for bargains and always bought things in bulk -- carting it all home, puffing and panting and pleased that she had saved a grand total of 40 pence by buying four dozen tomato tins all in one go.Whenever she spotted something useful she was convinced she would never see it again and would feel compelled to buy at least six.

"But where are we going to keep it all?" he would protest, not bothering to look away from his Indian film videos.

Television and the VCR were his only saviours. He would switch on the TV at 6 in the morning and doze in front of it until lunchtime. After lunch, he would sleep a bit, while the television remained on. He seldom had the volume up. He claimed it was distracting. He liked to just gaze at the pictures. In recent years, instead of BBC Open University or ITV daytime, the television had, almost permanently, been switched to an international Indian channel which carried commercial breaks of up to twelve minutes at a time, advertising everything from cooking oil to solicitors promising to facilitate divorce. The divorce ads were aimed at both sexes. Husbands were enticed that they would be shown ways to 'hide' their financial assets while wives were told they could wipe out a man who was planning to hide his money or to leave them. He marvelled at this modernity. Why couldn't his stupid sons make use of this facility and divorce their useless wives?

The Grumpy Old man's young wife had been cooking non-stop for four days. As a very rare occurrence she was expecting the entire brood, plus their wives and children to descend on Bank Holiday Monday. The old man was grumpy as usual:

"It will be so noisy and crowded. Why do they all have to come at once? The grandchildren are so badly behaved. No manners, no obedience! That's what happens when children speak only English. Speaking an Indian language always makes children better behaved."

"You are the first to complain that they don't come often enough. Now that they are all coming, why are you still grumbling?"

"They should realise we are getting on. We are not as young as we used to be...all of them, for one whole day. All that food to serve - and all that work -"

"I'll be doing all the work, what are you so worried about? You never budge from your chair except to go to the toilet and sometimes I think if the toilet could be attached to your chair you wouldn't even bother to get up for that. Anyway, I'm only preparing snacks and sweets. Your daughters-in-law are all so sweet and thoughtful.Between them, they'll be bringing all the food."

"Oh no! I hope Salma isn't making any of her lousy dishes. I tell you, I can't eat that sort of food. You'd better make sure I've got something else to eat," he moaned.

Salma was the second daughter-in-law, a Muslim girl from Kenya who despite having grown up in London, was an expert at traditional Muslim-Punjabi cuisine. He lived with the constant dread that she would, somehow, get his son to convert to Islam.

"I'm not cooking anything extra,"replied his wife."In any case, Alison is also bringing food so you can have some of hers."

Alison was the oldest daughter-in-law and she was Irish.

"No way am I touching White food.What can she make anyway? Sandwiches, huh!"

"Stop grumbling.Anyway, Ingrid always makes something vegetarian for us."

Ingrid was the youngest daughter-in-law -- a Goan girl who showed utmost sensitivity for her father-in-law's alleged Hindu customs. But the old man still lived in constant dread that she would, somehow, get his son to convert to Catholicism.

"I don't trust her cooking,"he retorted automatically. "Vegetarian it may be, but she will have used the same pots to cook meat and fish and God knows what else. My old mother would've had a fit."

"Times have changed," said his wife. "And you know that your own sons now eat meat and chicken - not in front of you, but they still do. You must let go of these stupid ideas…"

"So, you want me to start eating meat?" he twisted her argument.

"I didn't say that! Eat what you want to eat, but at least show some gratitude when your daughters-in-law, who have full-time jobs *and* young children, still have time to cook and bring us food."

"They are not *my* daughters-in-law. They are yours!"

She burst out laughing.

"Now you're being silly. You're jealous I'm closer to your sons than you are!"

"Don't call them *my* sons! Such high hopes I had for them! What do I get? A shop-worker, an assistant car sales manager and a TV repairman! At least they should have gone into their own businesses.Each one of them went out of his way to marry someone of a different religion, tainting my good family name, bringing shame..."

"What name? What shame? In this country who the hell cares about your family name? You're just another elderly Asian -- and one who's getting creaky at the joints... "

"Whatever you call it. Those disgraceful sons of yours...going after women of a different religion, just to annoy me. There was a time when a young man had *ideals*. He dreamed of a particular kind of wife...

DREAM GIRL

Satish Chandra, commonly known as Bachelor Satish, occupied a single room dwelling in Bombay Gardens. A childhood illness had left him with a pronounced limp, resulting in the unkind nickname of 'langra.' Satish had spent the past twenty years of his life in pursuit of an ideal, first class wife. In Satish's language, first-class meant a decent, virgin, Indian girl -- tall and fair-fair, with long-long hair. And, educated -- with at least a BA if not MA. Plus, an expert cook and housekeeper and, most important of all, one who wasn't inclined to answer back.

"If I throw a brick at her she should not hit back with a rock," he would explain.

But in spite of being in no doubt as to his exact requirements, the ideal dream wife - or indeed any kind of wife - had, somehow, completely eluded him. Satish worked as a cashier in the town's one and only bank. His job was a source of never-ending pride to himself, and to others, who imagined that having thousands of shillings pass through one's hands each day was, indeed, something that conveyed a high status.

In the Indian-African scheme of things, a man could have any number of shortcomings but beautiful maidens were, nevertheless, supposed to hold their breath in anticipation of being hand-picked by an eligible bachelor who could offer marriage and financial security. Never mind the pronounced limp, thinning hair and beer-gut. Or the minimal academic credentials, (a Junior Secondary School certificate with a hundred per cent mark in maths.) It was commonly acknowledged by all and sundry that Satish's continued bachelorhood was a direct result of his unrealistic expectations of the human female.

Naranbhai was often heard to say, "Ar-rey Satish Babu, as long she can roast a papard without setting it on fire, what does all this BA-MA rubbish matter?"

At one time, landlord Naranbhai had become embroiled in the search for Satish's 'Dream-Girl', as that non-existent, super-elusive female had rather disparagingly come to be known. Naranbhai liked to think of himself as a father to all his tenants, and Satish was his only bachelor tenant. So, if there was ever a fatherly duty crying out to be executed, this was it. Naranbhai had spread the word far and wide, carefully avoiding the interference of the toothless old-hag matchmaker whose efforts had resulted in the Mohini-Sohini fiasco. This time, Naranbhai was determined to go it alone, doing very well in the process, and resulting in many visitations by hopeful parents of virginal daughters.

But much to Naranbhai's annoyance and eventual exasperation, Satish always managed to find fault with the girls. Sometimes the hair wasn't long enough. At other times the girl was too outspoken, or had looked at him directly instead of lowering her eyes in a bashful manner. When the daughter of a well-to-do businessman from the next town had been presented to him he had rejected her outright on grounds of her not being able to speak English.

"I want smart, modern girl. I likes to speak the Ingliss," he had argued in his defence. But on another occasion he had turned down a 'modern' girl on charges of her not being able to read or write Gujarati:

"Not even educated in her own mother-tongue! How will my childrens learn own language if mother don't know?" he had challenged in his Ingliss.

"I see my perfect wife feeding my children with our kind of food and talking to them in Gujarati. But, speaking to me only in Ingliss, unless I want speaking in Gujarati. I want to speak Ingliss on all vital household matters, but at night, I want rumpy-pumpy in Gujarati."

Another potential bride he had been shown had, surprisingly, met with all his conditions and he would have said "yes" had it not been for her stupidity with the tea tray. As Mr and Mrs Naranbhai, Pandit Suddenly and Satish sat in her parents' small living room, she was called in for the regular inspection ceremony. This kind of summons always doubled up as functional servility. Rather than just walk in and twirl around like a Miss World contestant the girl, in accordance with the demands of decency, walked in head lowered, carrying a large rectangular tray with eight cups of tea. This she proceeded to place on a small table. As soon as she had lifted off the first two cups to hand to the guests, the rest of the tray, now one-side heavy, toppled over splashing tea onto the floor and spraying some of it on Satish's newly dry-cleaned white suit.

"It was just a small accident, baba," Naranbhai had tried to plead afterwards. "Doesn't mean she's not suitable. Accidents will always happen..."

"No, no, she wasn't using her brain. I don't like girls who don't use their brain for normal everyday tasks. If she can't even place a tea-tray on a table in the correct manner, how can she be entrusted with the future of my children?"

At that point, Naranbhai out of sheer disgust, had decided to wash his hands off the whole business of Bachelor Satish and his non-existent 'Dream Girl': "What does that boy want? He wants an apsara with long-long hair to suddenly descend from the sky holding English degree in one hand and seducing him in Gujarati with other hand, hain?"

Satish, although pushing forty was still a "boy" because he was unmarried. And, disgusted as he was with Satish's perfectionism in the matter of choosing a wife, the arrival of Shahbanu had added a fresh urgency to Naranbhai's aims to get the "the boy" married off, somehow. Under the pretext of ferrying her all over town in his khattara Ford Prefect, Satish was spending far too much time with Shahbanu. And, only a wife could put a stop to that sort of thing.

BLACK CAT

Until the arrival of Shahbanu and her vast collection of Elvis Presley records, Bachelor Satish with the large disposable income had been the only proud owner of a gramophone in Bombay Gardens. He possessed exactly twenty-five 78 rpm records consisting entirely of Indian film hits from the forties and early fifties.Whenever Satish was in, the records were played religiously, one by one, in exactly the same order. And then they were turned over, one by one -- fifty songs in all. Neighbours had got to know every single Satish song by heart, while the D'Sa children, who were mysteriously able to speak every single Indian language under the sun, (much to the shame of their mother who would've preferred them to be "smart-class" and speak only in English,) were able to run into the courtyard whenever it rained, singing along word-perfect:"Tak tina dhin, tina dhin, tak tina dhin, barsaat mein humse mille tum…"

"You'll catch your death - all of you, all at once! We can't afford eleven funerals!" Mrs D'Sa would yell.

Satish frequently counted his blessings, including the freedom to spend all his money on himself and to remain at the Black Cat - the sleazy local watering hole - for as long as he liked on Saturday nights without having to explain his whereabouts to a sulky wife. He often sat at a table with three others playing cards well into the small hours. While the other men rushed through the last few games for fear of being locked out by their wives, Satish felt free as a bird and found himself in the best possible situation to dole out advice - as only an unmarried man can do: "You don't be afraid like that. Go when you ready to go. Wife should be taught from day one that you in charge..." he preached.

The Black Cat had other attractions, not least of which was the barmaid, Maria, an object of never-ending fascination for Satish. Black but not black, brown but more like milky tea. She was a far cry from his Dream Girl. Short frizzy hair instead of the long-long straight hair he dreamed about, and certainly no BA MA.LLB. But she was, nevertheless, made of the stuff that kept dreams going until such time as Dream Girl might deign to descend to this earthly plane.

Married men always had that one extra drink to get another chance to grab at Maria as she brought it to their tables. Disillusioned bachelors with broken hearts cited Maria as an example of not how all beautiful girls are heartless and bitchy. She was everybody's and nobody's. She gave the impression of belonging only to herself, a fact that men, the world over, find inexplicably attractive. So when his married friends reluctantly headed home on Saturday nights, Satish usually stayed behind for a private drink with Maria.

The Black Cat operated a different charging structure for "Private Drinks". These could only be taken after a certain hour, that is, once the barmaid was off-duty, and they could be taken in her little room above the bar. Each drink cost twenty times the price of a normal, public drink. Needless to say, the barmaid's room consisted of only one piece of furniture: a single bed.

Satish considered his weekly private drink an essential part of his well being and hence a most necessary expense. It would, indeed, have taken a "Dream Girl" to make him break from this routine. This was human interaction at its best. You could have any amount that you could afford and there was no obligation to answer questions like "Who What When Where Why?" And, once in a while, when he was feeling generous, he would insist on treating one of his married friends to a private drink with Maria. He believed that sort of thing was good for married men. It taught them not to be too dependent on their sulky wives for sexual favours.

Naranbhai and the other men had a pretty good idea about Satish's Saturday night routine but refused to let that interfere in their dealings with the 'boy.' Pandit Suddenly, given to philosophical musings at opportune and inopportune moments had once remarked:

"Just because a man has one weakness, doesn't suddenly mean he is all bad. Satish has a very good heart. He could suddenly make a woman very happy, but he is such an idealist. Suddenly, no woman seems good enough for him."

"Boys will be boys. He is a bachelor. What do you expect? Once there is a wife, he will be straightened out. What is a healthy young man to do if there is no wife to keep him in check?" Naranbhai had agreed with his learned friend.

Naranbhai's useless nephew, the 17-year old son of his widowed sister Nalini, had befriended Satish at the Black Cat. Satish and Bharat - although widely differing in age - had, nevertheless, built up a good camaraderie based on their mutual lust for Maria. The Useless Nephew, Bharat, always allowed Bachelor Satish to go first, while he himself waited patiently in the bar below her room.

Satish would then emerge - some twenty minutes later - looking flushed and dazed and somewhat misty eyed, smug as a cat. He would thump the Useless Nephew Bharat on his back and say:

"Go on, your turn! She's still rearing to go...hot as hell...just like a well-buttered chappati. I made sure of that."

Satish felt some ownership towards Maria. As long as he went first, and the others only went after him, and that too with his approval and by his explicit permission, he felt no sexual jealousy over sharing Maria's sensual delights. A barmaid was, after all, public property.

In a strange sort of way that Satish hadn't really figured out, the thought of Bharat soon touching and feeling what he had himself just touched and felt, caused a delicious excitement within him - an inexplicable sensation that couldn't be analysed - well at least not while most of his critical faculties were taken up by thoughts of "Dream Girl."

TOO HOT TO HANDLE

One by one, the D'Sa children came down with chicken-pox, and Mrs D'Sa was temporarily driven insane between nursing them, giving her piano classes and baking the town's cakes. One by one the children made a recovery -- all except the youngest baby-boy who was still covered in the pox and ran a high fever. There was no money to send for a doctor and Mrs D'Sa, in a moment of despair, turned to Mrs Naranbhai for a small loan to have the child attended by a doctor. Mrs Naranbhai, although fully willing and able to lend her the money, decided instead to advise her of an old Indian method, tried and tested over the years and guaranteed to cure childhood illnesses as though by magic. The method involved the temporary theft of an iron object from a neighbour's house. The object had to be kept under the infected child's pillow for a whole week after which the illness was guaranteed to evaporate into thin air.

"Must be iron, and must be somebody else's, and they mustn't know you take," Mrs Naranbhai emphasised in a mixture of kitchen Swahili laced with basic English.

"But that is theft," Mrs D'Sa protested lamely. "I will have to go to Confession..."

"Yes, yes, confession-punfession, but what about your baby? Don't you want him to get better? And it is not real theft. You will quietly replace the object once the job is done."

What can a loving mother do confronted with such a convincing argument? And especially one that didn't involve getting into more debt?

Soon after Mrs Naranbhai's advice to Mrs D'Sa, Virjibhai the Compounder's older daughter, Bimla, suffered severe burns in an attempt to remove a pot of boiling milk from the fire. She would normally have used iron tongs designed specifically for this purpose. But the tongs had mysteriously vanished and had been missing for nearly a week. In that week, Bimla had managed by padding her hands with an old towel, or sometimes using the end of her skirt. But, on this occasion, the cloth had slipped and caused her fingers to come into direct contact with the intense heat of the pot, and the resulting pain had led to an uncontrollable scream, throwing the contents over Bimla while the scorching pot fell to the floor hitting her foot.

The news of Bimla's accident spread fast. Neighbours called in one by one with offers of homemade poultices and other remedies for the treatment of burns. Mrs Naranbhai, eaten up with guilt over her part in the disappearance of the tongs, prepared special meals for Virjibhai and his daughters while Bimla remained confined to bed.

On seeing Bimla's suffering, Mrs D'Sa could no longer live with her own guilt. She decided to own up to the theft of the tongs. In so doing, she completely disregarded the rules of the superstition which dictated that the stolen item must simply be placed back quietly and the theft never confessed, otherwise, the child's recovery would somehow reverse itself. But, Mrs D'Sa, being a good Catholic, decided to ignore that small detail in the interests of truthfulness and honesty, and her own, now rather precarious place in heaven.

On hearing Mrs D'Sa's tearful confession, Bimla was completely forgiving towards the distressed lady. She respected superstition and respected Mrs D'Sa for agreeing to enact an old Hindu custom in spite of being a Roman Catholic. She was also touched by the fact that whatever the woman had done, she had done for her child. A mother who was prepared to steal for her child was a mother to be admired.

Mrs D'Sa offered to pay the doctor's bills for Bimla's treatment but Virjibhai would not hear of it.

"My daughter is alive and well, and your son is cured of his chicken-pox, so no harm done," he said matter-of-factly, knowing that she had been unable to call in a doctor even for their own children, never mind foot the bill for other people's medical treatment. His employee, Dr Dawawalla, was providing full medical treatment and, under his expert care, Bimla's burns soon began the long process of healing.

Far from causing any ill feeling, the incident had only served to cement friendships between the neighbours at Bombay Gardens. It was the second Mrs Naranbhai who was now seen as the chief culprit and temporarily ostracised on grounds of being a trouble-making busybody. Why couldn't she have just given the D'Sa woman some money to pay a doctor instead of involving her in dubious, superstitious Indian customs? Those things only worked for Hindus. They weren't *meant* to work for people of other religions and beliefs. How could you be helped - or hindered - by a god you didn't believe in?

"I wish I'd never listened to that stupid woman," Mrs D'Sa said to Bimla after popping in to see her with a small heart-shaped cake, baked especially for her.

"It's all right, Mrs D'Sa," Bimla said gratefully. "I'm glad your baby-son is feeling better. What a pretty cake, thank you."

Shahbanu arrived with a new potted plant for Bimla and offered to cook lunch.

" No, no thank you..." Bimla began, uncertain how to proceed. It was common knowledge that Shahbanu never even cooked at home, so what the hell was she going to cook here? Everyone knew that mother and daughter lived on biscuits and coffee. It was part of Shahbanu's charm-school act to make promises and suggestions that were never kept.

"But what about Virjibhai and Kamla? What will they eat when they return?" Shahbanu quizzed, in her little-girl voice, with genuine-but-pretended concern.

"Mrs Naranbhai is sending food..." Bimla informed her uneasily, fully aware that Bombay Gardens was temporarily averse to Mrs Naranbhai's gestures of interfering goodwill.

Mrs D'Sa cut in angrily: "It's all because of that bloody woman this happened!"

But neither Bimla nor Shahbanu seemed game for a bitching session about the mistress of Naran Villa: Bimla, because she refused to have opinions about her elders and superiors. And Shahbanu, in keeping with her holy image, refused to see, hear or speak evil of anyone: particularly anyone whose husband happened to be a victim of Shahbanu's charms.

"I tell you, she *made* me do it," Mrs D'Sa persisted, refusing to buckle down and determined to have a full discussion on the subject.

165

"I'm sure she meant well, Mrs D'Sa," Shahbanu said. "She was only trying to help."

"Please call me Alda. Oh Shahbanu! You don't know what she's like. She was trying to make trouble between all of us. Why, only the other day, she was asking nosy questions about you, and all your male visitors, don't you know?"

Mrs D'Sa felt sure this last bit of information would persuade Shahbanu to abandon her holier-than-thou stance and resort to some good, cosy, old-fashioned, dirt-splashing.

But Shahbanu, composed as ever and butter-wouldn't-melt, simply said:

"It is understandable, Mrs D'Sa. In a small place like this, one always wants to know everything. Can't be helped..."

"But she wanted to know what the men do with you....."

"Whatever..." Shahbanu cut in firmly, and catching the end of her shocking pink sari she swept it round her thin waist and calmly strode off, leaving a faint fragrance of roses and jasmine in her wake.

Later that morning, Mrs Naranbhai wept tears of bitter fury with her aunt Kamini.

"Ungrateful, all of them! I give them the benefit of my wisdom and knowledge for free and they're all saying I'm some sort of villain," she sniffed into the end of her sari. And then, remembering her other favourite theme, she decided to use the occasion to have a good sniffle about that as well:

"No one respects a second wife, I tell you. Just because I am...."

"Never mind, never mind," the aunt consoled her. "That is the way of this world - you try and do good and it's thrown back at your face."

Aunt Kamini spoke with the superior air of one who had made supreme sacrifices all her life only to have them blow up in her face. On hearing her tone, Mrs Naranbhai sensed yet another film story from the silent era coming on and hastily got up from her place on the big swing.

166

"Must get on. So much to do! If I sit down to cry what's anyone going to eat today? Not just here, I also have to send food to Virjibhai's house…"

An hour later, Jannasani laboriously carried a big tray of food to Bombay Gardens in the scorching midday sun. Lunch, prepared by Mrs Naranbhai, for Virjibhai and his daughters. Bombay Gardens was only a short walk from Naran Villa, but laden with a heavy tray and the sun beating down on his head, it seemed like an eternity to the long-suffering, houseboy.

Jannasani was gone an unusually long time and just as Mrs Naranbhai was about to conclude that he'd probably made off to his village to feed all his own relatives on her delicious mattar-pilau, saag and cauliflower, he ambled back at the usual languid pace. Jannsani's demeanour gave no hint of urgency -- or the sad and shocking news he carried. There are those in this world whose chief joy is to be bearers of bad news -- to relish the impact that came from imparting such doom and gloom. Not Jannasani. His face remained without an ounce of sadness and his voice totally free of any gleeful anticipation of histrionics as he calmly announced:

"The boy - Mrs D'Sa's little toto - with the fever. He is dead."

CROSSROADS

Curious eye-witnesses saw Mrs D'Sa run a long way chasing after the van-cum-hearse that bore away the small coffin of her baby son. And, well-meaning but nosy eavesdroppers, heard her drunken husband demanding his dinner at exactly seven o'clock that evening.

Mrs Naranbhai sent her usual trays of food but Mr D'Sa despised vegetarian food. He had always said it was food fit for cattle, not humans. His voice got louder and louder and the neighbours, fearing that poor Mrs D'Sa would probably be in for a beating that night, hastily sanctioned the killing of a chicken and Mrs Naranbhai ordered Jannasani to go and cook it in the Bombay Gardens sakati. Naran Villa could not be contaminated by the cooking of dead flesh.

Mr D'Sa ate the chicken with relish while his children watched, waiting to be thrown some bones. They had already been fed on the neighbours' vegetarian food and shouldn't have been hungry but chicken was a very rare treat. One way or another everyone was fed. Only Mrs D'Sa refused to eat. She kept demanding to be taken to her child's grave. It rained heavily that evening and Mrs D'Sa was inconsolable. She was convinced that her dead child would get wet under all that mud and catch a cold.

The neighbours tried to soothe her, afraid that her hysterics would launch D'Sa into a beating session, chicken or no chicken. But Mrs D'Sa was so distraught that Virjibhai the Compounder called his employer, Dr Dawawalla, to give the distressed lady an injection to put her to sleep for a few hours.

Although Mrs Naranbhai had reacted to the crisis and rallied round with trays of food in her usual way, there was an element of smugness in her demeanor. That is not to say she was not genuinely distressed at Mrs D'Sa's loss, but she kept reminding herself, with the utmost satisfaction, that the Goan lady had disobeyed the rules of superstition and, as such, had caused her own child to die. She reminded herself, again and again, that she had explicitly impressed upon Mrs D'Sa the importance of secrecy, but that stupid woman, owing to some misguided

Catholic notion, had gone against her instructions and foolishly owned up to the theft of the tongs.

"Rules are rules, you see?" she said to her aunt Kamini that night. "You can't mess about with these things. These rules are handed down by our ancestors."

"Yes, yes," agreed Kamini Masi and immediately launched into the story of another woman who had displeased the gods and had had to face tragic consequences. Needless to say, the woman's character had been portrayed by Kamini Devi in a major film of the early 1930s. Mrs Naranbhai yawned several times but that did not deter the former Kamini Devi from describing each scene in great detail.

The widow Nalini arrived downstairs and managed to catch the last few sentences of Kamini's boastful recollection of her role of a lifetime.

"Some people can only live through what they've done in the past," she said to nobody in particular. "What are they doing today? Just hanging around and making trouble for anyone."

"Who are you talking about?" barked the younger Mrs Naranbhai. Although sick to death of her aunt's film actress stories, Mrs Naranbhai was always quick to react to any taunts against her ally.

"Nobody, nobody at all," Nalini said casually, and under her breath she muttered, "she's just a nobody."

At that point the older wife, Sushilaben, also appeared downstairs in complete contravention of house rules. She was supposed to remain confined to her quarters where she tended to the Mad Girl.

"What are you doing downstairs?" the younger wife asked territorially.

"I just came to ask you about the Goan people in Bombay Gardens. That lady, whose little boy died, how is she now?"

The older wife had not gone to the funeral because her Mad Girl could not be left alone, and Mrs Naranbhai, accordingly, concluded that the nosy old bat had just come down to hear all the gory details of a missed funeral. Mrs Naranbhai immediately assumed a lip-sealed, dignified pose in a crude imitation of the elegant Shahbanu, and said as quietly as possible:

"The doctor gave her an injection. She managed to go to sleep. Poor woman! We can only pray for her. God give her strength!"

The aunt Kamini, quickly realising the rules of this new tight-lipped game, joined in:

"Yes, poor woman. God, give her strength. Who knows where one goes after death, hain?"

Mrs Naranbhai readily took her cue and added: "Yes. Who knows? I prayed to God to give the baby a special place in their Christian heaven - or whatever they call it. I prayed to God to give the poor mother strength. No mother can bear that sort of grief easily..." and she wiped away an imaginary tear with the end of her sari, fully aware that the older wife would have registered the point about motherly grief, in relation to her own mad daughter.

If she had, Shushilaben chose to completely ignore that unkind allusion to disappointed motherhood.

Instead, she said: "The strange thing is, I heard that someone asked that Goan lady to do that old Indian tradition of stealing something made of iron but then she lost her nerve and confessed...."

Mrs Naranbhai did not like the way the conversation was headed:

"I don't know anything about that. Let us just remember her grief and pray for her. Anyway, I am going to bed now, " she announced hastily.

"I wonder how she knew about the superstition?" Sushilaben persisted, sensing the younger wife's unease and refusing to give up. "I mean she is Christian. They don't believe in these things, do they? Someone must have advised her. And, if they did such a thing, then they did wrong, because they didn't give her the full facts...."

There was a dramatic pause and Mrs Naranbhai could bear it no longer.

"I did, I did," she protested. "I did tell her not to tell but when Bimla got burnt..."

The older wife didn't allow her to finish the story:

"Those who don't know about these things should keep their noses out! If I had done such an irresponsible thing, I would hold myself personally to blame for the unnecessary death of an innocent child...." and she sniffled into the end of her sari.

Things had been tense between the two Naranbhai wives at the best of times, but some semblance of peace was usually possible owing to the fact that each woman had a staunch female ally within the household. But after the tragic death of the D'Sa child, the older wife assumed a position of moral victory. If there were any old Hindu superstitions to be handed out, then she, or her sister-in-law-cum best friend widow Nalini, were the best possible fountains of such advice: Nalini, because of her powerful dreams and she, herself, owing to her extensive knowledge and experience of all forms of alternative medicine.

What had she not tried in connection with Mad Girl's illness? OK, so none of these outlandish methods had made Kirti any better but, in the process of searching for a cure, Sushilaben had personally encountered every single healing system in the universe and, as such, considered herself an expert in these matters. From pigeon blood and feathers to cow-dung and urine: the Mad Girl had been fed every imaginable concoction dictated by almost every single belief system known to Man. And, when the cocktails of blood and urine and cow dung had failed, there had been scores of other rituals requiring various substances to be burnt and the ashes placed under her pillow. There had been forced feeding of unmentionable ingredients and forced starvation for days on end in an attempt to starve the "bhoot" (evil spirit) that was said to be in possession of her body. Various colourful characters of all races and religions, said to specialise in the chasing away of bhoots, had been summoned from all four corners of the African continent. They arrived in their multitudes, often uninvited, each professing to be the only one who had the key to this strange and mysterious illness. At first, Sushilaben had eagerly welcomed them all - quacks, hakeems, veds, yogis, saddhus, witch-doctors. By the time the Mad Girl was eight and showing no signs of improvement - if anything quite the reverse - Naranbhai had put an abrupt end to the unwelcome visitors.

Instead, he insisted on following the advice of his part-time Pandit friend who had recommended that the couple should concentrate on having another child. Only with the arrival of a new baby would the previous one be purged of the evil spirit. They tried day and night - Mad Girl Kirti's tantrums permitting - but Sushilaben failed to conceive. The Pandit then modified his prescription and said it would be enough if Naranbhai had a second child -- not necessarily from Sushilaben. It was then agreed that given these exceptional circumstances, and bearing in mind the Pandit's recommendation, Naranbhai should be allowed to take another wife.

The new Mrs Naranbhai arrived and, exactly nine months later, produced a healthy baby-boy. But Mad Girl did not get better. Another son was born to the Naranbhais, and then another, but the Mad Girl's condition grew worse.

It was around this time that the crossroads incident occurred. It had only happened because the younger Mrs Naranbhai, on the advice of her aunt Kamini, was making a first attempt at befriending the older wife.

"There is nothing a man hates more than both his wives getting on well with one another," Kamini masi had wisely advised her niece. "If the two of you stand united, he will feel undermined. That way, he will always give in to you. And, he won't be able to blame you for anything, because you are always nice to his first wife. In the old days in India, a wife always made sure she was on good terms with all the rivals - other wives, mistresses, rakhels and concubines."

Kamini Ben who had never been a wife was, of course, speaking from the mistress's perspective.

The second Mrs Naranbhai liked this radical scheme to extend more control over her husband and so approached the older wife with a garland of freshly cut gardenias:

"Here, I made one for myself so I made you one as well. After all,you are a married woman, so why shouldn't you wear flowers in your hair?" she said sweetly.

Sushilaben was at first very suspicious at this U-turn, but when the younger wife actually started showing an interest in the Mad

Girl's condition and offering possible solutions to her illness, the older wife was touched by the woman's efforts at making peace.

"Sushilaben, I know you must have tried everything, but when I was a young girl in my village in India, children with this condition were always taken to a crossroads. It must be on a dark night - no moon. You take the girl to a crossroad junction. You light a small lamp - must be pure ghee in the pot - and then you turn around and walk away. You mustn't look back. No matter what! Come home, wash your face, put the girl to bed and you also go straight to sleep. Don't talk to anyone. Next morning, girl will be fine."

Sushilaben considered the simplicity of the plan. No blood, no feathers, no elaborate rituals. What harm could it possibly do?

"Yes, but at night? All alone...?" Sushilaben seemed uncertain.

"But I'll come with you, na? We'll both go," Mrs Naranbhai said chummily to her new friend. "But we mustn't tell anyone. It doesn't work if you tell!"

There was just one problem with the scheme: there wasn't a single crossroads in town - only straight roads with mud-tracks leading off into settlements of the poor. There were T-junctions, and lay-bys, even roundabouts in true British colonial fashion, but no crossroads. Eventually, Jannasani was entrusted with the top-secret mission of locating a crossroads and then accompanying the two ladies and the Mad Girl on a dark, moonless night.

Jannasani eventually found a crossroads in a small neighbouring town, some thirty-five miles away. Mrs Naranbhai gave him some money to organise a taxi. A taxi came in the dead of night and pulled up, as instructed, some distance away from the house. Jannasani signalled to the ladies and they left Naran Villa stealthily, holding their saris above their ankles and gripping their wool shawls in their teeth. Sushilaben held the Mad Girl firmly by her shoulders, while Mrs Naranbhai carried all the lamp-lighting paraphernalia.

An hour later they were at the said crossroads. The taxi driver and Jannasani were asked to wait in the car while the women got out and led the girl to the centre of the junction. The night was dark and still. A filling station at one of corners of the junction looked like a derelict, disused shed, with the pumps turned off and the neon "Agip" sign with its black dog a ghostly shadow of its normal glory. A few small houses peppered off the main road and spreading into the bush, lay in darkness.

Mrs Naranbhai handed Sushilaben the lighting-up stuff while she herself gripped the Mad Girl's shoulders. The lamp had to be lit by the child's mother. That was an essential requirement of the ritual. The Mad Girl was strangely compliant. For once she wasn't struggling to get away as she usually did when someone attempted to perform any kind of ritual.

Sushilaben lit the lamp and it glowed in the pitch-dark street. It was a warm but slightly breezy night and the flame rose high and steady.The women exchanged a quick furtive look, wondering what to do next. Sushilaben felt she ought do something more - maybe say a prayer - but Mrs Naranbhai was quick to whisper:

"Now, let's go! No looking back, remember!"

A short walk brought them back to the car. They tumbled in, giggling with relief that it was all over. They hugged one another and each called the other "sister":

"Now we've done this together, we will always be sisters," they told one another, tenderly.

But that tenderness was only reserved for each other. For Jannasani and the taxi driver, Mrs Naranbhai reverted to her usual barking:

"Come on, what are you waiting for?Quick, start the car! Hope nobody's woken up and found us missing."

The two men looked at one another in despair. At last Jannasani asked:

"What about the girl? Aren't we taking her back?"

"The girl?" Both women panicked and simultaneously jumped out of the car.

"I thought you had her!"

"No, *you* were holding her! I was lighting the lamp."

"But you..."

"No you…oh no! Now look what you've done! I should never have listened to you! *You* had her…"

"No, *you* did! She must've been just behind....but you were the one who said not to look behind...oooohhh!" Sushilaben wailed. "What are we going to do? It's your bloody fault! You made me do it! You just have it in for me. What you would really like is to poison me and then have my husband all to yourself..."

The newly formed alliance lay in tatters while the women, Jannasani and the taxi driver ran to and fro in all directions searching for Mad Girl Kirti.

"She can't have gone far. She must be hiding somewhere here - - look in the bushes," the taxi driver tried to remain objective. It was one of the most exciting midnight jobs he'd ever had, even more exciting than driving Asian gentlemen into the bushes where they held assignations with African women.

Sushilaben was getting hysterical:"Kirti, Kirti! O my Mad One, where are you?"

Lamps were starting to be lit in the small windows of the houses lying just off the main road and a few shadowy figures could be seen in doorways.

The next morning the "Argus", the main English language newspaper, carried the following headline:

"ATTEMPTED ARSON: MAD GIRL AND TWO INDIAN WOMEN CAUGHT!"

It was reported that the women had been caught red-handed in the middle of the night, with matches, hovering near the houses of poor black people.

"Normal Indian method to get cheap land:set fire to the houses of the poor and then promise to build them new ones, provided they sell the land for about five shillings. Then these Indians set up their own palaces and the poor never get the houses they are promised."

More charitable sources concluded that the family had a mad girl called Kirti who had run away in the night, taking some matches with her. The women had simply come after her to make sure she wouldn't start a fire.

So what was that silly little lamp doing in the exact centre of the crossroads? quizzed the skeptical. What was a small, Indian-style, earthenware lamp doing in the middle of nowhere?

175

When the taxi-driver was interviewed he said he knew nothing about attempted arson, but that the women were performing some kind of voodoo ritual.

The newspapers changed their tack. Bloody pagans! Looking down on African religions, making fun of witch doctors and ancestor worship and then performing such meaningless doo-dahs dictated by their own holier-than-thou religions. Disturbing the well-earned sleep of hard-working Africans.

Reporters tried to corner Jannasani for an interview, but the wiry Jannasani knew only too well on which side his bread was buttered. Even without Naranbhai ordering him to do so, he was silent as the grave.

That dramatic night had ended when residents living near the crossroads had summoned the police and a police officer had finally found the Mad Girl sitting peacefully under a bush with a snake coiled round her neck.

The two Naranbhai wives were taken to the local Police Station for questioning, but the District Police Chief - a certain Mr Amin who preferred his name to be pronounced "Ay-men" - was a good friend of Naranbhai's, and the matter was soon cleared up. But Naranbhai's own head still throbbed with pain. He had done nothing all morning except sit with his head in his hands wondering what on earth had possessed the women – first, to become friends and then to carry out such a ridiculous procedure in the middle of the night? On being questioned by him, each woman promptly blamed the other and, much to his relief, the two wives were back to being enemies. The rumours of attempted arson and voodoo rituals gradually died away as newspapers became bored with the story.

But there was one small, significant change in the Mad Girl's condition. It was soon after this incident, that she had first started singing...

ALL OUT WAR

That crossroads incident had ocurred five earlier, and now, as Sushilaben seethed at Mrs Naranbhai's nerve at going about giving advice on supernatural matters, and that too to a Catholic, she wondered why the D'Sa woman had even taken all that rubbish seriously. What right had she to give such half-baked instructions to that poor D'Sa woman when, only five years ago, Mrs Naranbhai had so nearly brought disgrace upon the whole family by her stupid crossroads scheme? And, in any case, Sushilaben's own self-acknowledged expertise in all matters pertaining to the supernatural, coupled with her sister-in-law Nalini the widow's dream interpretation technique, was surely reason enough for Mrs D'Sa to have sought *her* expert opinion rather than go crawling for advice to the ignorant second-wife? Under the circumstances then, decided Sushilaben, it was not really surprising that the superstition had backfired.

"Those who don't know about such things should keep their noses out. They should know they are personally responsible for the death of an innocent child," Sushilaben was determined to discuss the circumstances of the D'Sa baby's death in full.

"Just what do you mean by that?" Mrs Naranbhai's temper was rising and the aunt Kamini decided not to try and restrain her. It was high time, she thought, the two wives had it out. There had been too much unspoken tension recently and, perhaps, the death of the D'Sa child provided the perfect opportunity for the two women to have it out.

"What do you mean? Repeat yourself, O rejected wife who lives on her husband's mercy. What did I just hear from your filthy mouth?" shouted Mrs Naranbhai.

"I choose to be a retired wife so that you can sleep and make babies with my rejected husband," the older wife replied.

While Mrs Naranbhai had stood up, the aunt Kamini settled down into a more comfortable position to enjoy the spectacle until such time as her intervention was required. She watched her niece Mrs Naranbhai firing the next salvo with the expression of one who had placed an enormous amount of money on this contender.

And that contender was in full flow at being told she slept with a reject:

"Watch your tongue!"yelled Mrs Naranbhai."God has punished you with a mad daughter and you still haven't learned your lesson?"

"Don't bring my innocent daughter into all this. I didn't produce her all by myself. Your beloved secondhand husband also had something to do with it, " the older wife retaliated, continuing, "You think Kirti is my fault? I tell you there is madness in their family. Wait till you have another one -- you'll soon find out."

"See masi?" Mrs Naranbhai turned to her aunt and pointed indignantly at the older wife."You see? She is cursing a child I haven't even conceived yet. Just because I have given *Him* three, normal healthy sons and she only managed one mad daughter, she hates me.

The older wife's ally, Nalini, decided it was her turn to speak:

"Nobody hates you. You hate yourself so much for marrying a man who was already married that you imagine everybody hates you," she said in wise tones.

Mrs Naranbhai would not have expected any different from her husband's sister; that woman had, from the very start, formed a close bond with her brother's older wife. The two women had always been more like sisters than sisters-in-law and Mrs Naranbhai had jealously concluded that this was because each had given birth to a useless child. Sushilaben had a mad daughter, while the widow sister had a sane, but utterly useless son, Naranbhai's Useless Nephew Bharat.

Since the older wife's ally had now made a contribution to the mud slinging, the aunt Kamini decided it was her turn to speak. But she had left it a bit late to rev up. The quarrel had already moved into top gear and all the women were shouting at each other all at once. The time for soliloquies had passed. Now it was a case of who had the loudest voice. And Kamini's voice had never been her fortune. Even so, she joined in with her crow-like reverberations unable to hear anybody but herself.

With all four women now yelling at the top of their voices, Naranbhai turned over in his bed uneasily. He had retired early having attended to various organisational matters for the D'Sa funeral -- not that his presence had really been required. In crises such as these, the upper and middle-class members of the Goan community materialised, as though out of thin air, and took care of the religious side of things. The same community that would normally not touch the D'Sas with a barge pole, with the exception of paying (her) a regular monthly amount for their daughters' piano lessons, had rallied along every step of the way with regard to funeral arrangements.

Naranbhai had found the experience of trying to help out even more exhausting than if he had actually had something to do.

He had just begun drifting into a relaxed, pre-slumber stage when the hawk like cries of his two wives and his sister were suddenly joined by the crowing of his second wife's aunt. He had hoped that the dispute - whatever its cause - would die down of its own accord, but now it seemed he would have to get out of bed and try and calm the women. It was not a task he cherished; like most men, he preferred a quiet life at home. Where his wives and the other women of his household were concerned, he would have given anything to learn the magic mantra that changes one, at will, into a mosquito.

Slowly he descended the steps from the upper floor. His arrival in the hall went unnoticed by the women who were really enjoying themselves now. There was shouting, wailing, crying, screaming, coughing, spluttering, spitting. From cursing descendants yet to be conceived, they had now moved on to various ancestors, long since departed.

Naranbhai was suddenly gripped with an irrational desire to leave them to it. He quietly slipped away towards the dining room and from there through the back door opening onto the backyard.

Jannasani squatted at the far end of the backyard, outside his little cupboard, smoking an exceptionally pungent-smelling cigarette that had less than half an inch left on it. Numbed by the war inside the house, Naranbhai became alert to trivial, inconsequential things. He stood some distance from Jannasani whose ability to sit in a squatting position for hours on end had never ceased to amaze Naranbhai. His own joints creaked even if he sat in a chair too long. The other thing that amazed Naranbhai about Jannasani was his ability to gaze into space for hours. Not anxious, not worried, not bored -- just still and alert, much as a cat waiting at a mousehole. Jannasani would squat until such time as he became sleepy and then he would sleep -- still squatting.

On seeing Naranbhai, Jannsani suddenly shot up assuming he was required for some late night task. The voices of the quarrelling women were clearly audible in the backyard. He waited for Naranbhai's orders, but none came. Master and Servant stood in silence and looked at one another. Naranbhai turned away to leave the yard by its backdoor and started walking in the direction of Bombay Gardens while Jannasani, with just a hint of an enigmatic smile, went back to his squatting position and his smelly cigarette.

SEEKING SOLACE

Shahbanu opened the door in a full-skirted dressing gown modelled on a design she had seen in an "English" film of the forties. If she was surprised to see Naranbhai at this late hour she certainly didn't show it. Instead she asked him in, as though he was expected.

"Sorry, sorry," he muttered, pointing to the parked Ford Anglia. "I know you have visitors...."

"No, not at all," she said sweetly. "That's just a friend of Saira's. They are in the other room. He teaches her, you see."

Naranbhai was too mentally exhausted to wonder what kind of teacher came home to teach at ten thirty in the night. Instead, he found himself pouring out all his domestic troubles to Shahbanu who, at that moment, struck him as an exceptionally rare and understanding woman. Then, thinking that he had moaned enough and feeling somewhat lightened of his burden, he got up to go, but she persuaded him to sit down and take another glass of pineapple juice.

"Please don't worry bhai-jaan," she said in her sweet, little-girl voice. "It happens in all houses. When women fight men become so helpless. All my friends....I mean my brothers and cousins...they all come here because they get no peace at home. Their wives, their sisters, their mothers just keep nagging them. Demanding money to make more jewellery, they want more saris, they want more trips to India....and the men, they just get fed up. That is why they come here."

"I see, I see," said, Naranbhai, feeling very pleased he now knew why the men only ever came on their own, and not with their women. And then, having just been at the receiving end of her benevolent grace, he realised all over again, just how reasonable and sympathetic Shahbanu could be. A cool stream on a hot day. A fragrant breeze blowing over the stifling stench of humidity. A soft, tinkling bell holding its own amidst a deafening roar. A patch of soft, cool, smooth silk on woollen coarseness. The coolest touch on a burning, feverish brow. A solitary dewdrop braving the heat and dust, shining defiantly crystal-like when everything around it was fast drying up. A dignified lotus, floating along, still immaculately white despite the muddy waters...

The list of many wonderful things that Shahbanu personified could have gone on and on in Naranbhai's mind had it not been for the slightly disconcerting sounds of the daughter Saira's giggles and muffled squeals from elsewhere in the house...

But Naranbhai chose to focus on Shahbanu, and Shahbanu alone. Whatever 'lesson' Saira was learning from her teacher at this unusual hour of night, was obviously on some subject of great amusement. Good, good! That's how education for girls should be. Light-hearted, not too serious and technical. Maybe he was telling her funny stories? No, no, he should not dwell on anything else. He should savour this delicious, private encounter with Shahbanu. She was, indeed, a rare gem. An understanding woman was a very unusual thing in this world.

"Come any time you like," she said to him. "I am your tenant, but you are like my brother. Like all my other brothers. Any time you feel it's getting too much over there, please come and relax here. I will serve you in any way I can."

Naranbhai swallowed hard, overcome with sudden emotion at her kindness and realising the stark contrast between the screeching voices he had just left behind and her own, soft, gentle, silky, slightly breathless, honey-drenched tones. Suddenly it all became too much for him. The sad events of the whole tragic day: the D'Sa baby's funeral, Mrs D'Sa's inconsolable grief, Mr D'Sa throwing chicken bones for his children to fight over, and the Naran Villa women scratching each other's eyes out.

He broke down and sobbed. He cried like he hadn't cried for years. Shahbanu gave him a glass of iced water and patted his arm while muttering a soothing verse from the Qur'an - or at least that's what he assumed it was, because it was in a language he didn't understand.

When he had calmed down, and was feeling self consciously stupid as only members of the human male species can feel after a genuine show of emotion, he experienced a mood of expansive generosity, and heard his own voice saying:

"I think you are paying far too much rent. Cut out the fifty - just pay the round-figure. You are more than a tenant, you are a friend," and with that his mouth quivered as he fought back more tears.

More sounds of muffled laughter from the daughter's bedroom immediately caused Shahbanu to raise the volume on Elvis Presley. Naranbhai put his fingers in his ears.

"Please, please," he protested. "Not so loud. Won't it disturb your lovely daughter?"

Shahbanu giggled girlishly and lowered the volume again.

A middle-aged man emerged from the direction of Saira's bedroom and said a polite good-bye to Shahbanu while nodding his head to Naranbhai by way of a greeting. Then, giving Shahbanu a wink he chided her with mock-accusation:

"You didn't tell *me* you were free! You know I prefer age and experience..."

Shahbanu shot up abruptly from her seat and started showing the man out, while at the same time turning her head back to Naranbhai, she muttered in mock annoyance and embarrassment:

"He doesn't give up! Thinks I should do Senior Cambridge exams as well...at my age!"

Not realising her mother had a visitor, the daughter Saira emerged from her room in a see-through red-and-black lace negligee. On seeing Naranbhai, she fled back to her room.

When Shahbanu came back into the house, Naranbhai assumed a conspiratorial voice:

"Sister, listen. Please don't feel bad but I must speak frankly to you. Your daughter is so beautiful, and that teacher - you know the one who just left - well, he is a man after all. I just wanted to say, be careful, all right? Please advise your daughter to be careful when alone with him. You never know with men, do you? Not all men are decent and morally upright like me. As a brother it is my duty to alert you. I feel very proud of Saira - like she was my own daughter. Well, you know the condition of my real daughter...."

And that last statement again reminded him of the scene at Naran Villa from which he had fled, and which he most sincerely hoped was now over.

"Yes, yes," Shahbanu said solemnly. "I will tell her to be careful. I really value your advice. Thank you."

Feeling much better at having been allowed to play benevolent landlord-cum-father again, (from having just been a cry-baby,) Naranbhai took his leave of Shahbanu some five minutes later, having issued a few more warnings on the need to be careful with male teachers who came home to teach young girls.

As soon as Shahbanu had bolted the front door and Naranbhai had walked some distance away, the daughter Saira emerged from her room and Mother and daughter squealed with hysterical laughter and collapsed on the plastic-covered sofa.

COUNTRY BUMPKINS

"Camilla, surely, not all Indians were the same?" I asked, after she'd told me about how most of them, after coming to the UK, droned on and on about a grand, mythical past. "Just because a few thousand people are expelled all at once, doesn't mean their circumstances were all the same, does it?"

"But that's just my point! All that in-fighting and rank pulling and then, along comes an Expulsion that treats them all like one big herd of wild animals. I think Expulsions are great! Suddenly, we were all given an equal second chance -- to start afresh in a new country. Hey! Why should I be the one who has to explain every single idiotic bigoted thing about East African Indians? These Indians -"

So, all of a sudden it's "these Indians." She's just finished having a go at me for "You Africans," and now it's about "*these* Indians" -- not including herself in that.

"You know, Baby, they come over here and talk of their big-big businesses and shops and industries, but I can tell you, over there, some of them -- no matter how rich -- were no better than the average Indian country bumpkin. Superstition and nonsense. Magic and witchcraft. They looked down on the Africans for witchdoctors and ancestor worship, but I'm telling you, no Indian would ever pass up on an opportunity to call on a quack: the men, if they wanted to make more money. And the women, if they wanted secret potions to keep their men from straying. And their own idiotic rituals dug out of obscure scriptures were said to be grand and noble. Narrow-mindedness passed off as "noble cultural heritage" ...

"Camilla, you really should write. I can tell you're seething to tell your story...."

"If I meet one more person who says 'you should write' -- I'll scream. No, I won't scream. I'll just say, 'you find the publisher and I'll write.' In this country, if it's on an Indian theme, unless it's something straight out of the Kama Sutra pandering to every Orientalist idea about the so-called exotic East, then just forget it....."

She stops suddenly. I can see she is very upset and angry. I lower my eyes with shame. I was one of those people who, for misguided reasons of my own, had made sure that Camilla's Indian princess story did not reach the right readers.

"Camilla, I'm sure you could write a terrific story -- it's all there....."

"Yes, we had it all," she says, as though talking to her self. "Half-baked pandits and illiterate matchmakers! And the same men who made the rule that unmarried young women were no better than prostitutes for the crime of being single, those same men spread their seed far and wide. And, far worse, if a young woman had independent means, like money of her own through an inheritance or something, then it was thought immoral that there was no man to spend it for her..."

"But surely, once the country was Independent, things improved? Surely all these Victorian-puritanical ideas died with the departure of the British? Ours was a very modern state, wasn't it?" I asked, without really having thought about it before. I hadn't realised the Indians had created moralistic super-structures of their own.

"What independence? Independence was a meaningless word for me. Even though I was one of very few Indians to actually attend the celebrations. But, at the same time as the country was getting its independence, I was being gagged and chained.....no, not by the new government, but by those who had appointed themselves custodians of decency and shame..."

THE JASMINE-SCENTED CURE

When Naranbhai returned to Naran Villa, some forty minutes after his impromptu visit to Shahbanu, the drawing room was in darkness. It looked like he hadn't been missed otherwise the lights would've been glaring full blast with all the women pacing up and down. He heaved a sigh of relief. That meant the quarrel was over and the women had retired to their respective quarters. He hoped Mrs Naranbhai would have gone straight to her own bedroom instead of coming into his.

Even so, he decided he should have some kind of believable story to explain his absence -- just in case......

His thoughts were interrupted by the sighting of Mrs Naranbhai at the top of the stairs. Surprisingly, she didn't seem angry -- just anxious.

"You're back? I saw you weren't in your room and Jannasani said you had gone to see if the D'Sas needed anything. I tell you, there isn't a landlord like you in the whole world. So kind and caring! Everybody takes you for a ride," she said flirtatiously, suddenly quite determined to take him for an altogether different kind of ride.

She was badly in need of sexual reassurance. Whenever she fought with the older wife, her only consolation lay in the fact that Naranbhai still slept with her whilst denying conjugals to the older woman for fear of her producing yet another mad, female child.

Naranbhai was pleasantly surprised by this reception, but his main source of pleasure was Jannasani's unexpected tact, uncommon intelligence and infinitely refined powers of discretion. Perhaps he had under-rated the man? Perhaps God had sent him a real friend and ally in the guise of a black African houseboy and he had never fully appreciated the fact? He toyed with the idea of increasing Jannasani's wages, then remembered he had just offered Shahbanu a reduction in rent. What would become of him and his family if he kept giving away all his money in this reckless fashion? Besides, if houseboys' wages were suddenly, and without sufficient explanation increased by the master, the lady of the house was bound to get suspicious. He resolved, instead, to give Jannasani that pair of nearly new trousers he had had in his wardrobe for ten years, in the hope of losing a few inches off his thickening waist. And, having made that decision to compensate Jannasani for his astute foresight and unfailing loyalty, he was at complete ease during Mrs Naranbhai's sexual puffing and panting. He was equally confident that given his second wife's past record, if there should be an outcome of this encounter, it could only be male. They already had a Doctor, Lawyer and Dentist. The fourth one, should he be conceived tonight, could always be dubbed "Chartered Accountant." But, alongside the reassuring feeling of Mrs Naranbhai only being able to bear boys, he was also ecstatic at the delicious warmth he felt after so recently being in the company of the fragrant Shahbanu. That warmth had made it possible to deploy a posture of languid submission to Mrs Naranbhai's lustful antics. Well, at least she always remained fully dressed for the act. For that alone, he was eternally grateful.

Still basking in after-glow laced with delicious, sensuous memories of Shahbanu's reassuring aura, Naranbhai was in an unusually good mood the following morning as he sat in an easy chair on the front verandah, doing nothing in particular except sipping sweet tea from a saucer and gazing into space. But the mood didn't last. Despite his new found strength and optimism he found himself searching for snags. He always did this when things seemed to be going well. His mind needed agitation. He decided to stew over all the potential problems that could plague his newest, still to be launched, business venture.

He would have to do his sums again and see how the figures looked. He grasped at the statuettes of his twin-gods in his right palm, the palm getting sweatier and sweatier as Naranbhai began day-dreaming about his great moment.....

But like every great dreamer, he had serious moments of doubt. What if it should all fail? What if he became bankrupt? He would have to sell Bombay Gardens to raise the money. The thought of giving up his extended family of tenants filled him with immense sadness. What would become of them? The quiet, even-tempered, wise and unassuming Virjibhai, his two daughters, the kindly Mrs

D'Sa and her brood, the limping Bachelor Satish - just like a son. And last, but by no means least, the beautiful Shahbanu and her graceful daughter Saira? Without any of these people he would be at the mercy of the women in his household with no other female subjects on whom to lavish his gallantry. There was something immensely soothing in wrapping oneself up in the imagined problems of others. It was extremely pleasing to think he could be of assistance to all his tenants. It was nice to hear Mrs D'Sa's piano. It was nice to discuss the effects of stomach acid with Virjibhai the Compounder. It was equally nice to caution Virjibhai on the pitfalls of rearing two motherless girls. It was nice to scold the D'Sa children when they were being unruly. It was good to hear Satish's twenty-five gramophone records over and over again. But, best of all, it was lovely to drop in on Shahbanu on the pretext of examining some new and exotic plant and then lingering a while…

Tears welled up in his eyes, and he had, finally, completely succeeding in turning his earlier light-hearted mood into one of bleak misery. If Bombay Gardens ever had to be sold then he would never be able to rest his eyes on Shahbanu's potted plants with their blazing colours and heady scents. Never again would he be able to wander into the Bombay Gardens' homely backyard and catch a glimpse of Bimla hurriedly rolling out chapatties in time for her father's packed lunch. Nor would he ever catch the delicious aroma of vanilla wafting from Mrs D'Sa's oven. It wasn't just a source of income. He had formed meaningful bonds with his many tenants. No, he would have to make sure that his latest business plan would not bankrupt him and force the sale of Bombay Gardens. A larger cash-flow was badly needed to prevent such a disaster.

He got up from his easy chair, feeling satisfactorily agitated and ready for battle. It was make or break. He would embark on his new business venture, somehow, and set about extending his glory and good name, no matter what the risk. He owed it to Shahbanu to prove to her that he could be more than just a cry-baby. As it was, all the men in Bombay Gardens were trying to impress her and he lived in the constant dread that Satish might, finally, buy a new car or the Panidt may perform some mind-boggling magic-trick and shoot up in that great lady's esteem. He clutched harder at his figurines of the twin-gods and hoped against hope that extra finances would materialise, somehow, to launch his biggest, most lavish venture yet...

DOCTOR DAUGHTER

Of all his tenants, Naranbhai considered the quiet, unassuming widower Virjibhai as the most trustworthy, and least likely to make trouble. True, Naranbhai was quite chummy with Pandit Suddenly, but now that the Pandit had shown such unbridled lust for Shahbanu, he was even more of a threat than he had been owing to his superior knowledge of English. Virjibhai, on the other hand, was, at least partially, a man after Naranbhai's own heart. *Partially*, because while he had shown all the right instincts in the upbringing of his older daughter Bimla - keeping her away from school and training her in the domestic arts, the best possible training for a good marriage - he had shown undue indulgence towards his outspoken younger daughter, Kamla. Kamla was being needlessly encouraged in her unladylike ambition of wanting to be the town's first lady doctor when she grew up.

"Arr-rey, Virjibhai," Naranbhai would say laughingly to his friend. "I have heard doctors have to study for seven years, *after* all their schooling. Seven years! She will be an old lady then - over twenty-five years old! Who will marry her then, hain?"

"I know, I know," Virjibhai would say affably. "But she is so bright. It would be a shame if she didn't do something with her brains. And women doctors are badly needed. Indian women don't like being attended by men doctors."

"But she can be stenographer or secretary. Or even nurse, or teacher."

"Yes, yes," Virjibhai would acquiesce, hastily adding, "but she loves the sciences you know. She's really good at..."

"Science-Vience, what? What can science do for human happiness? Nothing!" Naranbhai would say with profundity, as though the idea had just occurred to him that scientific progress and technological advancement were unrelated to the human condition.

The two men enjoyed an easy friendship mainly because Virjibhai specialised in never annoying anyone. Whatever the argument, he always managed to leave the other party with the impression that they had won it. As such, he was everybody's best, most understanding friend. So, this Sunday morning, when

Naranbhai appeared at Virjibhai's house - the two roomed dwelling which formed a right angle at one end of Bombay Gardens - he had every reason to believe that he would, at last, find someone who would be in favour of his new, extravagant, business scheme.

Virjibhai, was one of those unfortunate souls who, in money terms, was going to be worth far more after he departed from this earth. While alive, he could really only afford this two-roomed house and, if he was ever made to leave it, he had no idea what he would do. The rent was reasonable, the neighbours friendly, the landlord most cordial. Two rooms were more than ample for his humble requirements. What more does a small, three-person household need?

His job at Dr Dawawalla's dispensary, where Virjibhai was Compounder, brought in a moderate salary of which only a small portion was spent on rent, leaving a decent amount of money for food, clothes and other necessities. One of his largest items of expenditure was a life insurance policy - to take care of the girls in case anything should happen to him - and various savings accounts, including one for Bimla's marriage and another one for Kamla's future medical college expenses. Dr Dawawalla had been instrumental in guiding his employee through these sensible, far-sighted schemes. Naranbhai had rougly calculated the total amount that Virjibhai might have saved up until now, and, God forbid, if anything should happen to him, the girls would come into a hefty amount of money. Not right for mere *girls* to have those sort of independent means without a man to exercise some kind of restraining influence. Women who had not handled large sums of money were always bad news, not only for the neighbourhood, but also the wider community and the world at large. A lot of things were going wrong with the world because women were becoming economically independent and less and less likely to want, or need, a man. He intended to persuade Virjibhai to appoint him as a trustee for the funds, instead of that shameless prawn-eating Parsee doctor at whose surgery Virjibhai had worked since anybody could remember.

"Young girls, you know," he began carefully. "How will they cope with so much money....?"

The proud, prudent father was not to be persuaded so easily.

"Young, yes. Kamla may still be only ten, but she has the mind of a 30-year old. I tell you, I should know. It's true Bimla is a whole six years older, but she's a very simple-minded girl. Quite childish in some ways. Likes fillums and songs and just dreams of marriage. Now, Kamla, she just reads and reads and reads. Not just science. Whatever she can get her hands on. Even a ten-year-old Readers Digest, she will read from cover to cover and then start telling me about the Bermuda Triangle and Spontaneous Human Combustion and all such clever things."

"Spo...spont...human, yes, yes..." Naranbhai looked impressed. Bermuda Triangle sounded like a particularly sinister and bloodthirsty gang of thugs.

"Her English is very, very good," said the proud father, adding: "She writes all my official letters and fills out all forms, all by herself."

"Well, good, good. I will remember that for the future," Naranbhai said weakly, wondering how to broach the subject of becoming a trustee on the girls' inheritance. Then he had a brainwave:

"But *love* and all that? It's happening more and more to our girls. What if she falls in love with a bad-type and he cheats her out of all her money and runs away?"

"Dr Dawawalla will be in charge of funds," Virjibhai replied promptly.

"Yes, but he is not from our community. He might take the money and run away. Parsees are always dreaming of going to Canada you know? Or going somewhere or the other with a White Christian government. They only trust the Whites. After Independence, these Parsees and Goans will all go...wait and see..."

"Anyway," continued Virjibhai. "Our Raushan has also expressed an interest in being a guardian, in case anything happens to me...."

"Who? Raushan! That immoral woman who lets black men do it to her?" Naranbhai was clearly dismayed. "What sort of guardian would she make? See, Virjibhai, what I don't understand is why you always pick people of other communities rather than our own? They are all slaves of the whites and they'll all make off for foreign shores -- as soon as White countries let them in, they'll go running, even if it is just to drive a bus in Liverpool or clean the toilets in Canada."

"Yes, that's a point..." Virjibhai tailed off uncomfortably. Clearly, the matter of mistrusting Dawawalla had not occurred to him. Nor had the possibility that Raushan would corrupt Bimla and Kamla into marrying black men. Naranbhai waited calmly while these horrific possibilities sank into Virjibhai. He had planted the first seed of doubt, and seemed well on his way to getting what he came for.

After a few moments' silence, Virjibhai said: "I might consider splitting it into two. That way, whatever happens, one sister will always look after the other. But Dr Dawawalla must remain in charge of Kamla's share. He's a doctor after all. And she wants to be a doctor...."

"Too right! I want to be a doctor and I know my mind." Kamla had walked in with two cups of tea. "I don't want any man in charge of my money. In any case Bapu, it won't be necessary. I want you to live for thousands of years..."

Naranbhai ignored her remarks. "Did you remember to put sugar in that?" he barked instead, staring down into the cup of steaming tea.

"I don't know," she replied defiantly. "Bimla made the tea. I only brought it in because I wanted to hear you two talking about me...."

Naranbhai was stunned. The girl was too impertinent for her own good. A mere chit of a girl, wanting to listen in to grown-up man-talk about money! And to make matters worse, Virjibhai, on seeing Kamla, brightened up immediately and said: "Come in my darling daughter, come and sit down. Now our kind landlord Naranbhai here was suggesting that...."

Naranbhai looked embarrassed. He might have been able to pull the wool over poor Virjibhai's eyes, but not in a million years could he hope to out-do the over-wise Kamla.

"Yes? Just *what* was he suggesting?" she asked belligerently.

"Nothing, don't worry about it now", Naranbhai said sheepishly, and prepared to leave.

A week later, Virjibhai appeared at Naranvilla and informed Naranbhai that he had considered the matter of having two named trustees, and decided it made a lot of sense. And, he was happy to make Naranbhai the other trustee so that the girls would have double protection. Not that anything bad was ever likely to happen…

Aunt Kamini had overhead the conversation. Later, she asked her niece Mrs Naranbhai: "What is this Vima-Shima?"

"Life insurance. You get money when you die."

"What's the point? You mean they just give you money for dying?"

"Yes…"

The aunt considered the scheme for a while and decided it still didn't make sense: "And what happens if you *don't* die?" she asked.

"Don't be silly, masi! Everybody dies!" said Mrs Naranbhai.

ORPHANS

Kamla was always ravenous by lunchtime. As she set out on the short walk home from school she could think of nothing but food. She hoped her older sister Bimla would have cooked something delicious - she always did. Bimla had kept house ever since their mother died some nine years earlier. At that time Bimla was barely seven. But she had had to leave school to look after her father and the clever younger sister Kamla who showed every promise of some day being a highly accomplished and independent lady. For Bimla, her baby-sister Kamla's future success was all that mattered. She was immensely proud of Kamla, six years her junior.

Compounder Virjibhai's own ambition to become a doctor had been frustrated for lack of funds, but he derived almost as much satisfaction from preparing prescriptions as ordered by Dr Dawawalla. Apart from dreaming about making his younger daughter a doctor, working as a compounder was the nearest he was ever going to get to his own frustrated childhood dreams of someday becoming a doctor. He was filled with a sense of pride for being attached to the town's most popular doctor. Virjibhai had served Dr Dawawalla for many years. Employer and employee had developed a close relationship based on mutual trust and respect.

Dr Dawawalla, although generally unwilling to interfere in his employee's domestic arrangements had, nevertheless, been shocked that Bimla was being taken out of school to play Mother at such a young age.

"You could get married again, Virjibhai," he had suggested as tactfully as possible. Dawawalla was nothing but tactful when it came to other people's lives.

"What? And make my poor little girls have a stepmother? She's bound to ill-treat them. No, it's much better this way. Bimla is not that good at studying. It is better she concentrates on housework and leaves Kamla free to work hard in school. I'm going to make her a doctor, you know?"

In her nine years of playing housekeeper-cum-Mother, Bimla had become a very good cook. And now, as Kamla hurried home eagerly and hungrily, she felt a slight pang of guilt at having had such a fulfilling morning at school while her older sister would, as usual, have devoted the morning to cleaning the house, washing all their clothes and preparing lunch. She brushed off the guilt by reminding herself, as she did every single day on her way to and back from school, that one day she would make it up to Bimla. One day when she was a big doctor earning lots of money and commanding a lot of respect in the community, she would hand over all her earnings to Bimla, every single month. And wherever she lived - married or unmarried - Bimla would always live with her and be waited upon by an army of servants.

As Kamla approached the familiar back-entrance of Bombay Gardens a strange sense of impending doom gripped her. The backyard seemed quieter than usual. Normally, at this time, when various people were returning home for their lunch break, the neighbourhood hubbub would be evenly spread out over the entire backyard, but today, a strangely hushed noise seemed to be concentrated on only one part of Bombay Gardens: her house. Her footsteps hurried in that direction but she could not enter through the backdoor for the throngs of women who sat wet-eyed on the bare floor, whimpering and wiping their noses on their white saris.

As soon as they saw her they tried to embrace her all at once and started wailing louder. She was almost crushed under the weight of arms and bosoms as the women - most of whom she had never seen before - tried to all talk at once. Gradually, once she became used to the moaning and whimpering, she could make out a word here and part of a sentence there...

"Poor girls! What will become of you two? Oh God! Help them! Hey Ram, why them? What have they done wrong? O Bhagwan, Ya Allah, have mercy!"

The future lady-doctor-to-be Kamla had had enough of these meaningless histrionics. She tried to push them all back and raised her voice over their wailing:

"Will you all please stand back? Now, will *one* of you please tell me what's happened?" They all fell on her again with renewed hysteria while an unknown woman with owl-like glasses pronounced:

197

"Such pride - so outspoken! O Allah - it's all very well to talk like that when you have parents. But orphans, how can orphans ever look anyone in the eye and speak with such confidence?" And, with that she broke down and joined the chorus of the wailing women. The competition had begun in earnest over who could show the most grief and who could hug Kamla the tightest.

Kamla wriggled out of the multiple bosoms, somehow, and fled across the backyard to go round to the front of the house. Groups of men stood around talking in hushed tones. In the small sitting room, more white-sari-clad women sat on the floor and among them she recognised the new, fashionable neighbour Shahbanu. For once, instead of her usual shocking pink Shahbanu, too, was in white. And, nestling in her lap was the pale and almost unrecognisable face of sister Bimla. Every so often Bimla would pass out and Shahbanu, herself pale and without the usual shocking pink frosted lipstick, would splash a few fistfuls of water onto her face.

Kamla pushed past the muttering men and entered the room where she trampled over the seated women, beating everyone out of the way to get to her sister.

"What is it? Is she ill? Will someone tell me what happened?" she screamed at Shahbanu, who just shook her head and gestured languidly towards the other room.

Kamla fought her way to the bedroom but was denied entry by the men standing guard who informed her that Virjibhai's corpse was being prepared for cremation and females may not enter the room, in case they are in an 'unclean' state.

"We'll be ready in a while and then bring him out to the other room and you can pay your last respects," one of the men informed her.

Kamla froze. She stood quite still, unable to take in the truth of her father's sudden death, and unable to create an appropriate emotional response to her sister's half-dead form which was still being periodically splashed with water by Shahbanu.

When in shock, the stupidest, most trivial of things can suddenly assume an importance of gigantic proportions.

She ruminated how, just a few minutes ago, she had been starving and eagerly looking forward to lunch. That hunger had mysteriously vanished -- so much so that she thought she would never be hungry again. And why had she sometimes been so cruel? Why had she threatened to become a stenographer instead of a doctor if her father didn't, immediately, buy her whatever happened to have taken her fancy? And, more important, why couldn't any of those goodies provide any comfort now?

At that point, the tears started flowing freely.....

YOU ONLY DIE TWICE!

A week later, Naranbhai and his regular cronies sat on the front verandah of Naran Villa slurping sweet milky tea from saucers and speculating about the future that awaited mother-less-father-less Bimla and Kamla.

"The good die young, suddenly. It is God's way," said Pandit Suddenly.

"True, true," they chorused readily in agreement.

Dhanjibhai the grocer said: "So sad. I saw him going to work that morning. He looked fine," as though to say that anyone who had looked fine going to work could not have been knocked down so savagely by a fast lorry.

That fateful morning, Virjibhai had been deep in thought about the matter of choice for Kamla's eventual medical school. The country's brand new one, run by a progressive new religious sect, was fast gaining a reputation for being more a love-nest for young men and women than an establishment where medical skills were taught or learned. The one in the neighbouring country was stricter about segregating boys and girls but its qualifications were not internationally recognised as it was generally known that a few thousand shillings easily purchased a degree, armed with which the more ambitious tried to make off for England or Canada. What about West Africa? West African cities were larger than East African ones. They were sure to have decent medical colleges. Lagos, Accra, or perhaps Dakar? He would have to find out more. Maybe India would be best? Then Kamla could live with one of his married cousins and go to...or maybe, if he could save up enough, then London, Dublin or Edinburgh? Or then again.....?

It was while he was weighing up the pros and cons of London as opposed to Dublin or Edinburgh that the gigantic lorry had sent his body flying several feet into the air to land straight in front of an oncoming car that was going too fast to stop.

Subsequent inquiries had resulted in a deadlock between the car driver and the lorry driver. The lorry driver maintained that Virjibhai, even though he had seen the lorry, had been walking in the middle of the road. And, when his body flew up on impact, he was still alive.

"The car is to blame," said the lorry driver. "It was the car that actually killed him."

The car driver, of course, argued that the body that had flown straight at him from some height was already dead. How could you kill a dead man?

Both drivers were imprisoned for six months. The lorry driver's firm paid a fine to the police and got him off the hook so that he could get back to the vital job of delivering boxes of salty potato crisps to village dukas. The car driver decided a six-month all-expenses-paid trip to jail would not be such a bad thing since most of his friends were already there.

"Very tragic," said Naranbhai, "But now the main question is, what to do? Two girls - unmarried - not right for them to live alone, unsupervised by a man. The house is my property and I don't approve of that sort of thing. That is what I have called you all to discuss."

"Any relatives who could be called over from India to suddenly come and take charge of the young ladies?" asked Pandit Suddenly, whose favourite recourse in any crisis was to ship over relatives from India to come and exercise control.

"No, no," said Naranbhai magnanimously. "Poor girls. Enough shock losing father. Why should they have strange relatives in the house?"

Naranbhai's opposition to the relatives' plan was as much out of concern for the poor girls' well-being as it was due to the fact that Virjibhai, with his careful thrifty ways, had left a sizeable amount of money both, in savings and a life insurance policy. The policy was certainly worth enough to allow the two girls to live in comfort and go on paying rent to Naranbhai as well as affording Kamla's school fees. She had just turned eleven and it would be at least another six or seven years before she could gain entry to a medical college.

Naranbhai imagined himself moral guardian of the girls, and their soon-to-be acquired money. He had convinced himself that his interest in their affairs was purely out of concern for them. Such young girls would not know how to handle large amounts of money. Financial independence always resulted in women with lower morals. Having money made young women think they could do whatever the hell they liked.

"No," continued Naranbhai. "I propose that we should arrange a marriage as quickly as possible for Bimla - she is nearly seventeen, after all. Too old already, if you ask me. And we make it clear to the boy that he is to be a "ghar-damaad". Instead of taking her away to his house, he has to live in with her, because there is a younger sister to care for. That way Bimla is rewarded with a husband where she has lost a father, and Kamla gains a brother-in-law who will behave like a father. That is the best thing for them. Unmarried girls living on their own with so much money....no, I can't have that sort of thing going on in my properties. It is for decent peoples only, you know, like it says on the sign."

"Very right," agreed all the others. "Bigger girl must be married. Let us arrange it...."

Before they could move on with relish to the subject of a prospective bridegroom for Bimla, the younger sister Kamla appeared on the verandah from inside the house. The two sisters had been taken into Naran Villa for a few days by the kindly, nosy Mrs Naranbhai -- always first to rally round in a crisis and eager to provide support and comfort in the early days after Virjibhai's death.

On the day of the funeral she had been right behind Naranbhai when he had stood up in the full assembly of wailing women and hugging both girls to his chest had declared:

"You are all witnesses. From this day, I am telling you, I am their father. From today they are not orphans. They are *my* daughters. God has already given me three sons, *three*, you know? Now they will have two sisters."

"Three..." muttered someone in the crowd, but nobody was really listening. This public adoption of the orphan girls was far more status-enchancing than the fact of his real daughter, Mad Girl Kirti whom he had, as usual, forgotten. Besides, a truly sensational arrival at the funeral had just caused a sensation among the mourning crowd. As soon as Naranbhai declared himself father to the girls, his long-standing political opponent, Raushan, had come crashing in: "Yes, that's right! Appoint yourself their moral custodian and commit them to the same fate as Mohini and Sohini."

"Watch your tongue, woman! You're not from amongst us. You just follow your Sect and teach girls to have sex at the age of nine!"

"Stop being silly, Naranbhai. It is *your* religion and community that permitted the marriage of 8-year olds to men of 60 and over. Talk sense. We should be discussing the girls' future - yes, certainly. But we should be ensuring that they continue with their education. As Town Councillor I insist that I should....."

Before she could finish her sentence, Naranbhai said: "Yes, you stick to your Council and the collection of rubbish. These girls are from *our* community and poor Virjibhai trusted me with their future. His vima (insurance policy) is entrusted to me!"

The comment drew audible gasps from the crowd. It was common knowledge that Virjibhai had a big life insurance policy, but nobody knew that he had actually made Naranbhai a trustee.

With that dramatic revelation, the Naranbhais had taken both girls to Naran Villa where they were to live until such time as the elders could decide their fate. As chief mourners, the girls were instructed to remain inside the house, their bodies unscented and their hair uncombed, concealed from public view. But Kamla had broken all the rules by defiantly appearing on the verandah when Mrs Naranbhai and the other women had explicitly told her never to interfere when important men were talking about important matters. The men had just been discussing the matter of getting the older sister, Bimla, married off:

"Which girl must marry? Who are you talking about?" Kamla, still raw with grief, asked rudely.

"Nothing, nothing, beti. Just go and play. Everything will be all right, you poor child," said Naranbhai kindly while at the same time shooting a poisonous look at his second wife for having allowed Kamla to venture out onto the verandah in the midst of such a distinguished gathering engaged in settling the girls' future.

"No! If you are talking about us, I want to know. I have a right to know! Who the hell are all these people to decide our future, anyway?" Kamla had screamed hysterically.

Mrs Naranbhai tried to usher her away with hasty apologies to the all-male assembly. "Sorry, she is still very upset. Doesn't know what she is saying...forgive her..."

"It's OK," said Pandit Suddenly. "Very difficult for such young things to understand about death. Take her in and read Gita or Ramayan or something to calm her......"

"I can write a Ramayan about all of you! Look at you!" screamed the hysterical Kamla. "Sitting here and talking about us like we were a pair of caged animals and you are wondering how best to dispose of us. Until I am alive, no one, I tell you *no one* is going to make my sister marry anyone she doesn't love!"

Mrs Naranbhai dragged her away, kicking and screaming: "Now love-shove all that - you know that is for fillums only."

Mrs Naranbhai's ally, the aunt Kamini masi intervened:

"Look son," she said softly but firmly to Naranbhai. "They've just lost a father. Don't make more pain for the poor girls. Marriage, or whatever --later, later. When they are feeling better."

Naranbhai looked at her with renewed respect. She had provided an honourable way out. Instead of being seen to be buckling down in the face of Kamla's impertinence he could now do a dignified U-turn claiming that he had had the girls' feelings at heart and that marriage was, perhaps, not the best option at the moment.

Mrs Naranbhai, on seeing the effect of her aunt's words on all the men present, decided that this new liberal policy of leniency and total reasonability should be seen to be coming from her.

"Yes, whatever were you thinking of? Poor Virjibhai's funeral pyre still smouldering and you want his poor daughter to be decked out in bridal finery? What sort of man are you? I know how girls feel in these situations. I was one, remember?" and she wiped away an imaginary tear at a pretended memory of her own dear dead father.

"But she shamelessly said the word "love". Didn't you hear that, woman?"

"Thanks to fillums all young girls have the love dudu in their heads. So what?"

Naranbhai was not amused at having his authority undermined in the presence of his cronies. It was one thing to listen respectfully to an older aunt-in-law - especially one who had been a famous film star - but Mrs Naranbhai jumping on the bandwagon just buged him. He grew impatient with both women.

"OK OK, enough! All of you! Stop your cackling, get into the house and go about your business."

When the women had gone in, he sheepishly resumed his leadership role once again as he addressed his cronies: "What is it these days? Why can't a man make a single decision about anything without women cackling and jabbering all over the place?"

The other men "ummmed" sympathetically and went back to slurping from their saucers of tea.

RESTLESS SPIRIT

"Say it! Say you lied! Let me hear you say it and all!" screamed Mrs D'Sa and landed another savage blow on Number Three's bottom, whose faded khaki shorts had been pulled down for the purpose.

"I saw it! With my own eyes! Floating across the backyard. And then it stopped outside Kamla and Bimla's house and disappeared into the wall. I swear it! Cross my heart and hope to die!" whimpered the D'Sa child Number Three, ragged, urchin-like with piercing black eyes and in every respect identical to all the other D'Sa issues who had now come to be known only by number rather than name.

Mrs D'Sa whacked the child once more.

The other D'Sa Numbers stood in the vicinity of Naran Villa - the Naran Villa verandah being the scene of this latest drama - half hiding, half dying of curiosity to study Number Three's every expression of pain and anguish. They had all been through similar experiences and it was always a joy to see it happening to someone else.

"I'm sorry Mr Naranbhai," Mrs D'Sa wailed. "These children, you know. No sooner are they out of my tummy and they learn to lie. I am so sorry."

Naranbhai looked away embarrassed by her reference to children coming out of tummies. He began to slightly regret instigating the whole spectacle.

It had all come about because there had been rumours of a ghost - a brand new spirit, thought to belong to the late Virjibhai - hovering around and haunting Bombay Gardens. One family of tenants had already moved away in panic, and others had started to make threatening noises of looking at other properties. To make matters worse, Naranbhai had also failed to rent out the now vacant quarters of the departed family because the whole town was rife with rumours that Bombay Gardens was haunted.

It was commonly acknowledged by the townspeople that poor Virjibhai, still worried about his daughters, returned to the premises dressed in a white gown every night, but failing to see his daughters there, moaned and wailed until the early hours of dawn.

"What rubbish," the ex-film star aunt Kamini had said, most wisely. "If he never wore a white gown when alive, why the hell should he wear one now? Anyway, the spirit should know that *its* daughters are safe and well and now living with us. Why can't he just cross the road and come here and take a look?"

"But that's just it," said the superstitious widow Nalini, aunt Kamini masi's opposite number in the Naran Villa house system of friends and enemies. Nalini was always ready with a persuasive explanation for anything spooky:

"Don't you see? He can do everything except cross the road -- because that's how he died. He will never cross a road again."

"Of course he'll never cross a road again! He's dead isn't he?" retorted Kamini.

Naranbhai had had enough of these imbecile speculations. He was far more concerned about a mass exodus from his Bombay Gardens Empire. So, he had decided to investigate the origins of these rumours and it had emerged that thus far, only the D'Sa Number Three had claimed to actually having seen anything. The rest of the story had grown and taken root on the basis of this one sighting by a mere child -- and an urchin at that.

When Mrs D'Sa found out, she dragged Number Three kicking and screaming, to subject him to a public thrashing on the Naran Villa verandah. She planned to go on thrashing the boy until he relented and admitted to lying through his teeth - three of which had just been taken by the Tooth Fairy.

Number Three screamed and wailed in pain, his mouth wide open showing only dark brown gums where the teeth had once been. Mrs D'Sa continued administering the old hockey stick she kept for this purpose and her other children held their breath with excitement and a renewed sense of righteousness for not being at the receiving end of the dreaded weapon.

Naranbhai was just debating whether or not to order her to stop but then, realising that that would undermine her maternal authority, he decided to let her go on with the punishment. The child had, after all, cost him a lot of money in lost rent.

But the beating came to an end all too quickly, disappointingly for the other children who had now been joined by the three well-dressed Naranbhai boys - Doctor, Dentist and Lawyer. While the entire household had been gathered on, or near, the verandah to watch Mrs D'Sa - herself a frequent victim of her husband's leather belt - lashing out at the boy with a vengeance that was completely out of proportion to his crime, Mad Girl Kirti had, somehow, got out of her room. She now appeared on the verandah.

"Stop! Bas Karo! Stop it!" she said in a low voice in Hindi, fixing her gaze on Mrs D'Sa. Kirti looked completely sane and in control of herself. Her hair was tied back in a ponytail - unlike full-moon nights when it formed a mangled, matted mass over her face - her white dress spotless, her sandals correctly placed on her feet.

"Stop it!" she said again with force. Mrs D'Sa took a step back, waiting for someone to drag the Mad Girl away. But nobody moved. They were all in shock at seeing the Mad Girl, neat and tidy and speaking in perfectly normal tones. Nobody had ever heard her speak to anyone but her imaginary people.

"Don't beat the child just because of your own ignorance," she said in Hindi. "He did not lie. I have seen it too. The spirit also comes here. I see it when you are all asleep....." her voice had dropped to a whisper while the assembled crowd, ever-fascinated by the ghoulish, savoured this latest twist in the ghost story.

Partly toothless Number Three saw his chance and made off from the verandah to join the other children who, up until now, had taken such a savage delight in his pain. One of them had also filled up the customary pail of cold water in which the D'Sa minors rested their bottoms after their ritualised thrashings. Totally ignoring the bucket, Number Three had quite forgotten his recent trauma and was now determined to watch the fun as Kirti would, surely, be whipped by her father.

But the children were to be disappointed. Naranbhai had never been a violent man. While the D'Sas took violence as a necessary factor in the business of co-existing with one's parents, for Naranbhai, the idea of striking out at anyone - leave alone a mad girl - was unthinkable. And although fully aware of this fact about her husband, and despite the fact that Mrs Naranbhai the younger had not given birth to the girl she now rushed forward to shield Kirti as if she were her own daughter, and not the daughter of a rival wife.

"Don't you dare touch her!" she warned him sternly. "It is true. People like Kirti can see what we can't see. And children can often see what adults can't."

The older wife beamed at the younger one for her words of wisdom and her willingness to protect another woman's child and both women gently led Mad Girl Kirti away, leaving Naranbhai with the impression that the whole thing had somehow been his fault. The two allies - the widow Nalini and aunt Kamini - suddenly felt redundant. What was there for either of them to do if the two rival wives were suddenly going to become best friends? The allies decided to also put their arms round one another and remain good friends until such time as the two wives fell out again.

Mrs D'Sa shook her head and, tut-tutting all the way, led her disappointed brood clucking all the way back home.

On an upper floor of Naran Villa, the two wives suddenly found a common bond -- a belief in the supernatural.

"A puja, that's the only way," the Sushilaben said. "Restless souls are released that way - mukti, liberation from this plane."

"I agree," said the second Mrs Naranbhai.

The two wives were in agreement over something. No doubt, Naranbhai's little world stood on the brink of collapse, once again.

RELIGIONS OF THE WORLD UNITE!

The puja had been a grand affair. Eleven Brahmins had been summoned to chant the magic verses at Virjibhai's house, while Shahbanu, in her own house, had recited the Qur'an from cover to cover with the help of other Muslim women led by the special Qur'an teacher, Mama Safia. The offerings of dried fruit and nuts from the Quran reading had been brought over to Virjibhai's house and distributed to the puja guests. The puja offerings, consisting of fresh fruit and sliced coconut were offered to the women who had delligently read the Qur'an all afternoon. And even Mrs D'Sa, feeling partly responsible for the whole affair in light of the fact that it had been her Number Three who had originally sighted the restless soul, had had a quiet word with the local padre to perform a mini-exorcism on the Virjibhai premises. Ganga-Jal and Aab-e-Zamzam -- holy waters from the Ganges and from Mecca -- had been sprinkled in every room and also sprayed on the outer wall into which the ghost had been reported to disappear.

With Naranbhai footing the cost and playing host and Master of Ceremonies, three major world religions had joined hands in an effort to put Virjibhai's soul to rest.

That night Naranbhai had a dream. He thought he saw a face that looked exactly like Virjibhai's, saying to him: "Only when daughters are married can a father expect a place in heaven. Otherwise it is all hell. Who wants to go to hell? So, I still wander around on earth, you see?"

Naranbhai nodded in his sleep, beginning to see. The face disappeared and a voice said: "Marry her! Marry her, I tell you!"

Naranbhai woke up in a cold sweat and his mind started doing somersaults. Marry her? How can I marry her? He must've meant *get* her married.

Many years later, in 1972, this dream was to come back and haunt Naranbhai. But, for now, he was just thrilled that he could justify his original whim of getting Bimla "settled." And he couldn't wait to execute his new, modern method in the matter. He had decided that toothless matchmakers were the worst kind of evil known to man, and in the matter of arranging marriages it was vital that the two relevant parties conversed directly with each other -- for at least ten minutes -- before agreeing to tie the knot.

This new method appeared to him a bold invention of his own and he was determined to put it to the test. Let Raushan just try and interfere! This time, he had it on good authority, from Virjibhai's spirit, that arranging such a marriage was clearly ordained by the gods themselves. And then, with Independence just around the corner, who knew what would become of single Indian women?

Naranbhai had some serious thinking to do. His first thought was to give his useless nephew, Bharat, the ultimatum and demand that he take Bimla's hand. But then, remembering that Bharat was still only sixteen and hence a whole year younger than Bimla, he realised this would not please the gods. A husband had to be older, taller, richer and more educated than the wife. Or so the scriptures had decreed. Bharat only satisfied one out of four of those requirements: he was taller.

And, useless or not, Bharat belonged to the Naranbhai clan - a well-to-do family of industrialists - while Bimla's father, never mind the savings and the insurance policy had, after all, been a mere hand-to-mouth wage slave.

Naranbhai thoughts turned to other potential bridegrooms...

A GODLY ACT

The following evening, Naranbhai and his friends were assembled on the verandah. The usual cronies as well as three upstanding pillars of the Indian business community who admired Naranbhai's statesmanlike qualities and envied his ability to manage two wives under the same roof -- especially wives who sometimes behaved like one another's best friends. If they were always at loggerheads that would have been one thing. That, by itself, would require careful management. But, to actually navigate his way through rival wives who sometimes behaved like loving sisters, required a man of courage and wisdom.

Pandit Suddenly frequently marvelled at Naranbhai's management of the domestic situation at Naran Villa. He would list the points by sticking up his fingers, one by one. Naranbhai's foresight at installing other female relatives to provide moral support for each wife, his unquestioning sense of duty towards the Mad Girl when she could just as easily have been packed off to a madhouse to be cared for by big black female nurses in white coats. And last, but by no means least, his sense of responsibility to his widow sister Nalini and her sole surviving offspring, the Useless Nephew Bharat. And, as if all that wasn't already a plateful, his endless benevolence towards the tenants of Bombay Gardens: births, deaths and marriages. The Pandit, who was a something of a raconteur with leanings towards English Literature, would often joke: "Never mind that *I'm* the Pandit. What one needs is our dear Naranbhai in all situations: births, marriages and deaths. To hatch you, match you and despatch you!"

The men sat on the verandah sipping steaming hot tea from their saucers, and every so often between the slurpy sips, the subject always reverted to Virjibhai's untimely death and his restless spirit returning to haunt Bombay Gardens.

Naranbhai could no longer withhold the latest juicy twist in the ghost story. He lowered his voice to a conspiratorial whisper and spoke with pride of his dream. Virjibhai's spirit had appeared and had entrusted to him the task of getting the older daughter, Bimla, settled.

"Settled" could only mean one thing. One could only be settled if one was married -- even to completely the wrong person. Any other state of being was, by definition, a state of being unsettled, implying an immoral and nomadic existence.

The men were impressed by this fresh twist. So! Virjibhai's spirit had been restless because his marriageable daughter was unmarried! That explains it! That was why he kept visiting Bombay Gardens -- no doubt to attract their attention and to remind the community that it had, so far, failed in its duty of 'settling' the girl.

Even Pandit Suddenly, sometimes given to being contrary by virtue of his original thinking mind and, of course, his many English books, had to admit that the question of Bimla's marriage had now taken on a completely different complexion. Sure enough, unmarried women, particularly those of independent financial means, were bad news in any society. Societies that sported large numbers of single women were always the first to crumble and sink into debauchery. The only way to ensure that society remained morally upright and decent was to ensure that no young woman of marriageable age remained footloose and fancy-free. Where there was no temptation, there could be no debauchery. But in view of what Naranbhai had just told them, Bimla's marriage was no longer a necessity to satisfy neighbourhood demands for respectability. The marriage was now a religious duty, ordered by her father's ghost. Bimla would have to be married off... but ....to whom? Who would marry an orphan?

They all looked at Naranbhai feeling sure that their leader would have already thought of the perfect boy.

Naranbhai, aware of all eyes on him, took full enjoyment from this fleeting moment of expectancy. There was no feeling in the world as satisfying as having all the answers to a perplexing problem, answers eagerly awaited by those less fortunate beings who had not been blessed with his vision, his inventiveness and his leadership qualities.

Finally, he spoke:

"Now this Satish fellow - Bachelor - all these years of waiting for Dream Girl. We should talk to him and make him see there isn't going to be any Dream Girl. He should settle for Bimla. She is not bad looking. Long hair. Nice fair colour. No pimples. She is slim. Good character. OK, not very educated, but then she had to leave school to look after father and feed sister. What better training for a wife? And then bloody Satish himself is no BA, LLB, VD, DDT, whatever, is he? He should be told that it would be a noble thing to do. Satish must marry Bimla as a godly act of kindness, to help her out and to put her father's soul at rest."

At the end of his speech, the men sat deep in thought, mulling over the pros and cons of Bachelor Satish suddenly finding himself in charge of not one, but two young ladies of independent means.

After an aborted attempt at debate which led to a brief discussion in which everybody agreed with everybody else, it was decreed that Satish the Bachelor be summoned and bullied into accepting the match.

"I will evict him from my property if he refuses. With Independence coming, it's his duty to protect the girl," asserted Naranbhai, by way of summing up. "I'll just say to him that it is now his duty to make a decent woman out of Bimla, and to take on responsibility for young Kamla's moral upbringing. She is like a wild animal. Needs training and discipline. Father spoilt her too much with all this doctor-shoctor rubbish."

"But can we be suddenly sure Bimla will be ready to marry so suddenly?" asked the part-time Pandit, determined as ever to raise the other point of view.

"Of course she will! A girl who has just lost a father badly needs a husband!"

THE SUMMONS

The houseboy, Jannasani, was despatched to Satish's bank with the urgent message that he should report to landlord Naranbhai as soon as he finished work.

"Why? What has happened?" Satish asked in Swahili of Jannasani, the Naranbhais one and only servant who had either originally been christened 'Johnson' or had put in long years of service with a certain 'Mr Johnson.' It was usual for servants with unpronounceable African names to be given the names of their White masters. After 'Mr Johnson' went back to England, the house boy had, presumably, gone to work for a Punjabi family who could only say 'Jannasani' -- and the name had stuck. The Naranbhais had got him straight after the Punjabi family who had fired him for being frequently drunk and often not reporting for duty at all. And, it was bearing this fact in mind that the Naranbhais had insisted that Jannasani live in the closet-sized room at the end of the Naran Villa backyard. That was the only way to ensure his attendance at work.

"Why do they want me? What has happened?" asked Bachelor Satish again, getting impatient with Jannasani's dreamy ways.

"Si-jui Bwana. I don't know," he replied defensively with the air of one who was merely a messenger and as such should not be held responsible for any undesirable repercussions resulting from the message.

"But you must have some idea?" Satish persisted while at the same time reaching for a fifty-cent piece in his pocket. That was one of the advantages of being a bachelor -- a large disposable income.

"Tell me, has there been any meeting or anything?" asked Satish, now producing and rubbing the fifty-cent piece between forefinger and thumb.

"Yes Bwana. Meeting this afternoon. All the men. I only served tea. Talking Gujarati so I didn't understand." Jannasani replied evasively hoping the fifty-cents would double to a shilling. And then he'd only have to find another four for a private drink with Maria.

"Be afraid of God -- don't tell such lies! You understand every single word of Gujarati! All you guys do!" Satish still held on to the coin. "Come on! Out with it!"

"Just meeting.All the men. They said 'Independence is coming.' Then, that girl Kamla came out and shouted, saying her sister is not going to marry anyone. That is all I know."

"OK Jannasani. You go now. Tell your Bwana-Mkuba I will be there after work."

Satish was in a hurry to think things over. He had a fair idea what was wanted of him and he needed to be prepared, to have done his homework and to have explored the imminent marriage proposal from every possible angle.

Jannasani looked crestfallen. He had hoped to be pumped for more information so as to double his money. "OK Bwana. Maybe I will remember some more later on. Do you want me to come back if I remember anything else?"

"Crook! Rascal! No, get out! I know what I need to know, and it wasn't worth fifty cents, you rogue!" and with that he made as if to give the thin wiry Jannasani a friendly kick on his backside, while at the same time offering him a State Express 555 cigarette.

"Here,go on. Take this.You will remember me as a good friend always.See?Not all Muhindis are bad!" Satish said triumphantly.

Satish knew why he was being summoned to Naran Villa. He was never in arrears with the rent, and Naranbhai didn't usually include him in other social gatherings on account of his unattached status. An unmarried man, whatever his age, was still a "boy" and as such not considered suitable to join the men. The summons could only be something to do with yet another "Dream Girl." And since Mr and Mrs Naranbhai had long given up trying to find a girl for him, it could only be something to do with the most recent happenings in Bombay Gardens. And the most recent event had been the sudden death of Virjibhai, leaving behind two unmarried daughters. No doubt, he was going to be pressurised into taking the hand of the older one in marriage.

At exactly four-thirty pm Satish started the familiar walk from his bank in Main Street.The shame of being a car owner yet having to walk to work! More often than not, his car simply did not start in the morning. He limped all the way to the end of Main Street and down a side road full of soda stalls and fried snacks from where a small alleyway led to the Black Cat Bar. But today, he was headed straight home, resisting the temptations of the Black Cat sounds and smells.He carried on up the hill, past the posh houses of the teachers and doctors and then into the narrow mud track which was a short cut to Bombay Gardens. He was deep in thought and, with every step he limped forward, he considered the advantages and disadvantages of finally getting married. At one level he felt tremendously flattered.Over thirty-five and to be offered a girl of seventeen! She was sure to be a virgin and, even in the unlikely event that she wasn't, at least she would be obedient. She would look up to him and never answer back. Being an orphan, she would be eternally grateful.And, there was the added bonus of a younger sister, which meant he would get to exert parental authority even before any of his own children were born. That pleased him greatly.

He tried to remember what Bimla looked like but couldn't conjure up even a blurred image of her face. He attempted to have lustful thoughts about her but only Maria's beautiful ebony-milky-tea-coloured body,soon to be touched by Bharat --delicate, saffron-scented, fragile Bharat--accompanied the stirring erection.

Satish had lived next door to Bimla for ten years but couldn't for the life of him remember her face. The fact is, he had never thought of her in that way. She was just Virjibhai's daughter -- a kid turned young housekeeper, always covered in charcoal marks, hands wet from washing, unruly hair falling over her face as she sat in backyard, scrubbing the pots and pans in the afternoon sunshine. That was his strongest memory of Bimla because it was something he had seen almost every single day when returning to his one-room bachelor pad for a pre-cooked lunch.His meals were cooked and supplied by a middle-aged widow who lived approximately halfway between his bank and Bombay Gardens. Her kitchen would not have stood the test of even the most lenient health inspector.The daal frequently sported a floating cockroach posing as shrivelled up bark cinnamon while the dry vegetable curries probably had equal numbers of insect corpses mingling with mustard and cumin seeds. Satish remembered his arguments with the widow. He remembered accusing her of trying to poison him. He remembered threatening to cut her fee. And he remembered how, after every big scene, he always resumed their contract because her food was by far, the tastiest. He shuddered at the thought that the addition of insect-protein probably did much towards improving the flavour of cauliflower or bhindi. But, he quickly dismissed the possibility because he could think of no other way of keeping himself fed with good, home-made food, the only other alternative being the salty, greasy peanuts and chips at the Black Cat Club. He thought fondly of his routine of stopping at the widow's house to pick up his tiffin-carrier at lunchtime and then heading home to consume its contents. After lunch, on his way back to work, he would drop off the empty containers at her place so that she could fill it with his lunch the following day. His evening meals were light and usually consisted of peanuts washed down with a few glasses of the local brew. He felt a sudden wave of nostalgia for his bachelor days, like they'd already ended. The fights with the food-supplying widow and the excursions to Black Cat already felt like history.At that point he took control of himself:"No, I could never give up Saturday night cards or private drink with Maria. Bimla will have to put up with it! A man has certain rights."

Even as he thought it, he felt suddenly, and inexplicably, sorry for the hard-working, slender, young Bimla and wondered if he could ever learn to love her. But the wheels of love are often oiled by that substance which was the next item on his list of things to consider in favour of marriage:the matter of Virjibhai's savings and life insurance policy.He knew Naranbhai had recently muscled in as a trustee.It seemed incredible to Satish that someone as quiet and simple and penny-pinching as Virjibhai could have had so much foresight and financial acumen to provide for his nearest and dearest in the event of his death.

"Crafty old miser," thought Satish, and wondered if there was some way he could look up the particulars of Virjibhai's "Vima" as it was known, to ascertain just how much the girls were now worth.

BHAJJIAS & COKE

Naranbhai and four other senior men were already assembled on the verandah when Satish arrived, hot and sweaty from the early evening walk. Jannasani appeared with a bottle of Coca-Cola and a straw while Satish registered the fact that the others were drinking lassi, leading him to conclude, with some satisfaction, that the most expensive drink had been reserved for him. He was determined to make the most of his temporary elevation. Such opportunities for stardom were rare. A man being persuaded to take on a wife was indeed a hero of the moment and his every whim could be pandered to, as long as he looked like he might eventually say "Yes."

Satish had already decided to agree to the match, but there was no harm in letting them sweat a bit.

"Now, young Satish, listen here," began Naranbhai a shade too belligerently. The Pandit interrupted him to try and set a different kind of tone to the proceedings. Pandit Suddenly clearly believed in softening the blow:

"Satish, beta, you know we don't suddenly live forever?" he began philosophically and warming to his theme continued, "Life is but short. We come, then suddenly we go and then we are gone.......suddenly…"

At that point Naranbhai slammed down his stainless steel lassi cup in a way that made half the liquid squirt upwards and settle on his hand.

"Please let me do the talking," he urged Pandit Suddenly. "I am your leader..."

"Yes, but you were never properly elected. You just made yourself leader because you are suddenly the richest man with the biggest house," the Pandit protested.

Another man added his weight to this latest objection: "Yes, you only made yourself leader, whereas this sort of thing concerns everyone and should be done properly. The boy has to be convinced and persuaded properly. Not just ordered around," he concluded, urging Pandit Suddenly to resume his life and death, coming and going speech which all the other men were clearly enjoying.

Naranbhai shot him a hateful look. That's the way of this world. You give people your services and then one day, they stand up and tell you that you haven't been elected! Hey Ram! What next?

Satish was certainly not in the mood for the Pandit's philosophical musings peppered with numerous "suddenlys" so he turned to Naranbhai and said:

"Please, you were the one who summoned me here, so it would be best if you, yourself, told me whatever you had in mind. I am your tenant, you are the landlord and I am indebted to you for letting me live in such a beautiful little house for such a reasonable rent. Now, what can I do for you?"

Naranbhai felt himself swelling with pride for having had the foresight to choose such a morally upright tenant. In front of all the other men, Satish had upheld Naranbhai's right to be spokesman for the group. Such a public show of loyalty would not go unrewarded.

"Thank you, Satish. You are a most unusual young person showing much respect for those who deserve it. Now, gentlemen," he said turning to the others, "I trust you have no objections if I address *my* tenant directly as to what is required of him?"

The sarcasm was undisguised and its effect on the others caused the most pleasurable sensations in Naranbhai's swelling heart. He spoke crisply:

"Satish, you have been looking for a wife for a long time now. Dream Girl has not yet shown her face. But I put it to you that the Dream Girl was here, under your nose all the time. And now the time has come, and God has arranged your bhagye, your naseeb and qismat, so that she is finally ready to marry you. Her gunghat - her veil - has finally been lifted. Now we know who she is, and that is why I have called you here so you too may know. I am referring, of course, to Bimla - poor girl - daughter of our own, beloved, late Mr Virjibhai the Compounder, God rest his noble soul."

Naranbhai wiped away an imaginary tear with the end of his shirt while the others stared with awe and wonder at his powers of

220

oration. Elected or otherwise, he most certainly *was* leader material.

Such eloquence! And how nice to have brought God into it as well! What a marvellous reference to naseeb and qismat, because, after all, what could one do confronted by one's qismat? The script of destiny, undoubtedly, is one that no mere mortal can re-write.

"That's right, go on!" came a young female voice from one of the windows above the verandah: "Make your own stupid rules and then say it's qismat. God and qismat were invented by men like you so you could tell women what to do!"

Kamla had to be wrenched away from the iron-barred window by the women of the Naranbhai household.

Satish lost no time in raising his first pretended objection to the match:

"Bimla? To be my Dream-Girl? Be fair. Tell me, how can a man marry a girl like Bimla, sweet though she may be, when her younger sister has a tongue the length of the Kampala-Jinja Road? That is the first point I have to consider. Then there are many others....."

At the mention of numerous possible objections, Naranbhai shouted for Jannasani to bring another Coca-Cola for Satish.

"You useless fellow!" he shouted when Jannasani emerged with another ice-cold bottle. "Can't you see the man is tired and hot and thirsty? And you bring just one! Is it your money or mine? Why are you being so stingy? Go and tell Mama to fry some hot bhajjias as well," he ordered dismissing the servant, although Jannasani wanted nothing more than to hover close by and watch Satish squirm under their demands.

"Now, Satish," Naranbhai resumed his oratory. "To reply to your first objection. What do you expect when a girl hasn't got a mother or father to teach her how to hold her tongue? That is something that with God's grace and kindness, you will be able to do when you become her brother-in-law. Your presence will ensure that Kamla's wayward, scissors-sharp tongue is kept in check. As her brother-in-law, it will be your duty to shorten and tame her tongue and prepare her for marriage."

"I don't need to marry anyone, and neither does sister Bimla. I am going to be a doctor," Kamla's voice bellowed down at them again: "Why are we being held here? I want to go home!"

Kamla had repeatedly demanded to go back to their old house. Every time she said it and hoped Bimla would support her, Bimla just looked the other way and broke down in floods of tears.

Kamla registered with some dismay that Bimla had changed completely since their father's death. She seemed to have no will of her own and seemed more than happy to be mollycoddled by Mrs Naranbhai and all the other women. She seemed barely aware of Kamla's presence. As a result, Kamla felt alone in the world. It was all down to her. She would have to do something all by herself. She realised her sister was completely numb with shock and failed to understand the full impact of what they were all trying to do to her.

Kamla, who was nearing eleven, but with the maturity and intelligence of a 40-year old, had deduced that the community elders, led by Naranbhai, were perturbed about the girls suddenly having lots of money of their own. A husband was to be planted in the house to ensure that the girls didn't use their money to buy freedom or, in some other way, assert their riches to put themselves outside the rules of community. Kamla knew that Naranbhai's plans, allegedly executed by her own father's ghost had little, if anything, to do with Bimla's happiness.

"I said I want to go home!" she screamed again.

Once again, Kamla had to be wrenched away from the bedroom window overlooking the verandah while Satish's persuasion session continued:

"So, Satish-beta," Naranbhai continued in English. "What other objection? You said smaller sister's tongue too long -- well, you can see to that, can't you? What else you don't like?"

"Well, you know, I always wanted really long-long hair for my Dream Girl? Bimla's I don't remember. Is it long or short?" he asked

All the men fell silent as not a single one of them really knew the exact length of Bimla's hair since it was usually tied up in a knot to prevent it falling on her face while cooking or scrubbing pots.

In the end Mrs Naranbhai was called to help verify the exact length. She was able to report that Bimla's hair, when combed out straight, reached just below her waist.

The other men nodded approval, but Satish looked put out:

"You know, I prefer hair to reach below buttocks..." he announced, but then remembering Virjibhai's insurance policy, he continued in magnanimous fashion, "...but never mind. I'll let it go. Maybe if she puts more coconut oil every day it will grow longer," he said hopefully.

That provided the cue for Pandit Suddenly to enthuse about a certain wild berry, which when boiled, produced a thick froth in which hair could be rinsed to promote fast-growth. Failing that, starchy water drained from boiling rice was just as good.

The other men, either partially or totally bald, joined in with details of their favourite homemade remedies to promote hair growth and add silky lustre to a woman's tresses.

Naranbhai had had enough:

"OK, we are not gathered here to discuss beauty preparations for women's hairs. We are trying to arrange the wedding of our poor orphan Bimla to this decent young man..."

"The other thing is ejucaysen," said Satish, determined to raise more objections, and switching into 'Ingliss' for added emphasis: "You know I prefer B.A, or M.A. Settling with girl without ejucaysen is big sacrify for me."

At that point, the piping hot bhajjias arrived, complete with two freshly pounded chutneys-- one bright red, the other minty green-- and Satish, once again, found himself able to be charitable towards Bimla's lack of academic achievement. He had to manoeuvre the discussion, somehow, towards money.

"Pity-pity, you know. I always wanted working wife. Cooking, cleaning all that - yes. But that can also be done by servant. I want smart-smart girl who can go out and earn plenty-plenty money, so we have double-salary house. Double-salary is good, otherwise wife just eating up all my hard-earned money," he continued in 'Ingliss' as Jannasani was still fussing with bhajjia plates and chutney spoons. He was convinced Jannasani understood ever word of Gujarati. But unknown to Satish, and to all the others, Jannasani's English was even better than his Gujarati.

"Double-income - that is what I like," said Satish by way of summing up.

"When income double-double, then trouble also double-double," piped up Naranbhai, quoting his second wife's famous statement of a few years ago.

"Anyway, money no problem," Naranbhai added carefully in English while waving a dismissive hand at Jannasani to make himself scarce, and then resumed in Gujarati: "Money is no problem. Virjibhai made sure the girls will be OK. Of course they won't know how to handle money so I will be helping out with that, until you take charge," he added importantly with the air of one had just performed the most supreme sacrifice in history by agreeing to handle the financial affairs of another.

"Yes, but how much? I mean how much money?" asked Satish.

"Not too sure of exact amount...still to be settled. Enough savings to give Bimla a proper wedding, but there is more - some insurance....vima, you know..."

"How much?" asked Satish, without bothering to mince his words.

"Not sure. All in good time. At least be sure it *is* there!" Naranbhai replied evasively.

"But will I be getting a dowry?" Satish asked.

"Aren't you afraid of God?" Naranbhai was starting to lose his temper. "The girl has no mother or father and you want dowry?" Have you really no shame?"

"Now, now, calm down, please," Pandit Suddenly intervened again. "Whatever is theirs will be yours, suddenly. What's dowry when you will be getting all insurance and everything suddenly, hain?"

"He will not touch a cent!" screamed Kamla's voice. "The money is being saved for my studies. He will not be allowed near it. Tell him! Satish Babu, listen to me! They are tricking you into this marriage because they don't want Bimla and me to live on our own. You will get nothing from it. Nothing! Do you hear me?"

Naranbhai rose from his seat, flustered and embarrassed:

"She is still very hysterical about poor Virjibhai's death. Youngest, you know? His favourite. Very spoilt. Ignore her."

Satish got up thoughtfully. "Well, I don't know. There is a lot of matata here. I need time to think."

"Thinking is for cowards," pronounced the Pandit Suddenly. "Doing is for heroes - men of action, like you. Action, suddenly! Don't think. If you think, you will find many reasons suddenly to not do it. Anyone who is suddenly stupid enough to get married knows that if he stopped to really think about it, suddenly, it would never happen!"

"OK, OK," interrupted Naranbhai impatiently, despairing of Pandit Suddenly's circular arguments.

"That's enough! You may think it over Satish. No problem with that. After all it is a question of a young girl's life. Mustn't rush. Think it over and let me know tomorrow morning before you go to work. You see, if your answer is NO, I have a list of various other boys to approach..."

Satish felt a pang of envy and immense loss at the thought of Bimla and Kamla's ready money possibly falling into other hands.

"We only approached you first," Naranbhai continued, fully aware that his lie was having the desired effect, "... because you are no stranger to the girls. They have grown up around you, so it would be a more comfortable arrangement. They have been through so much, poor girls, how to inflict a stranger on them? Besides, wanted to give you first chance, because..."

Satish had consented to the marriage before Naranbhai could finish his sentence.

LESSONS IN SUBMISSION

Mrs Naranbhai went into gleeful fuss-mode over every little thing in the run up to Bimla's wedding. Ever mindful of the Mohini-Sohini disaster and generally given to morose pessimism on the lead up to any happy occasion, she had decided that a big wedding was exactly what was needed to raise everybody's spirits while laying poor Virjibhai's own restless, wandering one to permanent, peaceful rest.

Mrs Naranbhai, mother of three sons - the budding doctor-lawyer-dentist trio, and no daughters of her own - had decided to take a leading role in Bimla's wedding. It was a clear opportunity to reaffirm her status - as though there was any doubt about that - as First Lady of the house. She decided to fully savour the prospect of playing 'bride's mother', with the added bonus of getting the best of both worlds: all the excitement and unlimited license to fuss without the expense, because the wedding was being paid for out of the late Virjibhai's savings. She had chosen a lavish menu for the neighbourhood women to cook and she had ordered the finest outfits and the most expensive gold jewellery.

"Must do it in style," she had said to Bimla. "Show them girl, just because you don't have parents doesn't mean you are empty handed. Don't you remember what my husband said in front of everyone at your poor father's funeral? He said he was your father from now on - and what does that make me? It makes me your mother...so..."

Bimla had only a hazy memory of her father's funeral. All she remembered was resting her head in someone's lap and regaining consciousness, now and then, as ice cold water was splashed on her face.

They sat with the town jeweller, Soni, who had appeared at Naran Villa with an array of sample designs for Bimla to choose. Bimla was completely unused to choosing expensive jewellery for herself. She looked at the trinkets carved out of sparkling yellow metal in a detached sort of way, unable to believe that she, herself, would soon be able to wear such fine, expensive jewellery.

Mrs Naranbhai, on the other hand, was quite at home in the situation of sitting down, face-to-face, with an ever-hopeful jeweller and a glittering array of gold ornaments laid out before her:

"Nowadays, they hardly wear anything," she grumbled happily. "In my time, every toe had a ring, every finger, wrists, ankles, everything. Everything that could be covered in gold was covered, otherwise people would say the parents are paupers."

Mrs Naranbhai picked up the pieces one by one and dangled them before Bimla's eyes: "Come on, choose! Don't be shy," and smiling importantly at the jeweller she added: "Completely up to me to see it's all done properly. Who says they have no mother?"

The purchase of two dozen gold bangles - twelve for each wrist - was proudly sanctioned by Mrs Naranbhai. There is no pleasure in the world like shopping with someone else's money. Whether it was for herself or for anybody else, whether it was Naranbhai's money or somebody else's, Mrs Naranbhai was always in an expansive mood when engaged in the process of purchasing. It created in her a feeling of inexplicable goodwill towards the whole world, and one that made her extremely and quite unnecessarily familiar and chatty with the vendor.

"I have some exactly like these," she said fingering the bangles. "Only mine are thicker and heavier with red and green stones stuck in them. Oh, the weight! It's hard to raise my arms sometimes. From Ahmedabad, you know? Oh! You should see the jewellery shops in India. When I was getting married, my mother said..."

And she launched into yet another pre-nuptial anecdote narrated for the sole purpose of making her family sound grand and wealthy. Other women, who had popped in uninvited to witness the jewellery choosing ritual exchanged meaningful looks. All right, all right! Bangles or shangles - whether studded with rubies or emeralds or diamonds - in the end her first husband still didn't want her because she had spent a whole night with a stranger. Allegedly, chatting only. Whenever Mrs Naranbhai bragged about her own wedding, intending it to be taken only in reference to her nuptials with Mr Naranbhai, everybody else chose to take it as a boastful and somewhat fictitious version of events pertaining to her *first* marriage. (The marriage that had ended in a multiple car crash and the surreal, Bollywood-like mix-up of heavily veiled brides.)

The excitement of Bimla's forthcoming wedding had thrown the entire Naranbhai household routine into joyous disarray. Every single person, including the older wife Sushilaben and the widow Nalini, now quite recovered from the Mohini-Sohini double disaster, were behaving as though it was to be the very first Indian wedding on the African continent. Only Kamla, younger sister of the bride-to-be, had become more and more withdrawn and less given to verbal outbursts at the absurdity of it all. And, getting no help or support from her older sister Bimla, she found it even more difficult to speak her mind.

Acting on the instructions of her husband, Mrs Naranbhai had made sure the sisters didn't have too much contact in private. There were concerns over Kamla corrupting Bimla into her ways. And, Kamla trying to reach out to her older sister, was made none the easier by the fact of Bimla's ritual bridal seclusion -- an essential process for a bride-to-be in the two weeks or so leading up to the wedding.

Bimla was well hidden by Mrs Naranbhai, aided and abetted by the other women of the household. A bride-to-be should simply not be seen by outsiders -- it was supposed to bring bad luck of the most colossal proportions. But the women had taken Bimla's seclusion a step further than necessitated by tradition and hidden her even from her own sister. Bimla was always under the supervision of one or the other of the older women to ensure that no subversive, rebellious or revolutionary elements could corrupt her in these vital few days in the run up to the wedding.

All through those frenzied pre-wedding days, Kamla managed to gain access to Bimla only once, while Mrs Naranbhai was out at a protracted temple visit, leaving the ex-film star aunt Kamini to watch over Bimla. The aunt had fallen asleep while relating the plot of her one and only silent film, and Kamla tip-toed into the room where Bimla sat quietly sewing tinsel flowers on to a red sari.

Intricate emroidering and sewing was said to be good for a bride-to-be for three reasons. First, she would get used to keeping her head lowered, an essential requirement for the many hours of endless wedding rituals. Two, it would increase her powers of patience and forbearance. And last, but not least, the sight of a pretty, embroidered pattern gradually nearing completion would remove any last traces of doubt about the forthcoming marriage. If they have pretty clothes with which to occupy their thoughts, then girls were said to to be more likely to concentrate on the wedding, and not the actual marriage. But , most important of all, this was training for submission -- sexual submission: virtuous young women from respectable Indian homes were supposed to submit to the lust of strangers turned husbands by bringing their silver anklets up to their golden earrings.

Kamla stood silently for a moment feeling a lump in her throat at the sight of her older sister with her head bowed so submissively before the red nylon that was gradually being covered with gold tinsel flowers. She fought back the tears and decided to come straight out with it:

"Why are you going through with this? Listen to me! Can you really imagine a life with that Satish-langra, limping, good-for-nothing drunk and his khattara car and twenty-five gramophone records?" she had whispered softly but urgently, for fear of waking up the old aunt.

"Show some respect. And don't call him by his name. To you, he is "Brother-in-Law", and he is not a good-for-nothing. He has a good bank job," Bimla said sternly, not bothering to raise her head from a gold-tinsel petal that was causing some problems by refusing to sit in the position assigned to it.

"What's happened to you? Why won't you even look at me? Look, we are completely free. Our hands are tied only because ' *you* say nothing. Why are you staying here and letting these old witches fuss over you? Let's go - let's get out now! We'll be OK. We don't have to go back to our old house. We have enough money to rent another place. I sent a note to Dr Dawawalla and he can help us. But he says he can't interfere if you are marrying through choice. How can Satish be your choice? An old man who thinks he's a young boy! Look at his hair! Half of it has fallen out and what's left is grey but he still dreams of the perfect woman. Wants a young girl with long-long shiny black hair..."

The aunt Kamini stirred and turned over in the adjoining bed.

Bimla gave Kamla a sharp look and said: "I am marrying out of choice. I have always liked '*Him*.'" (Now he was going to be her husband she couldn't utter his name. He could only be 'He' or 'Him'.) "I have loved *Him* for years and my dream has come true," she said defiantly.

Kamla's head reeled. This couldn't be her sister. They had done something to her. One of the Naranbhai women must've given her some homemade concoction guaranteed to evoke submissiveness. That's what they did to the *satis* in the old days. Drugged them and then ceremoniously dragged them off to the cremation ground. Made them circle their husband's funeral pyre several times until they became so dizzy that all they could do was fall over it -- helped by the other women -- straight onto the flames. Afterwards they would be declared shining examples of Indian womanhood and shrines would be erected to commemorate their sacrifice.

Kamla shivered a bit. Bimla had even started speaking in flat, robotic tones, without emotion. Yes, they must have fed her some magic potion.

Bimla held up her sewing and said: "Look, isn't that nice? They say it's red but don't you think it's more like a cherry-red? More on the pink side, no? The gold shows up really well, no? Perhaps another row of flowers here? What do you think?"

Kamla swallowed hard. None of it was making any sense.

Bimla continued sewing the shiny flowers onto the cherry red nylon and didn't even bother to look up when Kamla left the room.

ETERNITY -- SIX MONTHS EXACTLY

Naran Villa and Bombay Gardens were buzzing with wedding fever. It was the one topic on everyone's lips. The shrivelled up aunt Kamini, who had never married, was not going to let that do her out of telling wedding stories. Not having had a real wedding, she decided to narrate the story of one of her fictitious weddings in a silent film of the early 1930s. As soon as she began the story, the majority of listeners muttered something about having to do something or the other and vanished. Only the D'Sa urchins - ever ready for a good yarn since their overworked mother never had time to tell them stories - remained glued to the spot. And Kamla. She remained sitting because she was too depressed and paralysed to move. She didn't mind aunt Kamini's droning tones, because her mind was somewhere else: how to stop her sister marrying the wastrel, heavy-drinking, balding, limping Satish?

The D'Sa children hung on Aunt Kamini's every word as though their life depended on it. She spoke in Gujarati, a language they had always understood -- and spoken --much to their mother's distress.

When Aunt Kamini had finished the story, D'Sa Number Four asked:

"Did you ever marry, like in real life?"

Kamini masi was thrilled to take questions from the audience:

"No, no, I couldn't. You see there were so many men in love with me, so many proposals.... If I had chosen any one, then all the others would've committed suicide, so their blood would be on my hands, you see...?" she produced a dramatic facial expression of the silent era, as though facing the camera for a crucial close-up.

"So you couldn't marry at all?" asked the child, sincerely dismayed.

"No, I couldn't marry. But there was one man I loved very much. I almost married him. But then, someone who was very, very jealous of my beauty and success bribed an astrologer to go to my beloved's house and tell his mother that if her son married me, then he would die within six months. The first-class badmaash crook astrologer said to her that *any* man who became

231

my *first* husband would die. So everybody was waiting for me to marry somebody else first. Everybody wanted to be my *second* husband. Nobody was prepared to be my first..."

The D'Sa children gasped at the story. This was even better than Enid Blyton! Astrologers predicting an untimely death was the juiciest story they'd heard in recent memory. Aunt Kamini explained the point again and again, and again and again..... They sat and listened, mesmerised. Only Kamla, suddenly coming to, shot up from her place and ran towards Bombay Gardens. She raced all the way down the short, narrow mud track that ran parallel to the open gutter. She entered the sakati through the back gate and sprinted straight to Satish's door.

It was lunchtime. He was sure to be in, consuming the cockroach-laden contents of his tiffin-carrier that was filled daily by the poor widow who cooked for him. One of his twenty-five gramophone records was playing the dulcet tones of Mukesh:

"Chotti si yeh zindagani re, chaar din ki jawani teri..." (this short life of yours, this short-lived youth, soon to end in grief...)

Kamla rattled on the door handle. Satish's unmistakable squeaky voice said: "Yes, who is it?" He was not used to lunchtime visitors. "Come in...."

He was shocked to see Kamla standing at the door. It wasn't done for young girls to visit a bachelor who lived on his own. Loud-mouthed hussy! Surely she come to offer herself to him? He would have to exercise the utmost restraint and turn down her advances. He would have to tell her he was soon to be married. He would have to fight her off as she reached for his trouser flies.

No, she hadn't come for his body. Instead, she stood some distance away, a serious expression on her face, while he carried on consuming his insect flavoured daal and rice.

"What do you want?" he barked between mouthfuls.

"There is something they haven't told you. Something nobody knows. I think you should know. When my sister was very young, an astrologer told my parents... "

MEHNDI AND SEX

In accordance with Indian tradition, Bimla's mehndi ceremony was held the night before the wedding, in September, 1962. Mrs Naranbhai had hurried the wedding all the more on the grounds that 'Independence' was coming in less than a month, and after that anything was liable to happen. By 'anything' she meant, of course, the inevitable carting off of all single Indian women for forced marriages with black men. The country had never seen so many Indian weddings in a single month, in the run up to Independence from British colonial rule.

The mehndi ceremony was a chiefly female affair. The bridegroom himself was not allowed anywhere in the vicinity of the bride's house. It was assumed that Satish was probably sitting all by himself in his one-room house, restlessly counting the hours to his happy day.

Naranbhai and a few of his close male friends remained confined to the verandah where they were served endless cups of tea by Jannasani while the entire house had been taken over by females of all ages, shapes and sizes, sporting costumes of green, red, purple and yellow. Mrs Naranbhai was extremely perturbed to see that Shahbanu, glittering in shocking-pink and gold, had chosen to hover on the verandah where all the men gazed at her in stupefied fashion. Such a shameless woman! Why did she always have to go and sit with the men? And what happened to grown men when confronted by Shahbanu's cheap available-to-all beauty? Mrs Naranbhai was even flustered because there was so much to do in the house that she couldn't stay near the verandah and keep an eye on Shahbanu's flirtatious antics. Every so often, Shahbanu's soft tones resulted in the men giggling girlishly. She sat near one, and then near another and flitted from man to man making smart remarks about every subject under the sun. Mrs Naranbhai noted with a great deal of bitterness, and fury, that Shahbanu had a built-in instinct for chortling whenever one of the men said something. No doubt, this resulted in each and every man thinking of himself as a first class wit and racconteur. Unable to watch any more, Mrs Naranbhai went back into the house to take charge of the ceremonies.

Bimla was dressed in an old yellow sari -- the idea being that the scruffier she looked the night before, the more radiant her bridal glow on the following day. For female guests, the mehndi ceremony was a far dressier affair than the actual wedding. It was only the bride who was required to be under-dressed for this ritual. For everybody else it was the perfect cue to get wedding outfits out of mothballs.

Pandit Suddenly had calculated an auspicious time at which the wedding ceremony should be performed. At exactly eleven minutes past eleven the following morning, Bimla and Satish were due to start the lengthy rituals of becoming man and wife.

The mehndi ceremony afforded the women of the town a rare opportunity to sing all the songs they knew - some relevant, some completely irrelevant to the proceedings. This was one occasion when musical expertise and lyrical accuracy were most benevolently overlooked in the interests of merry-making -- the singing was tuneless, the words all jumbled up. The dancing was no more than a bit of gentle swaying with the women forming a circle on the flat-roof terrace at the top of the house, the same terrace where Mad Girl Kirti performed her monthly sonnets to the full moon. Now, it was a terrace filled with sounds of giggling, chattering women exercising their God-given right to tease the bride-to-be -- an essential part of the mehndi ceremony and, for most young, virgin girls, the only authoritative source of something akin to a sex education.

Children still too young to exercise any curiosity about one of life's biggest mysteries, nevertheless, still had a grand time, running back and forth, squealing non-stop and clearly thrilled to be all dressed up. The unlimited supply of caffeine-laden Coca Cola contributed to their hyperactive antics. The commotion resulting from a general relaxation of household rules and other rigidities afforded children the perfect backdrop against which to compete with one another in terms of who could be the most disruptive and destructive of all.

While three girls worked on Bimla's hands and feet with the green-muddy substance weaving intricate patterns of flowers and leaves, Kamla stood well away from the bride-to-be. She refused to sing or dance and even refused to have any of the stuff painted on her own palms. It was customary for all the bride's close relations, but especially sisters, to also be adorned. Kamla's refusal to submit to such decoration was interpreted as out and out pig-headedness tinged with envy:

"Leave her. Younger sisters always get jealous when older ones get married," Mrs Naranbhai observed and then, turning to Kamla she added, "You are so lucky. Your sister isn't going anywhere far and you will be living with her. When my older sisters married they went away to other towns. I had no idea if and when I would see them again. Once a girl was married, she only ever returned once for the first ritual visit. Or then, the first birth, or if one of her parents had died. There were no comings and goings in those days. Goodbye to a bride really meant 'Goodbye'. I cried and cried when my sisters, one by one, left home. Even then, I was all dressed up and I had mehndi on my hands and my feet."

Kamla ignored the lecture and remained in her room studying her textbooks.

"What? She is studying today? Studying on the night before her sister's wedding?" quizzed a nosey woman friend of Mrs Naranbhai.

"Yes. Studying. She would be studying even if it was her own wedding, huh!" Mrs Naranbhai scoffed, and the two women enjoyed a private joke of a ribald nature as they speculated how Kamla would probably even be studying on her own wedding night while some poor bridegroom waited patiently for attention.

At that point, someone informed Mrs Naranbhai that the dreaded Raushan had turned up, uninvited, to the mehndi do. Mrs Naranbhai scuttled downstairs and arrived just in time to see Raushan knocking back almond and saffron milkshake laced with gin produced from a miniature in her handbag, while at the same time saying to a group of young women:

"Imagine! You are all soon to be ruled by Africans. Isn't it too bad that you people have not made more of an effort to integrate with the people who are going to be our rulers? Look around you! Do you see even one African guest at this ceremony? Did anyone think to invite even *one* African woman? Even *I* wasn't invited because I have an African husband..."

Mrs Naranbhai interrupted her at that point: "Raushan! Sweet of you! I'm so glad you took it on yourself to come uninvited. Very good of you to caution our girls about the coming dangers of a black government...see, girls? You must all get married quickly before you get carted off by black men, like our dear, dear, poor Raushan here!"

THE AUSPICIOUS MOMENT

The following morning Bimla was being got ready for the mandap - a temporary shelter erected on bamboo poles and decorated with mango leaves in the Naran Villa backyard - where the wedding ceremony was to take place. While the men busied themselves with the final details of the mandap, inside the house the women vied with one another to place the vital gold ornaments on the bride. One woman grabbed the anklets staking her claim to be the one to fasten them on, while another remained in firm possession of the fatter bangles known as *kangans*, that went at the end of the thinner ones, forming a sort of border at either end. Another woman possessively held on to the teeka - the forehead ornament which ran through the centre parting of the hair and ended in a medallion in the middle of the forehead - claiming she was the only person in the whole world who knew how to position it correctly. Mrs Naranbhai herself clutched the big nose-ring that had two small pearls and an emerald dangling from the centre - securing her right as "mother" to ply it through the bride's nose. It was, usually, the eventual removal of this vital nose-ring that signified the end of virginity. In fact, the commonest phrase to ascertain whether or not a marriage had been consummated was: "Was the nose-ring removed?"

The numerous gold ornaments had acquired an even bigger importance owing to the sad fact that the colour of the henna, so painstakingly applied during the mehndi ceremony the night before, had not taken. When the dried-on green muddy substance had been washed off, it had produced only a pale yellow impression, and the intricate pattern of flowers and leaves which had taken several hours to construct was now quite indistinguishable from the natural colour of Bimla's palms.

"That wretched Dhanjibhai," frothed Mrs Naranbhai, referring to her husband's friend and owner of the local general store. "First class crook! I always knew he adds other things to the mehndi to increase its weight. What are we going to do now? A bride with light-yellow mehndi is a very bad omen," she concluded gloomily.

Kamla surprised everyone by emerging from her room at an early hour fully dressed and made up in a manner befitting the only sister of the bride. It had taken no persuasion from anyone for her to get into her brand new clothes, made especially for the occasion, and she had even added flowers in her hair of her own accord. Mrs Naranbhai thought this strange bearing in mind the girl's mood these past few days. But she quickly brushed aside any doubts. Perhaps Kamla had at last seen sense and decided to relax and enjoy the wedding like any other girl her age.

At exactly eleven o'clock--eleven minutes to go to the auspicious moment--Bimla was finally ready and the women waited for her to be called out into the mandap. But a whisper had already risen among the gathering that the bridegroom had not yet arrived. It was customary for the groom to arrive first and take his position in the mandap, ready for the bride, who, flanked by giggling women, would be led out to sit alongside him.

At five past eleven there was still no sign of Satish. It was assumed he was probably still preening and to look his best. In keeping with the mood of teasing the bride from the night before, there was the usual, predictable, bitchy comment from one of the many women: "What ready-ready? Combing his hair or what? How many hair has he got left that it should take so long?"

The remark caused much giggling and tittering among the women.

A small party of men had been dispatched to Bombay Gardens to escort Satish over to Naran Villa on foot. One of these men now came sprinting towards Naranbhai:

"He is not at home!" he announced to the full assembly.

"Maybe he went to some other place to get dressed," said Naranbhai speaking more to himself than to anyone else.

"Where?" demanded to know the young man. "Where could he have gone?"

"A friend's house, maybe? Perhaps he didn't want to be alone. I'm sure he will be here soon," said Naranbhai vaguely, while at the same time registering the fact that the only friends Satish had ever had, the photographer Patel and the Black Cat Club manager Ahmed, had already arrived, sporting their best suits and ties.

At ten past eleven - a minute to go to the auspicious moment that the heavens had deemed favourable for the ceremony - there was still no sign of Satish.

At twelve minutes past the hour there was a general agreement that everyone's watches were probably five minutes fast.

The auspicious moment came and went.

Pandit Suddenly then announced that eleven thirty was equally auspicious if Satish came then, or eleven forty-five, or maybe even twelve-fifteen, suddenly, and who knows, twelve-thirty might also suddenly please the heavens.

Several auspicious moments came and went. And many more would come. There was no shortage of auspicious moments. There was no shortage of pandits prepared to perform the ceremony. There was no shortage of gold ornaments for the bride -- ornaments that kept being fussily adjusted and readjusted to kill time. There was no shortage of guests and certainly no shortage of food. In fact, there was no shortage of anything to suggest a wedding -- except, of course, the absence of a bridegroom!

By one o'clock, Naran Villa, despite the elaborate decoration of green leaves and red, white and blue bunting left over from when Princess Elizabeth had to cancel her visit, looked less and less like a house where a wedding was about to take place. More and more, it began to resemble one that had just hosted a funeral.

"Something bad must have suddenly happened," said Pandit Suddenly. "There must have been an accident, suddenly. He is not at home, and nobody has seen him. I suggest a verdict of 'missing, presumed dead.' "

Naranbhai decided that would, by far, be the best explanation for guests who were now no longer sitting with rapt attention in the mundap but had got up and formed small groups, gossiping and speculating about Satish's mysterious non-appearance.

"Please can I have your attention," he raised his voice over chattering crowd. "Owing to a tragic event, our bridegroom, Satish Chandra, is unable to make it today. The wedding is now postponed. Kindly go back to your houses. We will keep you informed...."

"Go back? What about lunch?" asked one of the guests.

Another said: "What tragic event? What has happened?"

Naranbhai shuffled about uneasily.

An elderly man spoke up: "How can he tell you what has happened? What has happened is this, my brothers: the bride has been rejected. Satish Chandra has failed to turn up because he no longer wants to marry this girl. Such shame! Who will marry her now? She is as good as a widow."

"Don't talk rubbish," yelled Naranbhai. "She is not even married. How can she be a widow, even if Satish - God forbid - is no longer in this world?"

"Excuse me," said Pandit Suddenly. "At the time of the wedding ceremony, the bride was in readiness to be wed. In spirit she was already, suddenly, his wife. And if he has, indeed, suddenly died during that time - and until we see the body we don't know that for sure - then she remains his widow and may not remarry. That would be extremely unlucky. But even if he is not dead, who would suddenly marry a girl who has been stood up by such a good boy, suddenly? He must have found out something about her character and decided against the marriage."

Another man spoke up: "You are covering up something Naranbhai. She is not even your real daughter so why are you covering up for her? If she has done something disgraceful then I think we should be told ..."

Naranbhai hung his head with shame.

Why did he feel such shame on her behalf? True, she wasn't his real daughter, but he had, of his own accord, decided to intervene and improve her life. What's a girl without marriage? Where would she be without a husband to watch over her? Why had he taken it upon himself to do such a noble thing? And why was God repaying him like this for all his kindness to the orphan girl?

"What about lunch?" asked another guest. "It would be such a pity to waste good food."

Mrs Naranbhai, silent up until now, intervened: "Brothers and sisters, it would be best if you each took your share of lunch home and ate it there. We will wrap it up..."

Naranbhai looked at her with renewed respect. He had always under-rated his second wife and called her a stupid woman when she tried to offer solutions to vexing problems but, on this occasion, even he had to admit that she had indeed suggested a wise course of action. The food would not be wasted, everybody would get their lunch, but they would eat it at home instead of consuming it in celebratory fashion in the grounds of Naran Villa.

Kamla shocked everyone by assisting Mrs Naranbhai and others to apportion and wrap up the food. She worked briskly , standing just outside the front gates and handing each person a folded up banana leaf and automatically saying good-bye at the same time, so there was no question of the guests lingering around the Villa.

Naranbhai watched the proceedings with admiration. The morning had been full of shocks: first the revelation of his second wife's untold wisdom in a crisis situation and now Kamla's calm, efficient, polite way of getting rid of unwanted guests. Yes, one should never be too hasty to judge people. The loudest and rudest people could sometimes sport great redeeming qualities.

When all the guests had departed Naran Villa assumed an air of immense gloom. The afternoon sun was high and in its glittering light, ragged pieces of red and blue bunting fluttered unceremoniously in the breeze, looking more like flying litter than the leftovers of festive adornment. The mandap itself, held up by four poles, collapsed in a particularly hard gust of wind. The sacred marriage fire, which had been lit on the night of the mehndi ceremony and around which Bimla and Satish were to have walked in the ritual of becoming man and wife, had long since choked on itself. In its place, a small pile of grey ashes -- give or take a cinder or two.

Naranbhai stood gazing at this scene of hopelessness - a marriage made in heaven had turned to ashes before it could even take place. Where the hell was Satish? And what would become of Bimla now? And how would he set about finding another boy for her if the matter of Satish could not be settled one way or the other? Was the boy alive or not? If dead, then that would look very bad for Bimla. What kind of girl was so unlucky that she killed off a man even *before* marrying to him? And if he had indeed died in some tragic accident like the one that had so cruelly ended Virjibhai's life, then why didn't anyone know about it yet? And, if he wasn't dead, then what the hell was he playing at? Where the hell was he? He'd better have a bloody good excuse.

Kamla changed out of her shiny outfit and made towards Bimla's room. In all this confusion she had completely forgotten to check up on her sister. The door of Bimla's room was open. But there was no sign of anyone in a red bridal sari. Kamla walked in and saw the back of a figure clad in a plain white sari sitting on the floor. She was about to ask about Bimla when the figure turned and she was shocked to see her new-Bride sister in full widow's garb.

"What is this? What have you done? Why?" Kamla almost choked, slowly becoming aware of Bimla's face beneath her newly shaven head.

"I am a widow now, so, I must dress like this," Bimla announced calmly. Her forehead, which had only that morning been decorated with marks of red, had now turned pink in her attempts to wipe out the festive markings.

"Who said you are a widow?" Kamla demanded.

"He didn't come to wed me. And only death could have kept him away. So he must be dead. And if he is dead, then I'm a widow," Bimla said in her usual flat, robotic tones.

"No, no no! He's not dead! He didn't bother to show up because he doesn't care. That doesn't make you a widow. Oh sister! When will you see sense? He has deserted you, and I say good riddance. You've been saved! We've both been saved! You are not a widow. The marriage never took place! One day, you will marry...."

"I'm already married! *He* died before the wedding...."

"No he didn't! He didn't show up because he was probably lying drunk with Maria. He will probably sleep there for three days and then he'll be too ashamed to show his face. Then he will move away and that's the last we'll see of the langra..."

She stopped as a sharp slap landed on her face.

That was the first time she been slapped by Bimla, or anyone else, for that matter.

"Making up such immoral rubbish about your brother-in-law? What Maria? Which Maria? I don't care if he has spent three nights with Maria or Theresa or Alicia. He is still my husband and my god, so kindly hold your tongue!"

The row had brought Mrs Naranbhai and the aunt Kamini into the room. Maybe it was because of the shaved head, but Kamla decided that Bimla looked positively menacing while defending her good-for-nothing husband-that-never-was.

Mrs Naranbhai rushed to Kamla's side, gently reprimanding Bimla: "Don't take it out on your little sister. I know it is terrible when the bridegroom doesn't show up, but that doesn't mean you hit your little sister. Who else has she got in the world but you, eh? "

"Little sister? *Little* sister?" screamed Bimla at Mrs Naranbhai. "Ask her, ask how she knows where my man goes - (she still wouldn't use his name) - and so what if he goes to Maria? A man is a man and he is free to go where he likes."

DOWN IN THE DUST

The weeks passed and there was still no sign of Satish. Naranbhai was just toying with the idea of enlisting the help of his Police Inspector friend to make some inquiries when, one evening, Satish turned up at Naran Villa as though nothing had happened.

"Jai Ramji Ki, Naranbhai! Long time no see!" he grinned. "I went to Congo for a few days. Just got back. Thought I should come here and see you, first, before going home. Have to pay my respects to a big man like you!"

Naranbhai stood there utterly stupefied. What on earth was the scoundrel playing at? At last he spoke but, much to his annoyance, he didn't sound half as angry as he felt:

"Err....yes, quite so, quite so. Good of you to come and see me... now, I need an explanation for your conduct..."

"I know, I know," Satish said impatiently. "I couldn't make it to the wedding owing to circumstances beyond my control. You see I'm still young and I'm planning to enjoy life. Please feel free to arrange her marriage elsewhere. No problem ..."

"What? Listen here, you! You gave me your word. I need to know why..."

"No reason, Naranbhai. I missed the wedding by mistake, but now I think it was probably for the best. Anyway I am making other plans to track down Dream Girl..."

"I will not have it! You hear me? Your marriage to Bimla is fixed. OK, so you didn't make it to the wedding. It was most inconvenient. But that doesn't mean it can't happen again. We can find another auspicious moment -- a simple affair this time. Just wed her and take her away," Naranbhai ordered.

"I can't," replied Satish.

"Why ever not?" snarled Naranbhai.

"Well you know, I only like long-long hair on a girl? Well, this one - I hear - her head is shaved. Be reasonable. How can I marry a bald girl?" he protested.

Naranbhai drew in a deep breath and said through clenched teeth: "Yes! Her head is shaved, yes! Shaved! Because *you* didn't turn up. The poor girl thought you were no longer in this world.

And, as any decent Hindu girl, she did whatever a widow has to do. Only for you! But don't worry, her hair will grow back again."

"But it will be a long time before her hair is long-long again. In the meantime, how can I bear to look at her?"

Naranbhai drew a few steps closer putting his face a few inches away from Satish's, and gnashing his teeth said:

"You do as you are told, now! This is your bloody fault! She is bald because of you! You didn't come to the wedding because you were in the drunken clutches of that Chauthari whore of a barmaid. Do you think I don't know?"

"If you know all that, then why are you still trying to dump this langra wastrel on my sister?" Kamla's voice spoke from behind Naranbhai and he spun around in surprise.

"Who told you to come here and interfere in man talk?" he shouted. "Go! Get inside!"

"I won't" she replied defiantly. "Not until you tell me what's in it for you. This man has said he doesn't want to marry my sister. So why are you forcing him? What sort of marriage will that be for my sister?"

Satish looked at Kamla with admiration. That sharp-tongued girl who had so irritated him in recent weeks now seemed a perfect image of beauty and sweetness.

"She is right, Naranbhai. What sort of husband would I make? A pretty useless one..."

"Even a useless husband is better than no husband!" barked Naranbhai. "Any kind of husband is better than no husband!"

Bimla, who had been listening at one of the windows above the verandah now came down like lightning, her bald head covered in her red bridal sari. She had thrown off the white one as soon as she saw Satish was alive and well. She threw herself at his feet: "Lord, please don't go. Take me with you, I beg you. I'll be your servant. You don't have to love me, just let me serve you. I will massage your feet, I will do anything you want me to do... anything..." she whimpered.

Satish hurried away as Bimla grabbed his ankle. She crawled on her stomach, crushing and creasing the tinsel flowers so painstakingly sewn on. Satish tried to wrench free of her grip on his left ankle, refusing to turn back and acknowledge her, refusing to see her writhing and squealing down in the dust.

Although a girl still waiting to be wed, she looked every bit the long-suffering abandoned wife as she lay in the dust long after Satish had broken free and marched on to Bombay Gardens to pack his belongings. Kamla felt her temples pounding as she watched the spectacle of her sister grovelling to be taken by a man who clearly didn't want her. Soon after this incident, it was heard that Satish had gone to India – no doubt, in search of Dream Girl.

THE "OTHER"

Camilla is now on to her third coffee and has ordered another sandwich. She keeps looking at her watch as though she's supposed to be somewhere else, and then seems to brush aside the idea.

"Sorry," I say. "Am I holding you up?"

"No, no," she says absent-mindedly. "I usually call in on my sister after shopping in this area. They're just a few minutes away, but don't worry. Unless of course you have other commitments.... are you married?"

"No. I was in a long-term relationship, but it ended. He went off with some other woman. I was the transition -- the excuse -- while he was breaking up with his wife.

"Typical Indian!" she fumes. "Indian men think they are doing someone a great favour by marrying them. If they can get it without being married, they'll never sign on the dotted line, I'm telling you! Indian men never respect you if you give them a blow job. Even if they are grotesque, they look for absolute perfection in a wife. All Indian men are...."

"Actually, he was English -- this guy I had the relationship with," I say, trying not to sound too triumphant. And little does she know I'm referring to *her* husband.

"Oh...pity. Still, I'm sure you'll soon meet someone else. You're still young. And you look so Indian, I'm sure another white man would go for you. They love the exotic. It's a funny thing about Englishmen. It's never straightforward. All their sexual appetites are fed by some kind of fantasy. If it's not the exotic Indian maiden straight out of position 137 from the Kama Sutra, then it's some childhood memory of nanny and fireside and nursery teas of jelly and custard..."

I suddenly feel reckless, and ask her straight out: "You've written a book haven't you? Have you tried to get it published?"

"For what? Who's going to read such a book? Who's even going to publish it?"

"Oh, I'm sure somebody would. I can't promise anything - but I'd be happy to show you some short-cuts to getting it to the right..." I can't believe I'm saying this after having sabotaged the only thing she submitted for publication.

She cuts in brutally: "Publishers! What do they know? My story is about Indians in East Africa. If it had been a story about Indians in India, it would have been issued and reprinted several times by now. They just can't cope with Indians living anywhere but India -- or Britain. Africa doesn't count, unless of course you write about wildlife, safaris, tribal dancers and, these days, AIDS. But, Indians living in small town East Africa and behaving exactly as though they were in some Indian village ...well, that doesn't sell books."

Suddenly, I feel very sorry for her. She has made a valid point. I had always imagined that the former colonial powers were generous in the extreme in promoting and bringing to light materials about African and Asian cultures that wouldn't otherwise have seen the light of day. But I'm forgetting something vital here. They've classified us as the "other" as though their culture were the norm and everything else a deviation. They acknowledge the "other" -- very much so -- but the "other" has to fit in with their definition of what it is to be "other." Years of systematic undermining of our cultures has led to us now being put in a showcase --on full view, brought to you by courtesy of this, that or the other do-gooding institute of culture and refinement. And there's a very clear idea about what is, and isn't "Indian," as there is of what is, and isn't, African. If it's a little Indian and a little African, then there's no convenient cubby-hole. It's almost as inconvenient as it used to be for a baby who was a bit of both. Yes, there is little or no recognition for Indian writers who write about the experience of being Indian in Africa. White European or American authors who had put in a brief spell as VSO or Peace Corps, were considered better qualified to comment on the plight of the African-Indians. I had always thought of the Indians of my country as businessmen, or industrialists and, mostly, shopkeepers. But writers? For me, Indian was an Indian was a Muhindi – big car, big house. Now, for the first time in my life, thanks to Camilla, I begin to see African-Indians in a new light.

CAW-CAWING CROW

In the weeks that followed the Bimla-Satish wedding fiasco, Mrs Naranbhai constantly reminded her husband that when it came to females of marriageable age, Naran Villa was definitely jinxed. First, she reminded him again of the Mohini-Sohini double-trouble. Already they had a Mad Girl caterwauling at all hours, and now there was Bimla as well, wailing and crying all day after being rejected by Bachelor Satish.

"It's all because of your habit of fiddling with these two naughty gods -- nobody else would even dream of keeping these gods in the house, leave alone carrying them around everywhere. I'm telling you, everything goes wrong because of your habit of clinging to these gods!" Mrs Naranbhai kept on at him. She was too tactless to have grapsed the basic rules of a marriage partnership: never put down a husband's gods, especially if he had inherited them from his dead mother.

Naran Villa and Bombay Gardens had barely recovered from the drama of Bimla's non-wedding when a fresh diversion presented itself. A mysterious figure in flowing, snow-white robes began to be seen hovering near the flowering shrubs of Bombay Gardens. Many people noted that the flowing white robes, worn by the mysterious wanderer, might well have been the same ones that were mistaken for Virjibhai's spirit. But nobody liked to say anything. It wasn't done to explode myths when they had provided such an honourable excuse to try and marry off a girl of seventeen to a completely unsuitable husband. In time, it was learnt that the mysterious figure was a certain Hazari Baba. He was supposed to be a mystic of some sort, but since mysticism was not really within anyone's grasp, it was assumed he was some sort of magician. Hazari Baba was by no means the first person in history to acquire such a reputation without ever having performed a single magic trick. Everybody assumed he must be a magician because he seemed to appear and disappear with relative ease. He seemed to have no identifiable means of support yet appeared extremely well-dressed. He was of no fixed abode but seemed, always, well rested. When he first appeared in the grounds of Naran Villa to examine some wild flowers, Mrs Naranbhai assumed he was a beggar - albeit a very well-dressed one - and immediately produced a cup of uncooked rice and some leftover stale chapatties from the previous night's dinner. Baba smiled at her and accepted the offerings most humbly, uttering profuse gratitude. Minutes later, he was seen feeding the same leftovers to black crows.

"Can't be that hungry if he's giving it all to the birds," Mrs Naranbhai grumbled to Kamini Masi. "They're all the same these down-and-outs. He probably has palaces and a big bank account somewhere, but still trying to sponge off other people!"

"Be fair," said Kamini Masi, slightly in awe of Baba's serene, majestic stature. "He never directly asked you for food, did he? You just brought it out yourself."

Baba continued hovering some distance away, in the grassy grounds of Naran Villa.

"What's he doing here? Why don't you just go and ask him?" Kamini masi egged her niece. But before Mrs Naranbhai could accost him, the Baba moved closer to where the women were standing and spoke in a soft, melodious voice:

"Visitors. You are sure to have visitors," he said in clear, refined Hindi.

"How do you know? Do you get visions about the future, or something, hain? Probably hallucinating because of your poor diet," she said mockingly.

"No, I eat very well, God be thanked. I just noticed the crow caw-cawing on your roof. It means visitors are imminent," he explained as calmly and as rationally as though he were explaining to a child the connection between the formation of clouds and a downpour of rain. From somewhere on the upper storey of the house the strains of the Mad Girl's voice cut through the noise of the crow:

O Bird of Prey, Devour my body
Relish every atom of this flesh, but
I beseech you,
Let these eyes remain intact
They have waited centuries
To see my Beloved

Have mercy on these eyes,
O Bird of Prey
Let my eyes first see Him
Then devour them, if you must!

The Baba moved towards the house automatically, as though hypnotised by some unseen force. He held up a hand, gently but firmly, as though to forbid any imminent interruptions.

"Who is she?" he asked with undisguised curiosity when the singing had stopped.

"My husband's first wife's mad daughter," answered Mrs Naranbhai. "She's always singing - whether the time is right or not - most embarrassing. Sometimes my husband is in the middle of an important business meeting and she suddenly starts singing - - no head or tail. But then she's mad. What can you do? Don't know where she learns all these tuneless toon-taan songs."

Baba was silent for a few moments. Then he asked, quite suddenly: "May I see her?"

"What for? She's not really allowed to see anyone, you know? And sometimes she can become very violent. Depends on the moon. Masi," she addressed her aunt Kamini. "Where are we in the moon cycle? When is full moon?"

Before Kamini could do any calculations, Hazari Baba's soft, even tones had gone up a fraction of a decibel as he implored Mrs Naranbhai: "Please can I see her? She can't harm me. It's really important I see her. I think I might be able to help her."

The Mad Girl's mother, the first wife Sushilaben, had overheard the conversation from her bedroom window which looked down onto the front verandah:

"Baba, really? Do you think you can help her? Of course you may see her. I'm her mother and I give you permission. This other woman has no authority over my daughter. She is just my husband's kept woman..."

Baba's face remained without emotion as he said: "Everyone is kept in some way. But the Keeper is the same. The only self-supporting woman is the one who puts her body -- or mind -- to good use, to keep men on their toes for what they've been hungry for since time began..."

251

Mrs Naranbhai suddenly moved as though someone had uncoiled a spring within her. "Watch your tongue you dirty old man! No way -- Sushilaben, listen to me," she barked looking up at the window. "I'm telling you, don't let this man into the house. Our husband is not even at home."

"I can always return when your husband is at home. I really need to see the girl ---what's her name? Why do you keep calling her 'The Mad Girl'?"

"Don't tell him her name," Nalini the widow with the dreams and premonitions had now appeared on the verandah and pronounced in cautionary tones. "Sometimes all these guys need is to know the first name and then they go and do their spells to bring the girl under control as their sex slave....my grandmother used to say, a girl's first name, a stray hair from her head or body, or a drop of her menstrual blood, should never ever fall into the hands of an enemy..."

Hazari Baba remained quite calm and serene. He asked again: "Please, can I return when your husband is home? I really need to see the girl..."

Just then, Naranbhai's friend and tenant, the part-time Pandit Suddenly, arrived in the compound of Naran Villa. On seeing Hazari Baba standing there, he let out a yelp of delight and diving down on all fours, prostrated at the Baba's feet. When he finally got up, his eyes were swimming with unshed tears.

Pandit Suddenly was nobody's fool. On spotting a potential rival, he decided the best policy was complete awe and subservience coupled with crawling respect.

"Baba? O Baba! How did you suddenly come, Baba? I heard rumours about some unknown person suddenly wandering around here. Didn't know it was you. What an honour for us!" he whimpered in a ridiculously emotional voice, deliberately put on to disguise his inner dismay at a real mystic having turned up on *his* patch. The Pandit had no intention of relinquishing his Panditry and have it usurped by some pretender. But in true British fashion, because he had read so many English books, the Pandit had decided that it was best to appear respectful towards this mysterious creature and learn all the secrets of his trade before exposing him as a fraud and trickster.

"Oh sorry," the Pandit whimpered, pretending to recover his senses, and realised that the women were gatehered on one side - hostile and suspicious - obviously awaiting an explanation:

"This is the one and only, err...err..." he hesitated.

"Hazari Amrohavalla," announced the mysterious sage.

"Oh yes, yes! Hazari Baba the Great, of Amroha. Saver of Souls, Mender of Hearts," he declared proudly, as though introducing an old friend and much-sought-after celebrity on stage. He had no idea as to the identity of the mysterious creature, but he thought this would make an impressive title. Moreover, *his* appearing to know the name would seal his reputation as a man of extensive knowledge.

"What's he doing here then? Whose heart has he come to mend?" asked Mrs Naranbhai.

Now that she had an intermediary, she refused to address the dubious Baba directly.

"Consider yourselves truly privileged, good ladies, that he has chosen to stand on your threshold and to actually speak. Normally, Baba only speaks twice a day -- once in the morning, and once in the evening..." Pandit Suddenly looked set to continue in this vein but the ever-practical Mrs Naranbhai immediately cut in:

"And where the hell is this Amroi-Shamroi place? Is it in Africa, or India? And what the hell is he doing here? Where does he live? And why are his robes so white? Which washing powder does he use?"

Before the Pandit could reply, Hazari Baba spoke again:

"My work takes me everywhere. I do not choose where I have to go. Today I'm here, tomorrow, who knows? Today you offer me stale bread. Who knows what - or even whether - I will eat tomorrow? My home is wherever the night overtakes me. The sky is my ceiling, the earth my floor. I rest wherever my feet get tired. But, I implore you, please give me a time when I can come back and see the daughter whose vocal chords drip golden honey and nectar."

"What for? Our daughter is not like a mirror in a barber's shop to be gazed at by every aandu-paandu. You're going to marry her or what, that we have to put her on show for you?" Kamini Masi had a way of twisting the mundane and sounding bitter about the most ordinary things in life. Unfulfilled ambition always left scars. And, women who had once been considered beautiful usually withered all the more when the accolades ceased.

The Baba simply lowered his head at the unkind jibe and turned around as though to leave. Pandit Suddenly immediately blocked his way and turning to Mrs Naranbhai and Kamini Masi said: "Please, please say he can return in the evening. Naranbhai will be home then, won't he? If anyone can help your mad daughter, Baba can. Such a pity about that poor young girl!" He was determined to join forces with the Baba.

Sushilaben spoke first: "Yes, he will be home. Baba, please come back at six." And then, addressing her rival the second Mrs Naranbhai she said with bitterness: "What is it with you? Any sign, any hope of a cure for my daughter and you have to put your foot in it! We've tried everything else - even your stupid Crossroads idea - so, why not this?

Mrs Naranbhai ignored the first wife completely and barked at the Baba:

"Listen here old man, and listen hard! Whoever you are -- mender of hearts or broken heads -- don't you dare step near this house again! I am the mistress of this house and those are my orders. Hanging around pretending to smell flowers and talking dirty about women - get out! Out!"

The screaming and shouting came to a halt when the widow Nalini suddenly remembered something: "Feet! Their feet always point backwards if they are not of this world. Did you check his feet to see if they are pointing the wrong way?"

"Er...no....no, I don't think...I didn't see..." Pandit Suddenly hesitated, immediately to be interrupted by Mrs Naranbhai.

"What 'no-no'? You practically threw yourself at his feet as soon as you spotted him. You were snivelling there for a good five minutes. You must've seen his feet!"

She turned around to check on Baba's feet herself, but he had disappeared. Mrs Naranbhai spun around, wondering why his retreating figure couldn't be seen in the near distance. Where could he have gone, so suddenly? A mild fear gripped her momentarily. Then she remembered that everybody else had seen him as well. Pandit Suddenly had even introduced the crazy man, so she certainly wasn't seeing things. And, the Baba himself, had spoken in poetic Hindi about various matters, something about the earth being his floor and the sky his ceiling...something like that, anyway.

The aunt Kamini, eager to stir things up, turned to her niece and said: "He said there would be visitors soon. He said when the crows go caw-caw on the roof, it means visitors."

Mrs Naranbhai was unimpressed: "So? Everybody knows that! You don't have to be a holy bloody magic-man to know that!"

AN INDISPENSABLE ASSET

It was soon after Baba's pronouncement that crows caw-cawing on the roof meant unexpected visitors that Jannasani disappeared for a couple of days.

"Typical!" fumed Mrs Naranbhai. "They've got to so much as hear the word 'visitor', real or imagined, and they vanish." It was Mrs Naranbhai's opinion that houseboys did not like visitors because it made more work and, that as far as she could remember, Jannasani had always done a disappearing act whenever visitors were imminent.

Two days later, Jannsani returned, accompanied by a young boy, and made no attempt to explain his mysterious disappearance. Instead he announced calmly, "This is Juma. My brother's son."

"Your brother's son? Didn't know you had a brother. But then you people have so many relatives. Everybody is a bloody dugu. So, this is your dugu's son, what of it? What's he doing here?" she asked, noting with some irritation that the boy had an immensely mischievous face and eyes the size of new potatoes.

"He's going to live here, with me. He will help me," Jannsani announced with a kind of finality that implied that Juma's appointment as junior dogsbody was a foregone conclusion.

"Who says? What gives you the right to go round hiring people to work in *my* house?" Mrs Naranbhai asked. Jannasani was really getting too bossy. She added: "If we need any more servants, *I'll* find them, *I'll* check their references. Why, this is just a toto!"

"No need for references. He is my brother's son. His parents died when their village was wiped out, in a single night, by giant killer ants. Not even a goat or cow remains…only this boy. He lives because he is clever. Juma, come, say 'Salaamu Mama' - "

Before Juma could obey orders, Mrs Naranbhai, feeling somewhat overtaken by events and for lack of anything better to say, asked, "Why is he named after a weekday? What sort of name is that?"

"He was born on a Friday - that is why he is called Juma. Very good boy. Very clever. Very clean. Will help us. No need for pay.

Just food, twice a day. He can sleep out in the sakati. When it rains, he can come into my room."

Jannasani could not be called pushy, or aggressive, by any stretch of the imagination, but he had a kind of languid, couldn't-care-less tone which always disarmed people into thinking that Jannasani's idea - whatever it may be - was, in fact, their very own and, as such, could do no harm. Or, at any rate, it couldn't do Jannasani any good.

Mrs Naranbhai paused to consider the advantages of a second servant, wage-free. It was sure to enhance her reputation as lady of a large house and, there was certainly enough work to keep him occupied. In fact, Jannasani hardly ever caught up with all his tasks, and if it hadn't been for her own hands-on approach to the running of her household, nothing would ever get done. Meals round the clock for a dozen people, endless visitors on the verandah and numerous cups of tea, demands for hot bhajjias, all the beds, sweeping, cleaning, dusting, shoe-polishing, washing, scouring, to say nothing of trying to keep abreast of the first wife's possible plots and schemes...

It might be nice to have a young boy to push around. Also, she could set the tone from the start. With Jannasani, she had lost it somewhat. Often, he behaved as though *he* owned the house with herself relegated to mere housekeeper.

Yes, a brand new servant - and a junior one at that - was less likely to answer back and possibly less insolent than Jannasani. But she had to make sure he would take orders from her, and not from his alleged uncle.

"When you say 'very clever', what do you mean?" she asked. She didn't want any scholarly types whiling away the time under the pretext of servant-hood just to get free meals and accommodation while doing their wretched school certificates.

"He knows a lot of things. He can repair things. He is very good at catching snakes. He knows how to handle difficult people. He knows all sorts of..." Jannasani listed Juma's many credentials painting him as an indispensable asset to any household.

Up until now, Mrs Naranbhai and Jannsani had discussed Juma as though he weren't even there. And Juma's head moved from left to right as though viewing a tennis match while the two held their dialogue. Mrs Naranbhai now turned her gaze on Juma:

"How old?"

"Eleven years and two months and thirteen days," Juma answered in Swahili, while pretending to count on his fingers.

"All right, all right," she said after a moment's thought, assuming that he was probably more like fifteen -- so difficult to tell with these people! "One week's trial!" she barked. "If he's no good, he has to go back to the village..."

"But the village is destroyed. And the killer ants might return," protested Jannasani.

"I don't care about your man-eating ants or spiders. He will go back to if I am not happy with his work," she said with finality.

Soon after the interview, the enemy sister-in-law Widow Nalini, taunted Mrs Naranbhai:

"That Baba person -- didn't he say there would be a visitor? Do you suppose he could have meant *this* boy?"

GOLDEN INDEPENDENCE
1962

Pandit Suddenly, addressing a potential devotee, was over-enthusing about Hazari Baba, just in case anybody imagined he felt threatened by this new Man of God.

"Even if it sounds like nonsense at the time, just think about it later. It's suddenly always true what he says. His every word is worth its weight in gold - suddenly - I tell you, it's pure gold!"

In time, this statement had been convoluted to mean something entirely different. It was mooted about that Hazari Baba knew how to make gold. And that was put forward as an explanation for his wealthy appearance despite having no visible means of support. It was whispered widely, and eagerly, that the Baba had inherited some ancient knowledge of alchemy -- a secret method that had been fiercely guarded by a tribe descended from the inhabitants of Persia, now resident in Zanzibar.

"No wonder!" said Naranbhai, on hearing the rumours. "The guy can touch anything and make it into gold so why the hell bother to work? No wonder he goes around sniffing gardenias. What else is there to do? Not like the rest of us, slaving, morning noon and night - "

"I haven't seen too much slaving from you," Mrs Naranbhai interrupted her husband. "All you do is sit in your chair and complain about the world."

"Women! Don't you see? Just because I'm sitting here, doesn't mean I'm not doing anything. Brain power. I have to think. I have great schemes in my mind. Wait and see," Naranbhai said.

"Your schemes usually mean a lot of trouble. The entire household goes upside down because of your schemes. I don't want any more schemes. Just live quietly, and learn to make do with what we have. Too much greed is bad -"

"Look who's talking! When did you ever learn to be happy with what you have? No, you must have this sari and those bangles and that necklace. Who is going to pay for it all? Am I made of money like that Hazari fellow? All these mouths to feed and just me to provide. Hey Bhagwan! What responsibilities a man must fulfil in these bad times when the world is changing...." As ever, he was clattering the figurines of his twin-gods in the palm of his right hand.

"Then you shouldn't get married so often," Mrs Naranbhai replied bitterly. "If you don't want to support people then stop going around marrying them!"

"I only married twice -- and with good reason. You make it sound like I'm getting married to a different woman every month!"

"Married or not, you are taking on everyone else's problems and ending up with extra responsibility on your head. Where is the need to feel so sorry for everyone? Why do you have to be everybody's guardian? It brings nothing but trouble! Why did you have to go and get into the middle of Virjibhai's Vima? Those girls have been nothing but trouble. And Kamla with her big mouth! You have no idea what I go through all day to get her to shut up. And now she's been going on and on about wanting to go to the midnight celebrations for Independence. And the older one - Bimla - just crying and whimpering all day for that wretched Satish."

"You have never seen it my way -- that is my problem. But wait, just wait until I become something big and then I'll show you all!"

"What big-big? Independence is next week, don't you know? And God knows what will happen after that? You don't even know if the new black government will let you do your big-big business scheme. Africans hate us. Even Jannasani has been strutting around with a party flag and chanting strange slogans. This is the time to be careful. Lie low - not talk big-big about grand schemes. We might be murdered in our beds by 10th October!"

The strange slogans she was referring to was the fact of Jannasani, on one occasion, when a political march had been going past, running up to the Naran Villa rooftop and shouting from the depth of his lungs: "DEEEEEE-PEEEEEEE!" – initials of the opposition Democratic Party. He had learnt the DP slogan from the D'Sa urchins, who chanted it non-stop while playing and chasing each other all over the Bombay Gardens backyard. Most

Goans supported DP because its leader was a Catholic. In the meantime, Raushan had been going from house to house urging Asians to vote for the other party -- an uneasy alliance between the Black tribal King and the new People's Congress. Her mouse-like husband, Sam, was a Congress man and tipped to be favoured for a cabinet post. She had been received very coldly at Naran Villa while campaigning for her husband's Party. Mrs Naranbhai had actually said to her:

"OK, so you want us to vote for People's Congress. For what? You think we all want to marry black men, like you?" And then, in an amazing show of political insight - not the kind that would usually be associated with the likes of semi-literate battle-axes from an Indian village - she went on to say: "Countries or political parties who have the word 'People' in their titles are the worst of all! They stand for anything but 'People.' "

Mrs Naranbhai was convinced that a PC win would result in a rounding up of all Asians into some kind of concentration camp in some mosquito-infested village on the outskirts of civilisation. In the months leading up to Independence she had been nagging Naranbhai to consider moving back to India. But he would not hear of it -- not least because he wasn't sure what he'd do with himself over there. He would only be a very small fish in a very big pond, despite his thousands of African shillings being worth quite a lot of Indian Rupees.

"Fine," Mrs Naranbhai had said with a great deal of bitterness. "Just hang around here, and wait to be killed by them -"

"Stop being so dramatic woman! All the political parties have said Asians are very important to the economy. They are offering citizenship -"

"Don't you dare even think about it! If you give up your British D passport and take a local one, I'm going back to India and I'm taking your sons with me!"

She had then tried to persuade him to take a short holiday in India - with her - just until all the Independence madness had died down:

"They'll all go on a rampage. Just look at the way they're behaving already! They'll just run around with axes. Look at

Jannasani, sometimes shouting "DP" sometimes singing songs in praise of the black King. What can peasants and servants know about politics? We should go away while all this madness is going on."

"No, no, I can't do that," he had said, offering no further explanation. "But, if it's making you nervous, you may take the children and go to India for a while. Later on, when everything's OK, you can return."

WHAT? Was she mad? Was she going to leave him alone in the house with the first wife, just because she was afraid of a post-independence mass slaughter of all Indians?

Independence came - and went - without much ado. The only direct repercussions of this momentous event in the Naranbhai household was that Kamla expressed a wish to attend the midnight ceremony. Mrs Naranbhai was horrified:

"What? You actually want to be there? What for? Asking for trouble! Don't you know as soon their flag is raised they will just run around killing all Indians?"

"That is ridiculous," said Kamla. "I happen to think it is an important historical occasion and I would like to be part of it. I have never been part of history. For once, something important is happening. It would be a shame to miss it. My father would have certainly allowed me to attend. I would like to able to tell my children and grandchildren about…"

"Hey Ram! Such shamelessness! An unmarried girl referring to her own children! Never mind children, even grandchildren already? Ram, Ram, Ram!"

WITNESSING HISTORY

"Do you know I was one of very few Indians actually present at the Independence celebrations? Yes, Independence had finally come but, nothing even remotely like independence, touched my life. We were plunged in our own little dramas. There was this mysterious sage...I can't remember his name, although I should because he saved my life....Anyway, all I remember is everyone was suddenly focussed on him. The Indians were envious of him and the Africans wanted to recruit him to work for them. But nobody succeeded in getting him. Even at the end, even after they were expelling the Asians, they were still looking for him... You see, he disappeared in such a way, it was so dramatic that afterwards I completely forgot how he came to be there in the first place..."

She can see I've lost interest. I want to know more about the celebrations and about the immediate post-Independence years in my country -- before I was born. And all she wants to do is ramble on about some Indian saint figure who, supposedly, saved her life....

"But tell me about Independence itself," I prompt her.

"Oh it was the most thrilling event of my life! Yet, little were we to know that exactly a decade after that, we would all be kicked out. Still, independence wasn't anything the Indians were too excited about. They were afraid. They felt "dumped". They had come to the country because the British had encouraged them to do so. Now the British were quitting, what would become of them? Naturally, they were scared. At Independence, many had the choice of giving up their British Protectorate passports and becoming citizens of the new country. Not many did. But, at the end of the day, those who kept their British passports had the last laugh. Those who opted for citizenship of the newly independent country were nearly all made stateless in 1972...."

"That's amazing! I didn't know that!" I said with genuine surprise. I had always been led to believe that the Indians who lived in my country chose to remain third class British citizens.

"So what happened immediately after Independence?" I asked. Of course I'd read all the history books in school and at university, but I wanted a first-hand account.

I'm now looking at Camilla with renewed admiration. Here was someone who had actually witnessed history in the making -- in my country -- something that had happened four years before my birth. I don't remember ever meeting anyone who had actually attended - or could remember even attending - that night of Independence celebrations. By the time I was growing up, Independence was already history -- and so much had gone wrong since, that we no longer referred to it as a major turning point in our history. Only one of my brothers - my favourite - said he was there. He was my favourite because I seemed to have known him from the day I was born. I should have known all of them because I was much younger and they must have all known me as a baby, but, somehow, *he* was special. He never explained how he came to be in the capital or how he got there. He can't have been more than eleven or so at the time. I asked Mama Safia once if the whole family had gone along to the celebrations, but I distinctly remember her saying that it was a late night affair and there were no special transport arrangements. They didn't go because they wouldn't have had anywhere to stay. And, overnight camping on the celebratory ground was expressly forbidden. And, I also remembered her saying that those who were lucky enough to live in the capital city -- mostly Indians -- had remained securely locked in their houses. It is for this reason I admire Camilla. She must have defied a lot of people to attend those celebrations.

"How exciting for you to actually be there! What happened exactly?" I asked her, all agog.

"It was like being in the middle of a big adventure -- I don't mean the Independence celebrations, but how I came to be there. At first I was expressly forbidden -- then the tune changed, for the silliest reason..."

She starts giggling. It's amazing for me that someone who had such a painful departure from the country of her birth could still laugh about it...

ANOTHER SERIES OF EXPLOSIONS

Pandit Suddenly arrived at Naran Villa early on the morning of 8th October, 1962. He looked as pleased as a schoolboy about to embark on a half-term treat.

"Naranbhai, I need Satish's car keys. He said I may use it while he is away..." he began.

"Why? You're never going out in all this madness....?" Naranbhai was genuinely startled. Pandit Suddenly, who had learned to drive in India during the War, was the only other driver in Bombay Gardens. Whenever Bachelor Satish was away, the Pandit was allowed to drive the banger-khattara Ford Prefect.

"Independence celebrations - tonight - I'm escorting our beautiful Mrs Shahbanu Hussein...."

Naranbhai's head reeled: "Are you out of your mind? Aren't you afraid to be out....?"

"I was, I was," said the Pandit sheepishly, "but when the lovely lady told me she had two passes to an enclosure immediately behind the VIP box -- given to her by a...a...err...*friend*...I decided not to be afraid. We will be with -- or very near -- the high-ups...so how can we come to any harm?"

It was too much for Naranbhai. The fact of Pandit Suddenly escorting his own beloved Shahbanu so late at night was bad enough. The fact of the enclosure near the VIP box, or that the coveted passes had obviously come through some government "high-up" hadn't even registered with him. He was only concerned about one thing: no way could he stand aside and allow the smug Pandit this kind of outing with a lady he had vowed to protect from all marauding hands and hungering eyes.

"I don't know if I'm free tonight you see..."Naranbhai began, carefully.

"No, no Naranbhai, you misunderstand. You are not required. I only need the keys so that I can drive Mrs Shahbanu..."

"There's a problem, see. Before he went away this time, Satish stressed that he was happy for anybody to drive his car, but that I should be present ...to err...to... to make sure nothing goes wrong. I'm not allowed to let the car out of my sight..."

"That's strange," said the Pandit, already smelling a rat. "Usually he's happy for me to use it from time to time...keep the battery going...such a khattara, anyway...who would steal it? It would fetch all of twenty shillings at Ali's Auction Mart..."

"Be that as it may," Naranbhai switched into bureaucratic-landlord mode: "I promised him I would not allow that car to move without my being present..."

"But that's difficult. She only has two passes for the event. That means you'll have to go into the crowd and sit with the common African people. I don't see how we can take you with us...." He trailed off and then had an idea: "I know! I'd better organise a taxi, since I can't have Satish's car," he said brightly.

"Taxi? Tonight of all nights! None of those fellows will be working. They need the slightest excuse to stop work. And today they'll all be drunk already! Are you really prepared to risk your life like that? Never mind your life, what about my tenant...I'm like a brother to her you know?"

No way was Naranbhai going to let the Pandit whisk Shahbanu away in a taxi!

"So, how else do we go? Are you proposing we walk all the way to the stadium and then walk back? You know Mrs Hussein, in her high heeled sandals, would never...."

"Of course not! How can you walk? The best thing would be for you to take the car, but I would have to come as well...."

The Pandit had no option. He had already promised Shahbanu he would drive her there. If that meant Naranbhai tagging along, then so be it. He thought of one more objection.

"But Naranbhai you know the car has no back seat? Satish removed it suddenly for me to have as a sofa. Where would you sit, suddenly?" he asked.

"Three can sit in the front...no problem. I am prepared to do my duty to Satish and keep an eye on his car. A promise is a promise, and if that means squeezing in tight into the front seat with Shahbanu, well then, what's a bit of discomfort to fulfil a neighbourly duty, hain?" Naranbhai said solemnly, trying hard not to grin.

The Pandit left, not entirely happy, but quite satisfied that the matter of tonight's transport had been resolved. At least he would be in the special seats with Shahbanu while Naranbhai would have to mingle with the plebs. The Pandit would be able to gloat, no end. That, alone, was more satisfying than if Naranbhai hadn't been coming at all.

That afternoon, Naran Villa could have become the scene of the worst marital row in the history of the equatorial belt had the second Mrs Naranbhai not had the foresight to make a move worthy of a world chess champion. She had overheard most of the conversation between her husband and the Pandit Suddenly and, without saying anything to her husband, she had cornered Kamla.

"You were saying the other day that you would like to see Independence?" she began in tentative fashion.

"Yes, very much. A degree of independence for me and my sister would be very good...."

"Hahahaha...funny girl!Very clever! No, I meant Independence *celebrations* tonight, at the stadium. You wanted to see the ceremony, no? Well, I have good news. The Pandit is driving Shahbanu there. My husband is also going, just to keep an eye on the car and make sure nothing goes wrong. So, if you still want to go, I suggest you join them..."

Given Mrs Naranbhai's recent views on Independence, it didn't take Kamla long to figure out the plot. She was to be Mrs Naranbhai's personal spy. Sure, the presence of the Pandit ensured there would be nothing improper between Shahbanu and Naranbhai but, men being men, you never could be sure. They might come to some sort of shared arrangement and keep one another's guilty secret. Although thrilled that she would be allowed to go out tonight, Kamla decided to make it difficult:

"No, it's OK, thanks for the offer. But once you'd forbidden me from going out I saw your point of view. I agree with you. We could all get massacred the moment the new flag is raised. I've gone off the idea," she said languidly, stifling a yawn as though it was already midnight, rather than the middle of the afternoon.

"Now, don't be silly! It's an important historic occasion. Young people like you should witness history and play a part in it. Actually, you look sleepy now. Go and have a nice long rest now, then you'll be able to stay up all night. Now, which dress should I ask Jannasani to iron for you for tonight?"

Kamla enjoyed her temporary empowerment: "No, leave it, please. Why don't you go with your husband and the others?"

"They are going in Satish's old khattara, and you know there is no backseat. How would I look crouched like a thief in the back in my expensive sari? It's different for you -- you're a kid. You could easily sit in the back and...."

"Thank you for your kind offer, but you know when I first planned to go it was really to take Juma. He and I were going to attend celebrations together. I wanted to treat him to something. He's a kid after all, almost my age. He never gets to go anywhere...." Kamla had brought a vital card into play.

"Juma? Which Juma? I didn't know you had a friend called Juma...." Mrs Naranbhai asked, genuinely puzzled.

"You know, Juma, *our* Juma..." Kamla explained.

"Juma? You don't mean the junior houseboy...Kamla! How could you...?"

It was the sort of information that would normally have caused Mrs Naranbhai to howl like a wild dog, beat her breast and proclaim the end of the world. She checked herself and added more icing sugar to her sickly-sweet speech on the importance of witnessing history.

"Oh, *that* Juma! *Our* Juma! Of course, he must go. It's *their* country after all. It's his duty to attend. How nice of you to think of him! You can be such a sweet-natured girl when you're not mouthing off. I'll go and tell him to be ready for tonight and I'd better give him one of my son's old shirts to wear...now, what would you like in your midnight picnic box, hain? Samosas or sandwiches? I think that boy Juma prefers samosas. I've seen him scoff a dozen at a time...now, let me see..."

Mrs Naranbhai was nobody's fool. She lost no time in telling Juma about the treat that awaited him tonight. That way, Juma would be the one to persuade Kamla to go along. Mrs Naranbhai was determined to make the outing as crowded as possible. There was safety in numbers. Plant as many agents as possible so that sources of information would be many and their stories could be checked against each other in case of irregularities. Then again, if it was a matter of Shahbanu's wily charms and her own husband's unashamed and unbridled lust, one could never have too many chaperones. And, in a move worthy of the most astute statesmen in history, Mrs Naranbhai had also had the foresight to extend a dinner invitation to the part-time Pandit and Shahbanu.

"It could be a long night. I want to make sure you both get a proper meal before you set out."

Who could refuse such a kind gesture? But her motive would have been plain as hell for anybody who knew her: she wanted to see what Shahbanu was wearing. Far better to see the real thing than to imagine that one's rival looked a great deal more fetching than they actually did. But, her main motive was of the stuff that goes into history-changing military campaigns. If her husband was going to be cooped up with the beautiful Shahbanu in the tight, cramped space of Satish's car, then she knew exactly what to feed him -- to feed all of them.

That evening, the Naran Villa dinner consisted of an unusually high number of various vegetarian dishes laced with raw garlic and onion. Every single dish was liberally sprinkled with both these odourous substances. And, thinking that her husband was sure to try and dodge his way round the slices of raw onion, she had also taken the extra precaution of cooking some extra food composed largely of flatulence-inducing ingredients. For these, she had conveniently overlooked adding the customary ginger and hing, or asfoetida, which was said to prevent such an embarrassing eventuality. Satisfied that her scheme would work through one, or both orifices of all three passengers, she felt a bit happier at the prospect of her husband being huddled close to Shahbanu for the long drive.

Mrs Naranbhai thought it best to say as little as possible to her husband while he spent some considerable time in getting ready for that night. A pile of clothes lay abandoned on the bed as he had changed his mind about outfits several dozen times. She went about her normal task as though there was nothing unusual about Naranbhai changing shirts every two minutes for a midnight outing with Shahbanu. Kamla and Juma were already dressed and they waited on the verandah...too excited to eat anything.

A fuming Naranbhai had to see Pandit Suddenly lead Shahbanu back to Bombay Gardens after dinner, for a quick touch-up on her make-up. He started trailing behind, car keys in hand.

"Hurry up!" said Mrs Naranbhai to her husband. "There will be a lot of traffic."

Kamla and Juma waited a few moments and then started walking behind him. He turned around: "What...? Why are you two following me? "

Mrs Naranbhai was still standing on the verandah to oversee things.

"What?" she shouted, before the children could reply. "Why shouldn't the children be treated to such fun? Is it just for you and the Pandit to enjoy? "

Naranbhai figured out the plot. You couldn't be married to some woman for ten years, and more, without knowing her mind's every single Machiavellian twist and turn. He scowled and carried on walking, the children fast on his heels.

Pandit Suddenly and an overdressed Shahbanu were already waiting by Saitsh's car. In the time that it had remained unused, the khattara-car had gathered a nice thick coating of reddish mud. Naranbhai's first bout of bad temper found an outlet:

"Pandit-ji, you only think about driving. Didn't it occur to you to get the car cleaned? How will my beautiful lady tenant here...?"

He paused and bowed to Shahbanu who was glittering from head to toe in shocking pink and gold.

"How can she step into such a filthy car in all her finery? You never think, do you? Didn't your English books teach you anything?" Naranbhai was determined to score points off the Pandit even before the outing had begun.

Without thinking, and as though automatically programmed, Juma at once produced a corner of his shirt tails and started rubbing the dirt off the driver's side door.

"Stop it!" scolded Kamla. "He didn't mean *you* had to clean it. You're not on duty now. It's your evening off and we're going out. See? You've dirtied your shirt now..."

They piled into the car. It was a two-door Ford Prefect of which only one of the doors worked. The Pandit unlocked it and pushed the seatback forward so Kamla and Juma could scramble into the back, where they had to crouch on the rusty metal floor from which the backseat had been removed. Naranbhai climbed into the driving seat and slid over to the passenger seat. Shahbanu went in next, gathering the folds of her sari in a way that showed more ankle and leg than would have been absolutely necessary.

The Pandit squirmed at having to say: "Move over some more good lady...more...you need to push closer to Naranbhai otherwise I can't get in." Naranbhai grinned like a Cheshire cat as Shahbanu pushed one side of her body into his. It still left a very tight space for the Pandit to climb into the driving seat. Eventually, after much shuffling and pressing and pushing, the door was shut and the Pandit attempted to start the car. The first attempt failed. On the second attempt, the car got into a melodic grrr-grr-grr-grr pre-starting drone that gradually faded and died.

"Turn the key properly, Pandit-ji," said Naranbhai, who had never succeeded in learning how to drive.

Finally, by some miracle, the khattara Ford Prefect started. Amidst crackles threatening to turn into explosions, the Pandit searched for the gear lever. Shahbanu was sitting on it. He thurst his left hand under her bottom and she squealed with delight: "Oh, Pandit ji, you *are* naughty!" she chortled, causing Naranbhai to wear an extra-stern expression and attempt to roll down the glass on his window. But he was squashed in so hard, and so tight, that there was no room for his arm to perform the necessary rotating motion. They'd only gone a few yards and it was already stifling hot. A stench of garlic and onions filled the car, now proceeding by a series of bumps and jerks and, eventually, giving way to a smooth, steady, 15 miles per hour.

When they were a mile or so from the venue, the traffic thickened to choking proportions, necessitating a slow crawl of the kind the old car hated. It stalled every few seconds and, finally, died with a whimper. As luck would have it, Mrs Naranbhai's other culinary precautions -- those to do with feeding her guests edibles that were guaranteed to produce flatulence -- chose this very moment to kick in. And, Shahbanu's jasmine and roses fragrance was quite powerless against the scents of nature. Kamla and Juma stifled their giggles. Only children can find funny what adults consider supremely inconvenient and embarrassing.

"You need to get out and push", said the Pandit to Naranbhai, among the deafening noise of car-horns. Everybody was impatient to get to the celebrations and a queue of cars, three-deep, had formed on a road that was really only wide enough for one car. And, to add to the congestion, there were huge throngs of people on foot, waving the new flag and singing their way to the stadium. They looked so happy and Kamla thought, with a pang, that that's how she would have liked to proceed to the celebrations. She wanted to walk with them, not crouch in the back of a seatless car surrounded by grumpy, flatulent, grown-ups.

"Don't be ridiculous!" barked Naranbhai. "How would I look pushing a car?"

"So, should we sit here all night?" shouted the Pandit, sending more onion fumes into the stifling interior and also beginning to lose his temper.

"Petrol..." Juma whispered, urgently to Kamla. "Tell them we have run out of petrol. It was already very low when we came out..." Juma knew not to speak directly to his elders and betters.

Kamla interrupted the argument: "We've stopped because the car is out of petrol! We should try and stop one of the other cars and see if any of them can sell us some..."

It was too late. Three men, from the cars stuck behind the khattara had come up and were making threatening movements with their fists.

"Calm down brothers," the Pandit said to the African men. "We have broken down....er...no....we've run out of petrol. You see I'm a Pandit. An upright, law-abiding member of the Indian community. We are very decent ...no violence, we don't believe in violence. Our Gandhiji said...."

The three men recoiled from his oniony breath and looked at one another and nodded. One of them said: "You see sir, right now your Mr Gandhi cannot help you! But we can, Mr Pandit. We can certainly help you! Just release the handbrake...."

The Pandit had to reach below Shahbanu's bottom again, causing her to flutter her eyelashes as he did so. Naranbhai looked the other way, gnashing his teeth and wondering why the Pandit's smelly breath was having a zero impact on Shahbanu.

And, before anybody could say anything, the three African men had swiftly pushed the car off the road onto a narrow, muddy roadside, so that it was no longer in the way.

"No need to thank us! Just say a small prayer for Mr Gandhi!" they said cheekily and jumped back into their car with a cheery wave.

"Now what?" said Naranbhai. The Pandit had no answer, so Naranbhai answered for him. "You'll just have to walk back to Bombay Gardens and get that little can of petrol Satish keeps for emergencies."

"Why me? Why can't you walk back and get it?" asked the Pandit.

"Because a man of my stature cannot be seen to be wandering about on foot at night. How would that look? I'm a landlord after all, whereas Pandits -- and holy types in general -- are supposed to walk miles and miles for all kinds of penances. It would be most fitting if you were to..."

"Naranbhai, no way!" protested the Pandit. There was a deadlock during which the stench in the car got headier.

Kamla offered a solution: "Pandit-Uncle and Naranbhai-Uncle...we're only a mile away from the stadium. Please, can Juma and I get out and walk there? I really don't want to miss the celebrations. There are so many people about, I'm sure it would be quite safe..."

"Keep shut young lady, unless you have an idea about how to get us out of this!" scolded Naranbhai.

"I do have an idea," she said. "The Kotecha family live close-by. They have a petrol station. It will be closed but they live right next door. I'm sure if Pandit-ji goes and asks they will give him some petrol. It will only take a few minutes to reach there...."

Naranbhai brightened: "Poor old Virjibhai was quite right about you!" he sighed "You are an exceptionally brilliant girl! Go, Pandit-ji! They'll never refuse to serve petrol to a holy man. Go right now...."

"But I don't know the house...how will I find it...?" The Pandit asked lamely.

"You just keep walking until you see the first building on your right. You can't miss it. It's only ten minutes' away," reassured Kamla.

The Pandit had no choice but to grudgingly get out and start walking towards the alleged Kotecha dwelling. Shahbanu moved her body away from Naranbhai, now that there was more space in the front. This, Naranbhai had not reckoned with.

As Kamla had expected, he said: "And now, Kamla, my dear child, as a reward for your brainwave, I have decided to let you and Juma walk to the stadium from here. Mind how you go, and you, boy, Juma! Keep an eye on her. I hold you responsible for her safety...we'll catch up later. Enjoy yourselves, children! Oh, here's a shilling -- buy a little flag each, OK? Show some patriotism! This is a very important night."

He couldn't wait to be rid of them. Kamla smiled to herself. She was cleverer than the rest of them put together. She and Juma would get to walk to the celebrations, just as she had wanted. She wanted to walk with the crowds and enjoy every moment of belonging in it. She didn't want to be a spectator, she wanted to be one of them — and proceed to the celebrations singing and dancing with them.

Noble though her intentions, Kamla was not entirely without wickedness. You had to be a little crooked to survive in a world where men made the rules and their emotionally insecure, needy women, reinforced them. The Kotecha house was actually miles and miles away. The Pandit would be gone forever and would probably end up completely lost. Naranbhai and Shahbanu would have many delicious hours alone, together, albeit laced with unwelcome aromas.

That was Kamla's way of getting even. And, to add insult to injury, she planned to tell Mrs Naranbhai, in great detail and in the most innocent of tones, what a crush it was on the front seat and how Shahbanu was practically in Naranbhai's lap most of the time. And then, when they ran out of petrol, how Naranbhai virtually *ordered* the Pandit to get out and walk all the way to the Kotecha house -- well over an hour away. And then, how he practically forced Juma and her to walk to the celebrations.

"He made us get out and walk, he did," she would say. "He said it was a *very* important historical event!"

THE MIDAS TOUCH

Mrs Naranbhai died many deaths in the immediate aftermath of Independence night. Shahbanu would have to be seen to even before trying to squeeze out the first wife. This fresh threat was far more urgent. But, Mrs Naranbhai was at a complete loss as to where to begin. There was no way Naranbhai would evict that wily Muslim tenant. She already had him dancing on her little finger. And then, a fresh idea came to her: that mysterious, elusive Hazari Baba chap. What if he really *was* a magician? Why not befriend him and enlist his help? She wished she hadn't been so hasty in dismissing him when he had requested an audience with the Mad Girl. She would have to bring him into their orbit under some other pretext. And, the Mad Girl would supply that pretext. Another bold U-turn!

In the meantime, speculation regarding Hazari Baba's alleged gold-making talents reached fever-pitch when somebody produced a scrap of a foreign newspaper which had been included in some packed goods from abroad. The scrap of paper showed a clear shot of a serene man with sparkling eyes, long hair and beard. He was clad in snow-white robes. Below the photo, a brief article stated that the "holy" man's fame was going from strength to strength and having lectured to packed halls all over the USA and Europe, the sage had currently gone into hiding, probably as a result of exhaustion. When the scrap of paper eventually reached Naran Villa, Naranbhai lost no time in jumping to conclusions:

"See? Just as I thought! He's made a lot of money by teaching foreigners to make gold - and then he has got into big-big trouble. So what better place to hide than this small place where nobody is likely to recognise him? All these holy types are crooks!"

"But he has never actually said he is holy. Or that he can teach you to make gold. If you read the article carefully, it says 'lecture'. Surely, that means the man is some kind of teacher, no?" said Mrs Naranbhai, adopting an unusually conciliatory tone.

"Woman! You can't even read English!" he barked. "All these chaps are just set to cash in. Big fashion for Gurus in America at the moment! All those rich American people buy them mansions and cars and sit at their feet smoking ganja and using that as an excuse for all kinds of immoral acts!"

"I still say it doesn't prove anything," said Mrs Naranbhai.

"What other proof do you need? The guy shows up here -- out of nowhere. Doesn't seem to do anything, or live anywhere - appears and disappears like a ghost. Can never be found when he is wanted. Turns up when we are having a crisis. Utters a bit of nonsense and then disappears again! That's the clearest sign of a criminal, don't you see?"

Later that day, both wives, looking like inseparable school friends, accosted Naranbhai on the verandah.

"What is it?" he asked impatiently. These joint representations by both wives could only mean one thing: they had already made up their minds about something.

Mrs Naranbhai looked at Sushilaben, and signalled her to speak:

"Last night, the Mad Girl kept calling out "Rangeelay, Rangeelay..." Sushilaben said.

"Yes, so?" Naranbhai looked at her uncomprehendingly.

"I was just wondering -- maybe that Hazari Baba character could shed some light on that name? I ...we...would like to send for him just to hear what he has to say..."

"All gibberish! What he says, what he doesn't say, what does it matter? He's a big crook! He has run away from America to hide here, in the middle of nowhere."

Mrs Naranbhai took up Sushilaben's case: "No, whatever he is, whoever he is, I agree with Sushilaben. We must call him here and listen to him, seriously. I think he knows something...about madness..."

Naranbhai was suddenly gripped by that all-too-familiar panic that took root in him every time the two wives were of one mind over something. This kind of inter-wife solidarity he could certainly do without. There was only one way out: surrender!

But he had enough presence of mind to resolve that if and when the Baba deigned to come, then he would also definitely invite photographer Patel. A new photograph of Baba, taken at Naran Villa, would be sufficient proof that the wicked man was hiding in an obscure East African country. And, if and when in the future the FBI or CIA or some such important organisation began an investigation, then Naranbhai would play a key role in catching the crook. It might bring a medal, or even a reward. And, it might just provide the big break Naranbahi so badly needed to recover his reputation after a series of disasters, personal and professional.

Jannsani was summoned and assigned the task of tracking down the elusive Baba and ordering him to report to Naran Villa at his earliest convenience.

THE BIG SWING

"Yes, my memories of Independence night are quite vivid. I wouldn't know where to begin.One day maybe I'll write my memoirs, or maybe I won't. Anyway, enough about me. Tell me more about that house you moved into in 1973," said Camilla.

It is obvious to me that although she is trying to sound casual about it, she has a definite connection with that house. I decide to spin it out a bit. She wants more clues about the Indian people who had lived in our house, so I will talk about everything else but that.

I tell her about the flat roof terrace secured by green railings -- or at least they must have once been painted green. I tell her about the semi-circular verandah at the front of the house. And my favourite place on that verandah. A big, swinging hammock which had once been covered in flowery plastic. It had tattered very badly. Seeing that it was my favourite place for studying, Mama Safia had had a new cloth covering made for that seat. But I knew about the flowery plastic of the old days because I'd seen a photograph of that seat in that old album. It had struck me as decidedly odd.

"Strange, isn't it?" I said to her. "Colour photos must have been so expensive in those days, you'd think at least a couple of family members would be sitting on the swinging-seat for the picture. It was just a photo of the seat, with nobody on it."

"Are you sure you haven't still got that scrapbook?" she asks again. I'm sure she's asked that question before. She continues: "After all, you didn't come out in the Expulsion. You came at your leisure. Surely you could have carried something like that? One scrapbook doesn't take up much space or weight. Something that was such a vital pastime in your childhood, how could you have left it behind?"

I decide not to answer. Instead, I chat about this and that -- the weather, the crowded tubes. I know this game. I have to appear reticent and she has to appear not too eager...

MADLY IN LOVE

"Tea, Baba?" Mrs Naranbhai asked when Baba had finished his fourth helping of lunch. How the hell could he eat so much and still be slender as a stem?

"Later, later," the Baba said softly. "Can I please meet the girl now? She, whose voice flows like liquid gold...?"

After a great deal of difficulty, and some six weeks of searching high and low, Hazari Baba had finally been tracked down by Jannasani. The servant had at once conveyed the urgent message that Mrs Naranbhai the Second, First Lady of Naran Villa, would like him to come to lunch at his earliest convenience. Hazari Baba had said he would be delighted to do so, provided he could get a few minutes alone to talk to the Mad Girl.

Hazari Baba's interview with the Mad Girl lasted exactly *twenty-seven minutes*. All that while Naranbhai and his women paced outside the room, wondering what the outcome would be - whether she would kick or scream, or scratch him - or whether she would simply break into song. Patel the photographer, camera in hand, waited with them, anxiously. But there was an eerie silence from within and only the very slightest murmur of voices. Hazari Baba emerged from the room looking as radiant and calm as when he had gone in and his demeanour gave no clue as to whether or not he had made an important breakthrough.

He glided past the gawking household members and headed for the big swing on the verandah. Patel positioned his camera. The others followed, fast on his heels, all eyes and ears in case Baba should start speaking while still on the move. But they were disappointed. Baba never spoke while moving. He never spoke while eating or drinking. He settled into the swing and began swaying gently -- deep in thought. Finally he opened his mouth and asked in a soft voice:

"What about that tea you offered earlier?"

Eight people scattered in various directions to order the tea for which Jannasani was already boiling water. When Jannasani walked onto the verandah with the single cup of tea, eight people followed, close-by in retinue fashion, eyes fixated on the cup, giving the impression of an important trophy rather than a mere cup of tea being carried in. And, as the Baba took his first tentative sip they held their breath. When he took the second sip, they relaxed. As Baba's sips got longer and longer and more thoughtful, it dawned on everyone, with some disappointment, that whatever he had found out, he was in no hurry to tell. But then Baba was never in a hurry -- for anything. And Baba also had the annoying habit of talking about mundane matters, especially if he sensed that people were on tenterhooks for words of wisdom. After a few contemplative slurps, he finally spoke:

"This Kenya tea is truly first-class. Aahhh...tea!" and he let out a beaming smile, just in time for Patel's camera going "futtuchutch".

Naranbhai sank into the easy chair opposite the swing. This Baba was infuriating, but at least the photo was safely in hand. The women hovered nearby. Shushilaben was about to go in and see whether the Mad Girl was OK, when the Baba, slowly draining the dregs of his tea-cup down his throat, put the cup down and said:

"She's in love. That's the problem."

They stared at him in disbelief. These holy guys said weird things at the best of times.

Naranbhai spoke first: "But she is mad. Who would love a mad girl?"

"I didn't say anybody loved her. I said *she* is in love," Baba clarified, cool as a cucumber, his luminescence growing by the second so that those who looked hard might actually have seen a kind of halo about his shoulder length, semi-golden locks.

They were all stunned into silence. Naranbhai was seething. All that pretended madness and that pointless singing at opportune and inopportune moments - all that expenditure on doctors and quacks and cures and remedies - and all the while it had been nothing more than illicit love-shove. He felt completely cheated and done out of vital funds. Somewhere in the house, Naranbhai kept a small notebook in which he had recorded every single item of expenditure connected to Mad Girl Kirti and the many cures that had been tried over the years. And now, this Baba too, would probably have to be paid something for his trouble. But Naranbhai felt he should first get his money's worth:

"OK, so who's the rascal? I want a name."

"His name is not important. She owes him something. What is important is that her madness will not vanish until she is reunited with him and can repay the debt..."

"Reunited? *Re* --? You don't mean she has already been with him?" Naranbhai felt completely betrayed.

"So to speak...these pangs of separation have unhinged her...." Baba said cryptically.

"Please explain!" Naranbhai barked. His friend, Pandit Suddenly, who had also been invited to lunch to provide a second opinion on Baba's prognosis of the Mad Girl, gave him a disapproving look. The Pandit was clearly bowled over by the Baba. Within a few seconds of meeting him, it was obvious to all and sundry that the part-time Pandit, something of a guru himself, had felt extremely threatened by the Baba and had decided that the best course of action was to play "chela" to the mentor and senior Guru.

"Naranbhai, with all due respect, that's not the way to speak to his Holiness the Serene Hazari Baba of Amroha, Saver of Souls and Mender of Hearts."

"I never knew heart-repair machines drank so much tea," said Naranbhai, still smarting at the possibility that there had been an illicit love affair going on right under his nose, under his own roof, and he had known nothing about it.

The Baba smiled. He had encountered many Naranbhais in his time. He never judged them, he merely observed. There were always those in this world for whom everything, however great or small, felt completely out of control if it managed to happen without their direct intervention.

Mrs Naranbhai stumbled in quickly: "Baba, please forgive my husband. He doesn't always think before speaking. Can you please tell us more about her love affair? Anything more we could do to help her?"

Sushilaben looked at her gratefully. Battle-axe second wife she may be, but in crises such as these she always showed herself to be more levelheaded than Naranbhai. It was very sweet of her to take such a conciliatory tone over the matter of the madness of her husband's first wife's offspring.

"No, there is nothing you can do. Her soul is trapped. Just let her sing. Let her be. She is singing his songs...their souls are enmeshed elsewhere -- in some other reality. Don't try to drag her away from that plane of blissful existence..."

Naranbhai had had enough. "I demand to know the boy's name, and I want to talk to him, NOW!" he yelled.

"He's not a boy," said Baba , " - although at one time he must have been. I was a boy once and so were you. Her Beloved is none other than the mystic-musician-poet Rangeelay Khan. He departed this earthly plane some 500 years ago."

Sushilaben, Kamini-masi, Nalini and Mrs Naranbhai stared at him open-mouthed but Naranbhai just shot up from his deck chair and immediately dug into the Baba:

"I know your types. All this bhoot-shoot stuff is what keeps you guys in bread and ghee. So you mean to tell me that a man who has been dead for 500 years visits my mad daughter in the night and makes her sing?"

"That is not what I said," the Baba said softly, totally impervious to Naranbhai's belligerent tone. "I said their souls are enmeshed. He sings -- through her. She can't have him physically, so she has given up her body to his soul. He permeates her entire being. There is nothing she can do. She and he are like one. It is not a conscious decision -- she didn't choose this. He chose *her* as his representative on earth. He departed this earthly plane before singing all the songs he wanted to sing. The soul yearns for whatever is left incomplete or unfulfilled on this plane, you know!"

"So, he chooses a mad girl to go on singing his toon-taan tunes? If he wanted someone who could sing, wouldn't he have picked on a more competent singer -- someone like Lata Mangeshkar?"

"Who knows? Perhaps he already has," Baba said quietly.

And then, determined to go on being obtuse, he added: "Maybe there are so many tunes that he has to have several representatives? Maybe all singers on this earth *are* his soul embodiments ...?"

"Now I've really heard it all, I really have. Holy men of the past looking to occupy the bodies of mad girls in the 20th century!" snorted Naranbhai.

Baba smiled. "There are many definitions of madness. It's all a question of who is being penetrated by whom..." he said softly

"Penetrate...you don't mean? No! Please, tell me, she's still a virgin, yes?"

"Depends how you define virginity..." the Baba was clearly enjoying himself. Pandit Suddenly felt he ought to intervene as he 'suddenly' sympathised with Naranbhai's distress.

"Please Baba, Your Holiness the Serene, Saver of Souls and Mender of Hearts. Pardon me for speaking frankly and so suddenly, but you know what he means. We are not as educated as you are. We are simple, humble people. What do we know about all this high talk of souls suddenly penetrating souls? What he means is, - you know - is she still a virgin, or has she suddenly done things with this ghost?"

"What ghost?" the Baba could be very obtuse when he wanted.

"This Rangeelay Khan character - you know the one who's been dead..."

"Yes, but who said he was a ghost?" Baba fixed him with twinkling, beady eyes.

"Well, when you die don't you become a ghost? A bhoot?"

"He is not dead. He's just in another time, another space. And, on this plane, he lives in Kirti's heart, mind, body.... his Being is manifested through her vocal chords "

A hush fell over everyone as they tried to grapple, as much with hearing the Mad Girl's real name being used in conversation, as with these new earth-shattering facts of life ....and death.

Mrs Naranbhai, practical as ever finally spoke up: "So what is the cure, Baba? Can his spirit be chased out from her body?"

"That might unhinge her completely. She may be happy as she is," Baba answered.

"Yes but *we* are not happy," complained Naranbhai. "This invisible soul-husband of hers, whoever he is, is causing us a lot of problems. She's caterwauling those meaningless songs day and night and embarrassing me all the time..."

Baba smiled an enigmatic smile.

Sushilaben dared to speak for the first time. As a retired first-wife, she was under strict instructions to never speak of her own accord in the presence of her husband and the second wife, particularly when there were guests.

"With all due respect, the songs are not that meaningless. I find the words are always quite appropriate. It's uncanny. Baba's theory really explains everything. I agree with him, we should just let her be, and live out her days whichever way God wishes..."

Sushilaben was clearly hugely relieved that her only daughter's inexplicable madness might, after all, be the result of some soul trickery on the part of some past holy man. That was a far more palatable explanation than the possibility that her own and Naranbhai's unbridled lust and the resulting illicit wedding-night (or afternoon) in the ruins of an old palace could have resulted in her only child being punished.

Her little speech emboldened her ally, Nalini the Widow, to speak: "But this mystic or holy man or whatever he is, he was a Muslim, no? Khans are usually Muslims. Why would he choose a *Hindu* girl to represent him on earth?" She said it more to the space in front of her than to anyone in particular. The Pandit and Naranbhai both fixed the Baba with a stern gaze which said: Go on! Let's hear you talk your way out of this one!

Baba's face was expressionless as they waited on tenterhooks for an explanation.

Proceedings were rudely - although for Naranbhai, delightfully - interrupted when Shahbanu arrived at the house wanting to borrow a hammer.

"I want to put up a picture..." she began to explain, but before she could finish, Naranbhai, his previous black mood completely wiped out, jumped up saying:

"What? All by yourself? Don't be so unreasonable, good lady! Don't make us all have heart attacks! What if you should hit your

285

finger or thumb by mistake? Can't have you disfiguring your bhindi-like fingers..."

And before anybody else could say anything, he had already said: "Go on home, please. I'll be there as soon as I can...."

The second Mrs Naranbhai had reached boiling point as she looked up and saw Baba looking directly at her. Despite herself, she lowered her eyes, bashfully. Bloody creep! He seemed to be able to read minds! On second thoughts, perhaps he *would* be worth consulting....? If he knew about making gold and silver, and love affairs with ghosts, then perhaps he also knew something about ancient, untraceable poisons?

A QUICK, SIMPLE AFFAIR

Soon after Independence, the toothless matchmaker appeared at Naran Villa: "What is this I hear, Naranbhai? Consulting all kinds of unreliable Muslim beggars in the matter of your daughter's madness?"

She had, on numerous occasions in the past, tried to persuade Naranbhai to get the Mad Girl married off, but the Mohini-Sohini disaster had brought all negotiations to an abrupt halt -- Naranbhai swearing he would never again have dealings with the old hag.

"All our elder have said it," continued the toothless old woman with her mouth spitting scented herbs in various directions: "A beautiful young woman running loose like that is bound to go mad, sooner or later! I heard that Muslim beggar-man told you the girl is in love with some dead man? Ha-ha! What do you expect?"

"So, what do you want me to do?" Naranbhai asked with some irritation and still smarting over the Mohini-Sohini business that had brought so much shame on his good name, to say nothing of the resulting election defeat some seven years earlier.

"Marriage. Being married and the love of a husband will soon cure her madness," the matchmaker said, with conviction. Also, business was a little slow these days since co-ed. schools had ensured that boys and girls would meet and pair-off without parental intervention. The Toothless Matchmaker lived in constant dread of the day when this kind of "love marrige" would be the norm and she would starve to death. And, to make matters worse, there was this loony in the vicinity, wearing a white gown with a beard to match, talking utter tripe and nonsense about love-shove.

She added: "Instead of concentrating on finding her a husband, you waste time with that weird Muslim Baba chap. He is completely mad, don't you know?"

"But who would want to marry my mad girl?" Naranbhai asked with genuine curiosity and, more than just a little pleased that there might, after all, be a way to rid himself of the daughter and her madness -- ever a thorn in his side.

"Make it worth the boy's while, and he will. Young men these days, they'll do anything for money," the Matchmaker replied her toothless mouth full of half-chewed herbs.

But the first wife, Sushilaben, absolutely refused to entertain the idea. She guessed it was probably a plot by the second wife, Mrs Naranbhai, to get rid of both mother and daughter from under her roof and then, extend a fuller control over her husband.

"And what sort of man marries just for money? Is it fair to abandon your daughter to a greedy man like that?" Sushilaben asked Naranbhai rebelliously.

The second Mrs Naranbhai lost no time in coming to his rescue: "What sort of mother are you Sushilaben? Marriage is the best cure don't you know? Don't you want to see your daughter happily married and well again? "

There was no answer to that.

Naranbhai found himself leaning more and more towards the idea of a marriage for the Mad Girl. He would have to discredit Hazari Baba to his first wife:

"See?" he challenged Sushilaben, "when we asked him how a Muslim soul came to possess a Hindu body, he had no answer. These holy guys think we are stupid!"

"I still think what he said makes a lot of sense," Sushilaben replied but, unable to offer any solid evidence to support the Baba's theory, could say no more about it.

"Yes, you *would* think that. Women love all that sort of thing!" he scolded her.

Later that afternoon, he teased his second wife: "Women! Just give them soul-shoal stuff and they lap it up! For all I know, you're probably carrying on with someone's soul behind my back," he said it half-jokingly, but it had been a long and trying day and Mrs Naranbhai felt hurt that he had lumped her in with the first wife. She wanted to be as unlike Sushilaben as possible.

"At least you have the courtesy to say 'soul' - whereas men don't even need that excuse. They can go to a woman, openly and unashamedly only for her body and then pretend to be in love with her soul."

Naranbhai noted with some satisfaction that she was still smarting over his impromptu visit, last week, to the delectable Shahbanu, to help her hammer in a picture-hook.

Just then, Patel the photographer stepped onto the verandah looking most perturbed:

"Naranbhai, that Baba of yours...the one who came to lunch the other day. I processed that roll and it's really strange, but all I've got is a picture of the swinging-seat. Nobody on it! I know he glides very quickly and noiselessly, but I tell you, he was definitely sitting there when I took the picture - yet - "

Naranbhai and his second wife both stepped forward to see the picture of the empty swing. Naranbhai was not impressed:

"Patel, you fool! He must have got up before you took the shot. I know how you fuss and how long you take -- this angle, that angle, look right, look left. And, before you know it, the subject has got bored and walked away!"

But Mrs Naranbhai was strangely silent. In her mind, there was no doubt that Hazari Baba had some very special powers -- powers she could do with. But, how to get a private meeting with such an elusive creature?

Three years later, the toothless old-hag matchmaker stood before Naranbhai with yet another suitable match for the Mad Girl. By now, Naranbhai was more willing to listen to any scheme that might bring about a cure for the Mad Girl. She explained:

"He is partially sighted. So he is having great difficulty finding a bride. He wants to marry because he says he must have a son. Ideally, he should have a normal wife who can look after him through old age. Not that he's old now. He is only forty...."

"But she is only sixteen - " muttered Naranbhai.

"So what? A man can be any age. You're not going to get someone her own age to marry her. Boys, these days! So fussy! I should know," the matchmaker said bitterly.

"Are you sure she might start feeling better?" asked Naranbhai. "What about all that singing -- that dead man's songs, like Hazari Baba was saying....."

"Oh!" exclaimed the Matchmaker, throwing her hands up in despiar. "You're not still going on about the silly beggar-Baba and his silly stories. Those things only happen in stories. In real life, women need to get married to feel better about everything."

"Are you sure she will get better?" asked Naranbhai, clearly keen for somebody else to make the vital decision for him.

"Guaranteed! Just after the wedding night, you wait and see. She will be a new person," the matchmaker was extremely positive, not least because the nearly blind chap had offered her a huge fee for locating a young, fertile bride for him.

On securing Naranbhai's approval, she hurried back to the prospective bridegroom:

"OK, there is some slight hysteria problem. Otherwise very good girl. Virgin, of course. Very beautiful. Fair. Long hair. Great singing voice. Wait till you hear her songs. She's a bit -- well just a bit simple, childlike. Don't expect her to behave like an adult. Otherwise, you will have full control over her...where else would you get that, hain? Girls, these days, they just come into your house and take over -- start telling you to do this, don't do that, sit here, stand there, eat this, don't eat that! Not Kirti. She's in her own world, poor thing. So innocent and so perfect err...well, at least her body is perfect."

The man was delighted. A docile, simple, childlike wife was exactly what he had dreamed about. He readily accepted the one and only condition that the bride's mother would accompany her to her new home as the girl needed a lot of care.

Some days later, the second Mrs Naranbhai was at her joyous best. She had ordered a special thick gold neck-chain to present to the matchmaker. She felt eternally indebted to the toothless old hag for ridding her of the first wife and the mad daughter in one master-stroke, especially as her plea to consult Hazari Baba had, so far, brought no response. She chided herself for being so silly as to think that that shifty Baba could have helped her. No, she was doing just fine -- without his help.

The Mad Girl's wedding was a quick, surreptitious affair. No guests. No grand rituals, no song or dance. Just a few mantras around the fire -- with Pandit Suddenly in attendance and another out-of-town Pandit to sanctify the ritual. The toothless old-hag matchmaker, once again admitted into the family circle, occupied a seat of honour during the proceedings for having successfully executed such a difficult and delicate bond between a man who was partially sighted, and a woman who was almost, completely, out of her mind.

All through the ceremonies, the Mad Girl remained strangely compliant and did as the Pandit asked. But Naranbhai wasn't taking any chances. That night, he locked the door from outside after pushing the bridegroom into the bridal chamber for the wedding night that was to take place within Naran Villa since the bridegroom's house was several hundred miles away, somewhere in Rwanda.

The night passed without incident. There were no screams, no laughter, and certainly no songs. At nine o'clock in the morning, Naranbhai unlocked the door and stood there. The Mad Girl was lying down -- her eyes wide open as usual. The bridegroom, lying next to her, stirred and sat up in bed on sensing Naranbhai at the door. Naranbhai posed the vital question, with a slight gesture of the head. He didn't use words. The blushing bridegroom nodded slowly -- again, no words, but a clear positive. Naranbhai never stopped to think how an allegedly partially sighted man had seen him so clearly as to respond to his unvoiced question.

Satisfied that all was well, Naranbhai went downstairs to break the news to his largely female household that the wedding night had been a success. The women giggled and tittered - all except Sushilaben, the Mad Girl's mother. She sobbed, but her tears were tears of relief. An hour later, the bridegroom came down, fully dressed. After heartily tucking into Mrs Naranbhai's halva-puri breakfast, he announced he was going out, 'on business.' He never returned.

Later, they found that the Mad Girl's wedding jewellery had vanished, as had the few hundred shillings she had received as gifts.

RHYME & REASON

Soon after the Mad Girl's first meeting with Hazari Baba, she had started singing a brand new song: *"How will it come, when death finally comes?"* and now she sang it with renewed strength and vigour, her powerful, lucid, voice piercing through the silvery night. The first verse of the song urged the Beloved to stay close on a dark and moonless night. It was a song about an abandoned lover bemoaning the spectre of a velvety, inky night that had gorged upon the blood of the setting sun to satisfy its hunger. As the night deepened and darkened, the sun threatened never to rise. But the night said, 'you must, you must' otherwise what will I eat tomorrow evening? Whose blood will I feast on?' And the distraught lover asked the Beloved to come closer, closer, as another greedy night opened its jaws to gobble up the sun....

On this particular night, as she sang it, the household looked on pitifully. They felt immensely sorry for her because, whereas previously she had only been a Mad Girl, now she was a mad *woman* whose husband had abandoned her after one night. And she didn't even know it! As they listened and felt sorry for her, (not because she was mad, but because her husband had walked out on her) a few Bombay Gardens' residents gradually wandered over, hypnotised by the catchy, new melody.

On seeing the small crowd growing, Mrs Naranbhai made the usual cutting remarks: "They all come like it's a free tamasha or circus." And, turning to her husband she said sarcastically, "See? If all your big-big business schemes fail, then here you have a way to feed all your hangers-on. Charge everybody to come and listen to this crazy girl..."

Mrs Naranbhai could have carried on this vein for centuries, if her aunt, Kamini Masi, had not suddenly changed the topic:

"See, what I can't understand is why her songs don't rhyme. Poetry should always rhyme, otherwise how can it be poetry?" she asked.

Mrs Naranbhai thought about the question for a moment and then said: "They don't rhyme, because remember, they aren't really *her* songs. Remember what that crazy Baba said, all those years ago? He said she is singing somebody else's songs -- some man

292

who lived hundreds of years ago. Maybe they didn't have rhyming in those days?"

Although the marriage cure had failed, Naranbhai was still keen to appear unconvinced by any theory that painted Hazari Baba in a favourable light.

"Rhyme-shyme nothing!" scowled Naranbhai on hearing this dialogue between the two women. "What that shady crook-Baba was saying was that the singer of those olden days -- something-Khan of somewhere -- left this earthly plane before he could sing all the songs he wanted to sing. Not surprising! Nowadays, we may tolerate it, but in those days, I tell you, who would have allowed him to sing such meaningless, rhyme-less toon-taans? They would have skinned him alive. That's probably how he died!"

"*No*, that is not how it happened," a soft, silky voice had spoken.

Naranbhai whizzed around and was staggered to see Hazari Baba standing in the moonlight. How did the fellow move without ever making a sound? And where the hell had he been all these years?

"What are you doing loitering here?" Naranbhai asked belligerently. "Never there when we send for you, and then slithering about quietly like a snake in the night!"

Baba ignored the question. Instead, he closed his eyes and began:

"Rangeelay Khan did not die because his songs were tuneless, or rhymeless. Quite the opposite. He died because the songs were too tuneful. So tuneful that a certain Princess of long ago, who had had some difficulty in falling asleep, found that his songs were like a soothing balm that would put her to sleep..."

"So? What do you mean?" asked Naranbhai, failing to see the relevance.

"I'm saying the Princess liked his voice so much she couldn't get enough of it. And then, when he was ordered to sing for her every single night, but refused to do so..."

"How do you know all this? Were you actually there, or what?" asked Naranbhai.

"In a manner of speaking...yes, and no," replied the Baba. "Anyway, I see that despite what I said, you forced Kirti into marriage. And, did it change anything? No, because it can't. Those whom God joins together no man can cast assunder."

And, before they could ask him what on earth he meant by that ridiculous comment, he launched into full flow:

"Let me tell you a story. In a way it's a story without a beginning, or middle, or even an end. Because, you see, it is still going on...."

The Mad Girl suddenly let out a sharp scream and fainted.

Two weeks later, her pregnancy was confirmed.

WHOSE BABY?

Seven months and some days later, a beautiful, normal, healthy, baby girl was born to the Mad Girl whose mental condition had deteriorated since her sham of a marriage. Now, there were regular outbursts. Fits of anger, followed by hours of whimpering, followed by cryptic songs. It had been a nightmare of a birth. In the end, the presiding midwife had relinquished all responsibility and ordered Naranbhai to send the girl to the big hospital for a caesarean. Naranbhai reflected morosely, that marriage had made no difference to the Mad Girl's condition. If anything, she was worse than before. All he had gained in return for the thousands of shillings spent on persuading the bridegroom, was this little granddaughter -- female offspring who, in the future, would bring more expense. But in a surprising twist of fate, the second Mrs Naranbhai suddenly expressed an interest in raising the girl as her own:

"Her mother cannot look after her. And her grandmother has quite enough on her plate nursing the Mad Girl. Please, can I have her? I've always wanted a daughter," she coaxed Naranbhai. It was agreed the baby would officially belong to the second wife.

Mrs Naranbhai was nobody's fool. Already resentful of Sushilaben's position in the house, she didn't want to provide any additional justification or brand new role as legitimate doting grandmother for the retired first wife. This baby, the newest acquisition of the family, would remain under her *own* control and hegemony.

"A little sister for my three boys - Doctor, Dentist, Lawyer" she said fondly, never missing an opportunity to remind all and sundry that she had borne THREE male heirs for Naranbhai. So, while the Mad Girl's breast milk continued to ooze out and soil her clothes and bed linen, an Indian wet-nurse was employed to feed the baby.

"*She* doesn't know any better," Mrs Naranbhai explained. "Everybody knows it's mine. Just giving birth to a child doesn't make it your own, you know? One night of lust, and others have to bear the consequences...."

Sushilaben sobbed helplessly at the way the second wife had twisted the facts of what might well have been the rape of the Mad Girl by her husband of one night.

If a lie is repeated often enough, it eventually becomes the truth. And, in time, everybody else also forgot that this beautiful little baby-girl had been brought into the world by the Mad Girl. Soon, Mrs Naranbhai had everybody believing that she'd had this baby herself. In time, she actually began to believe she had conceived and carried the baby in her body and then given it birth. She started to recount horror tales about what a long and arduous labour it had been. Ownership is like that. If you behave like you own something then, very soon, you do.

But undisputed ownership of the baby soon took the delicious edge off Mrs Naranbhai's latest acquisition. Although keen to possess the baby in order to undermine the first wife, she soon tired of the humdrum task of keeping the baby amused and entertained. And then she thanked her lucky stars that she'd had the good sense to allow Jannasani's little potato-eyed nephew Juma to join the household. Juma showed a God-given talent for looking after babies. Soon, the baby would be pacified by nobody but Juma. When she moved onto solids, only Juma was allowed to feed her. And, when she was in the mood to play, only Juma's antics amused her. And then, when nobody was looking, Juma would quickly carry her to the Mad Girl's room, where mother and baby would play for a bit. The Mad Girl's entire countenance changed on seeing the baby's face. Then, as soon as there were sounds of Mrs Naranbhai's flip-flop chappalls padding down the hallway, Juma would grab the infant and run out again. Even so, on most days, he made sure the Mad Girl had her baby for a quick, surreptitious suckle.

One night, as Juma was trying to clear out of the Mad Girl's room with the baby, Mrs Naranbhai caught up with him:

"What the hell are you doing here?" she barked.

"Nothing, nothing, just taking the baby for a walk..." he stammered, guilty as hell.

"A walk? In the house? Did you go near the Mad Girl's room? Did you?" she was holding and twisting his ear now. "Useless fellow! You do nothing all day except play with that baby. Is that work, I ask you? Is that what I hired you for? I took pity on you because you said your whole family and your village was destroyed by ants. A likely story! And what have you done for me in return? Just eat, sleep and play with the baby! You eat and eat. See how fat you're getting?" she prodded his round tummy, adding: "No more evening meals!"

Juma realised he was being punished, not for getting fat, but for disobeying orders and letting the Mad Girl feed her own baby. He put the baby to bed and when he came down he saw that the usual offering of leftovers after the Naran Villa dinner had not been placed on his tin-plate. He decided to go out for a long walk.

Kamla, who had heard the whole of Mrs Naranbhai's scolding from her upstairs room, suddenly felt at one with Juma who was, after all, nearly her age. She knew how it felt to have no mother or father, and now, to all intents and purposes, no sister either. Bimla had become somebody else, and Kamla felt completely alone in the world. She lost no time in stealing into the kitchen and filling some leftover puris from dinner into a large handkerchief, after which she set out via the back door to search for Juma, hoping he wouldn't have gone too far away. She caught up with him on the narrow dirt-track leading to Bombay Gardens and handed him the food, which Juma ate with undisguised relish. Looking after a baby all day was hungry work. Kamla promised him she would bring him scraps of food every night. But, she couldn't have known that in so doing, she was securing her survival in the drama that was to follow in less than six years from this time...

HAZARI BABA TELLS A STORY

Hazari Baba, who hadn't been seen since the Mad Girl's pregnancy and delivery, materialised early on a Saturday morning, when Pandit Suddenly was out in the shared backyard of Bombay Gardens doing his daily homage to the morning sun. As he finished his mutterings with closed eyes and turned the small can of water to pour the water over his face from a height, he became aware that the flow of water was being interrupted. It was pouring out all right, but it wasn't reaching his face. He opened his eyes in bewilderment to see the tall figure of Baba with his hands cupped together somewhere below the vessel, catching the water, and drinking it from his hands.

"What the -? Oh, now look what you suddenly made me do?" said the irritated Pandit. "I've spoken suddenly before finishing my prayers, now I'll have to do them all over again….and the sun is suddenly too high. It has to be done at the exact….." the Pandit rambled on.

Hazari Baba dried his mouth using the back of his hand and said, casually: " The sun? Too high for you Pandit-ji? If you want to pay homage to the sun, you could even do it at night. It's the same sun you know? High or low, seen or unseen from earth, it doesn't change you know?"

"No, indeed it doesn't Baba. Good of you to point that out to me," the Pandit said somewhat sarcastically, adding, "but rituals are rituals, and they have to be performed properly, at the proper time. Now, Baba, the sun is where it is. In a fixed place. But what about you Baba? Where are you these days? We hardly ever see you? Where do you live?" he asked as chummily as possible.

Baba smiled. "Everywhere is my house. Wherever you see the sky, there is my ceiling. And wherever the ground, there my floor. Wherever my hearts rests is home. Wherever I stop a while, that becomes my nest."

The Pandit chuckled. "Baba, you do suddenly say the nicest things. Very good, very good. But I meant, not just your *house*, but what about your things? Where do you keep your things?"

"Yes, things. That's where human beings come undone. Even the prisoner will tell you - even in prison, when a prisoner is moved from cell to cell - each time he moves he has accumulated more belongings. One acquires things -- that is the way it is with humans. Wherever they settle, they collect goods and chattels that bind their feet."

Pandit Suddenly was impressed, although he realised Baba had completely evaded the question. The Pandit himself was very fond of his belongings, such as they were, and the thought of ever being parted from even a single incense holder or tinsel-lined calendar depicting Hindu gods would have rendered him inconsolable.

They were interrupted by the D'Sa Number Three:

"Baba!" the child said. "Please tell us a story. You said something about a sleepless princess one day...."

Pandit Suddenly shot the boy a hateful look, "Don't interrupt suddenly when big people are talking!" he growled and then, turning his back on the child said: "Baba, tell me more about your methods. How is that you slide away unseen? Can you teach me? How does one become invisible?"

But Hazari Baba ignored the Pandit and said to the D'Sa child: "Stories are good for children. They can learn many things. Now, this is the story of the Sleepless Princess and Rangeelay Khan. The mystic musician....you'd like that one, yes?"

"Oh yes!" enthused D'Sa Number Three who had now been joined by various siblings: "The something Khan who possesses the Mad Girl's body and makes her sing. Please tell us..."

"He doesn't possess anything or anyone. He has departed this earth. His songs are left behind, that's all. They have to be sung."

"So how did he die?" asked the children, always game for anything even remotely ghoulish.

"He didn't die. He simply departed to another plane...."

The children were hooked, but their curiosity had yet to be satisfied:

"How did Rang....Rangee....Ranjy Khan depart, I mean what caused his...?"

Baba suddenly sat down cross-legged in the middle of the backyard. The Pandit leapt with surprise and made as if to go and fetch a stool from his house. Baba stopped him with a gesture of the hand and motioned him to sit down as well. The Pandit hesitated, holding his greying dhoti tighter around him, whilst Baba, in flowing robes of snow-white sat down happily on the dry, muddy ground of the backyard.

"Sit, Pandit-ji, and let me tell you all what happened..."

The Pandit had no choice but to obey and no sooner had the two men settled in a cross-legged position in the middle of the yard, than all the D'Sa children immediately surrounded them, soon to be followed by their parents. On seeing the entire group sitting on the ground in the middle of the backyard, more of the neighbours came out and joined them, without really knowing what was going on. Eventually, word reached Naran Villa that Baba was holding an impromptu audience in Bombay Gardens and the three Naranbhai boys, Doctor, Dentist and Lawyer were soon sprinting along to Bombay Gardens, along with the orphan Kamla. Mr and Mrs Naranbhai followed to see what all the excitement was about.

"I want to tell you a story," began Baba. "But it is a story without a beginning, middle or end...."

"Yes, no head or tail, just like you..." thought Naranbhai, but he kept his mouth shut because the entire audience, which had rapidly swelled, now gazed at Baba with hypnotic awe.

"Tell me friends, how can a man achieve what he had set out to achieve and still be put to death? How?"

They listened with their mouths opens, unable to believe that such a thing can happen.

"It happened like this you see. Once upon a time there was a Princess -- Princess Jagwati. She had not been able to sleep for a long time..."

The sun had reached its equatorial midpoint and Hazari Baba was still in full flow. Nobody had known the Baba to stay in one place for such a long time. They hung on his every word. Baba had woven the story with many colourful details. At appropriate points he had interrupted the story and sung the original songs as and when they appeared in the story, including all the atrocious songs sung by the half-baked musicians who had attempted to put the insomniac princess to sleep. His mimicry brought much welcome comic relief in a story that was, otherwise, completely and almost unbearably gripping...

Baba had reached a vital point in his narrative:

"Now, the Princess just could not accept the fact that the musician Rangeelay Khan did not want the prize -- marriage to her, that is. You see Rangeelay Khan was one of those very fortunate people who had already married the love of his life. He would not, he said, take a second wife - be she a Princess or a Queen - while his wife was still alive. And then, just in case anyone thought of killing his wife, he added that he would not take another wife under any circumstances. And should his wife die before him, he would devote the rest of his life to her remembrance. Now, you must realise that this sort of thing was very rare in those days when men could have many wives...."

Naranbhai fumed inwardly. He felt sure the Baba was having a go at him for having more than one wife.

Baba continued: "Rangeelay Khan said to the King, 'For my reward I want only that I am free to go back to my village and be with my wife. That is why I cannot marry your daughter.' The King was touched by Rangeelay Khan's devotion to his wife and immediately granted his wish. It would all have ended happily, except that the King's daughter, the sleepless Princess, just could not accept the fact that someone could prefer their own wife to *her*. She refused to believe that Rangeelay Khan did not want her, despite her beauty and the enormous fortune that would have been part of her marriage settlement. Now, there is so much wickedness in this world...." Hazari Baba paused.

"So what happened, what?" chorused the D'Sa urchins who had never been silent for such a long stretch of time, not even at school.

"I will return one day and continue the story. It should only be told and heard at night..." Baba started to get up. Everybody got up in dismay, creaking, groaning, gripping their knees and holding on to their backs. Nobody was used to sitting on the ground any more. Only Baba got up without so much as touching the ground - sprightly yet serene - and he began to glide away. While everybody else brushed off the mud and dust from their backsides,

Baba's robes remained as brilliant white as they had ever been. As his departing form disappeared through the back-gate at the end of the yard, Mrs D'Sa spoke first:

"Did you see that? Did you see? I must ask him what washing powder he uses...."

The Pandit, thinking this was a dig at his greying, yellowing dhoti, immediately retorted:

"Washing powder, huh! He doesn't even have a place to live in. He doesn't even have any possessions. He told me so himself. He probably waits for the rain to suddenly wash his robes. Washing powder!" sneered the Pandit.

Lunch was going to be late, for sure and Naranbhai, who liked his food to be on the table at one o'clock sharp, became grumpy:

"When women sitting around listening to stories how can any work ever get done?"

"So, if you're so worried you should have gone home to make the lunch," Mrs Naranbhai chided him.

Her aunt cautioned her: "What are you saying? Is that the way to talk to your husband? The day husbands start cooking, the world will end. Come on, let's go, I'll help you."

"In that case, I'll just pop in at Shahbanu's and make sure her electricity is working properly," announced Naranbhai.

"Her electricity is just fine," said Mrs Naranbhai with undisguised bitterness. "She has no difficulty keeping the current running through you..." she added sarcastically and before she could say anything else, Naranbhai said:

"Anyway, what's the point of my coming home just now? It's not as though my lunch is ready, with everybody sitting around listening to stupid stories...."

"See, see?" whimpered Mrs Naranbhai to her aunt. "He goes there openly now! You think they just sit and talk? He's punishing me for sitting around listening to stories instead of cooking his lunch. You see?"

"Yes, yes," consoled the aunt. "When a husband's heart starts pulling elsewhere, the best thing is to ignore it. He'll always return to you.... for food..."

"But what about her? *Her?*" whimpered Mrs Naranbhai, close to tears. "She never cooks or anything, and he still goes there again and again! I fill his stomach and he goes to *her* to fill his eyes with her cheap beauty...."

"And filling her as well, no doubt...." the aunt began and then stopped, adding: "Never mind, a passion soon spends itself. Best to ignore it. You'll see. He's flying high now, but he'll come crashing down to earth some day. Those cheap women only know how to excite. They don't know how to hold on!"

UNSUNG SONGS

As promised, Hazari Baba materialised in Bombay Gardens that night and resumed his story. D'Sa was annoyed. He had planned to beat his wife that night but now, there was no point. The children would be all distracted and enthralled by Baba and couldn't care less. D'Sa reckoned there was no point in beating their mother unless they were watching. He had convinced himself that he only beat her as a way of setting *them* a good example. So, deprived of an audience to watch his performance, D'Sa decided to remain drinking in the house and leave the others gathered around Baba for some tall yarn of yesteryear. Baba picked up the story where he had left off last time:

"On that very first night when Rangeelay Khan had been summoned out of the Princess's private garden into her bedchamber, the insomniac Princess Jagwati had not only fallen asleep for the first time in ten months, but she had slunk into delicious oblivion as Rangeelay Khan sang. Her attendants were so excited by this unusual sight that they immediately informed the King about the unknown musician. The musician was taken to the King who asked him to claim his reward. The musician said that all he wanted in return for helping the Princess to sleep was to be released from the obligation of having to marry her! He asked to be allowed to return to his village -- to the wife he loved very much.

The King was more than delighted to grant this humble request.

After Rangeelay Khan had left, the Princess woke up from her first sleep in months. It was well past midday and she felt completely refreshed and rested. Realising she hadn't felt so good in a long time, she requested that the unknown musician who had put her into that delicious stupor be presented to her. When told that he had gone back to his village, she was furious. She was already in love with the unseen musician, but when she heard that he had turned down the reward of marriage to her, (something the other contenders would have killed for) she was, understandably, enraged. How *dare* he? Anybody else would have jumped at the chance of marrying a princess, daughter of a powerful king. Who the hell was this unknown upstart to ask as reward only that he be set free from the obligation of having to marry her? The Princess paced up and down, getting angrier and angrier. By the time night fell, she realised she wouldn't be able to sleep. There was only one thing for it. She would have to tell the King to order the unknown singer to sing in her bedchamber every single night otherwise she would never be able to sleep again..."

Mrs Naranbhai looked up at that point and saw that Naranbhai had disappeared. So had Shahbanu. She could no longer concentrate on the story.

In Shahbanu's house, Naranbhai was seated on the slippery plastic-covered sofa while she went to fetch some sunglasses she had wanted him to mend. They had recently fallen and one side had come unhinged. Naranbhai had generously offered to make them "good as new" for her again. Now, as she brought out the glasses and sat beside him, leaning over to show him how they ought to look, his heart flew out of his body and he was suddenly overcome with emotion. He swallowed hard:

"You're the only woman - the only woman - who really understands me. Whenever I try to do something big, my wife - both my wives - just blow it to pieces. No vision, these women! For instance, this new business scheme I'm planning. Distinguished visitors from India will come and...

"Yes-yes, Bhaijaan," she interrupted, determined to refocus his attention on the matter in hand. "Very good. A man with your talents will always have bright new schemes. Now, about these glasses....I'd like you to fix this hinge so that...and then if you could just take a look at that leaky tap in the kitchen....oh! I nearly forgot. That backdoor lock needs oiling, I think.And then..."

He gazed at her with stupefied admiration. She really was a very, very good listener. If only all women could be like her. He wondered how a man could have two wives and still have nobody to listen? He felt very sorry for himself. And then, he broke down and sobbed. More and more these days, whenever he was alone with Shahbanu, he just wanted to cry.

CRISIS

"You've lived through so much history!" I sighed, looking at Camilla with renewed admiration. "I never imagined that the history of my country would would mean so much for ...err... those Indians who were chucked out-- err...your -- personal memories...sorry, I didn't mean it to sound like that...."

"Yes, I know what you mean. Sometimes I think we only became known to the world because we were kicked out. Otherwise, who'd ever heard anything about Indians in Africa? The things I could tell you! When were you born?" asked Camilla.

"I was born in 1966, four years after Independence," I replied.

"So you were only a baby in '66? It was a year of political troubles. I remember it vividly," she brightens up. "I was 14. It felt like war was going to break out. That was the year they deposed the tribal King. But, never mind the King, if you only knew about *my* troubles that year! That was the year of the strangest wedding I have ever attended...anyway, where were you in 66? In your village?"

"I guess I must've been. The village was an important settlement of the King's tribe. Once the King had been ousted from government, all tribe members were treated like criminals for having supported the King. You've never known a village with so many troubles! A year before that, it was apparently almost wiped out by giant killer ants. Luckily, Mama Safia and her family survived by seeing the ants early enough. They start with just one - or two - seemingly harmless and then, as soon as you turn your back, an entire army has arrived and taken over command! Anyway, she spotted the ants early enough, gathered up her sons, and fled to another village. Then, after the ants had left, she returned with the family. The village was full of skeletons and carcasses of animals, because these killer ants eat everything."

"Ants? Giant killer ants?" Camilla has a quizzical look.

"Look, I know you don't believe me, but it's true."

"No, of course, I believe you. It's just that ...well, it sounds so familiar. I used to know a little boy who claimed his entire family had been wiped out by the ants and that his village was destroyed...perhaps it was someone from your village?"

"A boy? What was his name?" I feel very excited. But she's not telling.

"No, maybe there wasn't such a boy. I don't know now. The trouble with being a writer is you make up so many things and then, at the end of the day, the line between fantasy and reality begins to blur. I'm sure I just made it up! But tell me more about the ants..."

"The strange thing is, Mama Safia never spoke about the ants as a tragic thing. Whenever she told me the story -- it had happened before my birth -- she always said the ants brought her luck. Strange thing to say, don't you think?"

"Not that strange if her family survived the onslaught and their fortunes changed."

"One of her sons -- the youngest -- left home after the ant incident. He told his mother he needed a bigger place, bigger challenges. He went to the city to look for work. Mama Safia always said that he brought back something with him that made her the luckiest woman on God's earth. I remember him from my childhood. I was always very close to him. He used to come back home to visit regularly, and then, when I was about five or six, he joined the army -- at the time of the military take-over...err...partial take-over. After that, I never saw him. We heard he was killed. For failing to carry out his duties. He was supposed to mind some prisoners but he let them go. Silly boy!"

Camilla is silent but I can see I have stirred something in her...

"Are you going to write the story of that Princess some day?" I ask, trying to sound casual.

"Hey!" she says, aggressively, "I have a lot to write about, you know? I don't have to recycle some old Indian legend! What I've seen, growing up in East Africa, will fill several volumes. I wish I had paid more attention, but we were so caught up in our own little dramas that the so-called Constitutional Crisis came and went without too many ripples for us..."

And then she starts giggling: "But it was a huge personal crisis for someone I know...it was quite tragic. I shouldn't laugh... but it was *so* funny at the time! "

And with that, she continues to chortle as some long-forgotten memory is awakened.

CURFEW, CURFEW!

1966

It was soon after lunch and, instead of the usual blinding sunshine and intense afternoon heat, the town had turned cold, grey and misty. There was an eerie silence. The streets were desolate and there was smoke rising somewhere over the hills. The strange hush that had suddenly descended on the town was broken by sounds of gunfire. But Naranbhai, more preoccupied with the previous night's episode with Shahbanu and feeling more than just a little sheepish as men were inclined to after a true show of emotion, was determined to 'set the record' straight with Shahbanu. He had left her place the previous evening, feeling and looking like a whimpering child. He could not leave her with that image. He felt that the sooner he could go over to Bombay Gardens and be his normal, gallant, dynamic self, the sooner Shahbanu would start looking up to him again. He resolved to discuss his new, top-secret business venture with her. Sound her out. Perhaps offer her a starring role. He badly needed her to look up to him again. But, as he prepared to go out, armed with the usual black umbrella in one hand and his figurines of the twin-gods in the other, Mrs Naranbhai intercepted him. He observed, with some bitterness, that his second wife had obviously been born with some kind of radar that always enabled her to block his path.

"You can't go out in this! We don't know what is happening," she said in urgent tones. But Naranbhai refused to be deterred. He wasn't going to postpone his image-enchancing plans just because of some gunfire somewhere in the distance. He set out as usual, walking briskly and waving his black umbrella left and right, finishing up huffing and puffing at Bombay Gardens some five minutes later. The residents always kept their front - and back - doors wide open during the day and went freely from each other's houses. Only Shahbanu's door required a knock for anyone to be let in, or even not to be let in, if the caller had chosen an inappropriate time.

Although Naranbhai had never once raised an eyebrow over the matter of Shahbanu's closed door, Mrs Naranbhai had often speculated: "What is this new English fashion of keeping your door shut? Obviously doesn't want to be interrupted...God knows what is going on in there - satin dressing gowns and see-through night-gowns and -- friends in high places, and --"

Naranbhai always managed to turn a deaf ear to such remarks. Mrs Naranbhai's objections were fading dimmer and dimmer in his mind as he crossed the Bombay Gardens' backyard in the direction of Shahbanu's back door. Just then, Mrs D'Sa came running into the communal backyard.

"Big trouble, Naranbhai, big mattata!" she said. "All those gunshots earlier this afternoon - haven't you heard? King. Arrested. Think arrested. Tony heard. BBC. Emergency. No more King. Curfew this evening. Sharp 6 o'clock!" Mrs D'Sa's speech always took a telegraphic form when she had something urgent and juicy to impart.

The D'Sa urchins leapt up and down chanting: "Curfew, curfew, curfew!" They were thrilled by the new word, although they had no idea what it meant. One of them asked his mother: "Mummy, what should we do for the curfew? Do we have to dress up? Will there be singing and dancing? "

"Dunderhead!" replied Mrs D'Sa, and proceeded to explain to her children what curfew meant. In so doing, she deviated from the truth, ever so slightly:

"Curfew means everybody, but everybody has to keep pin-drop silence from six in the evening, or else the askaris with guns will arrest and thrash you all! And all your teeth will end up in your stomach!"

"So, the King has been arrested?" asked Naranbhai. "His tribe won't like that."

And then, thinking he'd better take this sensational news back to Naran Villa instead of calling on Shahbanu just yet, he hesitated for a moment. He quickly changed his mind when he realised that Mrs Naranbhai would only get hysterical and predict that the King's tribe would soon go on a rampage killing and murdering all in its wake, and she would forbid Naranbhai from ever leaving the house again. Mrs Naranbhai, being a relatively new Indian settler, still had her Indian "habsheee-bansheee" views of native Africans. Naranbhai decided against going back home with the news and instead, went up to Shahbanu's closed door knocking at it with his usual rhythmic pattern: Rat-a-tat-tat -- tat tat tat! It was one of those little games he had devised for himself, believing that only his particular knock would cause the door to be opened -- a door that remained closed to all other intruders.

Shahbanu opened the door gingerly and heaved a sigh of relief at seeing that it was only Naranbhai. He took her expression of relief to mean that she was waiting just for him, and was, obviously, clearly delighted that he had decided to visit. On the short walk from Naran Villa, he had already rehearsed his little speech:

"Today I want to tell you about something very important. A momentous plan. Now, you tell me what you think. I want you to be by my side. My wife, you know, she doesn't really know about dealing with people. It's not that she's bad or anything, but she lacks a certain, shall we say... finesse...whereas you, you could charm the birds off the trees. That's why I would like you to...."

But he never got a chance to say a word.

EYES SHUT - EARS OPEN

After Shahbanu had opened the door, gingerly and without so much as a word, she just pulled Naranbhai into the house and quickly shut the door. His heart was racing. This was extremely forward -- and unexpected -- behaviour for someone of her refinement. She looked at him conspiratorially and placed a finger on his lips while at the same time saying: "Sshshhshh." For lack of anything better to do or say, he said "Sshshhsh" back to her, thoroughly enjoying the game. He had no idea what she was "shusshing" about.

A black silk burqa-clad figure, eyes concealed behind heavy black mesh, was seated on Shahbanu's sofa.

Shahbanu said: "Please Naranbhai, I have a very pious Muslim woman visitor, but don't tell anyone. Muslim women are not supposed to go out, you know? So, you haven't seen anything, OK?"

"OK, OK," said Naranbhai lamely, wondering what the big deal was, since he couldn't even see the woman's face. He sat down feeling decidedly awkward. Shahbanu ushered the burqa-clad woman to her bedroom and told Naranbhai to remain where he was. There was a great deal of whispering and shuffling. Naranbhai remained in the sitting room, feeling at a complete loss. He had quite forgotten his original mission of reinstating his strong, masculine entrepreneurial personality for Shahbanu's benefit. The minutes turned to hours and, every so often, Shahbanu would poke her head into the sitting room and say: "Sshhshhh." And he would say it back to her.

Some two hours later, he decided this wasn't getting him anywhere and that it was time to go, particularly since he wasn't going to get to be alone with his beautiful Shahbanu, not with that Muslim lady visitor still in the house. But every time he got up as though to leave, Shahbanu would step in from the bedroom and say: "Sit, Bhaijaan! I'll be with you as soon as my guest is comfortable..."

And soon, it was 6 o'clock in the evening.

Naranbhai was still waiting for her, oblivious to the curfew deadline. The curfew gongs came and went. Then, at around 8 pm, he began to get hungry and, realising that Shahbanu never had anything to offer in that department, he got up -- his thoughts turning longingly to the big evening meal that would be awaiting him at Naran Villa. Just as he was getting ready to leave, Shahbanu appeared again and protested:

"But the curfew has started - how will you go?"

"It's only a short walk - and nobody is really policing that mud-track. I'll walk quickly."

"But they have said they will even shoot at someone taking his wife to hospital to have a baby. They said everybody will be pretending to be having a baby ......"

Naranbhai would've liked to heroically dismiss her caution but felt himself less able to move at the prospect of being shot on sight: "Well, maybe, I'll just wait until it is darker. Wait till it goes a bit quieter -"

"It's too risky. Why don't you stay the night and leave at 6 in the morning, when the curfew lifts?" Shahbanu asked, matter-of-factly but, to Naranbhai it sounded like the most tantalising offer he'd ever had.

He stood silently, unsure what to do. In typical Shahbanu fashion, a packet of biscuits was produced and she offered to make coffee. Naranbhai gathered that that was to be his dinner. He mooched around uncertainly, while Shahbanu disappeared saying she had to do evening prayers. Suddenly, the charm of the visit wore off. He was in Shahbanu's house but unable to feel thrilled at the prospect of being so close to her. Eventually, the distant sound of a radio -- coming from the daughter Saira's room -- was turned off. She had, presumably, retired for the night. Shahbanu seemed to be doing some especially extended evening prayer. Naranbhai looked at the biscuits and his thoughts, once again, turned to the eight-course dinner that would be about to be served at the huge oval-shaped dining table at Naran Villa. Some small inner voice again urged him to leave, while the coast was clear:

"Yes, I'll leave -- in a while. How can I stay? All night? What will people say?" he said to no one in particular.

The clock on the wall ticked away as he sat alone in Shahbanu's little sitting room. Eventually, her prayers said, she emerged in a white silk sari carrying a pillow and blanket:

"Here, just rest here on the sofa. In the morning you will be able to go in safety. Not worth the risk, moving around in this curfew."

He had no intention of staying, but tired and hungry, he decided to lie down on the sofa. Feeling extremely uncomfortable on the slippery plastic-covered sofa he found his thoughts turning again and again to the neighbouring bedroom where Shahbanu was making preparations to sleep. He listened for every small sound and tried to interpret its meaning. He heard the tinkling of her glass bangles. He heard soft, padding footsteps as she presumably moved around the room. He heard the rustle of fabric. That, surely, was the sari being unwrapped from her beautiful form. Then there was a minute's silence. He was sure she was standing before a mirror in her choli and petticoat admiring her fine body. Then the tinkling of small objects being placed on a dressing table. He felt sure she would be unpinning and uncoiling her special figure-of-eight coiffure. Her silky tresses must now be cascading down her shoulders and framing her beautiful face in a sort of halo. With the sari off, he felt sure she would be getting into something delicate, fine and sensuous. Then again, it was quite possible she didn't wear anything in bed...

Was that a giggle....? Was she chatting to her Muslim lady friend in the burqa? Was the lady visitor still in the house? He toyed with the idea of needing something mundane -- like a glass of water -- and just knocking on her door. No! Knights in Shining Armour didn't do that sort of thing. She had asked him to rest on the sofa and it was his duty to remain here. Just for a while. Soon he would be getting up for the furtive, curfew-ridden walk back to Naran Villa. In a minute, in a minute, he said to himself, realising that the need to shut his eyes was fast over-taking all other needs Soon, he dozed off, regaining consciousness every so often, fully intending to make a move. "Five, just five minutes more..." he would whisper and turn over and doze some more. Soon, the house fell completely silent. Mother and daughter had apparently both retired for the night. And he still wasn't sure whether the Muslim lady guest in the burqa had left, or was staying the night.

RIDING OFF INTO THE SUNRISE

Naranbhai's eyes opened just before dawn and, forgetting that he was not at Naran Villa, started looking for a bathroom. Realising where he was, he cursed himself for not having put bathrooms inside the houses. He unbolted Shahbanu's back door and stepped out gingerly into the silent, chilly dawn -- the pale yellow light giving the dusty backyard quite an artistic touch. He stopped to admire the effect for a moment. His tenants were really very lucky to live in such a picturesque compound for such low rents. Just then, through the corner of his eye, he thought he saw some movement and a door being hastily closed somewhere behind him. No doubt, Pandit Suddenly had probably entertained a woman of the night who was now hoping to make an early getaway before the neighbours started stirring. At one time, he would have lost no time in banging on the door and demanding entry on grounds of decency and high moral standards having to be observed at all times. But, sailing in the same boat, he decided to let the matter go. Whoever it was, shuffling or muffling, he would overlook the matter and just make his way over to the bathrooms at the end of backyard. Once he was inside the small lavatory, the unusual sound of a motobike caused him to take a quick look through a crack in the wooden door to see what, if anything, was going on at the various backdoors which opened into the yard. As far as he knew, nobody in Bombay Gardens owned - or knew how to ride - a motorbike.

In the very early morning light, he saw a form in a black burqa, hastily leaving Shahbanu's house, while a strange man was revving up the motorbike in readiness to depart. The curfew would soon be lifting. The Black Burqa leapt onto the backseat of the motorbike and the bike sped away.

Naranbhai waited in the toilet for a moment, wondering why Shahbanu's pious, burqa-clad Muslim woman guest should not only stay the whole night but then, also, stealthily depart on a motorbike so early in the morning. He'd hardly had time to ponder the question when, still peering through the crack from inside the toilet door, he had the unexpected treat of Shahbanu emerging languidly from her house in a very flimsy negligee, her voluminous hair cascading down and enticingly covering her bra-less breasts. She was headead straight for one of the women's toilets.

This delicious - and unexpected - sighting completely eclipsed the matter of the woman in the burqa, leaping onto the back of a motorbike and riding off into the sunrise...

THE LOCK OUT

The reception awaiting Naranbhai at Naran Villa early that morning was far from cordial. Jannasani was up and about, making tea, and the rest of the household was stirring between bathrooms and bedrooms. Mrs Naranbhai was said to have locked herself in her room with a headache. Her aunt, Kamini masi, approached him in the manner of a colonel addressing an errant soldier:

"Aren't you afraid of God? Have you lost all your senses? " she inquired. "Openly spending the night with that woman and then daring to show your face here?"

"I didn't spend the night with anyone. I lost track of time and soon it was curfew. I had to stay put, otherwise I might have been shot," he said as matter-of-factly as possible.

"How did you lose track of time? Just what were you doing that time seemed to collapse like that?" Kamini Masi was determined to do her best on behalf of her niece. Before Naranbhai could answer, the widow Nalini appeared and had a go at Kamini:

"Who the hell are you to put my brother through this police inquiry?"

Fast on Nalini's heels, Sushilaben followed and remarked: "He knows what is best for him. I'm glad he stayed where he was. Do you want him shot? You want me to become a widow?"

"You're already worse than a widow," Kamini retorted. "He has already made you a widow by marrying someone else. Even then you have no shame. You stay here, and live on his crumbs and then have the audacity to sanction his immoral behaviour!"

"But I am his first wife, so I am entitled to live on his crumbs. And Naliniben is his sister, and equally, she is also entitled to live on his crumbs."

"Yes, that's right," put in Nalini. "We are both here, because we are entitled. But whose crumbs do YOU live on? Latching on to a married niece!" she added her voice rising.

Naranbhai left the women quarrelling and went up to the second wife's bedroom. Mrs Naranbhai would not open the door.

His persistent thumping brought the following muffled response from within:

"Why have you bothered to come back? Go, go and move in there for good! You'll never get more than biscuits to eat - "

"But it was the curfew, I'm telling you, I was stuck. She said it wouldn't be safe -"

"So, now *she* is the one concerned for your safety? Your well being is *her* business now?" Mrs Naranbhai's hysterical wails got louder. "Don't you know what emergencies have been happening in the country? All this going on, and no man at home! We could all have been murdered in our beds in the middle of the night, but do you care? Where are you when war is about to break out? Are you with your wife and children? No! You are over *there*, holding *her* hand!" And, with that, Mrs Naranbhai was so overcome with hiccups that the rest of her speech was quite unintelligible.

Aunt Kamini appeared outside the bedroom door and dug into Naranbhai again:

"See? Are you a man or what? How you torture and torment my beloved niece for that cheap Muslim woman across the road. Now, why do you stand here and pester her? Let her at least cry in peace. With all the pain you give her, she is at least entitled to shed tears in her own room. Leave her alone! Stop banging on her door!"

ANOTHER KIND OF CURFEW

Those who followed political events in the turbulent, newly independent country were soon to learn that the ancient tribal King had had to escape assassination by jumping over the palace walls. That was to leave the newish, upstart Prime Minister - soon to be President of the Republic -with more power than before. But the former PM did not forget those who had stood by him. Raushan's husband, Sam, was one such man and in the months after the so-called Constitutional Crisis, was amply rewarded by a meteoric rise from primary school teacher-cum-part-time politician to something high up in Government. From here he was permitted into the inner circle, where he became even closer to the PM who had now declared himself President of the Republic, with all opposition parties banned.

Naranbhai was understandably bitter at Sam's meteoric rise. His arch-enemy Raushan was now married to a powerful politician. In attempting to console him over this latest bombshell he remembered Mrs Naranbhai's famous words spoken at the time of Independence some four years ago: "Just wait and see! Once the country is handed over to the Blacks, every single one of them is going to become a politician of some sort. These guys all want to be chiefs. Everyone wants to be boss!" And now, still locked out of the marital bedroom, how he missed her wisdom, her biting remarks on every subject under the sun.

Mrs Naranbhai remained locked in her room for a full five days after Naranbhai's curfew adventure. In that time, Naranbhai's ardour soon subsided. True, he had returned from Bombay Gardens early that morning rearing to go, utterly eroticised by the sounds of Shahbanu's bedtime rituals and the early morning sighting of her see-through negligee, but Mrs Naranbhai's barking, sobbing and sulking had rapidly dampened any amorous intent. She remained in her room, whimpering, while Jannasani, lips sealed tight, dutifully carried up trays of food and endless glasses of water, tea and lassi. He would leave the tray outside her door, knock a couple of times to alert her, and some minutes later the door would be slightly, only slightly opened. The tray would be taken in, eagerly, which had caused the rival first wife to comment: "I see she's still got her big appetite for food! In her position, I would have starved myself to death."

"Yes!" retorted the aunt Kamini. "Just like you did when he married another woman over your head!"

On the third day of Mrs Naranbhai's self-imposed seclusion, Naranbhai's friend Pandit Suddenly teased him: "Yes, government has put country on six-to-six curfew, but we have heard your Mrs has suddenly put you on a full, all-day, everyday-curfew where her own bedroom is concerned."

Try as he might, Naranbhai had never managed to figure out just how news -- and particularly bad news -- travelled so fast to those who least needed to know about it. How was it that everything that was done, said or heard within the walls of Naran Villa so quickly became the main topic of conversation at Bombay Gardens? The Naran Villa-Bombay Gardens express-wire system would've put the likes of Reuters and BBC to shame. Quite apart from the servants, he thought bitterly, the D'Sa urchins were all set to become first class reporters when they grew up. The Naranbhai boys, Doctor, Dentist and Lawyer, sometimes played with the D'Sas and had, no doubt, informed their playmates that their mother had been confined to her room for a while, refusing to speak to their father. The D'Sa children had probably gone straight home and told their mother. And that lady, who had not for nothing earned for herself the title of "BBC, Bombay Gardens Bureau", had definitely tittle-tattled about it to the Pandit.

While Naranbhai seethed at his private shame being turned into a public joke, the Pandit was keen to discuss recent political events. But the ins and outs of the Constitutional Crisis and the resulting absolute powers of the former Prime Minister, now President of a one-party state, were far less scintillating than the many juicy rumours about the deposed King and his method of escape.

"They didn't get him you know?" said the Pandit, thrilled by the sensational events of the past week. "They said 'arrested' first, but no, even BBC got it wrong. He wasn't arrested. He escaped! I heard he jumped over the palace walls - missing the bullets by just a few inches. Mrs D'Sa was telling me she heard he had to

321

wear a black burqa to disguise himself. Some girl friend of his hid him in her house, all night, all through the curfew and from there, he was driven to Kenya and taken to the airport at Nairobi. He flew to England - dressed as a woman in a Burqa. That's one advantage Muslims always have. Whatever the law, whatever immigration rules, nobody can force a Muslim woman to lift her veil and show her face!"

"Yes, yes," Naranbhai said absent-mindedly. He was only half-listening. He was still fuming about how everyone had come to know that Mrs Naranbhai, apart from denying him his conjugal rights, was not even talking to him.

But in the days that followed, Naranbhai remembered his misadventure of over-nighting at Shahbanu's not as the night of the King's escape, nor the incident that put him in the doghouse with the second Mrs Naranbhai. He remembered it as the night that he had last seen the figurines of his favourite twin gods, Rahu and Ketu, together.

POISONOUS QUEEN OF THE NIGHT

Five days after the lock-out, Mrs Naranbhai decided it was time to forgive her husband, in return for certain concessions. She had enjoyed the five days of sulking, but then, remembering her aunt's advise, she realised that too much sulking would only serve to send her husband running back into that Muslim floozie's arms -- or, far worse, into the arms of his first wife. So, having decided to forgive him and planning to execute a fresh seduction campaign that very evening, Mrs Naranbhai decided to pick some fragrant flowers for her hair. The flowers, dubbed "Queen of the Night", only grew outside Shahbanu's window. They remained closed during the day and opened up only at sunset, giving off the most glorious, sensuous and seductive scent. She had tried, on numerous occasions, to plant the shrub within the grounds of Naran Villa. But, for some mysterious reason, the plant never "took" anywhere except immediately outside Shahbanu's front window in Bombay Gardens, giving Mrs Naranbhai a perfect excuse to loiter near the window and try to peer in on mysterious goings-on. Best way to see who was coming and who was going. In any case, Raat ki Rani flowers couldn't be picked any earlier than evening-time by those women who wanted them for the bedroom that night. The ancient scriptures had recommended fresh flowers as an essential aid in the art of seduction.

When she arrived outside the window, pretending to pick the flowers but actually straining to peep through the crack in Shahbanu's curtains, Hazari Baba crept up and startled her.

She barked: "Baba, you really have to stop this creeping around you know. Someone could have a heart attack! And where the hell are you when you are most wanted? Do you know how much food got wasted because you failed to show up the other day?"

"Food? Then it was obviously food that didn't have my name written on it. Everything we eat already carries our name - every grain of rice bears the name of its intended...just as these little flowers carry your name. Yes, they should do the trick," he said cryptically.

Mrs Naranbhai was stunned. She hadn't wished to discuss her sexual strategies quite so openly: "Baba! I just hate this big-big talk of yours. Where is the room to write a name on a grain of rice, hain, tell me?"

"A single grain of rice could have the entire history of mankind written on it."

"Baba, just stop all this big-big talk now. Don't you know what's happening in the country? The King has been deposed. Chased away by this dreadful government. A King, treated like that, just imagine!" she sighed.

"Kings are appointed by Man, not God. Only Man can oust what Man has put there ..."

Mrs Naranbhai failed to grasp this. Instead, she asked: "And why are you always here -- always hanging around here and there, but more here?"

She asked the question in the same tone that she reserved for Jannasani whenever a few ounces of tea or sugar went missing.

He ignored her question and said: "I see you are collecting Raat ki Rani flowers. They've been used since time immemorial. The petals dried, pounded and brushed through your hair are guaranteed to make an estranged lover succumb to your charms. Here, I've prepared some for you," he concluded while at the same time dropping the paper sachet into her basket of flowers.

Mrs Naranbhai pretended not to notice. She had always imagined that the flowers did their trick because of their heady scent.

"Me, I have no need to brush anything through my hair," she said dismissively. "My husband is completely devoted to me," she added.

"Good, good," said Hazari Baba in a matter of fact way. "Then you have no danger."

"Danger? What do you mean danger?" she asked, startled.

"Women who brushed heaps and heaps of that stuff into their hair, often ended up swallowing a few particles. It's lethal, but quite untraceable. It was a common method of suicide. And, for a slow death, just a small amount in a glass of milk every night does the trick. But just make sure you know who is at the receiving end. Sometimes, these things end up missing their target..."

He stopped suddenly and looked up at Shahbanu's window.

"I don't know what you mean," Mrs Naranbhai muttered, all flustered. She hastily put her hand over the small basket in which she'd collected a few flowers, to stop them blowing away in the breeze, and hurried back to Naran Villa.

SEEING STARS

It had been a full five days since Naranbhai had been allowed into his second wife's bedroom. He had mixed feelings about this. At one level, he was quite relieved that she didn't want him in that way anymore. At another, he was miffed that she should be the one to reject him, and not the other way around. So, he felt quite justified in playing the pining, wounded lover. In his mind, he could comfortably oscillate between pining for the beautiful, unattainable Shahbanu and then, every so often, alternate that with feeling left out in the cold by Mrs Naranbhai. Since his lock-out had been in force, he had started pacing about on the front verandah after dinner, admiring the moon and stars -- a time-honoured activity for frustrated lovers.

As he stood there humming a tune, Mrs Naranbhai suddenly appeared in a brand new sari with an elaborate garland of Raat ki Rani flowers in her hair. In her hand, she carried a smaller garland of the same, which she quickly slipped onto his wrist, pushing his arm towards his nose so that he could catch a whiff of the intoxicating scent and feel suitably aroused. He should have known his delicious, tragic, lonesome romantic pining moments were too good to last! Here she was, once again, his utterly undesirable wife, prepared to forgive him and, no doubt, about to embark on a fresh seduction strategy. Over the years, he had become used to this pattern of flaming rows followed by erotic reconciliations. He knew, only too well, that any wife could forgive a man for one night's transgression. If it had been more than one night with the same woman, then that would have been a very serious matter indeed.

"What are you thinking?" she asked seductively, as though nothing had happened in the last five days.

"I was just thinking about Bimla. How long can we have those sisters just sitting here? Must find a husband for her soon. Young girl like that, still unwed and a target for everybody's lust....must get her married...."

Even as he said it, he remembered the fiasco over Satish. And, then, the Mad Girl's disastrous one-night marriage. That, inevitably, brought back the memory of another bungle: Mohini and Sohini. Why? Why? Every time he tried to arrange a marriage it all went horribly wrong. He would have to reassert his glory in some other way…his grand business scheme, yet to be launched.

Just then, the Mad Girl broke into song from somewhere on the flat roof terrace. She sang of a bridegroom who came to wed her, witnessed only by the stars -- or were they fireflies? Was it a band playing, or were the flowers singing for joy? And there was mehndi, on her palms, the colour trickling down her wrists. But was it mehndi, or was it blood? How did one tell the difference?

The words of her song brought a sudden lump to Naranbhai's throat. He could have broken down and cried like an infant if Mrs Naranbhai hadn't said:

"There she goes again! The longer you just stand there, the louder she will sing. What are you doing out here, anyway?"

Naranbhai hastily brushed away a tear and turned to her:

"Nothing, nothing. Just admiring the stars," he said, a little embarrassed. "See how they all connect? If one star moves away, even slightly, then it loses its connection with the entire system. Just like humans…."

"Since when have you become so romantic, hain?" she teased. "If it's stars you want, then I'll show you stars. Just come upstairs with me!"

Naranbhai winced at her crassness. He tightened his fist over his twin-gods, wishing he could delay the inevitable and, being so preoccupied, didn't even notice that he had only *one* of the twins in his palm.

True, he was eternally grateful to her for having provided three healthy sons, but for some unknown reason, and especially since he had got to know Shahbanu, Mrs Naranbhai's sexual advances always caused an initial recoiling within him. Whenever she suggested sex he felt an automatic resistance to the idea. Once she'd had her wicked way with him, he felt quite relaxed, and even fully forgiving towards her. She had a way of smothering him that made him feel quite powerless. Inexplicably for one craving for so much power, it was a feeling he liked.

Later, lying beside her in bed, Naranbhai felt lighter -- an enormous burden had lifted. He was back in his second wife's good books. Soon, he would set about getting the Virjibhai girls off his hands -- before he embarked on his next big business scheme, otherwise the shrew, Kamla, was bound to raise the question of where all the money was coming from.

GOD DISAPPEARS

The following morning, Naranbhai was beyond consolation. Jannasani had had to abandon all his normal duties so that furniture could be moved, mattresses turned, corners swept and re-swept. But one of the twin-gods, Rahu, seemed to have vanished into thin air.

"Bad sign, very bad omen," muttered Pandit Suddenly. "You must immediately, and suddenly, dispose of the other one - Ketu - because without Rahu, Ketu brings nothing but bad luck. Just *one* should never be in your possession without the other one -- otherwise life will get imbalanced, suddenly. Bad, very, very, bad!"

The remark startled Naranbhai so much that he hurriedly threw the figurine of the other twin-god, Ketu, towards some bushes.

"No, not like that!" chided Pandit Suddenly. "It has to be disposed of properly. Tell Jannasani to bury it somewhere -- away from here --"

Mrs Naranbhai entered the drawing room, tired and dusty with searching for the missing god, Rahu.

"I say it's been stolen. Everyone knows your success and fortune have come from Rahu-Ketu, together, being so close to you. They've stolen one twin and now we'll all be ruined," she whimpered with extra-pretended grief. She had never liked his habit of fondling the gods but now that one had vanished, she decided to act as her husband's chief sympathiser. It wouldn't do to let anyone else appear more empathetic or understanding of his predicament. She had to carry his grief, and loss, as her own. She sat down on the floor and began to bawl with renewed determination.

Jannasani came back into the house after some hours of searching for the other god that Naranbhai, in a fit of panic, had just thrown into the bushes. Jannasani had been instructed to find, and bury it somewhere, away from the grounds of Naran Villa.

"I can't find it," he announced calmly.

"Oh no!" yelped Pandit Suddenly. "It *must* be found! Otherwise it will just lie somewhere near the house and suddenly bring bad luck! I told you not to throw it Naranbhai! It has to be disposed of properly!"

Naranbhai was about to start groaning with self-pity when a whiff of roses and jasmine announced Shahbanu's entry into the drawing room of Naran Villa. All of Bombay Gardens had also been searching high and low, in case Naranbhai had left the twin-god behind on one of his many mercy missions to his tenants.

"Bhai-jaan, O Bhai-jaan," she wailed in a mournful voice. "I've looked everywhere! That day, you know, when you were sitting on my bed..." she stopped just in time to catch a venomous look from Mrs Naranbhai and one of utter delight from the allies Sushilaben and Nalini. Mrs Naranbhai's aunt, Kamini masi, had also arrived -- just in time to hear this careless, off-the-cuff remark of Shahbanu's.

A one-minute silence followed. Mrs Naranbhai got up from her special wailing position and walked straight up to where Shahbanu was standing. The portly Mrs Naranbhai stood as erect as she could manage, but she still only managed to reach Shahbanu's chest, as the other woman was very tall and slender. Besides, whatever the situation, however dire the crisis, Shahbanu always managed to look more beautiful and dignified than anyone else. And now, here she stood brazenly, unashamedly, telling all and sundry how Naranbhai had allegedly sat on her bed. On such occasions, when Mrs Naranbhai felt she was completely in the right and totally entitled to everyone's sympathy, words somehow always came out sounding not quite as forceful as she would have liked: "When, I said WHEN was my husband in your bed?" She had intended it as a cool and level-headed question but it came out like the squak of a distressed hen, her voice completely cracking up on the word 'bed'.

"Mrs Naranbhai, please," said Shahbanu in sweet, reasonable tones sounding every bit like a loving mother correcting an errant and destructive toddler.

"He sat on the edge of my bed to drink some juice when he came to collect the rent. It's a sin for anyone to leave my house without at least taking one sip from a glass of water. It is our religion."

Naranbhai decided to step in and take the heat off the beautiful Shahbanu. Beauty should not have to get down there in the dirt and face the music.

"Yes, you know, our dear Mrs Hussein never allows anyone to leave without eating and drinking. I got off lightly. I had already eaten. But I couldn't refuse the juice - and you know I never consume anything standing up. It's against my religion. So I sat down on the edge of the bed - edge, mind you..."

"Religion! This is against HER religion, and that is against YOUR religion. You people use religion like it was there just for you! Everything is in the name of religion...."

She had made a valid point, but once again, much to her dismay, its impact was lost as her voice got hopelessly squeaky and out of control while Shahbanu stood erect and dignified with just a hint of a Mona Lisa-like partly bemused, partly disdainful smile in her eyes. That was the other thing about Shahbanu. Her mouth remained quite still while her eyes smiled, or showed displeasure, or invited, or rejected. Sometimes, at one and the same time, one eye showed love and the other, hatred. One eye said 'Come' the other barked 'Get out.' It ought to have been hellishly confusing but actually it did wonders for jaded, though still excitable, middle-aged males.

The aunt Kamini decided it was her turn to do her job as ally and show Naranbhai that she was earning her keep by sometimes helping to moderate things:

"Come on," she said, coaxing her niece. "You're just upset because your beloved husband's Rahu-god has gone missing. And now, Ketu missing as well! Our dear Mrs Hussein here and your husband are just like brother and sister. She always calls him "Bhai jaan", didn't you hear?"

"That's exactly what Muslim women do when they're carrying on with someone! All this Bhai-Bhai business means only one thing! It might fool you, but it doesn't fool me!" yelled Mrs Naranbhai, completely losing control.

Shahbanu ignored the outburst. Instead, she turned to Naranbhai with a neutral gaze and said: "Bhai-jaan, I'd better leave. Everyone is upset. It's only natural. I will go and do a special namaaz for the safe return of your beloved Rahu. Any God is my God - that is my religion."

At the mention of the dreaded word 'religion' yet again, Mrs Naranbhai let out a high-pitched wail: "There she goes again, bringing religion into everything!"

But Shahbanu had already slid away from view, leaving in her wake the slightest hint of her intoxicating fragrance. Naranbhai gazed with wonderment at that spot where she had stood, still charged with all the promises those eyes had just made. This often happened to spaces when Shahbanu had just vacated them. His mouth twitched and gave in to a sheepish smile as the faint smell of jasmine and roses reached his nostrils...

In a recklessly defiant mood, Naranbhai decided there and then where he'd be going later this afternoon for an extended visit, if Mrs Naranbhai didn't come to heel and behave herself: "A man needs peace and quiet" he thought, justifying the impending visit. "I deserve better than this daily ghit-phit ghit-phit of jealous, useless wives."

CONCESSIONS

Soon after the disappearance of the twin-gods, and Shahbanu's award-winning performance in the name of religion, Mrs Naranbhai decided that the Mad Girl's baby -- the one she had at first tried to raise as her own --was the root of all problems, including the political unrest in the country. Unable to score points off Shahbanu, it was far better to turn her venom on others. In any case, she had tired of the baby in the first few months and, nowadays, only Juma really looked after it. This irritated Mrs Naranbhai all the more because she had only allowed Juma into the household so as to have a second junior servant to boss around. Just barely a child himself, all he did was fuss around the baby all day. Playing with baby, making funny sounds at her, feeding her, changing, washing and boiling her nappies in the backyard and then painstakingly ironing them, bathing her, combing her hair, and then rocking her gently in his arms until she fell asleep. On top of that, the older servant Jannasani was often in the wrong place. *She* was the mistress of the household but instead of coming to her for orders, he went about his tasks as he wished and, whenever he was nowhere to be seen, the chances were he was hovering near the room of the first wife. This last fact infuriated Mrs Naranbhai no end! No doubt, Sushilaben was bending the servant's ear to aid and abet her in one of her plots to undermine the second wife. In a fit of anger,Mrs Naranbhai decided that the baby was to blame for distracting and subverting all the African servants.They should have been dancing attendance on *her* (as first lady of the house) but were all using the baby as an excuse to get out of normal duties. The baby would have to go!

"What am I running here? A sort of dharamshala or what, for mad people's offspring to be cared for by *my* servants? Who the hell knows where that baby came from?"

She had planted the first seed of doubt in Naranbhai's head. Up until now everybody had assumed that the baby was the result of the Mad Girl's wedding night rape by the rascal bridegroom. But, being unable to grasp the concept of rape within the sanctity of marriage, Naranbhai was almost grateful to his second wife for hinting that the baby *could* have come some other way. That crook Hazari Baba had, after all, spent a full *twenty-seven minutes* alone with the Mad Girl. Anything was possible with these wily, Baba types...covering up their lust with piety and pseudo-philosophical talk.

Mrs Naranbhai had nagged and nagged her husband, until, just for the sake of some peace and feeling he owed her something for that curfew night spent with Shahbanu, he had said:

"OK, do whatever you like. After all, if the baby *is* illegitimate we shouldn't be raising it here.Respectable household, after all.

Mrs Naranbhai had just been telling him that the baby ought to be given up for adoption. The nuns at some Catholic mission would take the child in and then find her a good home, with a good family -- perhaps in a neighbouring African country.

"Otherwise, just think," Mrs Naranbhai had gone on. "She may grow up mad, just like her mother. How can we have two mad girls in the house?"

And then, remembering that all time classic piece of wisdom she promptly clothed her intended treachery in a do-gooding mantle: "Moreover, even if she grows up normal -- more expense! Girls! It's a full time job to make sure they don't get pregnant. And then, who will marry her if they know her mother was mad? Worse, if there is no father. And, her father, probably not even a Hindu. We'll just be stuck with her. She'll become a shrivelled up old maid. What sort of life is that for a woman? Best to give her a new chance in life -- new parents, a new background, new past, new future. How can we stand in the way of her chances in life, hain? How can we be so selfish?" And she wiped away an imaginary tear with the end of her sari.

Unknown to the rest of the household, and in particular secrecy from the baby's grandmother, Sushilaben, Mrs Naranbhai summoned Jannasani and ordered him, under cover of darkness, to take the baby and leave it at the doorstep of the chapel attached to a certain mission hospital. She gave him a ten-shilling note for expenses and cautioned him that she would need to see a full expense report. She knew Jannasani was more than likely to hitch a lift to that remote outpost some nineteen miles away and then try and claim a bus fare from her. She knew he was more than likely to spend the night in some darkened doorway, and then claim a three-star hotel bill.

On receiving his orders, Jannasani had, as usual, looked at her without emotion. His face had a way of conveying that somehow, whatever the issue, whatever its rights or wrongs, he had been pre-programmed - since long before the universe itself had been created - to just carry out orders. "Ours not to question why, Ours but to do and die" could have been written by Janasanni -- had Janasanni known how to write in English.

JUMA VANISHES

The following morning, when Jannsani began his duties a little later than usual, Mrs Naranbhai looked at him meaningfully, not daring to voice the question. The slightest nod of Janasanni's head told her that he had, indeed, done exactly as instructed.

But then, just as she thought everything had gone off without a hitch, she was furious to note that the cheeky Juma with the new-potato eyes hadn't reported for duty that morning. With Jannasani starting late and that boy Juma doing a bunk, the household seemed in total disarray. There was so much to do, and everything was running horribly late. How on earth could she have lunch on the table by 1 o'clock? Naranbhai was extremely grumpy if his lunch was not laid at one, sharp. And these days, whenever he got grumpy, he stomped off to Shahbanu's house. Not that Shahbanu was ever likely to produce anything even remotely edible, and it was hunger for food that always forced him back to Naran Villa once his anger had cooled down. At Shahbanu's, a couple of biscuits were the most one could get in the way of bodily nourishment. Other kinds of hunger Mrs Naranbhai didn't dare think about.

"Where the hell is that clever-clever nephew of yours then, hain?"she dug into Jannasani."Now with that wretched infant gone, I was hoping to make him do some real work. He eats and eats and does nothing to earn his keep. Too much pombe -- lying drunk somewhere?You people start drinking the minute you're born - "

Jannasani shrugged his shoulders and said:"He had to return to his village."

"Why? What for? How dare he go without giving me notice? I will not, not, not give him a reference! Let him starve!" And then she said suddenly: "But I thought the entire village was destroyed by killer ants?"

Jannasani said nothing.A new light gleamed on Mrs Naranbhai's face. So far, she had not been able to come up with a good excuse to give to the rest of the family when they asked about the mysterious disappearance of the Mad Girl's baby. But now, that stupid, slippery chit of a boy Juma had, most kindly, though unwittingly, provided her with the perfect story.

Two hours later, Naran Villa was was once again turned inside out and upside down -- this time in search of the baby. Inspector "Ay-men" was writing out a report while various constables searched for the baby under the beds of the Naran Villa bedrooms and in the bushes and flower-pots outside. One particularly thin and wiry constable walked the entire length of the mud-track running alongside the smelly gutter all the way to Bombay Gardens. He was trying to see if the baby was, by any chance, being carried away amidst the empty cigarette packets, mango-skins, used condoms and sanitary towels slowly gushing along the smelly stream.

"I'm telling you, I'm telling you!" screamed Mrs Naranbhai. "That good-for-nothing boy with the potato-eyes has run off with the baby. He'll probably sell her to Arabs -- Slave Trade, you know? It still goes on. Straight to Mombasa and then a dhow to Oman or Zanzibar or Pemba, or somewhere like that!"

Inspector Ay-men registered with some irritation how Mrs Naranbhai, although completely ignorant and uneducated, could sound so authoritative on the mechanics of the East African Slave Trade.

Sushilaben just cried and cried. "It's her, I'm telling you it's *her*," she screamed at Ay-men and then pleaded with Naranbhai: "Don't you see? First she tried to take my daughter's baby away and make it her own. Then, getting tired of all the hard work, she dumped it onto the younger houseboy, Juma. He looked after it day and night, and she became jealous. She has killed it. I tell you *she* has killed it. She has probably also killed Juma -- I'm telling you she has buried them both somewhere here. Why don't you just dig up that backyard and see? And now she's blaming him for kidnapping the child. How could he, I ask you? That little boy, who never cared for his own sleep and danced attention day and night to every litle whim of my cute little...cute little..."

She broke down again, her wailing got louder and more mournful:"And just look at my poor unfortunate daughter! Disaster has struck, but she doesn't know. She can't even feel it.

Today, I thank God that she is mad. If she had been sane, can you imagine what her condition would be right now?" And, with that, Sushilaben's mournful wailing turned to screaming and rhythmic breast-beating.

A D'Sa urchin who had witnessed the entire episode, hurried back to Bombay Gardens to report the news. One by one, various Bombay Gardens tenants walked up the mud-track to Naran Villa, to offer condolences -- although they were unsure whether the condolences were for kidnapping or for murder. As more and more people arrived and the recriminations between the first wife and second wife got louder and louder, Inspector Ay-men needed an extra large handkerchief to mop up the sweat on his brow. Naranbhai looked at him meaningfully, as though to say: "*Now* do you see what *I* have to go through every single day?"

"OK, OK," said Ay-men, exasperated at being drawn into such a contentious domestic squabble instead of a proper, high-profile criminal investigation of the kind that would bring him a great deal of glory -- and medals -- and massive headlines in the 'Argus' when solved. "OK, I'll send out search parties for the boy. Where can he hide? Village, you said. A village destroyed by killer-ants? Where is the village, what is it called?"

But nobody knew the name of the village, or indeed where it might have been. Jannasani, the only person on this God's earth who might perhaps have known was, as usual, silent as the grave.

PICTURE A TREE

"Did Indians always have African servants?" I asked Camilla in my effort to learn more about the old days.

"Yes, usually," she replied.

"But if they were so prejudiced against Africans, then how come they didn't mind them working in their houses, being close to the children -- all that sort of thing...?"

"Don't know --" she replied unenthusiastically. "They can have enormous blind spots when it comes to being served. If somebody is polishing their shoes or changing the baby's nappies then the colour of his skin doesn't matter. Anyway, why do you only single out Indians? Did the whites ever have a problem with being waited upon by black servants? Did any white South African mem-sahib object to having her meals cooked by --?"

Feeling chastised, I fall silent. It's her turn to ask questions:

"Tell me more about those photographs," asks Camilla, predictably.

"I told you. Two identical girls in heavy saris. The other photo was that swing on our verandah -- with nobody on it. And the third photo was -- well, that was a really strange one. It was the picture of a tree...."

"Just a...a tree?" she interrupts a bit too eagerly.

"No, yes...no, there were some people near the tree. In fact the tree was all garlanded up. When I was a kid I thought it was just an Indian version of a Christmas tree, but now I think about it, maybe it was some kind of prayer ceremony. Oh, I nearly forgot! There was also a young woman, all heavily done up, near the tree. Just like a bride. But she can't have been. When Indian women dress up for a special occasion they can look so bridal! Tell me, do certain Indians worship trees?"

"That sounds like the same picture. I searched and searched for it at one time..."

"*You* were searching for that picture? Why?" I ask, genuinely bewildered.

"My life depended on it -- at one time. It hardly matters now..." She tails off, languidly.

A CONDEMNED WOMAN

It had been five years since Naranbhai had fondled the bulbous statuettes of both his twin-gods in the palm of his right hand. It had not been a particularly remarkable time, although politically, the country was going to the dogs since the former Prime Minister-turned-President operated like a king but flaunted the rhetoric of democracy and socialism at every opportune moment. There was widespread lawlessness coupled with severe shortages of basic foodstuffs. But, Naranbhai had not done too badly through the growing turmoil. If anything, minus the twin-gods life had become more stable than at any time during recent memory. Even his one-time enemy, Raushan, had been completely obliterated after being chucked out by her husband's new mistress. Naranbhai had actually been able to help Raushan with a small cash amount so she could take her children and go and live with her parents in South Africa. This kindly act had given Naranbhai untold pleasure. There was nothing quite as satisfying as being able to perform a grand gesture for a much-despised enemy and then watch them crawl with remorse. But, it would have been most unlike Naranbhai to remain satisfied -- or contented -- for too long.

A number of things still gnawed away at him. The Virjibhai girls, Bimla and Kamla, were still under his roof, and he felt completely frustrated at not being able to launch his new business scheme, just yet. His God Rahu may, or may not eventually turn up but it hardly mattered. Rahu, without his twin Ketu would be quite impotent. In the meantime, he had to somehow get rid of Bimla and Kamla. It was only after one, or both, the girls could be "settled" as far away from Naran Villa as possible, that Naranbhai would be able to do his accounts and see what was still left of Virjibhai's money. And then, he would be able to dazzle the town with his far-sightedness and entrepreneurial vision that would prove to all and sundry, but particularly to Shahbanu, that he was, indeed, a man of exceptional qualities.

It had been nine years since Bimla had been stood up by Bachelor Satish and she was already turning into an old maid -- aged twenty-five! In those intervening years, Naranbhai had tried many other avenues and, on one or two occasions, a marriage date and time had even been fixed. But, in each instance, the bridegroom pulled out at the last minute. There had been a potential bridegroom from the former Protectorate of Nyasaland who had done just that and, another one from Rhodesia, who had even appeared for all the pre-nuptial ceremonies and then backed out just as it was time to tie the final knot. Try as he might, Naranbhai could not understand why every arranged marriage for Bimla, far from being a disastrous marriage, didn't even get as far as actually taking place. OK, so she was an orphan, but she was armed with a reasonable dowry -- a larger amount of money than would have been normal for someone of her class. It was such a big responsibility to be in charge of two, unmarried, virgin females. Surely Naranbhai was entitled to his cut? And, with each passing day while the sisters remained under his roof, he was incurring untold costs: food, clothes...and...err...err...food, clothes....and...err... well. What about the strain from the ever-present threat that one, or both, might soon go morally haywire.

It was after a ninth prospective bridegroom -- one that was fairly suitable and one that even Kamla thought would make a good husband for Bimla -- had backed out at the eleventh hour, Kamla felt it was time to own up: "There's something you should know," she said to the Naranbhais: "I made up a story because I didn't want her to marry Satish..."

She proceeded to detail the bogus astrological prediction based on a film-story by the aunt Kamini. Sobbing and sniffling she confessed that she had put it about that according to the family astrologer, whosoever married her sister was certain to die within six months.

Both Naranbhai and his Mrs stared at her in disbelief. Finally, Mrs Naranbhai spoke.

"You did that? Such a dangerous lie! How dare you ruin her chances? You are evil!"

"I didn't know I was ruining her chances. I only thought that if her wedding could be cancelled then my sister and I could get on with our lives. How was I to know she was dreaming of marriage all along? How was I to know that her life's chief ambition is a loveless marriage? I thought I was doing her a favour..." Kamla broke down, sobbing.

Naranbhai grabbed her by one of her pigtails: "Now, even if we say it was a childish lie, who is going to believe us? Everybody, up and down the country, and all over Africa knows that whoever marries Bimla will die. After everything we've done for you!"

He stomped off, Mrs Naranbhai fast on his heels. How foolish young girls can be! Today, they're skipping and playing, and they think they'll always remain like that. What was a young woman without marriage? That, after all, was the sole reason God created woman -- for the comfort of man, in return for respectability and an improved status in society.

A SUITABLE TREE

One morning, Naranbhai ordered Bimla and Kamla to get ready for travel.

"You must dress up," Mrs Naranbhai said to Bimla. "We're taking you to get married."

Bimla's face lit up, momentarily, and then she blushed and fled from the room.

"Silly girl!" said a shocked Sushilaben. "Doesn't even want to know who she's marrying? Who is the boy?"

"You keep out of it!" barked the second wife. "It is none of your business. I have arranged everything. I am responsible for everything in this house, not you."

"Yes, but who is the groom....?"

"Never you mind," the second Mrs Naranbhai said bossily.

Kamla appeared where the women were talking:

"What is this I hear? My sister, getting married? To whom? And why do we have to go there? Why can't he come here? What's his name? What does he do?"

Mrs Naranbhai raised her hand: "Now, now be quiet, evil girl! Everything is taken care of. You can't always challenge your elders and betters..."

" I'm just asking WHO...? Do we know him...?"

"Kamla, who is getting married? You or your sister? Like a proper Indian girl, she hasn't raised a single objection or asked even one question. She just blushed and ran out of the room. And you? Just look at you! You want to know the whole history like you were the girl's grandmother...."

Kamla ran out of the room. She found Bimla upstairs.

"Don't you even want to know who he is? Aren't you even worried, or afraid...?"

"They have arranged it, so they must know what they are doing. Marriage is a serious business. It isn't for the likes of us to interfere. Our elders always act for the best...."

"Bimla, I can't believe this. Look what happened the last time? Don't you see? They're just trying to get rid of us. They've got our money and they want us out of the way. They won't tell me about your future husband, but they'll have to tell you. You have to ask more questions. It's my future too. Where is this place? Who is this man? Is there a school in this place? Ask them, sister, I beg of you, ask them...."

"Whatever they have done is for the best. They have been good to us. You know, I have only ever dreamed of getting married. There is nothing I want in life except to get married and have children. And, thanks to you, it might never have happened. Now, at last, somebody is prepared to marry me. I don't care who he is, or how he is. He is prepared to marry me. So, will you please stop interfering?"

Kamla stared at her in disbelief. So, it was back to this. What could one do against an older sister who was so blindly submissive to the wishes of elders, and supposedly betters? It is said when bride and groom are both willing then even God Himself cannot get in the way.

If it had been just Bimla's life then Kamla could stand aside, grin and bear it. But she knew that her own future would be tied to Bimla's and she would now be at the mercy of an unknown man, soon to be her brother-in-law and guardian.

But what Kamla didn't yet know was that she need not have feared the prospect of a possibly autocratic, dictatorial brother-in-law. She did not know that he was benign -- in the extreme -- despite being strong and upright. And she need not have feared any scolding, for he was silent...supportive... able to provide a cool shade for all those who came seeking solace from the merciless rays of the sun. And, in keeping with the guidance of the scriptures, he was also older -- as a bridegroom should always be.

To be exact, the said brother-in-law-to-be was, at least, four hundred years old.

He was, in fact, a tall, shady, broad-leafed, *tree*.

A SOLUTION, SUDDENLY

Pandit Suddenly, who had been somewhat eclipsed as holy man ever since Hazari Baba had become the area's favourite sage and story-teller, decided to prove his wide and extensive knowledge by coming up with an unusual solution for Bimla's hopeless predicament. The Pandit was accepted as something of an authority when it came to marriage and other vital, life-changing events. On numerous occasions, he had gathered a small crowd consisting mostly of females and read out to them passages from some obscure scripture or the other. There was that time when he had outlined, in the most pompous language possible, what the sages had said about the rules of conduct for a God-fearing Hindu wife:

"Be her husband deformed, aged, infirm, offensive in his manners; let him also be choleric, debauched, immoral, a drunkard, a gambler; let him frequent places of ill-repute, live in open sin with other women, have no affection whatever for his home; let him rave like a lunatic; let him live without honour; let him be blind, deaf, dumb, or crippled; in a word, let his defects be what they may, let his wickedness be what it may, a wife should always look upon him as her god, should lavish on him all her attention and care, paying no heed whatsoever to his character and giving him no cause whatsoever for displeasure....."

Given his expertise in the subject, the Pandit was, naturally, more than just a little concerned about Bimla's hopeless situation: almost married once or twice, but stood up at the mandap, quite literally. Far worse than a widow, but at least she was still a virgin. But, what use a virgin without the hope of remarriage? The Pandit had said that according to some obscure scriptures (that only he seemed to know about,) a girl in this situation could become a married woman again, and gain all the status and respectability that goes with that noble institution. Apparently, there was a precedent for this. In the old days, it was a frequent occurrence. Girls were often married to an inanimate object, usually a clay water-pot, but ideally, a tree. Then the pot was broken, or the tree felled, whereby she became a widow, but a virgin-widow. That way, the original prediction of the first husband dying was fulfilled, leaving her free to marry a second time. It was known as "Vriksha Vivah," he said, "Marriage to a Tree." And it was important that the ceremony be performed publicly, so that everyone could see that there had been a first "husband" and that "he" had died. But it had to be a particular kind of tree, not just any tree. For a start, it had to be the sort of tree with which no sexual union - however far-fetched its mechanics - was possible. So banana trees, which were aplenty in this part of the world, were ruled out. Many other kinds of trees whose branches could serve all kinds of immoral purposes were also ruled out. Apparently, there was only one kind of tree that was deemed completely safe for such a marriage. It was abundant in India, but nobody was sure if it grew anywhere in East Africa. And, even if it did, perhaps it was known by some other name. The Pandit offered to undertake the gruelling task of travelling - all expenses paid by Naranbhai - to locate the perfect tree.

Mrs Naranbhai had been instrumental in supporting the Pandit's scheme. More than anything, she badly needed to clear her household of all unnecessary female bodies. Once the orphan sisters could be got rid off, she could set about clearing out the first wife and the Mad Girl as well, eventually followed by the widow sister-in-law Nalini. Only then would she able to extend full and proper control over her husband.

"Yes, yes..." she had muttered vaguely, on hearing the Pandit's suggestion. "I did hear something like that once....it has been done..." She clearly hadn't a clue, but the Pandit was thrilled to have some support.

"Yes, that's right! A tree can symbolise suddenly all the benefits of having a husband. And, where no human husband is possible, then a tree can suddenly take his place. It provides shelter, food, respectability...suddenly!"

"But where will she live?" asked Naranbhai.

"Near the tree of course, once we locate a suitable one," said the Pandit.

"And her younger sister, Kamla?" asked Naranbhai.

346

"With her, of course. Once she's a married woman, she can rightfully take charge of the younger one and see to her correct moral upbringing," the Pandit said pompously.

Naranbhai, his second wife and the Pandit had decided to keep their plans secret until the right tree was found. After a search lasting several weeks, Pandit Suddenly settled for an old baobab with a very wide trunk. It was some two hundred miles away, in the middle of nowhere. There was a small village nearby, consisting of a few mud houses, a filling station and a small general store owned and run by an Indian. The shopkeeper, who had a wife and seven children, was approached and agreed to provide, for a low rent, a small storeroom at the back of the shop as accommodation for Bimla and Kamla. Once everything had been agreed, the forthcoming marriage was made public and everybody was informed that this was the antidote to release Bimla from the astrologer's prediction that her first husband would die within six months of marrying her. The tree would be felled three months after her marriage. After that, as a virgin, she would be free to marry a second time.And, her second husband would be quite safe against an early demise. The Pandit set about picking an auspicious hour for the ceremony, which would have to take place at the location of the tree, breaking with traditional custom whereby the bridegroom came over to marry the bride. This bridegroom could not only not be moved but, had his roots - quite literally - several hundred feet below the ground!

WEDDED AT LAST

When the end of Bimla's red sari was being tied round the tree, Kamla still thought it was some weird wedding ritual. Normally, the sari end would have been knotted to the bridegroom's scarf and, bride and groom together were then required to circle the sacred fire -- four times in one direction, with the man leading, and then three times in the other direction, with the bride leading. But, on this occasion, Bimla was asked to walk around the tree as the extra-long length of her sari, gradually unwound itself. When it was nearly coming off, she had to walk in the other direction and let it wrap around her body again. She had to do this a total of seven times while the others showered rice and rose-petals. When all the rounds were done, she and the tree were pronounced man and wife. Kamla thought it was a joke, prior to the appearance of the real bridegroom:

"So, where is he, this man who is supposed to be my new brother-in-law and guardian?" she asked Naranbhai.

"There! Can't you see him? There he stands, proud and dignified! A strong, silent type. A man of few words...thee hee-hee..." Naranbhai chuckled at his own wit.

"You've got to be mad!" screamed Kamla. But, at one level, she found the whole thing so amusing, that she decided to play along. All in all, she decided a tree was far less fraught with unknown dangers than a real man - and a complete stranger at that - might have been.

"So,what now?What happens now?" she asked, having decided to play along with the crazy tree game.

"That's the trouble with educating girls! They want to know everything. The bride hasn't asked a thing but *you* want to know what happens next! They're married -- husband and wife so, what do you think should happen next, eh?" Mrs Naranbhai asked sarcastically.

Kamla laughed,a little hysterically.Bimla glared at her, causing her to fall silent. Naranbhai spoke:"Now, you will both live here. There's a nice Indian shop nearby.The shopkeeper has agreed to let the two of you have a back room."

"Here?But this is in the middle of nowhere!What about my school?"

"All in good time, all in good time,"Naranbhai said, dismissing her with a wave of the hand."The important thing is for your sister to live near her husband so she can serve him -- every morning, and every evening...pay homage...show respect."

"To whom?To a tree?I don't believe this!" Kamla felt like she was in the middle of a particularly weird dream.

"Yes, yes. For three months-- just three months. Then you can both come back and live in Bombay Gardens, and you can start your school again. Three months is nothing. You'll soon catch up with school, clever girl like you..."

"But why *three* months?" asked Kamla.

"All the questions are being asked by the person whose business it isn't," pointed out Mrs Naranbhai." Three months because that is the minimum. After that the tree will be cut down and Bimla will be a widow - but a *virgin* widow...."

"This is mad! I don't understand..."

"Her first husband dies, remember?" Mrs Naranbhai said. "Thanks to you, we have to have a first husband who dies, just so she can find a second one..."

Kamla felt on the brink of madness.Perhaps it had finally happened? All these years of stress and uncertainty about the future had finally taken their toll on her mind?

THANKSGIVING(S)

Shahbanu and her daughter Saira rattled the padlock and chain at the big front gates of Naran Villa at 2 am. "Is anyone there, please? Please open up. This is an emergency! Jannasani! Jannasani!"

Jannasani was renowned for sleeping through almost anything. Sushilaben, the older Mrs Naranbhai was first to get up. She was a light sleeper, being used to being woken up by the Mad Girl's untimely songs. She opened the netted mosquito shutters across the window and looked down at the front of the house.

"Who is it? What do you want?" she asked.

"Please, quick! Open the door! He will kill me! Hurry!"

Soon the entire household was awake. Naranbhai was the last to come down. He wanted to put his arms round Shahbanu but, with all the females of his household looking on, could do no more than just stand beside her protectively.

After she had gratefully accepted a glass of cold water, Shahbanu announced, weakly, "I'd better go back home. I'm sure there's no danger now."

"Danger? Are you in any kind of danger?" Naranbhai asked, most concerned.

She broke down and started crying. Mrs Naranbhai, who was well aware of the sort of impact tears could have on a man, and particularly *her* man on whom she herself had used this gambit on numerous occasions, quickly ushered Shahbanu out of the sitting room: "You are in distress. Don't even think about going home! Here, come here, come upstairs and rest for a while," and she started leading her up the stairs, clearly intending to be alone with her in order to get to the bottom of the mystery. Once she had Shahbanu all to herself she lost no time in dropping the pretended-sympathy and barking:"What the hell are you doing in my house at this hour?"

Shahbanu said she had one of her migraines coming on, and could she please be left alone in a darkened room.

When the news of Shahbanu's headache reached Naranbhai, he lost no time in trundling to the room where she was resting to make further inquiries. No sooner had he arrived at the bedroom door, than Mrs Naranbhai appeared outside the door -- as though out of thin air. Ignoring her, he knocked on the door. Shahbanu emerged looking pale and drawn, a duppatta tied head-band fashion across her forehead.

"Oh, Bhaijan, I'm so ashamed I'm late with the rent. Just until the end of the week -"

"Please, please don't embarrass me. I wasn't even thinking about that. Tell me, what has caused this new headache? Is there anything I can do - err- anything *we* can do?" he added hastily, realising that his wife was hovering dangerously close.

"No, no, you have all been so kind. I'll have the money by the end of the week."

"Please, don't even think about money. That is not what I came to ask about."

Shahbanu's daughter, Saira, who had been aimlessly wandering around Naran Villa, now came into the room and burst into tears:

"Uncle, there *is* no money. We already owe money and those people are threatening to kill us if..."

"Keep quiet!" Shahbanu admonished her daughter, "Don't pay any attention to her. She's just being melodramatic. Girls, you know...."

"Who -- who is going to kill you?" asked Naranbhai, clearly thrilled at the prospect of being able to protect her from killers. "What is all this about owing money?"

"A few thousand shillings. My father borrowed it,and now they can't find him, they're after us,"the daughter Saira elaborated.

"Please,don't say any more," Shahbanu pleaded in a weak voice while at the same time clutching her head with both hands.

"No,tell me everything.Who are these people?Why are they threatening you?"

"When my husband was out of work, last year, we had to borrow -- and now, they want it back, by tomorrow. Otherwise they have threatened to take Saira by force..." Shahbanu broke down again.

Naranbhai was thoughtful for a moment. The rent was no problem. He could certainly wait -- even postpone payment indefinitely. But what was this about a few thousand shillings owed to some extremely menacing-sounding thuggy types of villians?

Finally he asked: "How much money do you owe?"

"Oh, more than I could ever find for tomorrow," Shahbanu said weakly.

"How much?" Naranbhai asked again, firmly, determined to rescue her, somehow.

She told him, and Naranbhai, although his second wife was hovering somewhere behind him, felt Mrs Naranbhai's whole being stiffen in anticipation of any plan to lend money to the beautiful Shahbanu.Even so, he did a few quick mental calculations.Virjibhai's savings and insurance money had improved his cash flow situation considerably in recent years.

"What time are they coming tomorrow?" he asked and then said in dramatic tones:"Tell them to come here, not Bombay Gardens! *I'll* be here to settle with them, and will have a few stern words to say. They are *not* to hassle my lone women tenants in future!"

"I can't let you do that! It's too much! How will I pay you back?" Shahbanu protested, rather feebly.

Mrs Naranbhai was about to open her mouth, but being the tactician that she was, she thought better of it. With a few, quick, mental aerobics she worked out that if Naranbhai was determined to 'save' the woman then there wasn't a thing she could do to prevent that. Opposition would only push him closer to the manipulative Shahbanu. She didn't, for a moment, believe Shahbanu's story. But, with her innate cunningness - the kind that is usual in women who have had little, or no formal education - she quickly realised that the only thing that would cure her husband of his infatuation for Shahbanu, would be to be duped out of a large sum of money. Here, at last, was a God-sent opportunity to stand back and just watch him fall out of love. And, when that happened, she would gather him up to her bosom and never even acknowledge that such a fascination had existed in the first place. Sure, it would mean the loss of a substantial sum of money, but then who said lessons come cheap?

She was a clever woman. Second wives, like second-borns, had to be much sharper than their predecessors and more tuned into the scheming, plotting ways of potential successors. So, Mrs Naranbhai remained quiet and dignified. Delighted that his wife was not going to interfere, and having allowed a sufficient pause for this eventuality, Naranbhai spoke with renewed confidence:

"Just tell those badmash ghunda thugs that I will be here, and the money will be here," he said in dramatic tones.

"No, please! I can't let you get dragged into all this. It would be better if you just gave me the money otherwise they might make up all sorts of things about you and me. If that gets back to my husband he will be so hurt. If they see you sticking up for me, they'll think -- you and I -"

She looked at Mrs Naranbhai and stopped mid-sentence.

Naranbhai considered this for a minute. What was the point of showing himself to unknown menacing types? Apart from his well-worn black umbrella, there was nothing in the house that even vaguely resembled a weapon. What was the point of having direct dealings with such unsavoury, thuggy-types? They might come back again and again and pester him for even more money. Far better, just give Shahbanu the money and let her deal with the baddies herself. After all, he only wanted *her* to feel indebted. Why show himself to her enemies and invite more trouble?

Later that evening, he handed Shahbanu a bundle of notes tied in a large white handkerchief. She wept profusely as she took it, with both hands cradled as though she were receiving a particularly fragile baby destined to someday form a new religion:

"Oh, Bhai-jaan, there can't be a better brother than you in the whole world! I will pay it back, as soon as I can. Thank you, thank you. May Allah cherish and protect you, and may He protect all those who are cherished by you. May you live a thousand years and may each year have ten thousand days. May your children fare forth into the world and do you proud and may their children inherit this world as masters and leaders.May my own house be struck by lightning so yours can flourish and prosper... "

"Yes, yes, all right," he said, slightly embarrassed at the eloquent thanksgiving in Urdu.

Mrs Naranbhai, close as ever, spoke for the first time: "No point in offering to have *your* own house burn down -- remember, that too is *our* house!"

And then she turned her eyes heavenwards in a silent, secret thanksgiving of her own.

REVISITING THE FAMILIAR

Within twenty-four hours of Naranbhai handing over the bundle of notes to Shahbanu, Bombay Gardens had witnessed one of the most dramatic episodes in its entire history. A man, understood to be Shahbanu's husband, had turned up and dragged her away, kicking and screaming. Afterwards it was mooted about that Mr Hussein had come back to claim his wife because the woman he had left her for had subsequently ditched him. And that abandoned by her husband, Shahbanu had, in the meantime, done her best to earn a living in the only way she had known. She'd had connections in high places through the oldest profession in the world and business was booming. Her husband had returned to claim his share of the booty and had dragged her back to his home in Congo -- or maybe even England or Canada. Nobody was too sure. But, as usual, the gaps had been filled in by wild guesses. There were those who believed that Shahbanu was in on it and that she and her husband operated by living separately.

Only Naranbhai refused to believe this. As far as he was concerned, Shahbanu was the victim in all this. The day after her husband had dragged her away, Naranbhai and his cronies had discussed the matter at length at their usual verandah forum.

"Isn't there anything more anybody could have done?" Naranbhai asked nobody in particular. "How can a man just turn up out of the blue and claim back a wife that he has abandoned for another woman?"

"He is her husband," said the Pandit, resident expert on a wife's duty. "He has full rights over her - not only under Islamic law, but under any law..."

"But in Islam it is easy to get divorced, no? Why did she have to go with him if she didn't want to?" the grocer Dhanjihai asked.

"Wanting or not wanting doesn't come into it," explained the Pandit. "A woman's place is by her husband. As for divorce - I don't know where you get these ideas that it is easy for Muslims. For men, yes. They can say 'I divorce you' three times, suddenly, in front of witnesses - male witnesses - and the deed is done, suddenly. A woman can do no such thing. She can only leave in disgrace. She can either be thrown out by the man, in which case he pays to evict her or then, she can leave of her own accord denouncing her right to his children, his property, all his worldly goods. Now, which woman would do such a crazy thing, suddenly, you tell me? And where would she go if she did? Her parents would refuse to know her..."

"Even though the husband had abandoned her for another woman?"

"Well, he hadn't really abandoned her. He had only married another woman. He was well within his rights. A man taking on another wife doesn't give the first wife grounds for divorce. It is every Muslim woman's duty to tolerate her husband's other wives..."

Naranbhai was wiping his tears again.

Sushilaben, Naranbhai's first wife was leaning out of the window of her front-facing bedroom, following the conversation below with great interest. She remained silent, but her look said it all:

"Huh! These men think only Muslim men have many wives!" she muttered under breath. Mad Girl Kirti who stared blankly at her mother. But there was a strange twinkle in her eye and the faintest hint of stagnant tears. For a split second Sushilaben felt as though the girl had understood perfectly. Then she checked herself for imagining things. A minute later the Mad Girl broke into song: it was a song about remaining thirsty in the Beloved's backyard. Like a plant wilting without rain. The lover admonished the Beloved:

For others you dig oceans
And I remain thirsty
Right here, in your backyard

The Mad Girl Kirti's golden singing voice made all the men on the verandah look up.

"Sorry, sorry, my mad daughter, you know," Naranbhai said, clearly embarrassed. "Doesn't know when to sing and when to shut up."

The Pandit resumed his summing up of the Shahbanu case:

356

"Well, she has gone with her husband, suddenly. She is his wife, so there's nothing anyone can do," he concluded as though privy to all the wisdom of Solomon.

Naranbhai found himself getting increasingly irritated with the man. It was almost as though he was enjoying himself just a bit too much at this tragic and dramatic turn of events. A married man had asserted his right to repossess his wife and the Pandit seemed to think that that was the way things should be, as did the second Mrs Naranbhai.

And, at such a time, amidst all the drama of Shahbanu protesting and wailing and being dragged through the dust, which person in their right mind could have brought up the matter of Naranbhai's recent loan of twenty thousand shillings to the woman?

Supposing, just supposing...? It was extremely painful for Naranbhai to have to believe that Shahbanu was anything less than a saint. It was easier to believe that Shahbanu's husband was a crook of the first order and had been involved in all manner of shady activities including pimping his wife to high-ranking black politicians....and at one time...perhaps even, the tribal King. Could she have been in on it? No, she could never do that! But a lot of men did visit her....no, no, her husband made her do it...but what if she had actually enjoyed it...? No, no! Nice women never enjoyed that sort of thing.

And then, there was his forthcoming big business scheme, a secret he had yet to disclose to friends and family. It had been designed for the specific aim of glorifying his image to the extent that Shahbanu would swoon at his feet. And now, with Shahbanu gone, where was the pleasure in launching such grandiose schemes?

Conflicting thoughts and emotions are the most tiring phenomenon known to man. As if to avoid thinking at all, Naranbhai suddenly felt bored with the male company on the verandah. He excused himself as though to go the bathroom, but headed straight for the bedroom of his first wife. As he appeared in the doorway, she was almost paralysed with shock. This hadn't happened for years: Naranbhai coming on his own to see her, without the second wife looking like she and her husband were joined at the hip.

He hovered at the doorway. The Mad Girl lay down on the bed and turned her face towards the wall. Suhsilaben got up to see what he wanted. He usually only spoke to her in connection with some new treatment for the Mad Girl, or when the second wife had been tittle-tattling about some real or imagined insult at the hands of her older rival.

"Yes, what is it?" asked Sushilaben finally.

"Nothing. Just came to see if you are all right? I mean..."

Sushilaben was quick to gauge his mood: "I am fine, but I feel very sad for Shahbanu. How unfair! I can't stop thinking about her. "

"I know," said Naranbhai quietly, sitting down next to her on the bed, "I can't stop thinking about her either. You know everything has started to go wrong since my twin-gods both disappeared. It's like all my powers disappeared with them..."

"I know, I know, " she said in the gentlest of tones. "Still, what could you have done? Shahbanu was a good, kind woman. We mustn't think badly of her. I'm sure she meant to return the money. But her husband turned up and dragged her away. What is a woman to do when a man marries another woman over her head, and is sanctioned by his religion to do so?" Sushilaben posed a rhetorical question. The irony was not lost on him. After all, hadn't he done just that to her?

Naranbhai pulled up both his legs and placed his head on his knees despondently.

"I feel so let down. I thought she was such a decent woman..."

"But she was, she was!" Sushilaben protested. "Such poise, grace, charm, dignity."

"But I never even realised that she might...she might... *cheat* me...." Naranbhai broke down. She knew he wasn't referring to the money, but Sushilaben thought it best to treat the whole thing as though it *was* only about the money. What was the point of rubbing salt into his wounds? What was the point of insinuating that all the while Naranbhai's heart -- and body -- had ached for her, she was in the arms of, and over, and under, and on all fours, with scores of others? And, that too in a house on which he had lowered the rent, as a special favour to her?

"No, of course she wasn't going to cheat you! What else could she do? Her husband needed money and as a loyal wife she had to provide it.....she entertained all those men because of his political activities. He made her do it, don't you see? What else could she have done? Opened a flower shop?"

"Nobody could teach her about flowers" Naranbhai said wistfully remembering the transformation of Bombay Gardens. What would happen to all those potted plants now? When your husband drags you back, hands and feet tied with rope, there isn't much time to worry about packing the plants. Naranbhai had been left with the bitterest taste in his mouth. Shahbanu, who had been such an inspiration for all his other tenants had, in reality, turned out to have such an unsavoury profession. Naranbhai recalled his disapproval of unmarried young women as tenants. But Shahbanu was married so it ought to be have been OK. Didn't marriage bring automatic respectability any more? What was the world coming to? Still, wasn't it Shahbanu who had inspired all of Bombay Gardens to pray and perform various other religious rituals bringing a distinctly holy feel to the whole place?

"So what?" Sushilaben said in answer to his question, and proceeded to rationalise Shahbanu's actions in a long speech that left Naranbhai open-mouthed.

"Look, she wasn't very educated," said Sushilaben, "but Shahbanu was astute. Life had dealt her enough blows for her to realise that people had strange notions of respectability and it was best to fit in with their expectations. And a public display of devotion is the most foolproof method of appearing respectable. She knew she lived in a world given only to outward appearances, and her every instinct told her it was her duty to appear holy. Whatever people see, they believe -- that's the way of this world. Shahbanu didn't really see anything wrong with her profession as a saleswoman for the world's oldest and most popular commodity, but she knew, with a positive certainty, that the very purchasers of that commodity are usually at the forefront of its condemnation."

Naranbhai reeled at the articulate and persuasive speech. Why hadn't he realised that he had a philosopher for a first wife? Why hadn't she shown him this side of her nature before? Had he perhaps not given her enough of a chance?

Sushilaben, encouraged by his attentiveness went on: "Besides, in walking out on her, her husband made a serious error of judgement. Just because he didn't want her, he assumed nobody else would desire her either. Serious mistake! A man should never think that!"

She finished with an enigmatic smile, but Naranbhai was too distraught to take note of those last words.

She continued: "Look, you also married another woman, and I stood by silently. Don't get me wrong, I understand you *had* to do it. But, I had to watch you go into your second wife's room every night. How did I get through that? With a new woman coming to live with you in *my* house, our old, faithful servant became my most valuable ally and support...see, one never knows where one might find true love..."

Naranbhai suddenly broke down and started sobbing noisily. Sushilaben thought it would be less embarrassing if she carried on comforting him about Shahbanu, rather than the latest bombshell she had just dropped on him. She put her hand on his arm and said in reassuring tones: "Well, we did whatever we could for her. God give her strength, poor woman!"

Naranbhai raised his head and looked into Sushilaben's eyes in a way he hadn't for well over a decade. And, as he did this, he felt the same first flush of youth that he had experienced when illegally consummating their marriage in those old ruins all those years ago. He realised, with something of a pang, that Sushilaben was in fact, quite a sweet and reasonable sort of woman. There was not a hint of that belligerence about her that he had come to associate with his battleaxe of a second wife; besides, this new, deep thinker-philosopher Sushilaben was, even now, not an altogether bad looking woman. And, with that thought upper most in his mind, he resolved to spend this night in Sushilaben's room.

WIFELY DUTIES

Within two months of Bimla's marriage to the tree, the country was plunged into political chaos. A partial military take-over resulted in different areas being under different governments. The cocky prime minister-turned president had fled the country but some of his loyal supporters retained control in certain provinces. The rest of the country had come under the dictatorship of a rather whimsical military man from the north, rumoured to love Indian food.

The remote village where Bimla and Kamla now lived came under the control of the samosa-loving dictator. He was an affable sort of chap, determined to mingle among his subjects and equally determined to gradually extend his control over the rest of the country. At the end of it all, he had plans to crown himself King - - not like the primitive tribal king who had been ousted some years earlier, but King in the old fashioned European way - complete with a jewelled crown and a court of jesters, advisors, story-tellers, dancers, snake charmers and....and magicians.

The Dictator's favourite pastime was to drive around in a jeep observing the daily life of his subjects - "My Peepole" as he referred to them. One day, as he was driving through a sleepy village with a large shady tree he was dumbfounded by what he saw:

"Most interesting, this is most interesting," he said to his Chamcha-Sidekick. "I am most interested in other cultures. What is that young Indian woman doing?"

Bimla's daily rituals of paying homage to her tree-husband, morning and evening, had already become a common sight for the locals. They had viewed the procedure on numerous occasions with a certain degree of amusement. She would appear at the tree at sunrise and at sunset. Her head covered in her sari, she would bend down and touch the roots with her right hand. After offering an auspicious red powder to the tree, she would sprinkle the powder into the middle-parting of her hair. Then she would lay a metal thali of fruit and nuts at the foot of the tree. The Dictator had never seen anything quite like this before, watched with as much interest and fascination as a young child might show on a maiden trip to the zoo.

"Very interesting indeed!" he remarked again to his Chamcha-Sidekick when the ritual was over and Bimla had gone back to the nearby shop behind which she and Kamla shared a storeroom.

"Do you suppose," the Dictator remarked to his Chamcha, "there is some kind of treasure buried at the root of that tree? Indians are famous for making gold and then hiding it. All this bowing of her head can only mean one thing. She is bowing to God. Indians give food to God before they give it to a starving passone. These Indians only have one God, you know? He's called *Gold*. I love them, these peepole of mine."

Then he frowned and said: "Gold and God, eh? What's the difference between the two? Just one letter. The letter "L". And what does that stand for? Pound! Do you know what a pound is?" he pointed a gun at the petrified Chamcha.

"Yes, sah! A weight. So many pounds of this, and so many pounds of that. That's what a pound is," said the dim-witted Chamcha who had had to leave secondary school after Form One, following a death in the family.

The Dictator thwacked him on the head with the gun:

"Fool! Imbecile! Pound is POUND. Money! Pound sterling! The currency with the picture of my beloved Majesty, Queen of England. Now do you follow?"

The Chamcha wasn't too sure, but decided to nod anyway. His boss clearly had a thing about kings and queens. He'd better agree. That, after all, was what he was paid for.

"Good, good!" beamed the Dictator. "You are learning faass. Stick with me and you will learn moa. I wonda how much gold these Indians have hidden away? ...eeh...how many of them are there anyway? If each paasone had one pound of gold, how many pounds that makes?"

The Chamcha was getting tired of these examination-style questions. Then he had a brainwave: "Don't know sah! How many pounds would depend on how many people."

"You Boffu! *That* is exactly what you have to find out!"

"Me, sah?" the Chamcha's voice quavered.

"Yes, you! Who else? I need to know how much gold is hidden under various trees in my country. And to know that, I must know how many lovely, lovely Indian peepole reside in my beautiful land. And how many know how to make gold..."

"What will you do when you have found out sah?" the Chamcha asked.

"What did your mother eat when you were in her womb? Have you no commasenss? Once I know who they are, I will demand...no request, that they teach me their secret gold-making recipe..."

A NATIONAL TREASURE

Soon after that conversation between the partial-Dictator and his dimwit Chamcha-Sidekick, some soldiers arrived and pinned a plaque to the tree trunk. They put a cordon around it. At the same time, a small hut was hastily erected and a 24-hour askari-soldier was put into place. From this day on, Bimla was not allowed to touch the tree, but merely hand over her offerings to the watchman who would place her tray of food at the base of the tree-trunk. According to the newly put up plaque, the tree had been declared the oldest in the country. It was said to be more than 400 years old and, as such, a protected national heritage. It was further announced that anyone caught tampering with the tree in anyway whatsoever, whether breaking off its leaves, or rubbing their body against its trunk or even pissing at its roots, would be carted off for a thousand lashings, or similar.

Meanwhile, when a little over three months had lapsed since the tree wedding, a small delegation set out from Naran Villa for the village two hundred miles away, to perform the ceremony of executing the tree, so that Bimla could be declared a virgin widow. Her first "husband" could be laid to rest, and the way paved for her second marriage. Naranbhai, Pandit Suddenly and Patel the photographer had only gone fifty miles when they were stopped at a checkpoint. A checkpoint? There had never been checkpoints on any of these roads before. It's not as though they were crossing a national border! The checkpoint was manned by armed soldiers. Soldiers had never been seen in this part of the country. Something must have happened. Some local, tribal crisis. If it had been some kind of national emergency, they would surely have heard something.

"Never mind," said Naranbhai. "We'll have to do it some other day. As long as she's been married for three months at least, it doesn't matter when we kill the tree..."

When they arrived back at Naran Villa, the entire household was on the verandah. The D'Sa children had also assembled. Mrs Naranbhai ran forward tearfully: "Oh thank God you're all right! We were so worried..."

364

Before Naranbhai could ask anything, one of the D'Sa children announed: "Military take-over! Raushan's husband Sam has become Head of Radio and Television. He helped the military, and now he's been rewarded."

Naranbhai's jaw dropped, not so much at this shocking turn of events, but more at the life-long mystery of how the ragged D'Sa children always knew of momentous political happenings long before anybody else. Even so, Naranbhai's first thoughts were not so much the matter of the tree, or how to release Bimla from her first marriage, but more whether his brand new business venture would now have to be shelved because of the rapidly spreading military take-over. The Dictator, originally thought to be no more than a crazy buffoon and only in charge of a couple of towns and four or five villages in the north-west, now seemed to have moved into the capital.

DEATH BY SAMOSA

Soon after the partial military coup, the new military dictator was heard to have said:

"I was taking a leisurely stroll down Main Street, and do you know what? For a moment I thought I was somewhere in India. Every shop sign had an Indian name, and almost every passer-by was in Indian clothes. Where am I asked myself? I am a very honest man of action, man of God. I had to keep pinching myself to check that I had not been transported by some magic carpet to the great Asian city of Bombay. Hee, hee, hee, hee, hee-hee-hey-hey..." his medals clinked as his heavily padded shoulders moved in time to the rhythm of his laughter. He always laughed a lot at his own jokes.

The word 'magic' had started to appear with alarming frequency in the Dictator's everyday speech. Magic and magicians were a top priority in the new scheme of things. Every single voodoo-antar-mantar-jantar practitioner in the marketplace and been rounded up and taken off to a special institution. Every single witchdoctor's clinic was closed with the witchdoctor being carted off to the same institution. But unlike the Salem witch hunt, this rounding up was about keeping the practitioners of these magic arts confined in top-security military jails where they were under a sentence of death to pass on their craft and skills to designated military men. The Dictator had wanted them to impart, in a few days, all that they had learned via the time-honoured technique of oral tradition over hundreds of years. Each and every trick and recipe had had to be demonstrated and then, when it was tried out by one of the military chaps and it happened to fail, the magician would not live to see the dawn.

The Dictator's comment about his country's chief city looking like something in "Asia", through a process of magic, was seen as harmless buffoonery - typical - of the kind that people had come to expect. If you woke up one particular morning and found that the Dictator had not made some momentous philosophical pronouncement about the country, or then again about other countries, or about this race or that, then you could safely conclude that he wasn't feeling tickety-boo that morning. The

Dictator's comments always became favourite family jokes and were repeated and chuckled over round the family dining table. Producing so much laughter and amusement, his half-baked sayings and pronouncements had even been welcome in these tense, lawless times, particularly by Indians who were keen to cite proof of the indisputable fact that whether leaders, masters, dictators or slaves, all Black Africans are, basically, dimwits.

Nobody, not even the doom-and-gloom laden Mrs Naranbhai, that most recent of Indian settlers who was apt to imagine shootings and massacres at the drop of a hat, had fully appreciated the wider implications of the Dictator's remarks about his capital city looking like a cross between Bombay and Karachi. Instead, when the remark had been reported to her via the usual Bombay Gardens Express Wire system, Mrs Naranbhai had chuckled: "He should be so lucky! When else would he, of all people, get to visit a first class place like Bombay?"

But, unknown to Mrs Naranbhai, the Dictator's remarks on his capital city resembling Bombay, had then led to his asking one of his side-kicks: "How many Indians in my beautiful country?"

"Don't know," Side-kick had replied languidly, hoping against hope that he wasn't going to be sent out to personally, there and then, count every single Muhindi head up and down the country and report his results by that evening. But *that* was exactly what the Dictator asked him to do!

"Oh no!" the Side-kick Chamcha moaned. "Please sah, have maahcy on me!" He was down on his knees.

"OK, since I'm a God-fearing man, and a man of action and not just words, I give you one week to make a form with questions. Make at least foa pages of questions. Find your friends to sit down at different places with the forms and ask all Muhindis to come and fill out this form. No, don't ask them to fill it out. Better still, treat them like they can't read and write. You guys ask the questions, and then fill out the form yourself. Pretend not to understand some of the answers. Take a long time to write down the answers. Make the gold-guzzling bastards wait as long as possible. Pay particular attention to the column that says: 'Occupation.' This whole exercise is for me to know how many

gold-makers there are in my country. And, when the form is
finished, don't let them sign it. Remember, we're treating them
like they can't read of write. Make them do a thumbprint. Yes!
That is a genius idea of mine. What is it?"

"Genius Sah!"

"Correct! Make them do a thumbprint, even if they are top
professor at University! Hee-hee-hee-hee-hee! And then just to
show goodwill, I will do some circulating myself. I'll turn up here
and there to show I am also involved in operations. Africans are
very hospitable people. These Muhindis are our special guests.
Now, can a host ever not know the exact number of guests in his
house? No, no, very pooa show! A host must always have an
EXACT idea of how many guests are in his house. So, I must
know each and every Muhindi in my country. I'll visit Muhindi
houses at random - actually I love their food - so that's not such a
bad idea. See? Another genius idea of mine! What idea of mine?"

"Geeenuous, geenuous, Sah!" the Chamcha was compelled to
respond.

Soon, it was rumoured that the Dictator had taken to driving
around in a jeep and calling at various Indian houses, at random,
and ordering that samosas - his favourite Indian snack - be
prepared for him, pronto. The woman who had been the first
recipient of such a call, had bragged about it to all and sundry:
"He just ate, and ate and ate and then clutching his stomach said:
"Aahhh--aaahhh...I'm dying, Mamma, O Mamma, I'm dying...!"

Mrs Naranbhai turned green with envy at the woman's story.
Naran Villa was one of the grandest houses in town, yet the
Dictator had not seen fit to call here and order his samosas. She
consoled herself that she had been saved the purchase of a brand
new dinner service, to prevent the household crockery being
defiled by the Dictator who was rumoured to have several kinds
of sexually transmitted afflictions. Needless to say, a number of
these were said to have been contracted by coupling with
mammals other than the human species.

After a few more weeks had gone by and the entire matter
forgotten, the Dictator's jeep pulled up outside Naran Villa at
exactly a quarter to one. The normal Naran Villa lunch was just

being laid and the sudden arrival of the Dictator threw the entire schedule into chaos. Samosas - which were not on the menu that day and which usually took the best part of the day to prepare - had to be hastily cobbled together, somehow. The resulting delay in lunch being served allowed the Dictator a fair stretch of time in which to explore the grounds of Naran Villa, as well as catch a glimpse of some neatly laid out barracks-style houses known as Bombay Gardens. Naranbhai hovered behind him, nervous and agitated as hell and unsure as to how to make conversation. On meeting famous people he meant to say all sorts of things but always became mysteriously tongue-tied when the opportunity came. As luck would have it, the Dictator caught sight of a serene and majestic figure in white robes, floating through the greenery, and bending down to sniff at some gardenias. Thinking it an extremely odd sight, he ordered Naranbhai to summon the man to come over. Naranbhai was thrilled at the prospect of the Dictator giving Hazari Baba a piece of his mind. Maybe the Dictator was going to scold - or even punish - the Baba for strolling around aimlessly sniffing at flowers when what the country needed was for men to work harder and harder and stop the Imperialist Conspiracy from taking over the African continent.

Hazari Baba was quite some distance away - and out of ear-shot - so instead of bellowing the command, Naranbhai waved his hand hoping to catch the Baba's eye to signal him to come over. But Hazari Baba, as was his wont, refused to look in Naranbhai's direction. He continued burying his nose into the gardenias, oblivious to Naranbhai, and equally oblivious to the seven-foot tall Dictator. In the end, Naranbhai yelled for Jannasani to abandon whatever he was doing and run over and fetch Hazari Baba. Jannasani emerged, black hands caked with white samosa dough, and immediately set out to obey orders. A tense silence followed as Naranbhai and the Dictator stood on the verandah watching, but unable to hear the exchange between the wiry Jannsani and the elusive Baba.

THE DIVINE WILL

"You are wanted, at the house. Get yourself over there -- pesi-pesi," Jannasani said, breathlessly and without making any concession to the custom of showing reverence and respect when addressing holy Baba types.

"Johnson," Baba began, being probably the only person in the vicinity, if not the whole world, who used Jannasani's original name. "Johnson, do you see this flower, right here, this one?"

Jannsani was never one to notice trees or flowers. He looked at it, slightly puzzled.

"Tell me, Johnson, do you see it?" Baba asked again.

"Yes, of course I see it, so?" grumbled Jannsani thinking life was really too unfair. He'd only been sent to summon the bearded man to Naran Villa. Nobody told him Baba would put him through some sort of gruelling gardening quiz and, that too, with samosa dough still sticking to his hands.

"The interesting thing about this flower is that nobody can tell it to grow. It can only follow its own nature pervaded with the Divine Will. The less that human beings interfere in nature's processes the greater the chance the Divine Will manifests and balances things out. So, like this flower, I know not where my feet may take me. One day I may well venture towards your master's house. But for now, leave me with my musings. Like that flower, I too come and go of my own will. No human being can tell me where to go. Only God decides my movements."

Jannasani gawked, trying to work out how to paraphrase Baba's English reply into Swahili for Naranbhai. He started running back to the house, still preoccupied with how to translate all that bit about the Divine Will and flowers growing as and when they like, not only for his master, but also the master of the entire country...

When he reached them, Jannasani said: "He says God decides his movements. Only God can tell him where to go."

"God?" said the Dictator, clearly put out that anyone other than himself should claim access to the Divine. "Go and tell him I *am* God and it is *my* divine will that he report to me this minute."

"That's right!" barked Naranbhai, keen to agree with the Dictator. "Doesn't he know that leaders of countries are just like God? Go back and tell him there is an important census going on, and he must be counted. Ask him if he has done his forms yet."

Naranbhai was determined to show the Dictator how law-abiding and politically aware he was. In referring to the Asian population census in this direct way, he hoped he had chalked up a few more points in the Dictator's book.

Jannasani's wiry form ambled back towards the gardenia bush:

"Census! Bwana and Leader want to know if you are aware of the Census and if you have filled out the paperwork....." he said to the Baba.

"I filled out my form long before the Universe was created. I have already been counted. God made this earth. Man made countries. I cannot be a signatory to anything that is man-made," replied Baba in his soft, melodious voice.

Jannasani frowned. What on earth was the man on about? Most Muhindis were a bit loopy in the head, but this one was the King of all Loops. Bloody Loop Guru!

He went back to report Baba's little speech but before he could open his mouth, the Dictator shouted at him:

"What have you come back for you useless man? No wonder you're just a servant! No brains!" And, with that, the Dictator tapped his gun at Jannasani's sweaty temple, and continued: "Wretched houseboy! Cooking and washing for Muhindis. Not like me. I am Master of my country -- Champion of Africa. Now, your orders were to send that hairy man in his Persil-White robes to present himself to me...GO!"

Jannasani hesitated, but when he reluctantly turned around to obey orders, he, Naranbhai and the Dictator saw that the Baba had vanished. The spot where he had been admiring the gardenia bush was in clear view, as was the land around it.

"Where does he live? Where?" the Dictator asked in urgent tones.

"Si-jui - don't know -" replied Jannasani. He was afraid to reiterate Baba's oft-heard pronouncement that the earth was his floor and the sky his ceiling. That kind of statement might well have caused the Dictator to shoot Jannasani on the spot.

The Dictator turned his gaze on Naranbhai who shook his head, in a gesture of helplessness.

"Most interesting, most interesting," remarked the Dictator and barked: "Cancel the samosas!"

And, with that, he jumped into his jeep and sped away leaving Naran Villa groaning under the weight of enough food to feed a banquet of a hundred and fifty!

ERECTIONS OF GOLD

The Dictator sped back to his Headquarters and immediately summoned his lackeys for an important meeting. These were not people who were allowed to advise him, or raise objections. This group of men served an even more vital function. They were appointed to furnish various pairs of ears so that the Dictator could test the full impact of his words on a live audience. In return for an erratically paid though generous salary, they were only ever required to say one word: 'Yes.'

"I have seen and heard interesting things in the last few days," the Dictator opened the meeting with the Yes-Men. "These Muhindis are not just Brown peepole who put sweet-smelling oil in their hair. They are not just peepole who wear different clothes and speak a different language. They operate all kinds of magic. Making things appear and disappear. Gold. They know how to make gold. They make tons of gold and then hide it somewhere, usually under the roots of a tree. Then they appoint one of their girls to guard the tree and place food by it, morning and night. They even have a girl who can make the moon bigger just by singing. And there's one man in white-white clothes and a long-long beard who only talks about flowers and then disappears into thin air. Magic! That is how they live so well. That is why they drive such big cars. That is why their women wear so much jewellery. It's not all good business sense and hard work, as they make you believe. They are summoning the magical forces to aid their prosperity. Now, there is nothing wrong with that. I want the peepole of my country to be prosperous. But are these Muhindis of my country? No, they are from India. But I have no problem in letting them enjoy my country if, in return, they shared with us their gold-making secret. Also, for my own pahssonal use, I would like to learn how to appeah and disappeah at will. I could have hours and hours of fun doing that. Now, how many of you would like to know the secret of making gold?"

All hands shot up in the air and a chorus of "Me, me, me" rose from the grinning yes-men.

"And how many of you would like to vanish into thin air at will?" he asked.

"Me, me, me also, me too, me," the chorus sang again.

"Good, good! So we are going to ask all our Muhindi brothers - now we know how many of them are in the country, their names, addresses, other details - we are going to call them one by one and request, I said REQUEST that they teach us their magical arts. If they don't know how to do magic, then they can give us the names and details of those who can. And, one by one, we'll invite them to our Command Post and request instruction in the ancient arts of India. Some of them, I hear, can have a continuous erection for 84 years. Eighty-foa years! Now, how many of you would like...?"

With uncharacteristic boldness, the chorus of "me, me, me" sprang up even before the Dictator, His Highness the Champion Liberator of Africa, could finish his sentence.

THINK BIG-BIG

Once the capital had been taken over, it was widely assumed that the military coup was complete, even though large areas of the south and south-east still remained under the old, partially defunct government. In the capital, the military take-over had only caused four or five days' disruption. After that, shops and businesses opened as normal. If anything, the situation felt a lot safer than it had done for a long time. Soon, apart from the presence of groups of soldiers here and there, there was nothing to suggest that the country was in political turmoil. The Indians were soon back to their normal activities and, the recent arrests of various people defined as "unlawful elements" in society had, if anything, made it easier for Indians to relax and enjoy life once again. But to say that Naranbhai was satisfied would be an overstatement. Life hadn't been too bad to him, and many of his past failures were now, somewhat, rectified. The girls Bimla and Kamla had finally been "settled." But Shahbanu's sudden, and unexplained departure had left a big hole, not only in his pocket, but in his ego. He still consoled himself that Shahbanu, owing to the dubious activities of her husband, had had no choice in the matter. She must have meant to pay back his money, but obviously didn't get a chance. Now, with whatever money was left, he felt the time was right to make his impact within his community and the rest of the town and country at large. The new Dictator had to be shown that certain Indians could still mount large operations and give the country a very good name. Yes, Naranbhai was now comfortably well off, and he was certainly the wealthiest man on his patch, but he felt that his real destiny had yet to be given a chance.

With Bimla and Kamla finally off his hands, and there being no other grand scheme to occupy his spare brain space, Naranbhai decided to implement his long-cherished business idea. In the past, there had been the question of money. But now, being a trustee for Virjibhai's girls had put quite a bit of spare cash in his hands. And then the recent political climate had been far from conducive to any kind of lavish merry-making. The previous President's constant references to "socialism" had sent shivers up

Naranbhai's spine. For Naranbhai, socialism was inseparable from Black Nationalism. And Black Nationalism could only be about hatred of Indians.

"These dumbos! Instead of hating the White man who ruled over them, they hate us!"

"Yes, but the Indians were part of that colonisation - you see it was arranged so that suddenly *we* would be hated -" the Pandit had tried to enlighten him.

But Naranbhai would never allow the Pandit to give him history lessons. OK, so the guy had read a few fat books in English, but that didn't make him an expert on business. Only Naranbhai had the vision required for an entrepreneur. And now, with a brand new Dictator in charge, and things more settled than they had been for a long time, this was the time for Naranbhai to show the world something new.

His new business scheme had the potential for cheering everybody up. This kind of thing might even help take everyone's minds off the political troubles and rumours of shootings and stabbings and put some festive spirit back into everyone. Diwali - the Hindu Festival of Lights - was imminent and he had a very special treat planned for his subjects. It was time to sound out his cronies about the scheme.

Naranbhai's gang of four, complete with associates and numerous hangers-on assembled on the Naran Villa verandah that evening. The recent curfew and State of Emergency had been lifted. The brand new Dictator, in a televised address, had urged the country to return to normal. He had asked people to have parties, to start going out in the evenings, to start spending money again. In his television debut, the Dictator had amused everyone with his sense of humour and peculiar turn of phrase.

"Eat, drink, enjoy! Spend, spend, spend! That is the way to improve our economy. We have been left in a very bad state, very bad state indeed by the corrupt practices of the previous government -- enemies of freedom. Now, we are all free. And you must see me as your Father. And I am ordering you to go out and spend money and enjoy yourself," the Dictator had said. And, if Naranbhai had had any lingering doubts as to the wisdom of launching his latest lavish business idea, this maiden speech by the Dictator had suddenly removed them. Who knows? The Dictator might even give Naranbhai a medal of honour in recognition of his efforts to enable people to "enjoy, go out, spend, spend..."

It was time to come out with the plan. Naranbhai broached the subject in a roundabout way. He began by announcing that the second Mrs Naranbhai had, once again, taken up her English conversation classes in earnest and this time she meant to stick with the lessons.

Dhanjibhai the grocer was smiling indulgently: "Yes, yes. My wife too. Wanted to learn English, but gave up. Can't have B-U-T being but and P-U-T being put. Too complicated for her."

Pandit Suddenly, the only person present with something like a fluent command of that language laughed with him. "Yes, it is a difficult and complicated language. Anyone who can master it can master the world. No wonder they ruled the world, eh?"

All the men laughed companionably and slurped tea from their saucers. All except an elderly Muslim man who had married four times. He looked clearly perplexed.

"This business of wives learning English...I mean what's the point? I, for one, would never allow an argumentative wife to learn to speak another language. Then she argues even more, in two languages!"

The men laughed louder.

Jannasani appeared with a plate of freshly fried bhajjias announcing that Mrs Naranbhai had sent these for the men. Her generosity in matters of food for her husband's friends caused the others to look accusingly at the Muslim man who had just made the scathing remark about argumentative wives.

Dhanjibhai finally spoke up: "Ingliss or no Ingliss, as long as a wife makes such good bhajjias, she may even speak Chinese, who cares?"

"I support her plan to learn English," Naranbhai finally announced to his friends, pausing between mouthfuls of piping hot bhajjias. "It could be useful in my new business venture."

Everyone stopped munching. A new business? One in which a mere wife, albeit an English-speaking one, had a part to play?

Naranbhai remained silent enjoying the dramatic effect of his mysterious statement. "Yes, my new work will involve dealing with lots of smart people from other countries, and she will have to be a sort of hostess, entertaining you know. She will have to learn all western manners and customs," he added, hoping to intensify the mystery.

"So your new work," Dhanjibhai finally spoke up, "it involves foreign people?"

"Yes, something like that," Naranbhai replied guardedly

"So what does that have to do with your wife?" Dhanjibhai asked suspiciously, while at the same time trying to conjure up in his mind an impossible image of Mrs Naranbhai conversing in English with foreign dignitaries...

"Parties. Smart parties," he replied evasively.

"Parties? Why these western customs all of a sudden? You yourself said those are for shameless people only," Pandit Suddenly raised a reasonable objection.

"Yes, yes, but sometimes you have to deal with those people to make money. And you have to entertain them properly otherwise they think you are nobody."

"So who are these people?" his friends asked.

"Rich people. Famous people. So famous that other people will pay money to see them. People will pay ten times the price of a cinema ticket. First they will see the film and then meet the stars of the film. Some people will have special invitation for cocktails afterwards - they will pay even more for the invitation - to come to Naran Villa cocktail party and meet the stars. You see? My old cinema is going to be like new. And, to celebrate the re-opening, I will bring the stars to the people. The scheme is sure to make me a lot of money."

"So you will pay for them to come all the way here?" asked the tight-fisted Dhanjibhai who was known to add various substances to his groceries to increase their weight and make their appearance more appealing.

"Yes, everything. Hotel and everything. Three appearances at the cinema during the showing of "Love in Himalayas" - the lead stars, Hero Kumar and Nirmala Natkhatti, in the flesh - and then big party here."

The men gasped in disbelief.

"But what is in it for them?" asked the Pandit determined to play devil's advocate. "By showing themselves like that, don't they become less popular? Everyone can see if they are fair or dark or tall or short."

"You don't know anything about it, Pandit-ji! Famous people nowadays don't want to be surrounded in mystery. They want to appear ordinary and human. It makes them more, not less popular. It's the new way. It's nearly 1972, man, don't you know? Even big-big Hollywood stars are allowing presswallahs to visit their big houses now and see them half-naked in a bath of bubbles. Even Queen - God Save Her - has allowed cameras into Buckingham Palace. Imagine!"

The men were deep in thought. It was, indeed, a clever and original scheme. A new breed of film stars had just sprung up in India and they were said to be kicking their arms and legs to get out and about and see the world. It was the new, educated, English-speaking breed of well trained Film Institute actors and actresses. No wonder Naranbhai felt unable to play host without a competent English-speaking wife by his side.

The wife in question, the second Mrs Naranbhai, however, had decided to embark on a project of her own. It had not escaped her notice that Naranbhai had, on more than one occasion, spent the entire night in the room of the older wife.

POISONED COCKTAILS

The news of Naranbhai's new business venture was soon talk of the town. It was reported and discussed with pride. The townspeople took a great delight in the fact that such distinguished and film personalities as Nirmala Natkhatti and Hero Kumar would be visiting their town. And, thanks to Naranbhai's business acumen, Indian communities from other towns and nearby countries would now arrive to catch a glimpse of their favourite stars. It was going to be very good for the economy. It was sure to lead to an increased demand for clothes and beautifying products, to say nothing of the extra shillings to be earned by renting out rooms for the weekend.

Soon, a crude hand-painted poster went up outside Naran Talkies announcing the exciting news that the brand new all-colour film "Love in Himalayas" would be premiered in the presence of its stars Hero Kumar and Nirmala Natkhati, special guests from Bombay, sponsored by Naranbhai. And, although the actual event was still a whole two months away, every ticket had been sold by the end of that first day, many to people who would sell them on at a profit of five hundred per cent.

The next few weeks were spent buzzing around with one and only one topic uppermost in everyone's mind: the Gala Premiere.

At Naran Villa itself, nerve-centre of all operations, preparations were well underway.

In the run up to the big event, Mrs Naranbhai enjoyed the unbounded kindness and generosity of all the neighbours and friends. They had earmarked her, chief lady of the house, as the key to an invitation to the Naran Villa Sundowner-Cocktail party which would secure an even closer look at the stars — an opportunity to see them eating and drinking and burping like normal human beings.

Even Mrs D'Sa, who had always had a policy of keeping a polite distance between herself and Indian culture, managed to get swept away by all the excitement. She arrived on the Naran Villa verandah, dressed in full black. Mrs D'Sa had only been seen in black since the death of her husband, a year earlier, caused by liver problems. She was now a much-changed woman. She looked calmer, younger and had a more upright posture, instead of her usual care-worn stoop. Her limbs no longer aching from nightly beatings, she had acquired all the fresh youthfulness of those who have big things to look forward to.

The death of a husband can sometimes be the most liberating thing. With nobody to drink her money down the drain, not only was she able to save, but the previously hostile Goan community that had kept her at arm's lenths for being married to a "crook" had now readmitted her in their midst. She had been shown some brochures about Canada where sparsely populated areas were crying out for settlers -- especially teachers. She had been persuaded to start training formally, as a music teacher, after which she could be sure of a job in Canada. She and her children were due to leave for Canada in just over a couple of months.

"Yes, Mrs D'Sa, what want you?"

Despite a few English lessons, Mrs Naranbhai was still more fluent in her limited Swahili. As a final parting gesture for having been their tenant for such a long time, and the Naranbhais having always been so kind to her and her children, Mrs D'Sa had volunteered to help prepare the many western-style snacks and canapes for the film-star cocktail party.

The older wife, Sushilaben, keen to have a say, decided to join the ladies discussing the menu for the party.

"But where will everybody sit? You don't mean they'll eat standing up? So bad for digestion," she asked, thinking it was a perfectly valid statement.

"You don't worry about other people's digestion. Just make sure you and your mad daughter stay away from everyone. What will people think?" Mrs Naranbhai shouted at her older rival.

"WHAT will they think?" yelled the older wife. "You think I produced the girl all by myself? You think your husband had nothing to do with it? You think she came with me as part of my dowry from my parents' home?"

She started to whimper, and her ally, the widow Nalini appeared from somewhere in the house and dug straight into Mrs Naranbhai.

"Don't you have any feelings? Are you made of stone? For once she has something to be excited about and you can't bear it, can you? Only God can understand you. Human beings have given up!"

Ex film-star Kamini masi, whose chief function within the household was to always stand by her niece, was quick to join enter fray.

"Those whose husbands have died should not talk to a married woman like that."

"And those who never even had a husband should keep well out of it," Sushilaben retorted.

"Those whose husbands have married another woman in front of their eyes should keep those eyes lowered," Kamini yelled hysterically, refusing to buckle down.

"And those who are at the mercy of their married nieces husbands' crumbs should not behave like they own the place!" The widow Nalini never lost an opportunity to remind Kamini of the inappropriateness of living in the house of a married niece.

Soon, all four women were talking and shouting at the same time, twisting the knife into one another to reawaken all their insecurities and reveal all their hopeless dependencies.

Mrs D'Sa listened to these exchanges in Gujarati for a while. Only half able to understand the language, and feeling sure she had heard it all before and would most certainly hear it all again, she turned to go. Just before she left she asked Mrs Naranbhai:

"About these cocktail snacks, shall I come back later? I have a lot to do before Canada, you know?"

Mrs Naranbhai chose to vent her anger on the innocent bystander:

"What cocktail-focktail? Can't you see my nerves are wrecked?" And, with that, she sat down on the bare floor to weep tears of bitter fury and despair brought on by feeling utterly out-of-control in what was to be a landmark event in the history of Naran Villa. Weeks of English lessons in which she was making agonisingly slow progress, weeks of preparation for a major star event, weeks of thinking and planning a new kind of party the ins and outs of which she still didn't fully comprehend had, indeed, proved too much for her nerves.

On seeing Mrs Naranbhai's dribbling, whimpering condition and fearing that she would make a fool of herself and bring much disgrace to his good name Naranbhai, reluctantly, handed over all arrangements for the party to the very posh, "Grand Hotel."

"Let it not be said I don't do things properly," he announced by way of justification.

While Naranbhai was completely distracted by his upcoming Gala Premiere, Mrs Naranbhai resolved to embark on a project of her own. For once and for all she was determined to get rid of Sushilaben. The sooner she could drive out the first wife, the sooner her unquestionable authority could be re-established. She observed, bitterly, how life had always dealt out things double-double. Never mind her own household having double-double ladies of the house, the country itself was under some kind of double-double government. Nobody knew which government was in charge where.

In the coming weeks, whilst the Dictator was determined to round up all opponents and finish them off, Mrs Naranbhai was equally determined to clip Sushilaben's wings, once and for all. But it wasn't going to be easy. Doing anything directly to Sushilaben would arouse too much suspicion and she herself would be a prime suspect. No, the way Sushilaben had legitimised her position in the house was through Mad Girl Kirti. It's the Mad Girl that would have to be dealt with, somehow. Once she could be got rid of, then her mother would have no reason to remain in the house. Mrs Naranbhai shook her head in despair as she recalled how a few months earlier she had been equally determined to get rid off Shahbanu and that situation had, miraculously, resolved itself. But, registered Mrs Naranbhai with a great deal of bitterness, that while the Shahbanu threat had evaporated into thin air, that lady's departure had somewhat backfired. It had sent Naranbhai rushing to his first wife for comfort. Yes, Sushilaben was now the thorn in her side. With that hussy of a Muslim tenant Shahbanu gone, Mrs Naranbhai's idea for someday testing the alleged properties of the poisonous Raat ki Rani flower had remained quite redundant. Still, there was no reason why this special, ancient, untraceable slow poison, originally intended for Shahbanu, could not now be tried on someone else...

ALMONDS FOR THE BRAIN

Mrs Naranbhai immediately began peace overtures towards Sushilaben: "I'm so sorry I shouted at you earlier, I mean, when Mrs D'Sa was here. I shouldn't have done that..."

"Never mind," Sushilaben replied, fully aware that the younger wife was up to something.

"You know, I'm under so much stress. I don't know why *he* makes such big-big fancy plans. What do I know about hosting Ingliss-style parties?"

"Yes, I understand, believe me. We are Indian women. We only know about breakfast, lunch and dinner. Don't understand about these other tit-bits. Why not just have a proper meal – curries, rice and puris instead of nibbling at fiddly tiny crackers that take ages to prepare and sit around turning sour in the heat?"

"I agree with you," Mrs Naranbhai said with a cordiality that spelt that the two women were, once again, in full agreement.

Round One accomplished, Mrs Naranbhai came straight to the point:"You know, Sushilaben, I've heard almonds are very good for the brain. I think your Mad Girl should eat more almonds..."

"I know, I know, but it's so difficult to make her eat anything. I have to force feed her. But she likes liquids...always thirsty!"

"There you are! Warm milk with ground almonds. Let me make that for her, every morning and every night," offered Mrs Naranbhai.

"Yes, please make it for her. So caring of you! Who says second wives are not understanding?" Sushilaben said with a bit too much sweetness in her tone.

In the days that followed, Mrs Naranbhai just couldn't believe how easy it had been to persuade the first wife that her mad daughter should have hot milk, twice daily, prepared by the hands of the second wife. But, as the weeks wore on, and the glass came back to the kitchen completely drained of its contents, the Mad Girl seemed to show no signs of being anywhere near death. Mrs Naranbhai increased the dosage drastically and soon she was adding as much poison as would have been sufficient to kill ten adults in under an hour.

ALL THE EXTRAS

The actual day of the film stars' arrival was a closely guarded secret. Naranbhai was not keen on too many people possibly getting a free glimpse of them ahead of the formal event. He hadn't spent all that money for nothing! No, if they wanted to see the stars, they would have to purchase tickets for the Gala Premiere.

His widow-sister Nalini had cornered him before sunrise on the very day the distinguished visitors from India were due. Naranbhai had risen extra early and was expecting to be joined by the Useless Nephew, Bharat, for the early morning journey to the airport. Bharat had never ever left his bed before midday at any time in his life but, this time, he had promised his uncle to be up and about at an early hour in honour of the imminent arrival of Nirmala Natkhatti, his favourite female goddess of celluloid.

It was getting close to five in the morning and there was still no sign of the Useless Nephew. Naranbhai went towards his sister's room to check on Bharat, when Nalini herself appeared at the door saying her son would be ready in about five minutes.

"Poor boy! To get up so early. He needs his sleep. I'll make sure he gets some sleep in the afternoon," she said and then moved closer to her brother, reducing her voice to an urgent whisper: "Anyway, I'm glad we've got a few minutes alone. I have to tell you about my dream...there's a plane crash and all your filmstars are falling out..."

"Not now, not now," Naranbhai said impatiently. "The sun hasn't even risen and you have to come here and start all your inauspicious jibbering-jabbering..."

He stopped suddenly. It wouldn't do to get all flustered on such an important morning. So, he calmed down, took a deep breath, and said coldly to her:

"Please tell that useless son of yours that I'm leaving in five minutes exactly. If he's there, he's there. Otherwise I'm going on my own."

The Useless Nephew surprised everyone by appearing on time, completely ready to accompany his uncle. They set off, in a special taxi well before dawn and under cover of darkness. The stars were expected on an early morning flight from Bombay that was to land at the country's one and only international airport some twenty miles away.

Naranbhai and his Useless Nephew stood in the viewing gallery for several minutes, watching scores of travellers coming down the steps of the plane, struggling across the tarmac with bags and boxes of various sizes. As the minutes turned to nearly an hour, Naranbhai realised that there was no Hero Kumar or indeed, the delectable, porcelain faced, backlit, Nirmala Natkhatti.

Eventually, when a full delegation of extremely tired looking people emerged with their airways' shoulder bags bearing large, vulgar, multi-coloured stickers advertising "Love in Himalaya," Naranbhai still refused to feel let down:

"Big people," he said to the nephew. "Big people always have other people with them. How can such big people move around without anybody?"

"Why not?" asked the difficult, Useless Nephew.

"Well, er... their lives may be in danger. Enemies Jealous of them for being famous."

The nephew looked unimpressed by this line of reasoning and if the truth be told, Naranbhai himself was not too convinced by his own argument.

As they stood just outside the customs' hall with Naranbhai holding up a primitively written name board, a young man in a brightly coloured floral print shirt and ridiculously outsize straw hat walked up to them. He introduced himself as "Director Babu" and said he was a film producer and director, keen to scout new locations in East Africa and also on the lookout for new faces for his forthcoming venture the like of which had never been witnessed in the history of cinema. He claimed to have worked on the script for a full twenty years.

Naranbhai looked him up and down and realised that that would have made the man around eight years of age at the time the alleged script had been started.

Another man, walking right behind the Director Babu, introduced himself as Secretary to the leading stars. He had a south Indian name consisting of at least seven syllables and could only speak in English. Naranbhai quickly dismissed the name as unutterable by civilised tongues and resolved to think of the chap, from now on, only as the Chappu-Mappu Secretary. And, fast on the heels of the Secretary, came the so-called male star, which brought home the distressing fact that the man was anyone but Hero Kumar. Naranbhai vaguely recognised him as the young man who had played small comic roles in exactly two films.

The female "star" turned out to be a wide-hipped young woman with a pinched-in waist -- more like a starlet-wannabe than a star. The Secretary explained that owing to Miss Nirmala Natkhati's sudden bout of chicken pox, her place had been taken by the second female lead in the film, a certain Rajni Devi - affectionately dubbed "Thunder Thighs" by the gossip rags. Alongside the said Rajni Devi-Thunder Thighs, and bearing an enormous vanity case was a frazzled middle-aged woman said to be her personal attendant, hairdresser, beautician, punchbag and general dogsbody.

Half an hour later, as mountains of luggage were being loaded into two taxis, Naranbhai found himself hit by the fresh realisation that he had to find accommodation for four, instead of just two people. How could he waste money on hotels for such ordinary people? They would have to be accommodated at Naran Villa, or Bombay Gardens. How was he goint to break the news to battleaxe Mrs Naranbhai that the guests weren't even stars but starlets and hangers-on? And, far worse, tickets had already been sold for an event that promised an "evening with the stars of the film."

Director Babu soon proved he was an incessant chatterbox. He kept chuntering on about something or the other: "Such a beautiful place. Look at it! So clean!" and he turned to look at the surrounding scenery through a frame constructed of fingers and thumbs, which he panned along at a steady speed. In the coming days Naranbhai was destined to witness this ridiculous habit of Director Babu again and again.

"Stupid show-off," thought Naranbhai. "What's he trying to prove? Are we to believe he is holding an invisible film camera in his hands at all times?"

Director Babu continued being captivated by the New World of East Africa through his finger frame: "There! That one is perfect for the song I have in mind. Oh! Just look at those flowers!" He continued to view the scene through his hand-frame while at the same time attempting to hum some alleged new melody.

Naranbhai wiped away a mass of sweat from his forehead. It was still only eight in the morning but his brow, for obvious reasons, was registering it as midday. The Useless Nephew, true to his name was being of no use whatsoever. Having quickly got over the disappointment of not seeing Nirmala Natkhati in the flesh, he had already started to console himself by flirting with Thunder Thighs Rajni. In a typical self-serving manner, he was far more pre-occupied with making sure he got to travel in the same car as the curvaceous Rajni. His uncle's angst about living arrangements for four people, not to mention the possible consequences of selling tickets under false pretences, was of no concern to him.

The Secretary with the unpronounceable name demanded to know which hotel they were being taken to. Naranbhai was all of a fluster as he replied:"All our hotels are unfortunately booked up. Very popular our town, you know? Lots of tourists. It is because of the wildlife..."

"Wildlife? Real wildlife?" Director Babu's eyes started flashing. "I always wanted to put lions and cheetahs in my film. Must re-write the script!"

The Secretary who was more concerned about practical matters than about Director Babu's blockbuster script, looked sternly at Naranbhai: "Where are we to be staying then?" he asked coldly.

"Err...err..I thought, my house, you know. But only two at my house. The other two, err... you... and this...err... Director...I will arrange something..."

Starlet Rajni Devi Thunder Thighs pouted: "House? What is to be happening here? How can I be to stay in somebody's house? Can't be seen with curlers in my hair -- I am star, don't you know? I need to keep mystery. "

"We are not to be staying in anyone's residences. This is most irregular practice. Hotail only! Please make all relevant arrangements," the tedious Secretary piped up again.

"Only one hotel in town and all booked up, sorry," Naranbhai attempted a nervous laugh only to met by a stony stare from the entire group.

To his complete surprise, the Useless Nephew came to the rescue: "Yes, all booked up. Impossible!" he said.

Naranbhai beamed at him with pride, little realising that the nephew wanted more badly than anything else, for Rajni Devi to stay at Naran Villa, preferably in a room not too far down the hall from his own.

The Secretary cut in, "These elements of disruption I was not at all to be expecting."

For lack of a better idea, Naranbhai decided to put all his guests in the still vacant Virjibhai house in Bombay Gardens.

With the unrecognisable "extras" safely installed in Bombay Gardens, he could go on pretending that the real stars were well hidden in some hotel. Only the Useless Nephew Bharat remained privy to Naranbhai's guilty secret: there *were* no stars.

As they arrived at Bombay Gardens, Bharat nudged and winked at his uncle: "Don't worry, Uncle. I'll think of something. Just keep going as normal..."

Naranbhai felt a lump in his throat as he realised yet again, that in times of trouble there was nothing like one's own. Blood was, indeed, thicker than water.

"Where are they?" Mrs Naranbhai had demanded to know, as soon as Naranbhai and his nephew were back at Naran Villa.

"Agents and assistants I have put in Bombay Gardens.The stars themselves, big people you know," said Naranbhai. "Can't expect them to come and rough it here.So much work for you. I put them in a big hotel... "

"Even more money!" said Mrs Naranbhai. "Then why did you ask me to prepare two bedrooms for the stars to live here? I was looking forward to having them..."

He still didn't know how to tell his second wife that the main stars had failed to turn up and he had a Gala Premiere looming over his head with tickets -- fifty shillings apiece --already sold. Unable to confide in his battle-axe second wife, he decided to confide in Sushilaben, his first wife. She had recently shown herself to be an exceptionally insightful woman. She was sure to understand. And she was sure to advise him well. Stealthily, he made his way to her room....

COPING WITHOUT GOD

As he approached Sushilaben's room, Naranbhai decided it was the loss of his beloved twin-gods that had caused all plans to go pear-shaped. The first wife, Sushilaben, who'd just seen him fretting on the landing as she stood in the doorway of her room, managed to draw him closer and whispered soothingly:"Don't worry. Just because the figurines of your gods have disappeared, doesn't mean God himself has disappeared."

Her whispered words were clearly having the desired effect and Naranbhai was soon whispering back some philosophy of his own. They might have carried on in this vein -- coming closer and closer to one another for the whispers to be heard -- had it not been for the sudden arrival of the second Mrs Naranbhai. She appeared as though out of thin air, highly suspicious of these hushed exchanges between husband and first wife.

"What are you doing?" she snapped at Sushilaben.This was the second time this week that she'd caught him khussar-phussaring with his first wife.

"Just passing - nothing. HE (all those years of marriage and now a semi-ex-wife, she still couldn't bring herself to say his name) seems upset because of Rahu and Ketu gone missing..." she began feebly.

"His being upset-shupset is MY business. He is MY husband. If he needs comforting *I* will be the one to do it. You just keep to your quarters!" she yelled.

She still couldn't understand how, night after night, the Mad Girl had swallowed the special milk with almonds and hadn't even so much as had a stomachache yet. And then, turning to her husband, she immediately launched into her usual nagging mode.

"Well, well, well!What's all this?Telling the whole bazaar your troubles before telling me! Am I dead? Why are you confiding in her? If she was enough for all your needs, why did you bring me here, hain?"

"Please, please," began Naranbhai his face crumpling at the prospect of more 'ghitt-pitt' between the wives, and now, no Shahbanu to escape to. Just then, the Useless Nephew Bharat appeared in the hallway. Bharat nodded silently and mysteriously at his uncle. Naranbhai brightened up at once.

"Come on, let's go for a walk, son! I need a walk," he said hurriedly and both Uncle and nephew skedadled away before Mrs Naranbhai could cross-examine them about the necessity of a walk in the midday sun.

Going out of the house was the best option. Naran Villa was full of eyes and ears. Conversations could be overhead, lip-movements could be read, outlandish conjectures made and far-fetched conclusions derived. As soon as they were a safe distance from the house, Bharat said to his uncle:

"It's all in hand. Everything -- all done and ready. Pukka! Don't worry."

"Are you sure? Have you got trustworthy people? They won't tell? And you understand about timing, yes? Don't mess up this one!"

"Uncle, what do you take me for? I promised you didn't I? You kick off the programme as normal, and leave the rest to me," he said in confident tones, and then quite unnecessarily added: "I've always wanted to do this kind of thing. I could make a profession out of it. In advanced rich countries - like overseas - people get paid for this kind of thing...it's a profession like so many respected professions. Do you know, some governments even pay agents to do hijackings and bombings just to divert attention from other scandals that might be about to break?"

"Yes, yes, I know - you're a born ghunda. And payment-wayment nothing! You've been living on my generosity since the day you were born. If we add it all up you've already been paid several times over!" And then, realising that the boy was actually going to be a sort of partner-in-crime, Naranbhai decided to tone down a bit.

"Still, instead of just making trouble for me, this time you're going to make trouble by special-order, yes? Just for ME, yes? Ha-ha! See? Nothing is good or bad. Just depends on whom you're doing it for, and why. Now, you *will* be careful won't you?"

END OF STORY

"That's right! Nothing is good or bad."

Naranbhai and the Useless Nephew Bharat whizzed around to see the majestic form of Hazari Baba standing just behind them in the blazing midday sun. Naranbhai's overtired mind did some quick somersaults as he rehearesed the practicalities of informing the Dictator that the elusive, slippery, crook-Baba had arrived and could be arrested, immediately. But, Naranbhai did not have a personal phone number for the Dictator and felt sure that if he rang a general one, it would result in untold delay. Naranbhai was still puzzling over the best course of action when he mechanically asked Hazari Baba:

"How did you get here? How long have you been standing there?"

"Time is immaterial," began Hazari Baba at his usual, languid pace. "I could have been here just a moment. And, then again, it could have been centuries. These are tricks of the human mind. Time is an illusion..."

"Have you never learnt to give a straight answer to anything?" Naranbhai asked, somewhat vexed that the crazy Baba might have heard every word of his conversation with the Useless Nephew. Still, never mind. Who would believe a half-crazed man who talked such nonsense all the time?

"What are you doing here?" Naranbhai asked.

"The story. I promised to finish the story for the D'Sa children. They'll be going away soon and they want to know what happened next - the Sleepless Princess - you remember? I was passing by so I thought I would just go over to Bombay Gardens and finish telling the story. For the past few years I've been telling the story up to the same point, over and over again. I think the time has come to move on and tell them the rest....maybe this evening..."

And, with that, he glided away towards Bombay Gardens.

That evening, Hazari Baba was surrounded by all the D'Sa children who hung on his every word. From across the backyard, Director Babu from India came out to see what the gathering was about, and realising that a story was about to be told, made himself comfortable. Soon, he was armed with a pen and an old school exercise book obligingly lent by one of the D'Sa sprog. Good stories were hard to come by! The best directors got their stories by hearsay. In India nobody would dream of paying a real writer to write a story for a mere film. Film stories were usually found by going to Hollywood movies or, by just ripping off some poor storyteller or a struggling novelist of yesteryear. How else does one get stories? The heroine's costume budget may well run into a six-figure sum; the stunt-and fight-man would want his full cut; and the choreographer and chorus dancers their measly shares but, would any film producer be crazy enough to pay a writer even *one* rupee for an original story? Little wonder that Director Babu was thrilled to have found an old-fashioned Indian storyteller in the interior of East Africa, of all places!

Hazari Baba had a special technique for telling stories. First he would ask one of the children: "Now, where did we get to last time?" Not only did it serve as a reminder for himself, but also showed him that the children had followed every single dizzying twist and turn in the story, so far.

D'Sa Number Four promptly said: "The Princess was angry that Rangeelay Khan loved his wife very much and would not take a second wife. So she told the King that Rangeelay Khan should be ordered to sing for her every single night, otherwise she would never be able to sleep....."

"Good, very good!" said Hazari Baba. It had been a few weeks since he had narrated that last chapter and the kid seemed to remember it as vividly as though it had only been told yesterday.

"Yes, and that was done. The Princess told the King that she needed the singer to sing for her every single night, and the King's messengers went to fetch Rangeelay Khan. But he declined. He said his place was next to his Beloved wife. When the Princess heard this, she became so angry and frustrated that she tried one last, desperate trick. She went to her father, the King, and said: 'Father, do you how he made me sleep that night? You assume it was his singing. But actually, as you know, he *was* in my bed-chamber, and we *were* alone. What do those two things together mean? A man and a woman, at night, with a bed close by and privacy? What happens?'

'I don't know,' said the King. 'What happens?'"

"Yes, what happens?" asked the D'Sa Number Two, all agog, and hoping against hope his mother wouldn't choose that very moment to yell that dinner was ready.

"Wait, be patient," said Hazari Baba raising his right hand. "The Princess told the King that Rangeelay Khan had not sung her to sleep.There was no song.He had put her to sleep by...by..."

Hazari Baba seemed to be weighing up his words to best put across the delicate matter of just what the Princess had accused Rangeelay Khan of doing.

"How, how? How had he put her to sleep?" interrupted the D'Sa Number One, who, being the oldest, had some idea of what might have happened but wanted Baba to say it.

"I will tell it you in the Princess's own words -- the words that she would have used for her father. She said: 'Father, that musician, Rangeelay Khan, did not sit on the other side of the curtain. He came into my bed. He lay beside me, and then on top of me, and then beside me again. It only took a few moments.'"

Hazari Baba paused at that stage, and then continued: "Now, children, in those days in India, they had different ways of measuring time. What the princess calls "moments" is in the fact the modern equivalent of about *twenty-seven minutes.*"

He continued with the story: "Yes, she told her father that the singer never sang, but did something else. She said, 'I felt something like a thousand delicate wings of a butterfly, flutter through my toes, and up towards my legs, and all over my body, and then the roots of my hair. And then, suddenly, quite inexplicably, I felt so, so, sleepy. That is how he made me sleep. There was no singing.'

On hearing this, the King went red with anger, and immediately ordered the arrest and execution of Rangeelay Khan. The Princess was dismayed. She did not want Rangeelay Khan executed. She was so much in love with him. She was only trying to get him to leave his wife and spend the rest of his life with *her.*

'Father, please,' she said, 'can't you just order him to live here and serve me for the rest of his days? That would be punishment enough, wouldn't it?'

But the King was adamant that Rangeelay Khan had betrayed his trust. He had tampered with the honour and chastity of a Princess and the punishment for that was death. In those days they buried you alive, in an upright position, inside a specially constructed stone wall -- like a pillar."

Hazari Baba allowed a pause for the full horror of his statement to sink in.

A sudden evening breeze made the children shiver. Scared as they were, no way was that going to be allowed to interfere with their savouring of this latest, most gory twist.

"Why? Why did they punish someone by closing him up in a pillar? How did they do that?" they asked.

"The would build a special pillar, put the prisoner in it, and then close it off. It took three or four days to die. A very slow, painful death. That was the standard form of punishment in those days, for serious crimes. And what the Princess had accused him of, was very, very serious indeed."

"But why was it a crime?" asked the D'Sa Number Five, a female. "What he did to her sounds so nice! She said it made butterflies in her toes and in the roots of her hair, so why was it a crime if it made her feel so nice?"

"You're too young, too young," said Baba. "What you need to know is this: all nice things have their rules. And Rangeelay Khan was thought to have broken those rules. But remember he hadn't really broken any rules. The Princess was accusing him of a horrible crime, just because he didn't want to marry her. He had successfully put her to sleep with his magic song, and she wanted his music forever. She wanted it to belong only to her. But music, you know, does not belong to anybody! It can never be chained! Even if you tie down the musician, you can't tie his music..."

"And then, then what happened?" interrupted all the children at once, less interested in the mysteries of music and far more on tenterhooks about the gory details of the fate that awaited Rangeelay Khan.

"Rangeelay Khan was thrown into the dungeon. He sang, day and night, for five days. Finally, the day of his execution arrived. The Princess was distraught. In keeping with the custom of that time, the victim was required to witness the punishment of the criminal. Stone by stone, Rangeelay Khan was closed off in the pillar.He went on singing.The Princess became drowsier and drowsier. No longer able to stand and watch, she slowly crawled to the pillar and laid her head against its cooling stone. His voice still reached her like a distant echo from somewhere in the depth of stone. She wanted to stop the proceedings. She wanted to tell the truth. She wanted a reprieve.But she was too drowsy to speak. She just lay there, half asleep until the singing stopped. It was presumed Rangeelay Khan had now, finally died, having used every last breath in his body to sing.

When the singing had stopped, the Princess suddenly woke up and screamed the place down:'He didn't do it! He didn't do anything! I was lying, I was jealous! Please, please, break the stone and set him free! He is innocent!'

The King was called, and the Princess confessed she had been lying, overcome with jealousy that Rangeelay Khan was so much in love with his wife that he wouldn't dump her for a beautiful princess. The King was outraged. Such an injustice had never taken place in his land. He immediately ordered the workers to break the stone wall and to pull Rangeelay Khan out. King and Princess watched anxiously as the pillar was broken, hoping against hope that Rangeelay Khan would only be unconscious. The King resolved there and then that the musician should be given half the Kingdom as compensation for the injustice he had suffered as the result of the vain Princess. The Princess herself was inconsolable. She accepted she was to blame, and resolved that if, when the pillar was opened and Rangeelay Khan had indeed passed away, then she too, should be put to death in the same fashion. At least that is what should have happened. But, fathers being fathers, of course the King had no intention of punishing his daughter. And, that was the biggest mistake of his life. Had he doled out just punishment then she would have been saved hundreds of years of anguish because, you see, people who tell such hateful lies have no way out -- none at all -- they can't even be poisoned, and death cannot come as the escape. This is one instance in which life becomes a bigger punishment than death and that person lives, again and again, unable to see a way out...driven insane by centuries of wandering...her spirit thirsting for reunion with the man she had loved, and so wrongly accused. The only way it could have been put right would have been for Rangeelay Khan, in another time and place, to actually do to her what she had accused him of doing, and the offspring of this consummation would...anyway, to get back to the story: Finally, when the pillar was broken, they all stepped forward eagerly hoping to drag out an unconscious Rangeelay Khan. But there was nothing there. No one. Not even a skeleton! Remember it had only been four days. Not enough for a skeleton. Just nothing! *No* thing! No Rangeelay Khan -- dead or alive!"

"How do you know all this Baba?" asked D'Sa Number One. "Did someone tell you the story, or....."

"Shut up," said the D'sa Number Four to her older brother. "What happened? Then what happened?"

"They just stood there in disbelief: 'He's disappeared! How could he have disappeared?' The King, Princess and all the workmen stood there astonished. Where could he have gone? They had not left the pillar unattended, even for a moment..."

"Dinner!" hollered Mrs D'Sa from her back door which opened onto the yard.

The children jumped with fright and in a reflex action turned around to see their apron-clad mother, summoning them indoors. But they were in no hurry to move. The story had reached a nail-biting moment. But when they turned back again to ask Hazari Baba the next question, he had vanished.

Director Babu stood in the middle of the backyard, chewing at his pen and vaguely scratching his head: how the hell was he going to make a film without an ending? He, more than anybody else, would have to find this crazy man and get the rest of the story.

Mrs D'Sa marched into the yard with military footsteps to round up her brood who had scattered in search of the vanishing Hazari Baba. The children ignored her and remained busy searching for Hazari Baba all over the backyard.They even searched the bathrooms. One of them stood on the shoulders of a taller one to see if he had left the compound. There was no sign of Hazari Baba.

"Dinner is getting cold - and I am not going to warm it up again and again!" hollered Mrs D'Sa.

KAMLA'S ESCAPE

"If you want to stay here and remain married to your tree, then you do that. I'm off! What sort of life is this? Not a school in sight, and for a brother-in-law I have a tree. And that shopkeeper, the way he looks at you it makes me so angry! Now, he's started looking at me as well...."

A sharp slap landed on Kamla's face: "Is that the way to speak of a man who has so kindly given us food and shelter so that I can remain close to my husband?"

"What husband? A tree? Are you mad?" screamed Kamla.

"Yes, I'm mad! You're the one who has put me here. Your hateful lies about the astrological fate of my husband meant nobody would marry me. So I had to be married to this tree. And now that I'm married, like a good Indian woman, my place is near my husband. I'm going nowhere."

"But they tricked us! They said the tree would be cut in three months and then we would be free to return to our old home and then...."

"They didn't trick us. How can the tree be cut? It's a national treasure now. My husband is a national heritage. He will be protected forever and ever and, with him safe and well, I will always remain in the blissful state of being married...."

Kamla and Bimla had these arguments everyday, and every single day, Kamla was gripped with an urgency to somehow get out of the remote village, and back to town so she could track down her father's old employer, Dr Dawawalla, and put herself in his care. She needed to start going to school again. And she needed the rest of her father's money that Naranbhai had put into his sale. Only Dawawalla could help her now. Every single day, she watched for an opportunity to escape. The only outside contact the girls had during this time was the once-a-month lorry driver - a middle-aged Indian man - who brought supplies for the shop, and occasionally left an old newspaper behind. Kamla would lap up whatever reading material came her way, even a month-old newspaper. It was in one of these old newspapers that Kamla read there had been a military take-over that had now reached the capital. And it was also in one of these newspapers that she had read about the forthcoming Gala Premiere, soon to be held at the newly re-opened Naran Talkies. So! That's how Naranbhai was spending her father's money! The same lorry driver, who had for nearly ten months been her only lifeline to the outside world, provided an escape route. While off-loading boxes of snacks, the back of his lorry was open. It was a very hot, airless afternoon. No one seemed to be around. The shopkeeper was busy counting in the supplies and the lorry driver was preoccupied with to-ing and fro-ing with the boxes. A few ragged village children played some distance away. Her sister, as usual, was fast asleep in the back room. She climbed into the lorry, not for a moment daring to think that she was actually making an escape.

"Just to see how it feels," she said to herself. She sat down on one of the boxes at the back, shielded by other boxes and sacks. She still didn't think she was getting away. If the lorry-driver should spot her while closing up the container, she would just say "sorry" and step down again. He would assume she was just playing. But he didn't see her. And soon, they were speeding away. For the first five minutes she was thrilled. Then she realised she would have to endure this dark, hot, airless ride for at least another four hours. Her heart sank. It sank further when she realised she had just assumed the lorry would be driving back to town. What if he was going elsewhere? Other villages? Other towns? She could be in this dark, airless container for hours...

GALA PREMIERE

It was a Saturday like any other Saturday, but when morning broke, Naranbhai for one would have far preferred it to be Friday, or Sunday, or any other day except the Saturday of the Gala Premiere. It had finally dawned on him that generally speaking, the bigger the idea the more prone it was to unintended consequences. His second wife's deeply philosophical comment kept running in his head: "When you plan big-big, trouble also comes big-big!"

By the late afternoon, there was a strange hush over town. The town's Indian population seemed to be almost completely hidden from view. A few shopkeepers were in evidence cowering behind their counters, but not a single female member of their household was on view, having been excused from their daily duties on grounds of special grooming rituals to prepare for the big evening.

Garlands were being strung, saris ironed, jewellery got out of boxes nestling in their hiding places at the back of cupboards and bottoms of tin-trunks. Every woman wanted to look her best, and every woman wanted to be ready in good time to ensure a good seat. But while everyone wanted to be sure of a good seat, they also wanted others to have arrived before them so that their elaborate, brand new costumes could make the fullest impact on the assembled crowd.

Just before darkness fell, the cinema building was outlined with tiny, multi-coloured bulbs, winking in turn to create the illusion of a constantly moving line of lights.

The first arrivals were full of questions and reluctant to be seated. Naranbhai cracked the whip: "The system is you go in and take your seat. I want everyone in their place and seated before the guests arrive. As they walk in, you will all rise and give them a warm applause. I will lead them onto the stage and introduce them one by one. They will say a few words and then the film will be shown. There will be a short interval..."

Once everyone was seated, the tension became unbearable. Some kept turning their heads round to see if the stars would walk up the aisle leading to the stage. Others, seemingly better informed, said: "No, not that way, stupid! They are already, here,

403

at the back, no doubt. He'll be bringing them out any minute now."

"Shhsshh!" hissed others, convinced that Naranbhai would only bring the stars out once the chatter had died down and an expectant hush fell on the auditorium.

Naranbhai wiped the beads of sweat off his forehead and stepped onto the stage. The primitive microphone gave off a deafening high-pitched tone. Everybody laughed good-naturedly. Any small technical mishap could be readily forgiven in this delicious anticipation of a sighting of their beloved stars.

"Ladies and Gentlemen....." began the nervous Naranbhai. "Today we have a very special thing here, so special that...."

"Get on with it!" shouted a youth from somewhere in the back rows. Others turned around and asked him to shut up. They were clearly enjoying this build-up.

"As I was saying," went on Naranbhai, "We have the most distinguished honour of having the most distinguished..."

Before he could finish his sentence, the crowd saw a man in a jungle-print shirt, straw hat and dark glasses step onto the stage and they broke into spontaneous applause.

The applause petered away. Nobody was sure just why they had applauded and Naranbhai was annoyed that the pushy Director Babu had pre-empted his cue:

"This is the distinguished director..." Naranbhai continued, but nobody was interested in the director's name. The whispers rose: "He's building up to it. Less important people are always announced first...wait for it..."

The Agent with the unpronounceable name was introduced as a most distinguished person who, always remaining behind the scenes, represented and dealt with the business interests of famous people. A mild applause followed, the crowd clearly puzzled at how such non-dynamic, ordinary-looking, slouchy postured man with a most unromantic name could get a job that allowed him such proximity to the demi-gods.

"And this is India's funniest man, Mr Soda Syfun, who will entertain us with his special jokes..."

They applauded politely, fully aware that Soda Syfun was a lesser comedian who had, with mild success, modelled himself on the inimitable Johnny Walker.

"Less important people always get introduced first..." they reassured one another, craning their necks to see if the magical shadows of Hero Kumar and Nirmala Natkhatti were already visible in the wings.

"And now - a very special surprise - the great dancer Rajni Devi, who will be performing for us tonight....a rare treat...very rare indeed...in the flesh..." Naranbhai clearly faltered at the word 'flesh.'

A few wolf whistles went up from the youths in the back row, more on account of Rajni Devi Thunder Thighs' revealing costume than any claim to fame. She had worn a black and red Playboy-style bunny outfit embroidered in gold sequins over black fishnet tights, topped off with an elaborate headwear of ostrich feathers dyed purple.

"That, ladies and gentlemen is our line-up for the evening, but first...."

A grumble was clearly audible swirling through the crowd, spreading like the faint odour of yesterday's boiled cabbage.

"Hey," a distinguished gentleman in the front row stood up to speak: "What about the stars?" he asked in a way that demanded an answer. He was not heckling, he was not whistling. He was simply asking a straightforward question in a business like way that prompted the crowd to echo and reinstate the question:

"Yes, what about them? Where is Hero Kumar? Where is Nirmala...?"

"Ah,...I should have said. Something I forgot to mention. Owing to a terrible sickness, Miss Nirmala Natkhati will not be joining us, but she sends her best wishes to each and everyone of you - personally - and she says........"

Naranbhai's voice was drowned in a chorus of protest. Another voice from the crowd shouted: "OK, so she is sick. Where the hell is Hero Kumar? Is he sick as well?"

"Please, please, I beg you, be silent, listen to me. It was just a joke. Joke, you know? Just teasing you. Of course they are here.

But first, the others are going to warm up the stage. Please be patient. We have lined up a great evening's entertainment for you...."

People were beginning to get up from their seats and tumble over other seated people who wanted to go on listening to Naranbhai's excuses. Stars or no stars, some people were clearly enjoying Naranbhai's squirming discomfort.

A man stood up and said: "We don't believe you. We demand a glimpse, just to reassure us that they will be appearing later."

Soon, general mayhem had broken out. Naranbhai ordered Rajni Devi Thunder Thighs to start dancing, urgently signalling to his staff to start the music over the cinema loudspeaker system. A screeching noise broke out, and Rajni Devi shouted:

"Wrong music! I'm not to be dancing to that!"

While Naranbhai tried to rectify matters, Rajni Devi announced she had a headache and would not dance at all. She marched off the stage wiggling her bottom in the tight, scanty costume of red and gold, leaving a stupefied Naranbhai watching helplessly after her voluptuous behind with its furry bunny-tail.

Naranbhai signalled to the comedian to take the mike and begin telling jokes. Soda Syfun obliged and, immediately, launched into his favourite, boring joke about his mother-in-law and the hot soup, but nobody was listening.

Director Babu stepped forward and bellowed:
"Please sit down, all of you! Listen! I am going to make a very big film based in Africa. First Indian film in Africa! With wildlife! Big budget! Completely original story. I need a new heroine. Any of you interested in acting?"

There was a momentary hush while various parents and daughters contemplated this new possibility.

Naranbhai looked at Director Babu gratefully and started to make plans for a grand talent contest in his head. But, within seconds, it all went wrong again. The same distinguished man who had spoken earlier, now stood up and said:

"That is all very well. A new heroine, and all that. That can all be discussed later. But right now, I think, unless you show us the real stars, every single one of us is entitled to our money back!"

The crowd surged forward and raised the distinguished man over their shoulders. They carried him high and started chanting:

"Money back! Money back!"

Naranbhai fled towards a back exit. He was barely through when he heard a loud crash followed by screams in the auditorium.

A ceiling fan, whizzing at high speed, had come crashing down, but not before its rotating blades had done a full slicing action on the downward journey and maimed or killed all who lay in its path...

HOLY & UNHOLY DEATH

Naranbhai had the vaguest memory of somehow reaching home that evening. Perhaps he had walked? Or, then again, maybe he had just got into somebody's car? Somebody must have driven him because he couldn't drive. Perhaps Jannasani had seen to it? Or maybe it was part of the useless nephew Bharat's grand plan to get the boss out safely?

Plan? What plan? He thought Bharat was just going to hire some trouble-makers to cause complete and utter chaos at the cinema hence 'forcing' Naranbhai to cancel the evening's proceedings without the need to explain that the big stars had failed to turn up. This could be followed by a further morality lecture on how badly Indian-Indians must now think African-Indians and no dignitary from India would ever dream of visiting again. And that would give Naranbhai the ultimate face-saving excuse to never mount such a project again. Far better than saying he had tried it once and it had been a monumental disaster. A bit of crowd rowdiness followed by a small fight would deem the premises unsafe for celebrities for many moons to come. The stars, who had never even appeared, could be excused as having had to make a hasty exit for their own safety, and to take the first plane back home. And nobody would've been any wiser. That was all that had been agreed with Bharat. Who on earth told the stupid badmaash-ghunda to loosen the fittings on a ceiling fan and create such a catastrophic tragedy?

That was the trouble with violence. It had a will of its own. Once you sanctioned it or even commissioned it, in whatever limited form, there was no telling where the spiralling roller coaster -- or ceiling fan -- would go.

Luckily for Naranbhai, at the start of the seventh decade of the 20th century, the compensation culture had not yet reached equatorial Africa. As such, nobody in their right minds could sue a cinema owner for a fast whizzing ceiling fan that had somehow detached itself from the ceiling to land on a few heads and bodies. So what? We are born; we die. Death uses whatever convenient excuse to reclaim its own. OK, not very dignified to die in a cinema (not like dying in a temple or a mosque) but still, death comes as the end.

When Naranbhai reached home, NaranVilla was deserted. The rest of the family was still at the cinema, or maybe struggling to get home amidst all the mayhem of police, Red Cross workers, emergency services. Only Sushilaben and the Mad Girl were at home. Even Jannasani had managed to wangle an attendance at the cinema on the pretext of helping out. Bharat was nowhere to be seen, and Naranbhai hadn't hung around at the cinema long enough to seek him out. He was so numb with shock that he hadn't even bothered to find out if any of his family members were hurt. He only had the slightest feeling of still being connected to the world. The rest of his being had taken off for somewhere else.

It is said that in the midst of dramatic happenings and momentous life-changing events, one is often preoccupied with some small, seemingly insignificant question: And that was exactly what happened to Naranbhai. He kept thinking to himself, over and over again: it was easy enough to tell if somebody else was dead. But how to tell if you, yourself, had just died?

A STAR IS BORN

As the minutes turned to hours, Naranbhai felt a strange kind of peace descend on him. There was a hush in the atmosphere, and for a moment he felt like he had got away with it. It was still only eight o'clock in the evening and there didn't appear to be any repercussions of the fiasco at the Cinema. But, as anyone who has experienced life in the myriad of twists and turns will confirm, that rare feeling of perfect contentment and peace that descends on one from time to time is seldom destined to last beyond a few minutes. So, within minutes of Naranbhai feeling at complete peace, his mood blackened as the first group of agitators appeared outside the front gates of Naran Villa. An unruly crowd was demanding justice for the families of the victims of the fan-crash and also demanding their money back.

"These people!" He grumbled to Mrs Naranbhai who had got back some minutes ago and had a thousand questions for him -- questions to which he had no answers. Far better to grumble: "Fillum, fillum, fillum-stars! That's all they think about. There are reports of the military government rounding up Indians who know magical arts, but instead of worrying about their future, they're worrying about Nirmala Natkhatti!"

All through the evening, the crowd gradually thickened and, by midnight, it had reached hysterical proportions. A giant sized moon hung in the black sky illuminating the dramatic scene with a powerful spotlight as though it were the climax of a major stage production. All the doors and windows of Naran Villa were locked from within for fear of a Bastille-type onslaught from the hysterical crowd. The Naran Villa gate had been chained and padlocked but some people had climbed over it and were helping others to do the same. Gradually, quite a large part of the throng - or most of the young males at any rate - were clustered on the front verandah demanding that Naranbhai come out and give them their money back.

A sudden hush was heard to fall on the crowd. There was a pause. The Director Babu in the floral shirt had arrived. The crowd looked at him with interest. Yes, he was one of them, but they had no quarrel with him. He was just one of the uninvited guests from Bombay. They had not been tricked by him, but by Naranbhai so they left him alone and decided to quieten down while waiting to see his next move. Would the gates of Naran Villa soon be opened to let him in? If that were the case they were determined to remain close behind and push their way into house.

But the gate remained closed and Director Babu remained standing at the gate. A tense silence followed, and then, suddenly, quite suddenly, the tension was broken: a crystal clear voice rang through the tension. Everybody looked up at the roof terrace where the Mad Girl gazed at the moon and sang:

> *You deceive yourself and hide from the world*
> *But how will you hide from yourself?*
> *How will you hide from God?*
> *O You, so blinded by greed*
> *Come on, come out and face the music,*
> *Listen to the cry of your soul, and face the music...*
> *Of death, but how will it come*
> *When death finally comes?*

As she sang the last line, Kirti leaned over the low, dark green railings that framed the flat roof terrace to prevent small children from falling over. A gust of wind blew her hair back from her face and the faraway look in her eyes made her seem like a mysterious beauty who had just stepped out of the silvery evening sky. The same gust of wind caused a heady whiff of the scent of a nearby gardenia shrub to reach the nostrils of Babu the Director. The combination of the three senses of sight, sound and smell, made Babu the Director realise with unfailing certainty that he had, at long last, met the fresh-faced, brand new heroine of his forthcoming film.

GOOD NEWS & BAD NEWS

The next morning, Naranbhai remained concealed from public view. The man who had once sat proudly on his front verandah was now hidden from all except his immediate family. He buried his face into a pillow and cursed his fate for the millionth time:

"Why me? Why does it always happen to me?" he whimpered into his pillow. "I think of nothing but doing good for the people and the first small thing that goes wrong those same people want my blood! Why? Why?"

Both wives stood near the bed exchanging helpless looks with one another and completely at a loss for anything comforting to say. Their allies, the widow Nalini and the aunt Kamini, stood near the doorway of the room, replicating the facial gestures of their proteges and both equally and, most unusually, at a complete loss for words.

Jannasani came in with the morning paper: "Bwana, I have made tea. I have made a seat for you on the rooftop. Nobody can see you from there. Fresh air, good for you!"

Naranbhai got up gratefully. He was dying for a cup of tea.

It's true what they say. In the end, everything is relative. The concept of a piece of news being good or bad really does depend on everything else that is going on at the time. So it came to pass that a staggering piece of news that would normally have sent Naranbhai into the deepest, blackest mood of uncertainty and a feeling of treacherous betrayal actually caused him to jump up from his deckchair and kiss the 'Argus' over and over again. He had expected to see a bold lead story on how a fairly prominent businessman (and landlord of an exclusive settlement known as "Bombay Gardens") had diddled members of his own Muhindi community by making them part with thousands of shillings under false pretences. But there was no such story. Instead, the paper had published a decent-sized, dispassionately written news story on how a ceiling fan had come crashing down at the town's only Indian cinema killing four people and injuring dozens of others. They had, quite erroneously, reported that the fan had crashed during the showing of an Indian film. Nothing had been mentioned about the stage-show, the unknown personalities from

India, or the heckling. But that wasn't the main reason for Naranbhai's boundless joy. The lead story in the newspaper was all about how the new military government of the funny, likeable Dictator with a penchant for samosas, had given all Indians in his country a deadline to report to Headquarters and voluntarily impart their knowledge of magic and gold-making to the government. Those who didn't know magic were no longer of any use, and they were being requested, in the politest of terms, to leave the country within thirty days.

But there was a great deal of confusion over whether or not the Dictator was in full control of the country, as indeed there was as to who was, and wasn't a magician. Rival governments from other regions had issued their own notices saying: "Ignore the Dictator completely! He lives in cloud-cuckoo-land. We are still in charge. Stay put!"

Naranbhai interpreted the whole fiasco as exceptionally good news. All the contradictory orders being issued by different regional governments at loggerheads with one another was no less than a gift from God! The entire Indian community was now sure to be focussed on its own precarious future. Who in God's name was going to bother about whether or not Nirmala Natkhatti had appeared, or not appeared, and who cared that four people died when a ceiling fan, in full motion, came crashing down? No, people were sure to have other, more important things on their minds, and he, Naranbhai, was once again clearly off the hook! His own personal twin-gods may have gone missing but, somehow, he was still loved and protected by the forces...

IN SEARCH OF GOLD

Naranbhai was still gloating over the news. He'd just downed the final drops of the delicious tea that Jannasni had served him, when a jeep came to a screeching halt outside Naran Villa. Four soldiers jumped out and started forcing the locked gate while shouting to be let in. Naranbhai's first instinct told him to hide in the bathroom but Mrs Naranbhai said: "What can they do? What have you done wrong? It's not YOUR fault that all the wrong people turned up from India! It's those trouble-makers who were booing and shouting. They are the ones who should be arrested. Go on! You have nothing to fear!"

Naranbhai decided that the practical Mrs Naranbhai always knew best and he should listen to her more often. He came out of the house and headed straight towards the soldiers, saying in clear, confident tones:

"I'm very glad to see you. About time too! Lots of trouble-makers at my cinema last night - big mattata - where the hell were you lot? Now, as I was saying - "

"We don't know about any cinema," said the leader of the group. "We want that Indian gentleman known as Hazari Baba - the magician - the one who makes golden erections for 84 years. We have reason to believe you're hiding him...here."

Naranbhai, still dazed from last night's fiasco at his cinema, was dumbfounded at the strange request. "Hazari Baba? Haven't seen him for ages - "

"It has been reported that he is seen loitering near this house - "

"Hey, you can search the house if you like! I assure you, you'll be wasting your time. I don't go in for those Baba types. Useless layabouts! Just goes around sniffing flowers. Why should I hide him here? I believe in hard work. The country needs hard-working men -- not men who go around sniffing flowers," he added with some pride, hoping the soldiers would be impressed at this show of patriotism.

They remained unmoved: "Where is he? Are you going to tell us or not?" One of the soldiers moved up to Naranbhai, and lightly brushed his collar bone with a gun.

"Wh...wh...what do I know?" Naranbhai mumbled and trembled, his eyes fixed on the gun. "Anyway, if he's a real magician, then surely he knows how to hide himself? As it is, he appears and disappears whenever he likes - "

"Exactly -- appears and disappears. He has powers. And he is needed. The Dictator has given us twenty-four hours to produce the man. Now, will you hand him over, or -- ?"

Hazari Baba was at the top of the Wanted list ever since rumours had reached the Dictator that, apart from knowing how to make gold (a useful skill for any government,) Hazari Baba also made magic potions to ensure eternal life. And, erections lasting 84 years at a time. There is nothing the Dictator wanted more than to live forever and ever -- and to attain such sexual prowess as an 84-year erection would surely deliver.

"Look, I'm telling you man, he's not here! He used to come sometimes to admire the plants. Why don't you try across the road? Bombay Gardens -- he goes there to tell the children stories and to look at the flowers -" Naranbhai thought he was being helpful.

"Stories, eh? I've had enough of *your* stories! If you don't produce Hazari Baba, I'm under orders to arrest you."

"Arrest? On what charges? I know the law! I have many friends in the police..."

"The police force has been fired. And there *is* a charge against you. Or, at least, we can make a charge. Operating a large public venue without due care and attention to the safety of your patrons. That ceiling fan was in very poor shape. And, it would appear the fan was deliberately loosened. Could have been done by you. You were charging big money for a fraudulent event. So, either you produce this Hazari Baba - in which case we are prepared to overlook the little accident at the cinema - or I have to place you under arrest."

"But what has Hazari Baba *done*?"wailed Mrs Naranbhai, unable to stay silent.

"That's just it. He's done nothing--yet--to help the government. We need him. We need his powers. And he has disappeared. We are sure he is hiding in your house."

"Then search for him!" screamed Mrs Naranbhai.

An hour later, when every room and cupboard in Naran Villa had been turned inside out and upside down and no Hazari Baba had emerged, Naranbhai was handcuffed and put into the back of an army jeep whilst his household looked on in stunned disbelief. Naranbhai had been driven away amidst the sobbing of the Naran Villa women and the curiously satisfied gaze of his Bombay Gardens tenants. Not that they were pleased to see him carted off to prison-- it's just that nobody could remember such a dramatic event in the recent history of Naran Villa. Not since the double suicide of Mohini and Sohini -- and disaster is always delicious when it happens to somebody else.

The first wife, Sushilaben, had completely risen to the occasion and beaten her breast, allegedly, out of grief for the second wife: "She's so young. Such a short time she had with him. Her children are still so young. At least I had his youth, what happiness has she seen, poor woman?" she said to the assembled crowd of tenants and then, turning to Mrs Naranbhai, she added: "Have patience, sister! You must be strong for your children -- your three strong, lovely boys. Otherwise what will become of them? You will have to wait for your - err.. our - husband until he has served his sentence. You must be strong. Here, drink this, it will calm you....*warm milk*, very good for the nerves..."

And, with that, she took the glass of luke-warm milk that Mrs Naranbhai, herself had prepared, as she did every morning and night, for the Mad Girl, and helped Mrs Naranbhai drink it...

As the stomach convulsions began and Mrs Naranbhai rolled about on the floor wailing and screaming and clutching at her stomach as though it would fall out of her body, everybody agreed that her husband's arrest had affected her very, very badly...

UPRIGHT IMPRISONMENT

Even as they were pushing him into the back of the jeep, Naranbhai kept muttering in shocked disbelief: "But what is the charge? What have I done? What?"

"Manslaughter. That fan was deliberately loosened to fall and create a diversion. Selling tickets under false pretences!"

"I never..." Naranbhai began, then remembered how the Useless Nephew Bharat had assured him that everything was in hand. He should have known that when Bharat talked of things being 'in hand', it usually meant things were soon going to get completely out of hand.

It was a long drive -- the prison was over two hundred miles away. The jeep had stopped, just once for the driver and soldiers to relieve themselves in the bushes. Naranbhai was denied this privilege because his hands were tied behind his back. When he asked why someone couldn't help him with his zip, one of the cheeky young soldiers was horrified: "What do you take me for? I don't play with men's trouser zips!"

When they arrived at the prison, Naranbhai was shoved into a cell that offered standing room only, alongside some 40 or 50 other men. Most of the upright prisoners were either political dissidents or small time crooks unable to pay the appropriate fine. The entire area stank of sweat, stale urine and faeces. Naranbhai looked at his surroundings in shocked disbelief. He had imagined, as an Indian, he would be locked up in a cosy private area of his own, with a hard single bed and a commode and a daily supply of the morning newspaper -- to say nothing of the option of Indian vegetarian meals. Most of the other prisoners had perfected the art of sleeping in a standing position. The fact that they were packed liked sardines actually helped in that they could lean on one another's bodies for support. Naranbhai found himself thinking about Jannasani - of all people - because Jannasani, whatever his surroundings, and at moments both opportune and inopportune, had always known how to fall asleep -- in almost any position.

KAMLA AT BLACK CAT

It was the discomfort of a very full bladder that finally caused Kamla to wake. It was pitch dark. She had no idea of the time, or of how many days she had spent in the airless lorry container, since her escape from the village. She realised they were not moving. They were obviously parked somewhere. Perhaps outside the driver's house? Where? Where did he live? She didn't dwell on the question for too long. Her only concern at the moment was to urinate, somehow, without soiling herself. She got up and tried to pace around in the pitch dark lorry container, but kept bumping into boxes and sacks. Finally she panicked as she realised the lack of air and the fact that she could have been locked in here for days. Her stomach growing more uncomfortable and swollen by the minute, she fought her way towards the door to try and feel for a catch that could be opened up. There was a catch, but it wouldn't give. The container was obviously chained up and padlocked from the outside. It was as she realised this and panicked a little more that she felt the trickle of urine, quite involuntarily, making its way down her thighs and towards her ankles. Soon, the soles of her plastic chappals were squelching. She was disgusted with herself. She sat down and wept. She wept at the humiliation of sitting in her own urine. She cried tears of bitter fury at everything that had happened since the death of her father. Naranbhai's determination to take over and run their lives; his belief that unmarried women were like dynamite, just waiting to go off; her sister's submissiveness in the face of age and authority. And then that dreadful, sweltering hot village where she had felt marooned. The shopkeeper tiptoeing into their room every night. The covers on her sister's bed rising and falling in the darkness, and the shopkeeper's wife's sullen face in the mornings. The wife could not take it out on Bimla since her husband had obviously taken a shine to the girl, so she vented her anger and frustration on Kamla, assigning her various chores and barking after her if she so much as put a foot wrong. Kamla cried until she felt dizzy. Finally she got up and resolved to bang on the door and cry for help. It was now impossible to get out of the lorry unseen, so she may as well make a noise, get some help and get out. Later on, she could offer some plausible explanation like how she'd only been playing with the boxes and the lorry had suddenly moved off.

She started thumping her fists at the door for what seemed like an eternity. She could hear distant strains of African music, but nothing else. No one had come to investigate the thumping or her faint cries for help. Finally, she gave up and sat down again, her nostrils just beginning to catch the smell of urine. But the smell did nothing to dull her gnawing hunger. If anything, it reminded her that she was now reduced to the basics of the human condition: the need to fill the stomach, and the even more urgent need to empty it.

Kamla was just trying to rip open a sack of what she hoped would be edible when there was a sudden rattling at the door. She shot up, ready to make a run for it. The door swung open to reveal that it was early evening. The lorry driver climbed in to take out some boxes when his eyes fell on a bedraggled young woman.

Before he could say anything, Kamla had shot past him and jumped off the lorry. She paused for a moment to take in her surroundings and saw that they were on the main road adjacent to the alley that led to the Black Cat Club. Her ordeal already forgotten, her heart filled with joy as she realised she was in the right city. She started running…and she didn't stop until she got to Dr Dawawalla's surgery.

THE DOCTOR

The evening was getting cooler, but the sweat poured down Kamla's face as she reached Dawawalla's surgery. She was tired, hungry, thirsty and penniless. The compounder let her in and said the doctor was with a patient. She would have to wait. She heaved a sigh of relief. When she had first read about a military coup reaching the capital, she had imagined there would be soldiers marching in the street (with a band) and there would be a huge army presence everywhere so that life would never be normal again. But now, seeing that the town was exactly as she had left it, despite everything that had happened, she felt a huge sense of ease.

She looked around the dispensary wistfully, and remembering her father milling around among the powders and coloured liquids, the tears welled up in her tired eyes. The events of the past few days and the excitement of escaping from the village had finally taken its toll on her youthful vigour. She sat down in the small waiting room full of sick people, glad to be at her destination -- and more than just a little glad to be sitting down in a normal place, with light after what might have been days of being locked up in the dark.

"Yes?" asked the young African compounder through his dispensary hatch.

"Dr Dawawalla. I wanted to see Dr Dawawalla...."

"Oh, he's going to Canada, for good. There's no doctor here at the moment."

"But he's got my money...he..."

"I don't know about any money," the young man said impatiently. "He is leaving for Canada soon...now, if you'll excuse me, there are still some people waiting to be seen..."

Kamla sat there stupefied. How could Dr Uncle Dawawalla have just gone off like that? And what arrangements had he made for her father's money to be returned to her? What about medical college, what about, what about...?

It was just possible Dawawalla hadn't yet left the country. She vaguely remembered that he lived in one of the smart houses in the European Residential Area. It was well over five miles away.

But she felt sure that finding Dawawalla would solve all her problems. Perhaps he would take her to Canada with him.

Dawawalla's servant opened the door and called his master. As she entered the house, she noticed that most of it was packed up. The shelves were all empty. But of course! They had said he was leaving for Canada soon. Dawawalla was taken aback to see her, almost as if he had been caught red-handed. But she was so relieved to see him that she didn't notice anything untoward in his manner. She felt sure that the look of dismay on his face had something to do with the fact that she had turned up at his doorstep, by foot and all by herself, so late at night. In fact, she was so relieved at finding him that she even failed to notice that he was looking at her in a very different way. Always the exceptionally kind "uncle" figure, today his eyes seemed to rest on various parts of her body. But overcome with exhaustion, she just sank into his embrace, unaware that it was anything but avuncular.

"Oh, Doctor Uncle! You don't know what I've been through...they married my sister to a tree...and now she refuses to leave the tree...and...I ran away...I was trapped in the back of a lorry for...for...I don't know how many days. Uncle, now I've found you, everything's going to be all right, isn't it? Isn't it?"

"Yes, yes," he said reassuringly, starting to take off her badly soiled dress. She felt sure it was because she stank of urine. Of course he had to take it off. He had taken her clothes off many times, when she had been examined by him during various childhood illnesses. He was taking it off because he was going to give her some clean clothes...

She went on whimpering: "And you'll take me away with you? They say you're going to Canada. Canada - that sounds so nice. I can come too, can't I? And I can go to school there....and medical college. You know, I haven't been to school for months and months..."

She gradually lost consciousness.

Kamla found herself in a big bed when she woke up. She was naked. Then she remembered she was in Dawawalla's house, and quite safe. The house was completely quiet. He must have gone to work. She sat up and felt a bit strange. There was some dried up blood on the sheets. "Another period? Already?" she thought. She pulled herself up with some difficulty and felt a dull pain between her legs. She put it all down to the ordeal of the past few days. She found the same dirty dress lying in a heap on the floor and wondered why Dawawalla had not given her a clean shirt or something. She had no choice but to wear that dress and under it, all her soiled underwear. She emerged in the near empty drawing room, where Dawawalla's servant stood with a bunch of keys in his hands:

"I have to lock up now," he said without emotion. "Are you leaving soon?"

"Where is...?"

"He left for the airport," the straight-faced servant said.

"But..." began Kamla, unable to take it in.

"He had to go to Canada. For good," the servant reminded her.

"But what about me? And my money? My education money....?"

The servant seemed to be debating whether or not to say something. Finally he said: "What about your money? Didn't you make him pay you before he....?"

Kamla stood there uncomprehending: "But how could he have gone? What about me?"

"What about you?" said the unemotional servant. "They all come, and stay a night and then leave in the morning. So I thought you would do the same....."

It was only on hearing those words that Kamla understood the reason for the soreness between her legs, and the spots of blood.

With the servant hovering restlessly to lock up the house and hand the keys over as per his instructions, there was no time to think. Her only hope was that she might find someone sympathetic in Bombay Gardens. It's the only other place she knew, or would be able to find on foot. She remembered Shahbanu. Shahbanu had always been good to her...

She moved languidly, dragging her feet in her plastic sandals, for the long walk to Bombay Gardens....

HOME AGAIN?

When previously exciting places suddenly seem utterly devoid of charm, then one can be sure that one's childhood is well and truly at an end. To find disappointment and disillusionment is the clearest confirmation of adulthood. Kamla looked at the unkempt yellowing buildings and the rusting door locks surrounded by thirsty, half-dying potted plants and wondered why she had ever thought of Bombay Gardens as the green playground of her golden childhood. It was here she had learnt to stand and to walk; it was here she uttered her first words. As a motherless toddler this was the very earth that had been trodden by the pitter-patter of her tiny, shoeless feet. This very backyard was the vast playground of her dreamy childhood, a time when everything had been vibrant, ever alive with limitless activity and adventure. Yet, today, it stood eerily silent, in a semi-squalid state of neglect. Where had all those lovely green plants gone? Perhaps it was true what she had always heard grown-ups say: childhood was the best time of life. Now she was really and truly a woman deprived of all wonder and innocence - thanks to Dawawalla's unbridled lust - why did the world suddenly seem so yellow and rusty, so devoid of the innocent joys of life? Where was everyone?

She thumped hard on Shahbanu's door, but she could see there were no curtains on the front window and peering in she saw that the place was completely empty, save a few sheets of crumpled old newspapers obviously discarded during packing operations. Nestling somewhere between the sheets of old newspaper she noticed the sequinned, shocking pink clutch bag that had been Shahbanu's badge of co-ordinated fashion for a good few years. Now it lay, discarded and unwanted amid empty cardboard boxes and old newspapers. How good it had looked tucked casually under Shahbanu's arm. And how sad and out of place it now looked lying amidst yellowing copies of old Sunday Nations.

She walked round to the back gate and entered the communal courtyard, hoping to encounter some signs of life. The once chaotic backyard-sakati looked strangely tame in the stark light of day. No Bimla scrubbing pots at one end, no D'Sa urchins chasing each with sticks and stones. No sounds of Satish's gramophone and no Lata Mangeshkar - with a complete command over three-and-a-half octaves - piercing the scorching afternoon heat. Her eyes wandered to the D'Sa backdoor. Various packing cases were cluttered up carelessly. In a few moments, a smart middle-aged woman emerged in a brightly printed floral dress, fussing over some crystal glass-bowls that had be packed just so, otherwise they would break. Kamla stood still, watching the operations with detached interest. Gradually she realised she was looking at a much-improved and well-groomed Mrs D'Sa. She had only ever seen that woman in full black. For most of Kamla's childhood Mrs D'Sa had seldom been out of her mourning garb. Now as she stood over a young servant while he followed her instructions on how to secure several bulging suitcases with rope, Mrs D'Sa looked nothing like the creased, care-worn woman who had so often been at the receiving end of her husband's merciless leather belt. Her entire stature her changed. She stood more upright and her manner had a new authority and confidence.

It was some minutes before Mrs D'Sa noticed the intruder in the backyard. It had only been ten months or so, but the changes in appearance between girlhood and womanhood were pretty transformational. So, Mrs D'Sa could be forgiven for not immediately recognising Virjibhai the Compounder's younger, extremely outspoken and spirited daughter. Instead she said: "Yes? Looking for someone? Can I help you?"

Kamla burst into tears as the clear, polished voice of that Goan lady triggered off a plethora of childhood memories. The cakes and biscuits and treats that Mrs D'Sa, despite the greedy eyes of her own eleven children, would set aside for Kamla because her mother had died before the girl had learnt to walk. The women of Bombay Gardens had all played second mothers to her, while her older sister, Bimla had taken over from the real mother. Suddenly the thought of Bimla being stuck married to a tree in that village in the middle of nowhere - the same Bimla who had been a mother and whom Kamla had now so heartlessly ditched - brought floods of tears that couldn't be stopped. A puzzled Mrs D'Sa looked at her. She moved closer to the girl: "Who are you? Why are you crying? What do you want?"

"Ka-kam-mm-la," Kamla sobbed. "It's me. I - "

"Goodness me! Kamla! Look at you, so grown up! Young lady or what? Oh my God, but you're beautiful! Come, come give me a big hug - now, now, big hug, come on."

Kamla's sobs turned into loud wails as her head fell on Mrs D'Sa's shoulder. In the next few minutes much was said, but nothing was understood. Both women had urgent things to communicate to the other but each was obsessed with momentous events of her own.

"We're going, you know? For good. And I am allowed to take my belongings because it was all decided even before the Expulsion - oh! You probably don't know...the Dictator is rounding up all Indians, especially those who can do magic. The Pandit is waiting, eagerly, to be summoned. He's feeling quite insulted they haven't come for him yet. That proves he has no real knowledge of anything, isn't that funny? And those who don't have any magic are being thrown out. But we had already decided to go. So good to be going of our own free will-- not booted out like others. See, I'm even allowed to take my things? Others have to leave everything and just get out! Unless they are magicians. Imagine! How ridiculous! I'm so glad I already made the decision to go. To Canada. Winnipeg. Do you know where that is? You were always the so-so clever one. How's your school? When are you becoming a doctor, eh, Kamla?"

"I went everywhere, everywhere. Bimla is trapped in that village. Married to a tree. You know she was tricked -"

"Oh yes, Bimla! Your sister! How is she? Happily married now, eh? At last! Everything always works out in the end. You know, D'Sa died, man? Died on me, just like that - these men! Just go and die when you least expect it -- now I'm going to Canada....."

"Dawawalla, Dr Dawawalla, do you remember? He -- well, do you know what he did to me -?" Kamla tried to make her voice heard over Mrs D'Sa's Canada prattle.

"Oh yes, that kind, kind Parsi gentleman. Always had a soft spot for you. How is he? I've heard he's moving to Canada. Canada is great! Oh, by the way, you know Naranbhai had a major flop with his latest business scheme? All bogus people

425

came from India. And Mrs Naranbhai was soooo jealous I'm going away to Canada for good - and not like the others...people have to leave everything - even cars..."

"It hurt so much - so much I can't tell you. I didn't even think it was real. I thought I was dreaming. I thought he had taken my dress off because I had done pee in my pants. And there was this black servant -- so superior! He treated me like I was..."

"Oh, talking of servants. You know Jannasani is going to be a big-big man soon? He's going to be chief site supervisor when they start building a school here. No more Bombay Gardens you know...new quarters for teachers of Islam. I've heard he might be converting soon. Imagine all our houses being knocked down....but we will have a nice flat in Canada...so what do I care? Everybody has nice houses in Can....."

"I was sure Dawawalla would help me. That's why I fell into his arms. And what he did to me! Do you understand what that's done to my insides? My faith is shattered in everything. He just... just - " Kamla broke down and cried some more. Somewhere inside her she realised she wasn't getting through to the other woman.

"Oh, and listen to this," Mrs D'Sa continued with undisguised relish. "Shahbanu took Naranbhai's money and ran away. But the fool still believes that her villain husband came and dragged her away, against her will. She had them all eating out of her hand. Men are such fools! Their brains are in their goolies. If their goolies were cut off then all the world's problems would be solved in a minute..."

On seeing her burst into tears again, Mrs D'Sa embraced her fondly saying: "Oh, you poor, poor girl! So many memories! No wonder you are so upset. You're probably thinking of poor Mr Virjibhai - such a nice man - God rest his soul and grant him a place in heaven. Never mind, everything will be OK. Imagine! Dawawalla and I could be neighbours in Canada! No class distinctions there, you know? Everybody is the same and everybody can make a lot of money. I'm a proper music teacher now...."

Kamla gave up trying to tell Mrs D'Sa about what she'd been through. She dried her tears, asked: "So, where is Shahbanu - err... I mean Mrs Hussein?"

"Who knows? I tell you, her husband came back only because her business was doing so well...she supported herself in such a sinful way...!"

Kamla was about to say: Sinful? What's so sinful about that? Shahbanu had male visitors and charged them good money. What did you charge your husband for beating you whenever he felt like it?

But, she thought better of it and instead asked: "Do you know where Raushan is?"

"Oh Raushan! What a mattata! Big promotion for her husband, Sam. When men get promoted they always want a new wife, take it from me. Where have you been girl? Don't you read the papers? Sometimes they say the Dictator is in control, sometimes the papers say he's been overthrown by Sam Passo. The last I heard, Sam Passo was running the Broadcasting Station. Determined to show the Dictator that he is on his side. But don't think he'll last. What a mess! I'm so glad we're moving to Winnipeg. That's in Canada, you know? I've been knitting away like mad - 40 degrees below zero in Winnipeg. Can you even imagine that? But lots of Catholic churches -"

Tiring a bit of Mrs D'Sa's incessant chatter about irrelevant matters, Kamla made an instant decision to go to the Broadcasting Station and find Sam. Dawawalla had gone with her money, but at least Naranbhai could still be punished. The radio and TV station would be the best place to complain about Naranbhai since there were no other authorities left. She would tell Sam about Naranbhai embezzling her education money and performing outrageous acts of injustice against girls -- like marrying them off to a tree. She was convinced the tree-marriage story would strike a chord with Sam. It had all the potential of becoming a sensational news story to divert attention from the country's political troubles.

She said a quick good-bye to Mrs D'Sa. That other woman, bade her a fond farewell and waved for ages as Kamla walked away, with Mrs D'Sa actually believing she'd had a really good chat with the girl and that they'd caught up on everything.

A HOT NEWS STORY

There was an armed guard at the entrance to the modern television and radio building. Kamla walked up to one of them and said: "I need to see the boss, please. He is a personal friend. I have vital information for him about one of the Indians. A hot story!"

They were amused. They had never seen a young Indian woman turn up by herself at the broadcasting station with a "hot story".

It was much easier than she had imagined. They searched her -- there wasn't much to search -- and showed her in. Thirty minutes latershe was sitting down in a chair in Sam's office, crying. He looked on helplessly, finally offering her his handkerchief. In between the sobs, she talked - incoherently - about her late father's insurance policy. About her wanting to be a doctor. About her and her sister being sent off to live in a village where there were no schools. And that she was roaming around like a stray dog, because Dawawalla had embezzled her father's money, raped her, and then made off to Canada. And, by the by, she mentioned about her sister being married to a tree......

She told him that the husband Naranbhai had chosen for her sister, Bimla, had had a preservation order slapped on it.

It was that point Sam jumped up from his chair. He shook her by the shoulders and said: "Stop crying! Explain to me, again. Your sister was forced to marry a tree...?"

She told him the story. Sam's eyes brightened up. Here, at last, was a way out. Here was his chance to show the new Dictator that he could go after the Indians like a hound dog and get to the bottom of their mysterious, treacherous practices. He would expose the entire race as evil and backward. He would find good reason why these people had no right to live in such a beautiful and advanced country. He would run the story on every single news bulletin on television and radio. It would lead to a shaming of all the Indians and Naranbhai would be placed under arrest. Sam would get all the credit for breaking the story and the Dictator would reward him by making his position secure in any new government.

429

"Proof. I need proof that such a wedding took place," said Sam.

Kamla was hesitant. Finally she said: "What sort of proof? I am the proof! I was there! It was my sister who was getting married..."

"But something - something we can show..."

Kamla jumped up from the chair. "There is a photograph! Patel the photographer was there. I knew he took pictures...but I don't have ...they'll be at Naranbhai's house...you know, Naran Villa, near Bombay Gardens?"

"Then go there and bring the picture. We will have it blown up and splashed everywhere. We will say, not content with exploiting us, they are now exploiting our trees....forcing our trees to get married without consent from the government...Ha! They say African men will marry their girls by force. But, *they* are forcing their girls to marry African trees! Yes, I can see it - I love it, I love it!"

Exhausted, but elated that here, at last, was a solution, Kamla started to make her way to Naran Villa, over five miles away. On the way, she worked out her strategy. A confrontational attitude was not going to help. She would have to make some sob story and gain entrance to the house somehow. Then she would have to look for the photo. As soon as she'd found it, she would run back to Sam's office and then everything would be all right. Naranbhai would have to return her money. She would go to school again. And Bimla would be rescued from the village. She started running...

Kamla had thought that Raushan would have been her only hope but now she was thrilled -- and energised -- she had found an even better person than Raushan: Raushan's ex-husband Sam -- a powerful man, high up in the government, who had promised to help her if she could provide at least one picture of Bimla's strange wedding.

She arrived at the gates of Naran Villa and was puzzled to see a huge crowd of people and some soldiers milling around the house. She stepped back slightly thinking they may well be looking for her at Bimla's request. She disappeared into the crowd, and heard their murmurs.

"Stranger and stranger things have started to happen at this house. Last night, when the Mad Girl was singing, the film director - that guy in the flowery shirt - said he had found the new fresh-faced heroine of his next film. And today, the heroine's father was carted off like a common criminal, such shame! His first wife screeching like a hyena and his second wife writhing like a wounded animal. Hey Ram!"

SLOWLY GOING MAD

Kamla stood transfixed to the spot. It was a few hours before she walked away from Naran Villa, totally at a loss in trying to make sense of anything she had seen. Should she go back into the house? Creeep in unnoticed amidst the wailing women and go straight to the cupboard on top of which the photo albums were kept? Some sixth sense told her to stay away from the house. The women were all wailing and beating their chests. Mrs Naranbhai herself was rolling about on the floor of the verandah as everyone looked on helplessly. Nobody bothered to call a doctor to see to Mrs Naranbhai's convulsions on the floor because, it was said, there was no cure for grief.

The unruly mob that had gathered outside the house had slowly dispersed. She was tired, and beginning to look completely bedraggled. Her tightly plaited hair had come undone. Loose strands of hair hung over the face. The rest was starting to get matted. Her dress was covered with dirt. She stank of urine. She walked away, languidly, alongside the smelly gutter again. Her mind was blank. There was nothing in particular that she wanted to think about. And a song that she'd once heard the Mad Girl sing came into her mind for no reason at all. And she began singing as she walked:

"How will it come, when death finally comes?"

And then, surprised at herself that she could remember the melody and the words so vividly, she sang louder as she walked. The singing soothed her. She hadn't even known she could sing. It was as though someone else was singing through her. For lack of a better idea, she just retraced her footsteps to Bombay Gardens. Desolate as it was in the early evening light, it was still the only place she knew. She would just put her head down somewhere in the backyard and fall asleep. Morning would bring some other solution. She entered the backyard again. Nobody had bothered to lock the gate for the night. And, just when she thought she had the entire yard to herself, she saw a dhoti-clad figure emerge from one of the houses and start throwing odd things onto a pile in the middle of the yard.

JOAN OF ARC'S DIWALI

"Those mother-fucking bastard-shits are NOT suddenly getting their hands on my things," the Pandit declared hysterically. One or two tenants still left in Bombay Gardens were shocked by the Pandit's language. He had never been known to use such expletives. He kept repeating the statement making free use of the word "fuck" while assembling a pathetic looking pile of belongings that, according to him, were far too valuable to fall into the grubby, blood-stained hands of the "mother-fucking bastard-shits." He threw his things, one by one onto the higgeldy-piggeldy pile of odds and ends: a stained old mattress, incense burners, pandit-style books on astrology and other astrological paraphernalia, dividers, compass, logarithms, scrolls and scrolls of Vedic charts. And then, quite blasphemously, he even threw on a few figurines of his beloved Hindu deities, along with some tinsel-covered calendars depicting a colourful, though serene, image of a beautiful Sita flanked by the brothers Ram and Lakshman. It was their release from a fourteen-year exile that was the story behind the Hindu festival of Diwali: "I would rather burn them with my own hands than let such sacred things fall, suddenly, in the hands of those mother-fucking bastard-shits."

With each layer of bric-a-brac, he splashed a generous amount of petrol. Then he disappeared into his house for a bit, and emerged again with piles of clothing, pots, pans, a small box-fridge, some old film magazines, a few issues of Readers' Digest and Newsweek. All of these were thrown onto the pile. Then some old, tattered textbooks from his Indian schooldays. All the front covers had gone. Only Bernard Shaw's "St. Joan" still announced itself as such. He added a half broken, rusty old bicycle that hadn't been ridden since 1946. Alongside that he added a bicycle pump and an old tool-box which contained nothing of use whatsoever, apart from a few rusty screws and a handful of bent nails. Finally he brought out his sun-topi (British colonial style sun-helmet) and placed it on the top with the same care and attention as though he were placing the fairy atop a Christmas tree. Christmas? Sorry, wrong festival. Yes, that too had its origination in the principle of light, celebrating the lengthening of days in the northern hemisphere, but here, so near the equator where days and nights were of equal length, Christmas had very little to do with lighting levels. Anyway, this was still only October. This time of year was nearly always Diwali time and the Bombay Gardens sakati always managed to host the best fireworks display in town. Whereas Naran Villa had been the headquarters for all other ceremonials, Bombay Gardens, owing to its vast, flat sakati was always given precedence for Diwali fireworks and landlord Naranbhai's entire family had always attended these celebrations. In the past, the Roman Catholic D'Sa kids were the ones who most enjoyed Diwali. They were given lots and lots of crackers and rockets by Naranbhai and others, and D'Sa Number Three was once heard to observe that Diwali was far more fun than Christmas. At Christmas they had to wear their best clothes - making it impossible to pursue any of their normal activities - put in a midnight appearance at Church, and then behave themselves for the rest of the following day. At Diwali they could run around ragged as usual, setting off fire-crackers in the unlikeliest of places causing girls and women to scream with fright. But tradition dictated that children - of whatever faith - could never be scolded for merry-making at Diwali, so they got off scot-free. Yes, Diwali was indeed their real Christmas! Had it had been a normal Diwali, and the D'Sa children had not already departed with their mother for Canada, the backyard-sakati would be full of loud-bangs and crackling sounds and the squeals of delighted children. At the end of all the fireworks there would be a huge bonfire, and traditional Indian dancing.

There was still going to be a bonfire. But it was the Pandit Suddenly's bonfire - an empty and defiant gesture of the powerless against the powers that be - with just a handful of onlookers. There had been radio announcements, repeated again and again, that any Asians found to be destroying their property or belongings (and particularly their *cars*) would be shot on the spot. The Pandit's reaction had been: "Let them shoot me, suddenly. Nobody can suddenly kill an already-dead man!" And, with that, he doused the little pile of belongings with more petrol from a can -- the same can that Satish had kept for emergencies and for which, ten years earlier in 1962, Naranbhai had expected the Pandit to walk all the way to Bombay Gardens on Independence night...

The flames shot up and sparks crackled as the Pandit's paraphernalia slowly disintegrated. He stood near the fire, his face ablaze in the bright orange light, his eyes glistening. The flames rose higher and higher, and then quite suddenly and without a warning, Pandit Suddenly seemed to leap into the fire and let out a monstrous yelp as the heat engulfed him and his thin cotton vest and balloon-like dhoti caught fire. The onlookers stood around helplessly. Nobody was going to leap into the fire and risk being roasted.

Kamla stood some distance away, still singing and staring without emotion into the fire. Yes, the decrepit Pandit with his views on the duties of a good Hindu wife had, most carelessly, splashed his dhoti with petrol. Yes, she had stood behind him. And, maybe -- just *maybe* -- she had pushed him into his own bonfire. So what? Hadn't he pushed young women into similar fires? Hadn't he always extolled the ancient practice of sati whereby widows had willingly jumped onto the funeral pyre of their husbands? The Pandit's cries were drowned in the crackling fire. And Kamla just there, singing the Mad Girl's latest song:

How will it come
When death finally comes?
Will it feel like the first kiss of lovers
Or the stabbing pain
Of love torn asunder?
Will it whisper the summons
Coaxing, cajoling, tempting,
"Come! I have come for you!"
Or will it scream its command,
"Stop! Your Time is Up!"
Will it come with the first strain of Spring
Or with the first yellowing cry of Autumn?
Will it come by water
Or will it come by fire?
How will it come

When death finally comes?

As the flames of the Pandit's bonfire rose higher and higher, Kamla began to feel a sense of peace. It was this wretched Pandit's idea that her sister should be married to a tree, and now he was being gobbled up in a fire that he had set alight. She mused how those who thought they had ready answers for every single one of life's conundrums were, themselves, so powerless, so fallible. Just as she began to calm down and enjoy her song, a group of soldiers suddenly appeared in the courtyard and grabbed her:

"Don't you know it is illegal to destroy your belongings?" their leader shouted.

"They're not my belongings. Nothing belongs to me. Nothing." she said in a flat, unemotional voice.

They handcuffed her and frog marched her to a jeep. Their leader radioed back to HQ:

"We've got her. We've got the Mad Girl. She was watching the fire and singing....yes, crazy, completely crazy...wild hair...dirty dress...not like a normal Indian girl at all...completely mad...."

"I'm not the Mad Girl! I'm not mad," screamed Kamla, finally shocked into being again.

"Yes, yes, they all say that. All mad people say they are not mad," the soldiers humoured her while bundling her into their jeep. As the jeep sped away, the Pandit's fire continued to glow in the backyard, casting an eerie orange light all over the now desolate sakati.

THE BIG SLEEP

Hazari Baba had appeared in the backyard of Bombay Gardens as the flames rose higher and higher on the Pandit's Diwali bonfire.

"Hey, you!" shouted one of the soldiers. "Clear off!"

"I can't help it, sorry," said Hazari Baba. "I can't help it any more than the moth can help being pulled to the flame. Where is the one who was just singing that song...?"

"Song? What the hell -? Wait, wait," said another. "It's that Indian magician who always talks nonsense. The one we've been looking for. Get him!"

Baba's hands were tied with a rope and he was put into the army truck to be driven some fifty miles away to a makeshift dungeon which had been hastily commissioned as a "Guest House" for all Indian magicians. Here they were to remain until such time as they had taught their magic skills to the Dictator's men.

Afterwards, nobody could understand how Hazari Baba, who was such an expert at appearing and disappearing at will, could not do so on this occasion. He was thrown into a dark, dank cell measuring seven feet by four. And, he was told he would live here until he spilled the beans about the magic trick that enabled him to turn everything he touched to gold or, failing that, he at least instruct the army on the secret art of the continuous 84-year erection. But Baba refused to speak. Instead, he sat down cross-legged in the small cell with the same expression on his face as though he were sitting on some plush carpet in an ornate palace and preparing to perform for a King. He didn't say a word, but he sang, continuously, from the moment he sat down. He refused food and water. The guards looked on bemused for a while, thinking that sooner or later he'd get fed up with singing, and get fed up with the cell, and decide to co-operate.

After about two days of non-stop singing, a disturbing thing happened. The guards began to feel very, very sleepy. One by one they slipped into a languid state, so much so that, when a fresh, interesting new arrival was brought in to be thrown into the cell adjoining Baba's, they hardly noticed her. It was said she was

437

Mad. But the Dictator believed that mad people sometimes had magical powers. So his men had instructions to catch and lock up every single loony in the country. And this particular Mad Girl was famous. She was well known in her locality for singing, unfailingly at Full Moon.

"Every time she sings, the moon becomes so big," the Dictator had remarked. "Normally it is small. And sometimes it disappears altogether - and then reappears like a thin, needle-fine crescent. But, when this young woman sings, it becomes a shiny globe - almost as big as the sun. No, she definitely knows some magic. A big moon is not always a good idea. It throws too much light everywhere. Certain activities need pitch-dark. The moon becomes big and bright and then all my men who have important duties to perform at night, can be seen so, so clearly..." the Dictator provided, by way of explanation. "Arrest her, lock her up. Get that magic out of her. Learn how to keep the moon away...learn from her how we can order up the moon as and when we need it."

And so. the Mad Girl - or someone who was *assumed* to be the Mad Girl - had come to occupy the cell next to Hazari Baba's. She paced about as agitated in hers, as he sat serenely in his, with one solid stone wall between them. He sang and sang while the guards dozed and dozed. Apart from Hazari Baba's powerful singing voice, a strange hush fell over the whole prison. Only Kamla's voice bellowed out every now and then:

"Oh shut up, can't you? How can you sing at a time like this? Just get up and tell them that I am not who they think I am. Only you can verify that I am not Mad Girl Kirti. I need you to speak yet all you do is sing! Bloody idiot!"

Their cells were alongside each other. She could not see him, nor he her; she could only hear his singing and it was driving her up the wall. Finally, she became tired of screaming. The guards snored contentedly as Baba sang. It was the same song that Rangeelay Khan had sung for the Princess some four hundred years ago.

And it went on for four days. Baba singing and the guards snoring. Kamla was hungry, thirsty, tired, but nobody was awake to bring her food or water. How the hell did Hazari Baba keep singing on and on without food or water? She grew increasingly weak and eventually became feverish.

Baba's singing never stopped, but she thought she heard his voice speaking clearly, over the singing:"You will be just fine! He will come for you soon, and you will be safe. Don't be afraid. I have to go. If you wake up and see I'm no longer there, don't worry, you will soon be free. I must go. I have to tell the story, many more times. Somebody will need to hear this story, in less than a year from now. A lonely soul - a child who was torn from the bossom of her family. My stories will be her only childhood memory. I cannot deprive her of that....I must go....I must go...."

Her forehead ached. Finally, she could no longer pace about, leave alone stand up. She sank to the ground and crawled to the wall joining Baba's cell. Her head leaning against the cool stone wall, her ear pressed against it, she babbled deliriously. She wanted to get up, to do something, but a strange drowsiness overcame her. The strains of Baba's song drifted in and out of her consciousness. She was a little girl again. Her father worked as a Compounder, and her sister cooked all her favourite food. She would run home from school and tuck in greedily....

Baba's voice sang on:
A cradle of fragrant sandalwood
Rocked by the evening breeze
Sleep, beautiful one, sleep
As though you are dead
For death may well come
But how will it come
When death finally comes?

SLEEPING SICKNESS

On the fifth day, a new soldier reported for duty. He had arrived ahead of his other colleagues and, on arrival, was astonished to find that the duty soldiers were fast asleep while a bearded man in white robes sitting all alone, in a small, padlocked cell, singing. How on earth could his robes remain snow-white in such filthy surroundings? Was there a new magic washing powder that nobody had heard about?

In the adjoining cell, a young girl in a very dirty dress lay unconscious, her head resting on the cool stone wall that divided her cell from the singing apparition.

The young soldier shivered. There was something going on in this prison -- a new kind of sleeping sickness, perhaps? As a little boy, he had known of entire villages being wiped out by this kind of thing, said to be caused by a fly. Perhaps the flies had a nest here? It was best to get out before the ants followed. The flies and ants worked together. Once the flies had put everyone to sleep, the giant ants came along to pick the carcasses clean. He remembered how the ants had eaten their way through every living thing in his village some years ago.

Suddenly, he recognised the face of the girl. Maybe she was still alive? Maybe he could revive her? He carried her out, and his soldier's uniform ensured that a passing truck would give him a lift back to Naran Villa...

When the rest of the other guards arrived at the special underground prison, they beheld an even stranger sight. They saw the slumped form of various soldiers snoring in unison. And, a cell, which was still securely padlocked from the outside, was completely empty. They'd been told that the gold-making Indian man was being held here, and they had been promised some delightful tortures that they would have to carry out on him to get him to spill the beans on his gold-making recipe. They had also been told that a Mad Girl was being held here and that, she too, had some magical powers -- like making the moon grow bigger and smaller. They had looked forward to the double-delight of a gold-making Baba and a girl who could change the size of the moon at will. But, all they had was five or six soldiers, fast asleep.

The new guards felt completely cheated and betrayed. But, instead of raising the alarm, they quickly agreed with one another to report back that everything was quite normal. This could be a good life -- a very good life with nothing much to do, except sleep.

A SORT OF FREEDOM

In another prison, some three hundred miles to the north, Naranbhai had been standing up for two weeks. The Prison Warden appeared out of the blue and unlocked the cell, asking Naranbhai to step out. Any time any one person was asked to step out in this way, it created a sort of domino effect. With one body gone, all the others suddenly found another few inches of space and quickly started huddling closer as this was the only way to stand for hours on end.

"Visitor for you. A lady. In my office," the Prison Warden said.

Naranbhai's heart started beating 'fast-fast'. He had known all along that there had been some terrible mistake. Of course, someone had come to tell him that everything was going to be OK and that a major campaign was on for his freedom. His name would be cleared in no time at all. Perhaps his battle-axe second wife - or maybe his beloved Shahbanu had organised a movement...? Yes, it had to be Shahbanu. His beautiful, sympathetic Shahbanu had come back from wherever her husband had taken her, to fight the campaign for Naranbhai's freedom. She was probably so guilty about taking his money and running away, that now, God-fearing woman that she was, she had come to him in his hour of need. It was good that he would meet her in the Warden's office -- away from the hell-hole. He wouldn't have wanted her to see his living conditions. As it was he felt completely filthy and smelly and wondered how the rose-and-jasmine aroma of Shahbanu would cope with his dishevelled, prickly, unshaven, unwashed presence.

He was mystified at seeing the slender young woman who stood in the Prison Warden's office. It certainly wasn't Shahbanu, yet she looked vaguely familiar. But he couldn't place her.

"It's me...", she said, softly.

GOD IN CHAINS

It's nearing six o'clock. I've been with Camilla since a little after two in the afternoon. Neither of us seems to want to end the meeting. I'm still fascinated by her, because this is the woman I had wondered about so much, some years ago. It's easy to idealise our rivals and think they have superhuman properties. Yet, here she is, with all the insecurities and doubts of any ordinary woman. An ordinary woman. I say 'ordinary' in that the wives of lovers are at first always imagined as *special* and *powerful*, only because they've got someone one wants.   Actually, Camilla is an extraordinary woman because I'm sure she's had the most amazing life. And, she can write. Perhaps some day she will write about it. But, in some curious way, I sense she is equally fascinated by me -- as though I hold the key to some secret she is trying to fathom.

There's a lull in the conversation. It must be twenty to, or twenty past six and the angels must be passing. It must be because of the angels that I have this sudden need to confess. I must come clean. First, I must tell her that I hijacked her manuscript. Then I must own up about being her husband's illicit lover for nearly five years. How do I begin? My throat is dry. Even so, I have this sudden need for one of those cigarettes I just made her put away....and I don't even smoke!

I can't bear the burden of this guilt. Let whatever happens, happen....

"Camilla," I began, nervous though determined. "There is something I should...."

Whenever I'm nervous, I have this habit of pulling out this chain I wear round my neck and running its cold metal along my chin and through my teeth.

"Camilla," I continue, "you have to know some things about me........I'm the woman who made sure your story did not see the light of day. And, your husband..."

She's not listening. I'm talking about what I think are sensational revelations but her eyes are focused on my mouth: "What's that thing you wear on a chain?" Camilla interrupts, with a distinct panic in her voice.

"Oh, it's...it's nothing," I say, utterly puzzled that she is more interested in a piece of jewellery than in what I've just been trying to tell her.

She suddenly reaches out and grasps my hand to stop the movement of the chain across my chin and, before I know it, she is holding the figurine of my little Indian God between her thumb and index finger, her eyes wild with excitement:

"Where? *Where* did you get this?" she demands.

"I...er...I don't know. I've always had it. It's some kind of Indian God, I think. I don't know the name, but I've always worn it. Anyway, I'm trying to tell you something...."

"*Who...* who gave it to you?" she asks in the tone of someone who has apprehended an errant schoolgirl with a piece of stolen jewellery.

"Nobody gave it to me. I've always had it..." I stutter, mystified by her excitement.

Camilla is seized by fresh sense of urgency. She shoots up, gathering her shopping bags. The waiter is putting chairs onto tables and has started mopping the floor. I thought she has got up so abruptly only because the café is soon to close. Instead, she grabs my arm and says: "Baby! Quick! Let's go! Let me give you a lift. I first need to stop off somewhere...then I'll drop you anywhere you want. It's only a twenty minute drive to these people I'm going to see and my car is just round the corner..."

"What people? Don't tell me you know the people who lived in that house before we moved in? Thanks, but I can't. Some other time, maybe? I've got plans this evening..." I trail off, not sure what to make of her behaviour. Had she heard what I'd just told her? I'm dying to confess, and I think I have confessed. But I want acknowledgement. And forgiveness. Why is she so excited by the little god-figure I've always worn?

A confession is supposed to make one feel better. But I'm utterly confused. Am I still guilty? Does that mean I should do exactly as she says...do I still owe her something?

A lift would be quite nice. It was Saturday and the tube would be unbearably crowded with shoppers. Oh! I can't bear it! She's being so nice to me. I was the wrong doer. I was the one who had

had an affair with her husband. And I had done her an even bigger injustice by sabotaging her story, making sure it didn't reach any of the judges for that competition. Suddenly I felt I should do exactly as she says. I must serve her, in some way, for the rest of her life.

Camilla's voice interrupts my remorseful thoughts: "You have to come right now Baby! I can't explain it, but I feel it's going to be too late if we don't go now..."

THE END IS NIGH!

The weather, true to its British summer habit, offered up an unrelenting drizzle that continued unabated into the early evening. Not that more clement weather would've made any difference to the Grumpy Old Man. He was, as usual, plonked in front of the TV.

"But you are not even watching it! Let's have some music. They have such nice songs on Sunrise Radio," his young wife tried to suggest a change of activity.

The Grumpy Old Man carried on staring at the flickering, silent images of Bollywood. His wife was reaching the end of her tether -- how on earth could he understand a film with the sound turned down?

She suggested: "Why don't you go for a walk? You could have gone and collected your parcel -- I'm dying to know what it is! But they'll be shut now. You should've gone in the morning. Why didn't you go? I tried to go for you, I couldn't find the card..."

"I threw it away! I don't need any parcels! I'm happy with my film...."

And he continued to stare at the screen. A beautiful woman in medieval north Indian costume slept while a bearded musician, seated behind a diaphanous curtain, sang....

"See?" grumped the Old Man. "How innocent she looks! Who would believe she is completely and utterly mad? Kitty Complex -- ha! Mad, mad, mad!"

" Look, why don't we have the radio for a change...?"

"You and your radio. It's goes on all day in the kitchen like a non-stop mantra. Isn't that enough?"

"Why can't you do something with me for a change? Something we can both share?"

"I share my life with you. What more do you want? My soul? Women!"

She felt hurt: "Yes, you have done me the biggest favour in the universe by sharing your grumpiness with me. Thank you. Any other woman would've walked out by now."

"Go on then, go! What's stopping you?" he barked angrily.

"One of these days I might just do that. Back to India. Back to my people."

"What people? They're all dead. And how can you live there? Soooo English now, aren't you?"

She fought back the tears and decided to visit the Muslim woman next door. They'd had their differences in the past and she tended to keep her distance but, right now, she badly needed to interact with another human being without it feeling like constant war.

"I'm going next door for a while," she said to the Grumpy Old Man.

"Crooks! All of them! Why do you have to mix with them?" he snapped back.

"She's a good woman. So poetic! And she's pious and God-fearing."

"Oh yes? I know all about that kind of piety. All for show!" he said bitterly

"I don't care," his wife replied, "I like her. You used to like her too, remember?"

"I remember nothing of the sort! Muslims are not to be trusted, never!" he grumbled.

His wife shook her head slightly and went out of the front door. It wasn't entirely unknown that highly charged infatuations of yesteryear can sometimes turn sour -- and that too in a few months. In this case it had been nearly thirty years!

When the Grumpy Old Man's wife returned a couple of hours later, he seemed to have dozed off -- the remote control still in his hand. She went to take it from him when she noticed that something was wrong. His mouth was half-open and he wasn't breathing. She immediately ran to the neighbour she had just been visiting.

The next few minutes had a strange fossilised quality. Things seemed to be moving, but at the same time everything seemed frozen into a single image. The woman from next door was making her a cup of tea while the woman's son-in-law was hovering somewhere nearby, mobile phone in hand: "Aunty, don't worry. They're on their way," he kept saying in reassuring tones.

When the ambulance arrived, ten minutes later, grumpy old Mr Naranbhai was already dead.

On someone's death, one's first thoughts can range from the sublime to the ridiculous.

Grumpy old Naranbhai's much younger third wife, Bimla - previously married to a tree - hovered dangerously close to both:

"Sushilaben got all the youth and vigour and romance, the nosy-bat-evil-busybody second Mrs Naranbhai got all the status and reflected glory from his financial prosperity. I just got endless washing, cooking and having to put up with his grumpiness," she whimpered.

The Muslim neighbour, Shahbanu Hussein, a podgy, portly woman of around sixty years of age, tried to comfort her: "Now, now, that's what marriage means. It means being there for one another -- through good times and bad, and you did your duty."

"But that's just it," wailed Bimla. "There were no good times. When he was on good times I wasn't his wife. Everybody else got the good times -- even you."

As soon she'd said it, she wished she hadn't, and with that she broke down again.

The woman from next door, once the elegant, green-fingered Shahbanu Hussein - a previous tenant of Naranbhai's Bombay Gardens, and now his portly neighbour in North London - took the jibe calmly. She realised Bimla was upset and Shahbanu was still very good at turning on the sympathy full volume.

It didn't strike Bimla at the time, but in later years, she constantly remembered that although Shahbanu's waist and hips had somewhat thickened, her eloquence had survived the ravages of time:

"We get whatever share is marked for us. In his final years, you were destined to be with him. It's easy for anyone to stand by when the going's good, but those who stick through the bad times are the real salt of this earth. The universe is full of little parcels with different names on them. No matter how much you try to get someone else's, you can only get the one Allah addressed personally to you."

But, of Shahbanu's entire eloquent speech, Bimla registered only one word -- even in her state of grief and shock. And, that word was 'parcel.'

THE THIRD WIFE

Twenty-eight earlier, when Naranbhai had served his upright imprisonment for a fortnight, the guards had informed him he had a lady visitor. At first, he didn't recognise the young woman. Even when she said, "It's me...me..." he couldn't place her voice. It was a voice that hadn't been heard too often. It was the voice of one who was not used to speaking her mind. It was some while before she identified herself as Bimla, the late Virjibhai the Compounder's daughter whom Naranbhai had married off to a tree. What on earth was she doing here?

She came straight to the point: "I need you to marry me..."

"Yes, yes, I know, I know, I've been trying all these years to get you married, but something or the other always blocks my plans, honestly." What a cheek, he thought. Tracking him down in this hellhole and ordering him to sort out her life! What could he do for her stuck in here? Then he remembered she was still married to her tree, and he said, guiltily: "We *were* going to come and cut the tree, honestly, but..."

"No, I don't mean arrange my marriage to anybody else. I'm not talking about the tree. I need to get married to you," she said firmly.

"What? Are you mad? Don't you know....? I already have two....?"

"Yes, yes, but that's all over now. Sushilaben has taken Mad Girl to India with the Director Babu. The Mad Girl is going to be a film star. Bharat has gone with them, to be her secretary. And your second wife, she died -- half an hour after your arrest."

Naranbhai stared at her in disbelief. Sushilaben? India? Mad Girl a film star? Mrs Naranbhai, his precious second wife and mother of three sons, dead?

"How do you know all this?" he finally managed to ask in a dazed voice.

"I went there. I have been asked to get out of the country. I have no magic secrets, so I am not allowed to stay. I thought I would be OK as the wife of an African grown tree. I assumed the tree was a citizen, but the Dictator's government says marriage to a tree is not recognised. I pleaded and pleaded that I need to stay wherever my husband stays and if he stands with his roots deep in this African soil, then where can I go? But they just laughed. I even met the Dictator in person, to plead my case. You should have seen how much he laughed. He almost had a seizure and his chamchas got quite worried he might die or something. Basically, I cannot stay here. And I can't go anywhere because I don't have any papers. I went to Naran Villa and found your three sons. Very distressed -- the poor children. Jannasani was doing his best to look after them but....and then I realised how we can help each other. You are now a single man. I can be mother to the Doctor, Dentist and Lawyer. And I can get you out of here. You must marry me... you have to! It is because of you I'm in this mess...."

"Have you no shame? Proposing marriage to man - a much older man - and that too by yourself, without an elder to intercede on your behalf? What's the world coming to?"

"You can take your world and stuff it up your....." she began.

Naranbhai covered his ears with his hands. So! The ant had grown wings! This snivelling woman who never dared to say "boo" had suddenly found her vocal chords. And, how she talked! She was unstoppable: "All those years you kept arranging marriages for me. Did I ask you to do that? And now, when I'm in need, and I'm asking you directly to marry me, you accuse me of shamelessness. You don't see the hopelessness of my situation, do you? Married to an African tree, but no longer allowed to remain near him. How am I to do my duty as a good Hindu wife? You must marry me, you must! It's the only way I can get out! And do you know something else? It's the only way YOU can get out. I am being expelled. As my husband, you would be expelled with me. I know these are crazy times, but even *they* can't have it both ways! They can't order your expulsion and still keep you in prison, don't you see ...?"

Naranbhai was beginning to see.

TWINS: REUNITED

Parcel. As soon as Shahbanu had referred to destiny's little parcels, 'parcel' was the only word that had registered with Bimla. The shock of somebody's death can make one behave in a most peculiar fashion. Just two hours after Naranbhai's death, the third Mrs Naranbhai, previously known only as Bimla, daughter of the late Virjibhai-the-Compounder, (and at one time briefly married to a tree) was suddenly determined to start clearing out some of his things.

"Plenty of time for all that later," they tried to tell her, but Bimla was adamant she needed a clear out. Shahbanu offered to help and Bimla accepted gratefully. While rummaging through Naranbhai's things, the women came across a brown paper parcel, wrapped in one of his old shirts and pushed to the back of a closet.

The sight of the parcel brought a smile to Bimla's face. Crafty old, grumpy old thing! So, he *had* gone and collected his parcel from the post office, but why hadn't he said anything about it? She told Shahbanu how he had pretended not to be interested in the parcel. How he had grumbled all afternoon, saying mysterious parcels by post were nothing but trouble and more than likely to contain a bomb.

Bimla drew the parcel out carefully, with a kind of ceremonial reverence. She removed the outer wrapping of thick brown paper to reveal pink bubble plastic. She removed the plastic and it revealed white tissue paper. She tore off the white tissue paper and it revealed more brown paper. She hurriedly tore off the brown paper. Years of habit had forced her to open things carefully, even if she was never going to reuse the paper. Once the inner brown paper had gone, it revealed a thick plastic bag -- more pink bubbles, more tissue paper, more brown paper and, at last, the all-too-familiar figure of Rahu, Naranbhai's personal God of Bounty, one of the twin-gods who had gone missing in 1966. The bulbous, little gold statuette that Naranbhai had carried cupped in his palm at all times some twenty-eight years earlier, now looked strangely out of place.

Bimla froze while Shahbanu squealed with disbelief at the familiar Rahu figurine.

"Oh, how we searched and searched for it at the time!" was all she managed to say before becoming pensive. The sight of the familiar, bulbous figurine, although missing for more than two decades, transported her back to the days of Bombay Gardens. A lump came to her throat as she recalled the memory of a middle-aged Naranbhai fondling the statue while drinking his juice. Her heart was suddenly pierced with nostalgia for a bygone youth as she recalled those early days of how easily she had manipulated Naranbhai and had him eating (biscuits only) from the palm of her hand. And how her helpless female act had never ceased to have the desired effect on him. And that idiotic Pandit Suddenly who had provided "competition" for poor Mr Naranbhai. And how the suspicious, forever insecure second Mrs Naranbhai would watch her every move.

Bimla had very different memories of her own. She remembered him pretending to read the Argus, or talking with his cronies whilst slurping sweet tea from a sacuer. She recalled his many attempts to marry her off and make her respectable. Perhaps he meant well? After all, what was a young woman without a husband by her side?

It was some minutes before Bimla noticed a neatly folded piece of paper within the package. It was the headed-paper of a well known Indian film Production company and on it clearly typed in Hindi:

Dear Father,

I had to take Rahu. After all, if He is a God, then is He only your God? Is He not also my God? Within a month of taking Him from your room, Director Babu spotted me and catapulted me to name, fame and wealth. I did 200 films in 10 years. Your Rahu stayed by me day and night. But now, I think I should return Him. I think the time has come for him to be reunited with his twin, Ketu. And, together, they will perhaps restore a balance -- if not for you, then for my daughter. You took her away from me but she will return, somehow. I have a feeling she needs Him to balance out her life...because, you see, all these years she has had Ketu by himself. He was tightly gripped in her fist at the time she was sent away... it's only right she should have the pair. Sorry for any inconvenience. Kitty Complex (your "MAD" daughter, Kirti)

Bimla wrapped her palm round the Rahu figure and held it to her heart. Hot tears silently poured down her cheeks. Shahbanu put her arms round Bimla's shoulders, and let out a long, mournful sigh....

At that very moment, sitting in a Wembley coffee shop, Camilla had spotted a very familiar figurine on Baby's chain. And, she'd had this sudden, overwhelming urge to take this woman calling herself 'Baby' to the house of her grumpy old brother-in-law Naranbhai...

The doorbell rang with an urgency that should have made everybody jump. But Bimla remained frozen. Shahbanu got up and answered the door. As soon as Bimla saw whom Shahbanu had brought into the sitting room, she cried out:

"Kamla! Where on earth have you been? I tried calling your mobile all afternoon, but it was switched off...."

She stopped suddenly as she realised her younger sister Kamla, (who now preferred her name to be pronounced "Camilla") had a stranger with her.

Kamla went up to her sister and put her arms around her. On opening the door, Shahbanu had told Kamla the news of her brother-in-law, the Grumpy Old Naranbhai's sudden death, earlier that afternoon. Kamla made a futile attempt to comfort Bimla, but Bimla just brushed her aside, saying:

"You hated him! What use sympathy now?" and then, becoming aware of the stranger in their midst, she asked: "Who is this?"

"This is Baby. She says that *is* her real name! Look! Just look at her face! Who does she remind you of? Now, do you see what she's wearing on that chain round her neck?"

Bimla showed no surprise or pleasure. Instead, she quickly gathered some of the brown paper and pink bubble paper around the Rahu figurine, threw in the letter from Kirti and then, without even saying 'Hello' just handed the whole thing to a stupefied

Baby who was struck by seeing that the two gods looked almost identical.

"Here -- you may as well have the other one..."snapped Bimla, as she shoved the stuff into Baby's hand. And, with that, she complained she could feel a headache coming on. Shahbanu led her upstairs to rest.

Baby and Kamla sat alone in the small front room. It had started to rain heavily. Baby was still examining and comparing the figurines of the two gods, while at the same time trying to make sense of the letter the third Mrs Naranbhai had just handed her. She looked up at Kamla. In answer to Baby's unasked question, Kamla said: "They are twins. They should always be together."

And before Baby could ask another question, Kamla said:

"That short story I wrote was nothing -- it was just a teaser.
I've written something much more important. Maybe you'll see it on a bookshelf some day..."